Seni Glaister has worked in bookselling since 1988 and was the co-founder and CEO of The Book People. *The Museum of Things Left Behind* is her first novel. She has four children and lives in Sussex.

The Museum of Things Left Behind

SENI GLAISTER

4th ESTATE • London

4th Estate
An imprint of HarperCollins Publishers
1 London Bridge Street
London SE1 9GF
www.4thEstate.co.uk

First published in Great Britain by 4th Estate in 2015
This paperback edition first published in 2016

1

A catalogue record for this book is
available from the British Library.

ISBN 978-0-00-811899-0

MIX
Paper from
responsible sources
FSC **FSC® C007454**
www.fsc.org

FSC™ is a non-profit international organisation established to promote
the responsible management of the world's forests. Products carrying the
FSC label are independently certified to assure consumers that they come
from forests that are managed to meet the social, economic and
ecological needs of present and future generations,
and other controlled sources.

Find out more about HarperCollins and the environment at
www.harpercollins.co.uk/green

Printed in Great Britain by Clays Ltd, St Ives plc

For my brave and brilliant father
Prof. David Glaister

The Characters

THE PROLETARIAT

The Postman	Remi
The Stationmaster	Vinsent Gabboni
Patron of Il Gallo Giallo	Dario Mariani
Patron of Il Toro Rosso	Piper
The Clockmaker	Pavel
The Potter	Elio

THE VISITORS

British VIP	Lizzie Holmesworth
American Consultant 1	Chuck Whylie
American Consultant 2	Paul Fields

Alieni theam faciunt optimam.
(Strangers make the best tea.)

CHAPTER 1

In Which a Letter Stands Out

HIGH ABOVE THE CITY, in the dustiest, windiest, sparsest corner of the north-west quadrant, Remi was sorting the mail. He had arrived out of breath at the sorting office. He glanced at his stopwatch and noted, with a flicker of irritation, that he was at the upper end of the time he allowed himself for this short journey. The early-morning rain had added an element of risk to some of the sharper corners, and on several occasions he'd had to slow almost to a stop to avoid injury to himself or damage to his bicycle. Happily, though, he lived on the same level as his workplace, and his commute was generally a straightforward three-kilometre cycle ride on the slippery paths that snaked through the tea plantations from the small home he shared with his mother. In a month or two, with the onset of the harsh summer sun, these paths would quickly mould into dusty, deeply grooved channels. In turn the channels would soon evolve into narrow ruts, which would hug his bicycle tyres so snugly that he could

1

ride much of the way with his eyes closed – a feat he had often attempted with considerable, albeit unrecorded, success. Even in the wet spring months his journey to work was not strenuous; his bicycle could probably still find its own way through sheer habit, and this was certainly the easiest section of his day's circuit. That morning, however, his journey had been interrupted not once but twice, on the first occasion by a neighbour, who needed help with a stuck pig, then shortly afterwards by a second neighbour, who held the firm belief that a problem shared was a problem halved. Remi had wondered, as he pedalled furiously to make up for the lost seconds, whether the sharing of a problem exactly doubled it, providing it with two minds instead of one in which to fester, and he further worried that the problem, like the simplest of organisms, was simultaneously dividing and subdividing in his brain and that of his neighbour.

As always, however, Remi's most pressing concern had been his prompt arrival at the office for, despite the absence of a supervisor's watchful eye or any sort of mechanism to monitor his comings and goings, Remi's deep commitment to the state had engendered within him a work ethic unlikely to be rivalled within the whole of Vallerosa. In his decade of postal duties he had never been late for work, notching up instead some two hundred hours of unpaid overtime through his systematic early arrival. This uninterrupted record of excellence counted for little, however, and the banked hours bore no currency other than within his own conscience. Had he been pushed to verbalize the seriousness with which he approached timekeeping, he would probably admit that if he were to stray from his self-governed schedule on more than one or two occasions, he would not hesitate to sack himself.

The sorting office – a basic construction with lofty eaves and a trill of natural light that flitted down from windows too high to provide a view in or out – served multitudinous roles and could, just by a change of the swinging sign outside, transform itself from postal hub to the country's only ticketing office to the bureau of the registrar and back again. With the ticket sign hoisted, citizens would come here from far and wide to receive their allocated quota for state-organized events, including the busy annual season of *festa*, dances and sporting competitions. Not long ago these duties would have been fulfilled far below in the official city buildings surrounding Piazza Rosa but the president (who had pledged his life to the rigorous execution of his responsibilities but occasionally had difficulty separating valid solutions from denial) had taken exception to opening his curtains in the morning and looking down upon slowly shuffling queues of people. Queues, the president was quite sure, were a symbol of need, the physical manifestation of demand outweighing supply and, most worryingly, a queue might suggest, to any rational man peering from his balcony above, a failure on the part of the president accurately to judge and cater for the requirements of his people. So the issue of tickets had been moved as far from the palace windows as possible. Now occasions such as the Annual Blindfolded Hog Chasing Finals or the Spousal Waltz would cause an unobtrusive and unobserved queue to snake as far as the eye could see.

On the first Monday of each month the sorting office sign would be lowered and replaced with the Owl and Viper insignia representing the city's official registrar. On those mornings the office was commandeered by Benito, the *notaio*, who issued, in painstaking brown-inked calligraphy, the hand-drafted certificates of birth, death and marriage. The queues for these services were inoffensively short, but the same president who had been insulted by queues forming in Piazza Rosa had been equally upset by the notion of grieving widows and widowers sharing a small reception room with eager soon-to-be-weds or, even worse, the smug and self-satisfied contentment of new parents. As it had been impossible to allocate a separate reception area to each distinct need, he had relocated the office in its entirety to the new postal sorting office at the top of the hill. While this did not negate the possibility of a newly bereft widow sitting beside a recently endowed mother, it successfully removed the possibility of the incumbent president being troubled by this notion. As it happened, there appeared to be less and less likelihood of such offence being caused as, in recent years, it had come to the attention of several officials, whose role did not specify a requirement to notice such things, that the registration of deaths was using considerably more ink than the issue of marriage certificates, and the issue of marriage certificates seemed to be using considerably more ink than the registration of births. But it would be a little while yet before anyone felt concerned enough to raise the matter through the ranks of government and bring it to the notice of somebody with enough seniority to act upon it.

On ticketing days, and on the Mondays that fell to the service of the *notaio*, there was no mail service. Furthermore, much longer-lasting interruptions to the important job of postal delivery took place every five years. In the summer of years ending with 0 or 5, red and black bunting would be nailed to the front of the sorting office, and for a whole two-week period, the building would become the balloting headquarters from which the city's volunteers mounted and executed their political campaign. This period was fast approaching and Remi's underarms were already tingling with anxiety at the thought of the disruption his beloved postal service would suffer if – as had been rumoured recently – the campaign were to become one of above average complexity.

But on most mornings, such as this, the office was Remi's domain, a sanctuary in which correspondence could be allowed to negotiate the most delicate part of its journey, the transition from letter sent to letter received. The brass name plates were Remi's to polish; the visiting cats were his to spoil with saucers of milk and scratches behind the ears; the single teacup, saucer, plate, fork and knife were his to wash up; the kettle was his to – meticulously, according to a detailed list of tasks – descale every other month. Remi's routine had varied very little since he had perfected it nearly a decade ago but the diligence with which he approached every last detail suggested that the job was as exciting and agreeable as if he were performing it for the very first time.

The mail awaiting him was about average for the time of year, a smallish bundle at the bottom of a large grain sack. Having prepared his morning cup of tea, Remi set about the preliminary stage of his role. Removing his shoes, he set them neatly by the door. After clicking each of his knuckles, he took the sack and spilled the contents onto the polished linoleum floor, spreading the mail out as he went and occasionally separating small clusters with the aid of a socked toe. Then, with the deftness of a croupier, he began to shuffle each of the assorted envelopes into one of the eight quadrants.

Armed with the basic topography represented by the eight meagre piles of mail on the floor of the sorting office, any transient traveller would find himself very quickly able to navigate the dark and otherwise confusing labyrinth of alleys, moss-covered steps and steep gullies that interlinked each proud district. The four principal quadrants, north-west, south-west, north-east and south-east, further subdivided into a top and a bottom region, belonging either to the *alto*s or to the *basso*s. Vallerosa's landmass, as any number of bleary-eyed and disoriented travellers can confirm, is made up in its entirety of a steep and craggy gorge, to which the medieval city has tenuously and surprisingly adhered since its founding fathers built their first hovels on a small plateau halfway up the side of the ravine; they had made their dangerous escape across Europe pursued by fervent Catholics who, luckily for the escapees, had had no fortitude when it came to mountain climbing, despite their very close relationship to God. Here, legend will tell you, on the far side of the mountains – mountains considered insurmountable by the weaker-spirited – the nimble pioneers believed they had at last found sanctuary. Settling in this heaven on earth at the centre-most point of the world, they gave thanks for this safe haven. Finally harboured from the wrath of an all-powerful regime, they collapsed in exhaustion, hidden from view in all directions by the mountains that cut them off completely from the rest of the world for more than half of the year, yet blessed them with a plentiful supply of clean water from below and verdant pasture above.

Through the middle of this unlikely outpost, half a mile below the shed in which Remi now toiled, the beautiful river Florin rages from west to east, thundering its pale blues, greys and greens through the centre of the country, carving an ever-deepening crease through the nation's belly. The river's source, the bright winter snows and cool spring rains from the slopes of Italy's high mountains to the west contribute generously to both velocity and volume; within the last hundred years, three generations of formidable engineers have built a trio of impressive dams to harness the energy of this plentiful resource. First Hydras, then Gorgons and, most recently, Chimeras have been built, each more ingenious than the dam before; between them these masterful behemoths turn the great turbines that feed the country's modest electrical needs. With its excess energy stripped and redirected to boil kettles, to flicker and hum in light bulbs and refrigerators, the Florin continues its journey more sedately, though always with the capacity to surprise, towards a series of inhospitable bends between sheer granite cliffs, that mark the end of its journey through Vallerosa, where it passes quietly into Austria.

The four lower quadrants, each nudging the river's craggy banks, combine to form the *basso*s. From here, where the lowest homes dip their toes into the spring floodwaters, the city, carved from a solid seam of red granite, rises chaotically upwards towards the magnificent Piazza Rosa to the north and the slighter, quieter, humbler Piazza Verde in the south. Despite their difference in grandeur, each has claimed the largest, flattest areas on either side of the river to house the country's municipal buildings. From these piazzas the city continues to clamber upwards, on either side of the river, meandering through the *alto*s, the higher houses scrabbling and clawing their way ever more precariously; the foundations of many appear to rest on the roofs of the tier beneath them. At the highest point of the gorge the anxiety of the buildings to take a foothold lessens and the dwellings dwindle in density, petering out as the steep gorge softens to join the plateau above. Despite the distance from the river beneath them, even the uppermost homes have chosen to turn their backs on the green expanse of the mesa and instead crane their necks to look down upon layer after layer of houses beneath them, and these houses scrabble for a view of the river below. On a still day the rush of water as it crashes from Hydras, then again from Gorgons and Chimeras, can be heard from every corner of the country: the natural acoustics provided by the land's topography, the giant loudhailer that forms its mouth at the lowest point, will allow a man snoozing in his chair after lunch high in the *alto*s to set his watch to the bells chiming in Piazza Rosa way beneath him. That is, if the bells were allowed to chime.

These geographic distinctions – the *basso*s, the *alto*s, from the north and west to the south and east – entirely satisfy the needs of all the country's citizens, even though from time to time the government has attempted to issue new labels to describe the eight regions more accurately. Indeed, on one occasion a bill that introduced a complex postal code system that could pinpoint an address to its very street had been drafted but it had subsequently been mislaid and no replacement scheme had – so far – been adopted. Without the impetus and intervention of Remi it is doubtful that one ever will and so, for the time being, the eight quadrants remain.

And now, high above in the sorting office, with a neat pile of letters to represent each quadrant, it was Remi's job to shuffle the post into the order of his delivery route. His fastidious nature and eye for detail insisted that he should hand-deliver each letter to the correct address. But he knew, too, that this must be balanced with the knowledge that it was his duty to be efficient with time, the currency by which he was paid and the yardstick by which he was measured; if a letter happened to appear in the pile after its designated drop-off point, he would simply post it through the first available door, trusting that the resident would pass it on to the correct recipient at his earliest convenience. In the summer, when homeowners leave their doors and windows open to encourage safe onward passage of any air current, Remi would take the letters

9

into the homes and stand them against a vase or milk jug so that they would not be missed. The people of Vallerosa were neighbourly by nature and were in and out of each other's houses all the time. The arrival of a letter to any citizen was always noteworthy, and any intermediary handler who redirected a missive to its correct address would probably be invited to share the news so all were happy to play their part in the safe forwarding of mail.

On a normal day (which this was not), with his mailbag adequately ordered, Remi would carefully attire himself in his uniform. To the Velcro strip above his left breast pocket he would stick the smart insignia of the post office and, to complete his transformation, don the navy blue peaked cap of the postman. Standing in front of the mirror, he would tweak and tug his uniform into its neatest possible configuration, polishing his teeth with his tongue and peering closely at his reflection for unruly nasal hair or other signs of personal weakness. It was undeniable: he was a good-looking, clean-smelling man with decent prospects. That he was still single was as mysterious to Remi as it was to his mother. There was nothing in the reflection that stared back at him that indicated why this should be so. Despite his bachelor status, he was comfortable with the man who eyed him squarely in the mirror. Proud to be an upstanding citizen with purpose, he saluted himself and received the returned salute with a grateful smile. At the threshold he would bend to attach his bicycle clips to his trouser hems and step into his shoes, which, with their rugged crêpe soles, were ideally suited to the long cycle ride ahead of him.

Today, however, as already noted, was turning out to be far from routine. Having emptied out the post and spread it with his toe, as usual, one letter had immediately jumped out at him, his attention seized by its unusual colours. Remi could not have noticed its significance sooner had it been accompanied by a vision of blazing angels and a heavenly choir. Indeed, a well-aimed shaft of light from the window high above was now pointing it out to him. He dropped to his knees and crept forward on all fours. Fishing out his prize, he remained on his knees, barely able to contemplate this trembling fissure in a sea of the prosaic. He scrutinized the envelope with a curious, then greedy eye, scanning every detail. As the full significance of the letter began to sink in, the colour drained from Remi's face and re-formed as two pink spots high on his cheeks. He held the envelope in both hands, holding it up to the light and then to his nose, inhaling deeply and picking out the exotic scents absorbed on its long journey. Among the dirty whites, greys and browns of the everyday post, the pale blue of the aerogramme was distinct enough to mark it out as unique, but the almost weightless paper and those two neatly affixed stamps, one gold, the other blue, each bearing the foiled outline of the profile of Her Majesty the Queen of England, were enough to make Remi's hands shake. Never had he held such a precious delivery. The address revealed its intention. With 'Vallerosa' neatly printed as its closing directive and a double wavy line beneath it, drawing it to the attention of the postmen of many nationalities who had ensured its safe onward passage, the address insisted, politely but firmly, that it be directed without delay to the country's Parliament Hall, the home of the government.

Breathless, he bundled the mail into his satchel, barely cognizant of the order as he stuffed it in. He dressed hurriedly, buttoning his shirt with one hand while smoothing his hair with the other. He slapped the Velcro badge to his chest, at an inappropriately jaunty angle. He jammed his feet into his shoes, and only slowed to stow the precious letter between his string vest and chest, then tucked his shirt tightly into his trousers.

Off he went into the fresh morning air, heart soaring and palms tingling with excitement and anticipation. Remi pedalled furiously for the last twenty yards of the steep hill, which allowed him to freewheel, at pace, along a dark alley, then diagonally across Piazza Rosa. He bumped over the cobbles, his bell ringing clearly in the quiet of the morning square, and leaped off, the bicycle continuing without him until it came to a clattering halt against the railings of Parliament Hall.

'I have a letter! A letter for our president! I must deliver it at once! Look, it has, it has … a foreign stamp!' The two guards knew Remi well, drank with him frequently and would probably be joining him for their regular light lunch of cold boar and bread later that day, but nevertheless each reached for his gun holster as the postman ripped at his shirt, buttons flying. They took turns to scrutinize the letter, looking closely at the address, the stamps and back again at the trembling postman. Undeniably, the seal of international airfreight was a persuasive argument and one that, upon lengthy reflection, neither felt able to resist.

On the understanding that both men would accompany him until responsibility had been passed to a senior minister, Remi was allowed to enter Parliament Hall. As they pushed the double doors to enter, all three experienced a prickle of excitement as the building swallowed them.

CHAPTER 2

In Which Treason Is Narrowly Avoided

THE OFFICE of the minister for the exterior was an efficient one, run by the extremely busy Mario Lucaccia, whose intense industriousness manifested itself in an empty desk with just a notepad and a careful alignment of recently sharpened pencils, ordered by size and poised for action. The interruption to his morning was regrettable as he was on the verge of implementing a groundbreaking directive, the nature of which had eluded him for some years. He tutted audibly. With barely a pause and a brusque wave of the hand, the young minister swiftly passed Remi on, through an internal door that was partly shrouded by a heavy brocade curtain. It led to the larger and more cluttered office of Signor Rolando Posti, the minister for the interior.

'What have we here, Remi-Post?' the world-weary minister enquired, peering up at the visitor from beneath his once-impressive eyebrows.

'I am here, with your kind permission, to deliver a letter from the United Kingdom of England, sir.' Remi shuffled a little but took comfort from the presence of two palace guards and one minister for the exterior.

'A letter you say. And how can you be so sure?' The minister reached for the aerogramme and studied it carefully.

'Oh, I know a letter when I see one, sir. It is my job to know these things.' On safe ground now, Remi shuffled a little less.

'It is, is it? And at what point, Remi-Post, does your job end and my job commence? For is it not within the remit of my job to recognize the difference between a letter and a formal application from a foreign entity?' The minister for the interior let the possibility hang in the air.

'A formal what, sir?' Remi knew immediately that this was outside the realm of his training and fell silent, his mouth agape.

The minister continued, 'And as such, if it is determined to be the latter rather than the former, it requires an altogether different procedure. And here is a conundrum that immediately becomes apparent, Remi-Post, a quandary that a postman such as your good self needn't ordinarily concern himself with, but I shall enlighten you because it is the wish of our president that wisdom is shared for the collective understanding of our entire nation and for the evolutionary betterment of future generations.' He paused. 'If it is just a letter, we needn't worry our president with it. He is a busy man with an election to prepare for, and it is our job, as ministers, to act as filters and remove all that is trifling or troublesome from his immediate concern. If I were to go now to his chambers and interrupt his work with just-a-letter I cannot begin to second guess the consequences, but they would be grave.' Signor Posti sighed heavily for dramatic effect. 'If, however, it transpires that this is indeed a formal application from a foreign entity, and I were to hesitate before presenting it to our president, or to presume I had the resource or acumen to deal with it independently, then he would be quite correct to consider my action, or my non-action, as an act of gross treason.'

He glowered at the men in the room. The palace guards were almost imperceptibly retreating, a backwards halfstep at a time, in a silent bid to put distance between themselves and these treasonous associations. Signor Lucaccia, meanwhile, who had been listening intently to the exchange, was now eyeing the older minister. The younger minister's scrutiny sported a glint of nervousness and he was chewing his lip anxiously, but he knew, too, that there was much he could learn from studying the older man's handling of the situation. All the power was in the interior, everybody knew that, and progressing from his own inferior ministerial duties would be easier if he took his lead from this sagacious elder statesman.

Signor Posti drew himself up in his chair and looked coolly at his audience. Now was a time for decisiveness and clear thinking. A letter would be quicker to deal with, but there was no precedent for receiving one at Parliament Hall and the stamps upon this communication certainly appeared to bear the mark of the United Kingdom's most senior stateswoman. The minister was a cautious man, and his caution was one of the virtues that had earned him high office. It would be safer – both for the sake of his career and for the sanctity of his country – to assume this was not just-a-letter but an official communiqué. In this instance, hasty action would mitigate any potential risk to the president. With the first part of the decision already made, it was now simply a case of determining the correct protocol.

Swivelling his chair, Signor Posti turned slowly and deliberately to the shelves behind him and heaved one of the tomes back to his desk. He wetted his finger and flicked through the pages, conscious of four pairs of eyes upon him as he scanned the headings and sub-sections, many of which he had authored over the years. After several tense moments he found the right page and, smiling knowingly to himself, began the laborious task of form filling. This required the dispatching of the hovering minister for the exterior for two fresh sheets of carbon paper to allow the execution of the paperwork in triplicate. Glad once more to have volunteered interest, the less-experienced man hurried off importantly.

Remi jigged from foot to foot, anxious to learn his fate and, if protocol decreed it, to take hold once more of the important document. A lifetime of training had prepared him for this very scenario and, while the minister before him had an evolved understanding of the machinations of Parliament, he alone understood that the royal blue of the *par avion* sticker, fixed jauntily to the left-hand corner, insisted upon the most urgent of handling at all times.

But, as anxious as he was, his strict sense of hierarchy ensured that he must do nothing to interrupt the process of government. As patiently as possible, he observed the complex ritual, quietly respectful of the enormous amount of bureaucracy his not just-a-letter had already generated.

At last, the postman's conscientious approach was rewarded. After a brief discussion between the two ministers, who huddled forehead to forehead in a corner while they decided on the best course of action, Remi was invited to hand-deliver the not just-a-letter to its final destination, proceeding further into the echelons of Parliament Hall, using another, narrower, flight of stairs. Shaking with excitement and accompanied now by two guardsmen, one short, eager minister for the exterior and one tall, craggy, breathless minister for the interior, he hesitated, then politely rapped on the carved wooden door of his president's private chambers. Upon hearing the call from within, he was barely able to still the knocking of his knees.

CHAPTER 3

In Which a Formal Communication From a Foreign Entity Is Delivered

UNTIL TWENTY-TWO MINUTES past ten, when Remi's bicycle had bounced its way, riderless, to a halt in front of the railings, President Sergio Scorpioni had been contemplating life and the complex paradigms it dealt him. Each new dawn seemed to reveal to him another bewildering puzzle to solve, and nightfall brought disappointment and impotence in place of the sense of completion and resolution he craved. Today his own dissatisfaction was the source of his troubles. 'To what do all men aspire?' he asked himself. 'Great wealth? Good looks? A beautiful wife with generous hips?' Pausing for effect, even though the conversation was playing out in the confines of his own mind, he answered, 'No, the ultimate status symbol comes in the shape of a position of power.' And there he was, appointed to the highest office in the land, with all its associated amenities and privileges. At his disposal he had catering staff and cleaning staff, he had a dozen vice-presidents, who were the clearest thinkers and his dearest friends in the land, yet he remained unfulfilled.

He shook his head and chewed his lip as he surveyed the material manifestation of his power. As a centrepiece, his sumptuous private chambers boasted an intricately carved mahogany four-poster bed, with a firm but forgiving mattress on which to rest at night, several goose-down pillows on which to lay his head, cool cotton sheets and warm angora blankets, surrounded by the finest bombazine hangings.

Throughout his chambers the floor was covered with layer upon layer of hand-woven carpets, each overlapping the next and telling its own elaborate tales. Their rich and complex threads wove the stories of many lifetimes, winding together the narratives of peasant childhoods with high holidays, of marriages made in Heaven and useful lives reflected upon from the comfort of an old age well accounted-for. Carpets owned by his mother, stitched by his grandmother, trodden on by his father and forefathers before him.

His desk, carved, like his bed, of the very finest hardwood, was solid, vast, and shone with decades of polish. With inset inkwells and a large blotter that was regularly refilled with a clean sheet, that desk had been the seat of power for his father, and his father's father. And look! It was all his! As he paced from bed, to desk, to window and back again, in a circle that showed, after four and a half years of office, a faint trace of a path in the carpets, he tried to count his blessings on his fingers. 'One, I have my health. Two, I have the tools for change. Three, I don't have to make my own bed in the morning ...'

It was no good, his face crumpled and his fingers balled into fists as the full weight of the responsibility that was attendant upon his comfortable life came crashing back upon his shoulders. As he continued to pace, his lips formed silent pledges but the acid that rose from his stomach, giving him almost constant pain in his lower chest, came from a dark, dismal place that countered those promises and told him that he would never, ever, be as successful as his father.

He stopped at the window, resting his forehead against the damp glass and allowing a little pool of condensation to gather there. Below him, Piazza Rosa was gloomy. Puddles from the previous night's rain had gathered between the cobbles, and wastepaper clung miserably to the rims of gutters, refusing to be swept away out of sight but lingering to add to the forlorn landscape. Plastic webbed chairs were tilted forward against moulded white tables, and metal shutters were drawn at the majority of shop windows, giving the country's finest meeting point an air of neglect and dejection. Sergio looked at his watch, which showed twenty-five past ten, and then up at the landmark clock opposite him. It remained stubbornly, accusingly, at ten to seven and the painted clay figurines, crafted to represent the finest attributes of Vallerosa, who should have been lining up to announce the next fifteen-minute interval, had long been stilled. Today was the beginning of spring, a time of festivity, traditionally used to commence courtship and slaughter the last of the

21

winter pigs, but no one was celebrating. Even Franco, the town's alcoholic, would have been a welcome sight, but not even he was prepared to liven up the square with his clumsy lurching and unintelligible mutterings. Sergio scanned the piazza, his eyes sweeping across the left edge, with its arched walkway, along the grand façade of the town hall and clock tower and back down the right edge, but all was damply silent.

Inside, the electrics hummed, the ancient heating system clicked and sighed, and the building itself creaked under the oppressive atmosphere of a period of celebration when the public had chosen – unanimously – not to celebrate.

The winter months were dismal, as for any city that thrived on its long, hot summers, whose very livelihood depended on clear blue skies by day and clement nights. Each year, work in the tea plantations remained at a standstill until the sun heaved itself over the mountaintop to awaken the first shoots in April, when labour could once again resume. A sluggishness of pace that was forgivable in the unrelenting summer sun took on a less condonable tenor, tinged with apathy and inertia, when the days shortened and the thermometer seldom rose above twelve degrees.

The red façade of the city's main square that, under the kind light of the summer months, shone with every tone from a pale, dusty rose to a deep, bottomless burgundy, looked tired in the winter, shrinking in fear from each day's onslaught. The flaking plaster and crumbling stone glared accusingly at the president, reminding him of the enormous cost involved in maintaining the piazza in its present state, let alone restoring it to its pre-1900s glory.

He returned to his desk and took up his pen. After allowing it to drink thirstily from the ink, he resumed writing. His current train of thought was complex and the recent round of pacing had done little to unlock his dilemma. He reread the last passage he had written.

Choice exists to liberate your electorate. But, what a responsible leader must ask is, does his constituent really hanker after choice? No, of course they don't. What the constituent demands – nay, deserves – is flawless leadership. And providing that flawlessness is evident throughout government, elected or otherwise, if perfection has already been attained, then how can further choice ever equate to liberation? That choice, that freedom, which the democratic world so craves, is redundant if the only choice the state can proffer is that between perfection and mediocrity. What, then, are you offering your people? Your people are the backbone of the society, yes; they are the bedrock of the country, the foundation on which any great nation is built. They are the flour, the eggs and milk, but without the wooden spoon, they cannot be the pancake. They are the proletariat, not the elected, and as such they cannot possibly begin to interpret the discourse of politicians. Nor are they equipped to decipher the devious ruses that politicians will utilize, the depths to which they'll sink, in pursuit of a vote. And why are they unable to enter the twisted mind of a power-crazed despot, hell-bent on seizing control of a country? Because the state has governed in such a way that its people only understand fairness, citizenship, fellowship, a society working together for the benefit of society. This country's people have not been educated in the art of insidiousness. You give your people a vote without giving them the warped mind needed to make an educated decision and they are in danger of choosing to exercise their vote for change just because they can. You, through the so called tools of liberation, have given them the very rope with which they will unwittingly hoist themselves from the petard.

Sergio flexed his writing hand and leaned back in his chair, which groaned beneath him. He rested his eyes and immediately, uninvited, the image of his father sprang before his closed lids. He rubbed them with the back of his hands and opened them again, preferring the look of his writing to the ever-wagging finger of Sergio Senior. He sighed deeply, wiped away the small beads of sweat gathering on his upper lip, and continued.

Give an honest man the choice between good and evil and he might inadvertently choose evil, because he has no experience from which to recognize the traits of the perfidious.

As Sergio came decisively to this conclusion, a resounding thud in his heart seemed to echo his thinking. He took up his pen to begin writing once more when, startled, he realized the noise came not from inside his head but from somebody knocking repeatedly at the door. Glancing around the room to assure himself that there were no visible traces of his inner turmoil, Sergio barked permission to enter.

Expecting a butler with a tray of tea, as was customary at this time, he was surprised to find he was giving audience to a posse of visitors. Their sheer numbers as they filed through the door gave him a moment's anxiety that, as foretold in any one of his recent nightmares, a coup might be unfolding before his eyes. But quickly he recognized them all as friends, the young postman, whom he himself had promoted, his trusted minister for the interior, the younger, ambitious minister for the exterior, for whom he had high hopes, and two palace guards, who were hanging about in the background, onlookers, it appeared, rather than active protectors of the realm.

After an awkward silence, Remi stepped forward and, unsure whether he was presenting a letter, a not just-a-letter, or an official communication from a foreign entity, simply held out the blue envelope to his president. He was not quite far enough forward for Sergio to reach it without standing up, and even when the president had pushed himself up from his chair and leaned across his desk, there was still an unmet gap of some inches. It seemed that the stalemate might never be broken. Sergio stretched further but Remi, clearly terrified by the proximity of the president, dared not look at him and affixed his eyes instead to the intricate pattern in the carpet.

Sergio relented, and came around his desk to pluck the letter from the postman's hands. At this moment, perhaps unsure that he wanted his adventure to end, Remi clung to a corner and Sergio had to use surprising force to tug the envelope away. Flustered, he retreated to the safe haven behind his desk and took a long-handled letter-opener from beside the blotter.

One of the ministers, either interior or exterior, made a murmur as if to excuse the party but Sergio silenced the onlookers with a wave of his hand. He removed the elegant letter-opener slowly from its leather sheath, inserted the tip into the top seal and, with unhurried decorum, used the blade to separate the three gummed sides. The letter tumbled out to its full length and the president read its contents from top to bottom, taking in the London address, the velvety quality of the flimsy yet luxurious paper, the superb penmanship, with its loops and curves, unlike any he had seen before, and the evenly applied ink of the signature. Some of it was almost impossible to decipher but he peered at the English words, identifying several as his eyes flicked from one line to the next. 'Please ... visit ... research ... success ... Duke of Edinburgh ... 5 June ... for one month.'

A slow smile spread across Sergio's face, softening his features and letting the careworn frown disappear. His only regret, which passed through his mind at lightning speed, was that his father (who had made it quite clear that his son would probably amount to nothing) was no longer alive to witness this triumph. For a triumph it most certainly was, and that it had fallen during Sergio's tenure allowed the president to take this success as a personal one.

His country had finally been recognized beyond its borders and, as clear as the blue ink with which the signature had sealed its intent, a visit from British royalty, of those distant but hallowed islands in the North Sea, was imminent and had been humbly begged by, presumably, the personal secretary of the Duke of Edinburgh, to whom the letter referred on a number of occasions.

He put the letter down. Placing a hand firmly on either side of it, he leaned forward and looked thoughtfully at each man before him. 'Gentlemen,' he announced grandly. 'It seems we are to expect a royal visit later this year. Sound the fanfare. I shall be making an address to the people on this matter of national importance at …' he glanced at his watch, then calculated the time he would need to write a short speech and change into his formal attire '… noon. I shall speak to them from the balcony. That will be all. Carry on.'

The five men hastily backed out of the room, leaving the president to the solitude of his chambers. As soon as he was sure he was alone, he punched the air and danced a little jig on the spot.

Meanwhile, the minister for the exterior headed directly to the press office, the minister for the interior went to the army's control centre while the postman made for Il Gallo Giallo to ensure that word quickly spread. Within the hour, those at home, or in either of the city's two bars, downed tools, drinks, laundry or children and headed out into Piazza Rosa to hear the president's news.

CHAPTER 4

In Which News Travels Fast

THE OPPOSITE END of Piazza Rosa from Parliament Hall, the north-west corner, was home to both of the city's bars, whose perpendicular proximity was separated at the narrowest point by a mere five feet or so. That their walls didn't touch was thanks to the narrow cobbled path that carried most of the pedestrian traffic from the piazza to the residential area and on, through a slow ascent of zigzags, to the tea plantations above.

The bars each occupied approximately the same square footage. Il Gallo Giallo benefited from the generous arched frontage afforded by the walkway that spanned the west face of the piazza; in this shaded area patrons could enjoy their tea or beer without being drained by the full force of the sun. On the other hand, Il Toro Rosso, while only ninety degrees away, offered a very different climate: it enjoyed full afternoon sunshine on its apron, offering clients a distinct advantage in the winter months and early evening, when a drinker might enjoy the last of the sun as it reached over the mountains and into the valley. A free man, in a different city, in a different country, but faced with the same choice, might choose to spend his lunchtime at Il Gallo Giallo and his evenings at Il Toro Rosso. Or his winters at Il Toro Rosso and his summers at Il Gallo Giallo. But this wasn't a different city, or a different country, and where you chose to drink wasn't a simple matter of ergonomics or personal comfort.

Inside, the bars barely differed. An equal number of bar stools had popped their red vinyl seat covers to reveal tired yellowing foam. The twelve or so tables in each were topped with thin slabs of a similar red stone, probably quarried from the same pit in the nearby foothills. During the summer months the cool stone offered respite, and it was said that by leaving your bottled beer atop any of the tables for just a few minutes, the beer's temperature would actually drop by a degree or two. During the winter months the stone was a curse but the patrons of both bars knew better than to lean their exposed wrists or hands on the inhospitable surface. Both bars were decorated in a similar fashion – that is to say, minimally. A few sparse mirrors shouting the copy lines of long-forgotten tobaccos and liquors hung on nails, and similar drab once-white curtains, never closed, were suspended at the window of each bar, sharing the view of the dark alley between them. The ninety-degree angle at which the establishments sat ensured that the drinkers in one bar couldn't view those in the other, although when the outside tables were occupied in both, it would be easy to imagine that the occupants were all patronizing the same place: the chairs often spilled over the boundaries and met across the alley.

Most residents of the city rarely referred to the bars as either Il Gallo Giallo or Il Toro Rosso, knowing the first as 'Gallo' or the Old Bar, and the second as 'Rosso' or the New Bar. There was little to choose between them as far as age went either: although Il Gallo Giallo was older by a full five years, they had both opened to custom in the mid-1800s, which meant that their shared history had them as close siblings, rather than relatives separated by a generation.

Il Gallo Giallo, the Old Bar, was run by a taciturn land-lord, whose job it was, he felt, to slam beers down in front of his customers, allowing the top centimetre to slop onto the table below, and to leave teas cooling on the counter before delivering them at a less than satisfactory temperature. The tea was never strained, but drunk so dark and bitter that to the uninitiated it would be completely unpalatable. Those drinking in the Old Bar, however, had earned their right to consume their tea there, and to issue one word of complaint either about the manners of Dario Mariani, their landlord, or the tempera-ture of the tea was unheard of.

By contrast, a young man, with traces of naïve optimism still visible on his face, ran the New Bar. He had inherited his position from his father, who had taught his son every-thing he knew before retiring, and then dying, both grace-fully and considerately. His son, Piper, had been an attentive student and had learned the lessons of beer, tea, and of the illegal but much practised habit of fortifying the local wine into something that would chase the cold away from your kidneys in the winter. But he had aspirations above and beyond those he had acquired from his beloved father. Piper had a secret ambition to beat his rival. How he could judge his success in a battle that the other showed no interest in entering, he had not yet ascertained – perhaps by a gradual migration of loyal customers from the Old Bar to his, or through some as yet unimagined innovation … He lay awake at night, considering it.

In truth, though, a truth that Dario took for granted and Piper refused to acknowledge, there was no competition between the bars. A century and more of tradition was so firmly rooted that it was unlikely that anything would shake the unwritten rule that, come lunchtime, the men of government, heads of state, the police and the army – anyone who donned a uniform – made their way to Il Gallo Giallo. Within its yellowing walls you would find, too, those who aspired to a life in government and who were considered – either by themselves or others – as on the up.

Il Toro Rosso, on the other hand, was home to the labourers and farmhands, the teachers and health-workers, the artisans and musicians, and the students who lacked political ambition.

There was no edict that suggested this was where you belonged, and those whose instinct drew them to one or the other were probably unaware, at the time, of the partisan statement they were making when they went, at any age, for the first time to order a drink. But the distinction was inherent and abided by comfortably without the prejudice that similar apartheid might afford in other European countries. That is not to say that one could not choose to drink with a man from the other bar, but habitual practice suggested they were probably more likely to meet on the three or four tables that inhabited no man's land between the two establishments. As such, these were often the most prized positions to occupy.

Today Remi entered Il Gallo Giallo, breathing in the scent of hops and tea while looking around to see who might be there to hear his news. He hung up his hat next to those of Mario Lucaccia and Giuseppe Scota and sauntered slowly, luxuriously, to the bar with affected patience and the quiet smile of a man who knows he has a story to share with a willing audience.

He told his tale in the smallest detail, with only the tiniest embellishment, describing the onion-skin quality of the perfumed paper and the gold-leaf emblem of the royal stamps, his immediate ascent through Parliament Hall and his private audience with the president, who had read to him, word for word, in the flawless hissing articulation of the English language as if he himself had been raised among the British nobility.

'Oh, yes, the president's English is word-perfect. Not a thotthage in thite for the president.' The postman mimicked a peasant's pronunciation of the country's second or third language, depending on the number of years they had been immersed in pursuit of a full and useful education.

Remi continued to regale his audience with the contents of the letter, that none other than the royal Duke of

Edinburgh, brother, he thought to the King himself or uncle to the Queen. One of the two. Anyway, a senior royal, certainly, who had set his sights on visiting their country, for he had heard such fine stories about it around the globe.

Draining his cup of tea, and pushing it back across the bar, he waited for a refill. Immediately speculation was rife, and the topic of conversation bubbled across the bar and out onto the adjoining pavement, trickling to those standing at the mouth of the alley and across into the New Bar. It was as if Remi himself were being carried above the heads of the drinkers, a victorious matador at the annual Bull Fling. His words seeped through the New Bar, gathering a momentum and meaning all of their own as they were taken, doubled and passed on.

By the time the president greeted his audience from the balcony there were very few who hadn't heard one of the many unofficial versions of the extraordinary news.

CHAPTER 5

In Which a President Addresses His Nation

ANGELO, SERGIO'S CHIEF OF STAFF, had masterfully managed to intercede just in time to pull the president back from the potential error of donning full military uniform. However, Sergio's smart black suit was decorated with a scattering of medals to add a sense of sobriety to the occasion. As the president slid open the long windows of his sitting room and stepped onto his balcony, he felt his mood lifted by the formality of the occasion and the splendour of pageantry. Behind him filed Angelo, Mario Lucaccia, the minister for the exterior, and his ten other senior ministers who now fanned out at either side of him. They stood to attention, their arms straight at their sides, their feet shoulder-width apart, as was the custom when the president made any public address.

Despite the dull spring day and the ceaseless drizzle, a curious crowd had assembled in Piazza Rosa, propelled by the contagious enthusiasm of Remi the postman. By the time the president had taken his position, at least

34

fifteen hundred people were gathered in the piazza. As he approached the front of the balcony, the onlookers allowed their conversation to peter out and turned instead to fix their eyes on him.

'Ladies and gentlemen, serfs and servants,' Sergio began, using the protocol that had been introduced by his father. 'Today is a day that has been much anticipated but always expected. A day when, finally, the rest of the world has decided to look kindly upon our statedom.' Here, Sergio looked up from his notes and, with all the confidence of a gifted orator, spoke from his heart. 'A day that marks a turning point in our history and is, perhaps, the end of the beginning of our history and the start of the middle.' Losing his drift, he returned quickly to the notes. 'A day when I have had pressed into my hand by our very humble servant Remi, the postman, a letter that bears the royal insignia of the British Isles and Her Majesty's Great Britain.'

Here, he held up the letter, as if, from one storey below, the audience might be able to read for themselves the contents. With one arm raised high, he thrust his chest forward, allowing his deep baritone to ricochet off the piazza buildings, which provided natural amplification to the row of basic microphones in front of him. He drew a breath, then announced grandly, 'It is my very great privilege to inform you that we shall be receiving a noble visitation from Britain's far shores. No less than the royal Duke of Edinburgh himself shall begin a month-long tour of our humble state on June the fifth of this year. I therefore declare that the four days preceding the visit, from

June the first to June the fourth, will be devoted to preparation. I ask that you all join me and my government to ensure that we come together to use this opportunity to showcase our country not just to Britain and Europe but to the rest of the world.' Sergio paused, then continued, 'June the fifth, when our royal visitor will arrive, will be marked by a day of celebration. We shall have just enough time to fortify some wine and fatten some pigs.'

At this, the susurrus of assent could be heard. General calls to celebration were open to misinterpretation, but specific detail – permission, they gathered, to turn a goodly portion of their wine reserves into something a little stronger – they could interpret very clearly. As the men turned to each other to discuss the specifics, Sergio became aware that he had lost their attention. 'Carry on!' he bellowed into the microphones, then retreated to his rooms.

Inside, he brushed the raindrops off his jacket and started to address his men. Angelo dropped into a chair to take notes and began scribbling.

'Right, men. This is an opportunity for you to shine. First, we must form a committee. It will meet once a week until our preparations are well under way, then daily, of course, for the first crucial days of June. Agreed. Now, we'll need you, Roberto, to look after the budget for the event. Perhaps we'll form a separate working group to deal with the finer details.' Roberto Feraguzzi nodded. 'And you, Enzo, I'll need you to ensure the first-flush tea is harvested and ready for consumption.' Enzo Civicchioni grinned enthusiastically, patting his pockets for a non-existent pen with which to take notes that he'd only later mislay. 'And you, Alix, you have a crucial role to play – that of national security. I cannot stress heavily enough the gravity of the situation. I suggest we are on Code Red between now and our visitor's safe departure. Agreed?' Alixandria Heliopolis Visparelli saluted smartly. 'Mario Lucaccia, you are, of course, essential to proceedings, as minister for the exterior. What finer opportunity than this to showcase our country to the outside world? You, like-wise, Settimio. This is a once-in-a-lifetime opportunity for you to realize some of your goals, touristically speaking. Giuseppe Scota, you may not think there is much of a part for an education minister to play but I see you as vital in bringing the students to the occasion. Exclude them at your peril.'

'Of course,' agreed Scota, already dreaming of the opportunities this might afford some of his older students.

Sergio continued, 'Decio, there are many aspects of your role that will come into play. I want you in from the start. We've got health and safety to consider, not to mention the ongoing physical health of our visitor. I want absolutely no illness lurking to sabotage proceedings. You must see to it that everyone is well, understood?' Dottore Decio Rossini smiled and agreed.

'Vlad, I want you to work with Giuseppe Scota. Education and employment go hand in hand, as always.' He scanned the room full of expectant faces. 'Pompili and Cellini. This is your moment. This will be the best *festa* in the history of Vallerosa. You understand? That is a command.'

The two men nodded gravely.

'And I'll need you, Rolando, on board too. Detail, detail, detail. Proper planning will prevent a poor performance, yes?'

'Yes, sir. Of course, always, sir.'

'I think that group should just about cover it. Those mentioned will be required to satisfy a quorum. I apologize to those of you who cannot be part of the committee on this auspicious occasion, but I'm sure your expertise will be called upon in time. Sometimes it's better to keep an operation a little leaner, just to ensure that we're working as efficiently as possible. The rest of you, consider yourselves back-up of the very finest order.' Sergio smiled at his men.

They looked at each other, trying to find a common expression that fell neatly between congratulations and commiseration.

'That will be all, then. Those of you not directly involved in the proceedings are dismissed. The rest of you, let's gather for the first ever meeting of the Committee to Ensure the Safe Arrival, Visit and Return of our VIP. That will be the ...'

'CESAVROV?' interjected Angelo from the corner.

Sergio considered this. 'Hmm, that's not going to run. Work on it, will you, Angelo? Table it for the first meeting. OK, men, on with your day, please. I know it's a disappointment but only committee members are now required.'

'Sir?' said Angelo, from the corner. 'According to my minutes, everyone here has been appointed to the committee.'

'Have they?' The president frowned the most fleeting of frowns. 'Of course they have. You will find that is because they are indispensable. There is not a man among them who could be spared from a visit of such national importance.' Sergio used the moment to appraise them slowly, his gaze sweeping over the assembled group. Drawing himself tall, he dismissed them with a curt nod that interrupted any possibility of his eyes misting with tears. 'Well, carry on, then. What are you standing around for?' He ran a finger around his collar to loosen it a little.

The twelve men filed out to take their places at the boardroom table and begin the serious business of planning.

SEVERAL HOURS LATER, whoops and hollers could be heard from the assembled group and Sergio flushed with pleasure. A breathless Angelo came flying in. 'It was tough, sir, but I do believe we've cracked it. The project will be named the Planning for English Guest and the Safe Undertaking of Security …'

Sergio thought for a moment, then a slow smile spread across his face, revealing itself eventually as a triumphant grin. 'PEGASUS,' he murmured, rolling the word around on his tongue and trying it from every angle. 'Yes, excellent work. That, Angelo, will most certainly fly.'

CHAPTER 6

In Which Enough
Tea Is Grown

SHORTLY AFTERWARDS, in the opulent surroundings of the Upper House, the Special Furthering of Agricultural Development Committee was gathering for its monthly appraisal. Eleven of the twelve quorum were assembled around the vast cherry-wood boardroom table, six positions marked out to each side of the president. Each member sat straight-backed, awaiting the moment at which the discussion would be initiated by the president, but no deliberation could begin until the tea had been poured. In front of each committee member sat two bone china teacups, a pair of identical silver tea strainers and a small, lidded china pot. Angelo, the president's chief of staff, the cabinet member responsible for the care of Parliament Hall but also for the day-to-day care of the president, discreetly opened the proceedings by preparing Sergio's tea. With minimal fuss, he poured it from pot to cup, then from cup to cup, through a fine-meshed strainer. Expertly, with a trained eye and an accomplished hand, he filtered it back and forth. With each passing, the dark green liquid took on a lighter tone until, with an almost imperceptible nod, Angelo indicated that it had achieved the requisite tint of amber and, as such, was ready for drinking. Then each committee member began to strain their own tea, with less precision and a lot more haste, catching up with their leader in time to join him as he leaned forward to take his first slurp.

Oh, the first taste of afternoon tea! It didn't matter how many times the ritual was performed, the first sip always delivered a powerful shock to the system. Sergio slurped the liquid noisily through his teeth, allowing the bitter flavour to coat the inside of his mouth and marvelling as the aftershocks ricocheted through his upper jaw and settled somewhere beneath his eye-sockets. He grimaced and sucked in both cheeks to lessen the impact. After an involuntary shake of his head his entire upper body shuddered, allowing the effect of the tea to cascade through his frame, working its magic on every area that called for special attention, from his stiff knee and ankle joints to his cramping toes. As the president savoured the moment, the committee members joined in with the noisy ceremony, adding their own facial tics, scowls, lip smackings and flinches to the ritual.

'Aaaah,' pronounced the president. 'That's better. Shall we begin?' He glanced around the room, taking a mental register of his staff, beginning on his left with Dottore Decio Rossini, minister for health (mental, physical and metaphysical). The doctor's pallid, doughy face sported heavy brown bags under the eyes. His shirt, slightly fraying at the collar, bore the unmistakable yellowing stains of fatherhood on both shoulders – he had seven small boys. While Sergio eyed him, the weary doctor stifled a yawn and wondered where he would find the energy to keep trying to produce a daughter for his wife. The president noted his physician's exhaustion but appreciated the reasons behind it and allowed his eyes to travel beyond him to Signor Vlad Lubicic, minister for employment and personal development. Vlad had telltale purple bags but his eyes today were dreamy, preoccupied, and he'd barely touched his tea. There had to be a significant new woman in his life, of that Sergio was certain. Excellent. The president made a mental note to find out who she was and, if appropriate, to hurry proceedings to their proper conclusion. It would be more efficient and a better use of ministerial time to bring the pining phase to an end as quickly as possible. And an official wedding was always good for the nation's morale. Third on his left sat Signor Marcello Pompili, minister for recreation. Hair slicked back, rosy cheeks pumiced to a shine, keen, bright eyes glinting with vigour, Signor Pompili sat forward in his seat with a youthful ardour that radiated gusto. Yes, an excellent advertisement for the role, an outlook to be encouraged and replicated. Sergio's appraisal continued to Signor Cellini, minister for leisure. What he observed here was far less encouraging. Where his colleague Signor Pompili shone, Cellini drooped. His shoulders slumped; his body language told of dissatisfaction or worry. His Adam's apple leaped feverishly up and down his throat, sending out little signals of anxiety, and his eyes darted around the room, stealing glances at his colleagues and at the president but managing to avoid contact with either. Signor Cellini was brother-in-law, of course, to Signor Roberto Feraguzzi, minister of finance, seated now to Sergio's right. Feraguzzi was a cool customer and, apart from the almost imperceptible tic that tugged occasionally at his upper left cheek, there was barely an anxious bone in his body. He chewed his inner cheek from time to time, in a subtle bid to disguise the tic, but Sergio knew that this meant nothing. His face had twitched for as long as the president had known him. Of much more concern was the remote but entirely plausible explanation that Feraguzzi had knowledge of a pending financial crisis and had chosen to share it with brother-in-law Cellini, whose face was less able to smother his emotion.

Between Feraguzzi and Angelo there was an empty chair, the usual seat of the minister for agricultural development. That they were assembled to hear from him made his lack of punctuality doubly irritating. Sergio's eyes rested on the empty chair and glared accusingly, prompting Angelo to speak out.

'Mr President, Signor Civicchioni sends his apologies. He will be joining us a few minutes late today, but he will bring with him a special report from the American consultant, who is available to meet with the committee today, should you wish it. I understand that the report was late being prepared because the typist was late for work due to problems of a feminine nature. I understand, however, that a second typist was subsequently drafted in

43

and the completed report will be available for inspection at any moment.'

Sergio nodded and allowed his eyes to travel further on to Commandant Alixandria Heliopolis Visparelli, minister for defence. Alix had no interest in the Special Furthering of Agricultural Development; he cared nothing for the difference between an output and a yield, and he had not initially been invited to sit on this committee. He had, however, persuaded Sergio that he should be recruited to it, and of all members, he paid the closest attention at each of these gatherings. While he had no interest in crops or herds, he had a very grave interest in the comings and goings of the American consultant, and this assembly was an excellent one for studying a potential enemy at close quarters without allowing him to know he had been identified as a possible threat. Since these meetings had first convened, Alix had been known to throw in trick questions to flush out any ulterior motive on the part of the American consultant, but these cunning ploys were normally met with a frown from his president, who insisted, somewhat naïvely, Alix thought, on assuming everyone was a friend to their nation until proved otherwise. That Alix seemed to be uniquely suspicious made him more determined to be vigilant; he always double-checked the firing mechanism on his handgun before appearing at the committee table. Even now, as Sergio appraised his team, Alix's eyes roamed in the other direction. He was preparing an escape route, should he have to rescue the president from an attempt on his life.

To the right of Alix sat Signor Lucaccia, minister for the exterior. That they were seated next to each other was the unhappy accident of the very first meeting. Since then, the men had assumed the same positions. If Alix and Mario had been able to choose, they would each have sat on the same side of the table (in order not to have to look at each other) and as far apart as possible (in order not to have to sense each other). Instead, they were destined to sit shoulder to shoulder for at least an hour each month and both men visibly bristled with discomfort. Alix was doing his best to lean into some of the vacant space allowed by the missing minister for agricultural development while Mario leaned heavily to his right, rubbing thighs with his neighbour, the minister for education, Professore Giuseppe Scota. Sergio glanced sympathetically at the professor, who looked as if he resented the intrusion into his personal space by the young exterior minister, but Scota returned the kind look with an almost imperceptible shrug. Both the professor and his president understood the rift between the two men. It was said that there were only two things worth fighting about in Vallerosa, pigs and women, and the two men had fought over both. Nothing could be done to heal the rift.

As Sergio shared his quiet moment of understanding with Scota, Civicchioni, the errant minister for agricultural development, entered, trailing a flurry of flying shirt tails and the flapping ends of a loosely knotted tie, while clutching armfuls of unstapled loose-leaf papers that drifted from him as he rushed to take his seat. Sergio nodded permission to him to join them and added a

45

cursory study of the late arrival to his mental register. Today Civicchioni was agitated, partially undressed and harried. The big lock of curly brown hair that obscured his right eye added a moderately incompetent and slightly insane look. Sergio noted with satisfaction that this promising young man was behaving true to form.

'Mr President. May I?' As he patted and prodded his paperwork into some sort of order, he grabbed a gulp of unstrained tea, wincing while swilling it around as though it were mouthwash. With an appreciative smack of his lips, he used the palm of his hand to push the escaped lock of hair to the top of his head as he launched into the purpose of the gathering that afternoon.

'You will all be fully aware that under section four, article five, sub-section twelve, particle b of last Tuesday's emergency agricultural meeting, I have been asked by our esteemed president to meet with our American consultant, the expert who has been contracted to this government to review and enhance our agricultural policy.'

At the mention of the visiting American, Alix allowed an audible hiss to escape from his lips. With one enemy practically sitting in his lap and another central to this discussion, he bristled with an urgent need to kill somebody. Sergio was quick to sense his defence minister's simmering displeasure and managed to catch his eye, silently holding up four fingers in admonishment. Alix hung his head in shame, and muttered quietly to himself the mantra, 'Restraint is a powerful weapon.' He looked his president in the eye and half smiled an apology. The president empathized, as he himself had suffered from moments of weakness in which he occasionally struggled to live consistently within the strict teachings of their shared military guru, General Isaak von Bunyan.

(*Restraint Is a Powerful Weapon* is the fourth book in von Bunyan's six-volume military compendium; its title loosely but not absolutely translates as 'Avoiding Military Conflict Through Ingenuity and Psychological Camouflage', a thesis studied in depth and adhered to by both Alix and his president. This masterpiece of warfare avoidance had for some decades been widely credited with the shared success of Vallerosa and Switzerland in their unblemished records of peace. If asked to compare the success of each country, it could probably be argued that Vallerosa's interpretation of the Eight Rules of Camouflage is perhaps even more successful than that of Switzerland: not only has it successfully blended with all its surrounding countries to avoid conflict, it has done such an effective job that half of its neighbours think of Vallerosa as a poor and undesirable province of their own state, while the other half have failed to notice it exists at all. And, while on the subject of comparing success in this area, any one of the assembled men, whether followers of General Isaak von Bunyan or not, could have pointed out that Vallerosa had never knowingly harboured a war criminal or condoned the laundering of money.)

Enzo Civicchioni continued with his briefing: 'You will all remember that our American consultant was initially contracted to us for six months. His contract has subsequently been reviewed and renewed on a number of occasions, and he has now been helping us to shape our agricultural policy for, let me see …' he glanced down at the handwritten notes scribbled in the margin of his document '… Yes, here we are. Our temporary contractor has now been engaged by this government for two full governmental terms.

'Further to this, it is my understanding from various discussions with our esteemed president and ongoing discussions with our finance and employment ministers, that it is still our government's belief that the American consultant is best equipped to find an export market for this great nation's produce. Now that we have followed his advice and altered the methods by which we farm our lands, and having done everything asked of us to assist our American consultant, we are confident that we might soon be in a position whereby our very desirable produce should be paired with an appropriate overseas customer.'

After another gulp of tea, he continued, 'You must understand that while I had no dealings with our American consultant in the earlier years of our relationship, this being my first term of office, it is my understanding from those who have championed these discussions,' here he nodded towards Feraguzzi, 'particularly Signor Feraguzzi – who has been able to combine the expertise garnered in his previous role as minister for agricultural development with his current role as minister of finance – that by continuing with the policy set out under the aforementioned section four, article five, sub-section twelve, particles a, b and c, we should soon find that the many years of hardship and sacrifice endured as we implemented the changes should bear fruit. I do believe, in fact, that Signor

Feraguzzi may be able to add a little flesh to that fruit, if he would elaborate a little.'

Civicchioni took the opportunity to regulate his breathing as he passed the baton to the minister of finance. He also used the moment's pause to wink at Vlad, who blushed in response, indicating that he had understood the message conveyed in the wink. Now Vlad suppressed a shy smile and concentrated fiercely on the blank piece of paper in front of him while Signor Feraguzzi cleared his throat to speak.

'Esteemed president, gentlemen, colleagues. For the last twelve fiscal reporting periods, our export portfolio has remained constant at zero. When you take into consideration the marked depreciation of our currency and unprecedented inflation of almost all other economic measures, which is unsurprising given the consistently volatile backdrop against which we must compete, managing to hold our exports constant has been a sizeable challenge. However, we have set our sights on more aggressive growth and, in the grand tradition of our forefathers, we have our eye on the bigger prize. With this in mind, following detailed discourse with our American consultant and much high-level analysis, it is my estimation that, with a successful export contract in place, we should be able to realize an export income in excess of twenty million American dollars.'

Feraguzzi paused to allow a ripple of applause to complete its circuit. 'There's more,' he continued. 'Against a backdrop of considerable financial instability, our import portfolio has similarly remained constant at zero.

However, it is our intention to continue with our policy of zero imports while simultaneously increasing our share of the export market, allowing us quickly to establish ourselves as a nation in control of one of the most impressive GDPs in the world!' Feraguzzi stopped briefly to allow this ambitious statement to sink in.

'But the good news does not stop here. I would now like to invite our American consultant into our meeting, with the permission of our esteemed president, to present to you his most recent findings.'

With that, Angelo jumped up and threw open the double doors to allow the American consultant to enter. The American's readiness at the door suggested he had long been prepared to be called for. He strode in alone, yet managed to convey the air of a man with an entourage in his wake. Exuding calm and confidence in his pressed chinos and neatly ironed, monogrammed shirt, he brushed past the seated ministers. Without waiting for an invitation to join them, he took the position recently vacated by Angelo, forcing the chief of staff to retire to a chair in the corner to continue with his note-taking.

Before speaking Chuck Whylie swept a cool hand across his hair, in an unnecessary move to correct any stray locks. With a polite cough into a closed fist, to indicate that he was going to speak, he began his address.

'Mr President, it is indeed an honour to join you once more. You know, sir, I have been coming to this fine country of yours for many years now and I do believe this is the twenty-fourth occasion on which I have addressed your government. Before I begin today I would like to reiterate that I am profoundly proud of our association and acutely proud of the work that we have been able to undertake together.'

Whylie nodded encouragingly while he allowed his message to sink in, a mannerism he deployed habitually to allow the foreigners an opportunity to assimilate his words. This impersonated – pleasingly, he thought – the rhythm and flow of a speech to the United Nations, with built-in delays for multilingual dissemination. In the small, tea-scented boardroom, the attendant audience were unsure of their collective purpose during these pauses, so allowed their minds to wander far enough afield to be returned to the room shocked and confused by the next burst of speech, thus reinforcing Whylie's misapprehension that his interludes were necessary for the assembled company.

'Of course I do not act alone. My partners back at Client Opted Inc., together with the not inconsiderable team of expert advisers that have taken your country on as a special project, are truly honoured that we have been able to work so closely with you. We think of this relationship not as one between two distinct nations on opposite sides of a great ocean, or as one between buyer and seller, contractee and contracted, employer and employee, biller and billed. No, indeed, we think of ourselves as partners, as equals, and we take our shared responsibility for the economic future of your country very seriously indeed.'

Another generous pause allowed enough time for Alix to imagine exposing the interloper as an assassin but not before he himself had taken a non-fatal bullet intended for his president.

'You are, in fact, one of our top ten clients on a global basis.' Chuck nodded, smiled, and took the small round of applause graciously. 'And it is not without some sadness that I see this project beginning to draw to a close. But we understand, as you understand, that this separation is only possible because of our success. We never intended to leave until the job was well done, and I have an impressive set of figures in front of me that suggests the job is nearly done well.'

Nine expectant faces stared at their American consultant. Trained on his ruddy cheeks and suspiciously immaculate manicure were the tiredly interested eyes of Dottore Rossini, the smiling, aloof eyes of Vlad Lubicic, the ebullient, excited, shining orbs of Signor Pompili, the cautious, defensive slump of Signor Cellini, the alert businesslike scrutiny of Signor Feraguzzi and the barely concealed suspicion of Alix. Civicchioni was too personally involved in the project to maintain any impartiality and held himself back from interjecting. Instead, having borrowed a pen from Angelo, he focused on scribbling notes into his margins. 'Partners! Top Ten!' he scrawled, emphatically ticking and underlining the praise as it was dealt. Signor Lubicic and Professore Scota were now not looking intently at the American but instead stared jealously at the laptop that Whylie now prodded to life with a few stabs of his index finger.

'I would like, if I may, to give a brief résumé to contextualize our progress. More than a decade ago, when I first joined you, we were asked by the dear departed Sergio Senior to analyse your strengths and set forward a proposal that would allow you to compete in a global market. What foresight that man had! He understood immediately when Client Opted Inc. set out to explain that not only had you picked the low-hanging fruit but eaten it and forgotten to replant the pips! What we found here was, I'm going to have to admit now to you, disheartening at best.'

Vlad used this latest pause not to be disheartened but to revisit a walk he had taken the previous night with a young woman upon his arm. He sighed and smiled to himself, already imagining the next and the many walks beyond it. Whylie resumed talking and Vlad tumbled back to earth.

'Even the untrained eye could recognize that your output was simply too negligible to take to the market, and what you did have was cut so fine between your various crops that we had to wonder whether there was anything worth saving. I, of course, was much too young to express it – hey, I was practically in short trousers – but, let's face it, my boss and your previous president, they spoke the same language. You were nothing more than bit players. A bit of this and a bit of that.'

He stopped to allow his audience to catch up. Dottore Rossini used the break to do a mental walk-through of his hospital, wondering whether he might be able to call in for a quick ward-round between this meeting and his siesta. If the American consultant could just talk a little faster, with a touch more fluency, they would all get out of the Special

Furthering of Agricultural Development Committee meeting sooner and achieve more in all of their respective roles, not just those of an agricultural nature. But the doctor had long worried about the American consultant's mental health and knew he should set an example by being as patient and generous with him as he could.

Chuck Whylie, having punctuated one of his uncomfortably long silences with a round of nodding, returned to his soliloquy, having sufficiently damaged any momentum his talk might have gained. He took to his feet and banged his fist on the table to emphasize his point and elicit greater engagement from those whose eyes were politely trained on him. 'The thing is, gentlemen, you simply had nothing substantial to take to the world stage with any credibility at all. Oh, don't get me wrong, I'm not going to stand here in front of you and knock the great effort you made. You had a ...' he sought the right word '... an interesting assortment of produce, some of which might have found a niche market, if anyone else had known what on earth it was!' He laughed alone, so quickly continued: 'It was then that we set about maximizing your potential. Together, our goal was to plant three thousand hectares of a single crop with commercial prospects. At that time, with a total landmass of 3672 hectares, you had just fourteen hundred given to tea plantation, yet that was the crop you recognized as your core strength, a national symbol no less! But your output was here,' he stretched out his left hand, 'and if we could establish a market with a USP that was going to really give us something to work with, the demand was going to be here.' His right hand reached considerably higher. 'And, boy, were those two numbers a long way apart.'

The American consultant rested the heels of both hands on the table in front of him and leaned forward, deliberately making eye contact with each of the assembled group. 'I left you a challenge, if you remember, to set about converting the high land that was at that time little more than waste. And I know, for the sentimental among you, that that was a tough call. People get emotionally attached to the strangest things, a little bit of pasture here, an orchard or two there. But what was it really good for? Nothing!'

He shook his head sadly at the memory. 'But, hey, guys, I've got to hand it to you! You know how to rise to a challenge. By the time I had next returned, not only had you substantially increased the size of your plantation, but had doubled the number of plants you were growing per hectare. What a great achievement that was! And I think, as we take this little jog around Memory Park, we should applaud that achievement.' The assembled group were in collective mourning for the loss of their orchards so the American consultant clapped alone. 'But none of us will ever forget that terrible realization when we analysed the results of the first significant year. We just had to face up to the facts. Your best, our best, just wasn't good enough. With the greatest will in the world, we needed more. We knew there was a market for it, but we weren't even going to get a nibble without a bulletproof strategy behind us.

'So, phase two of the review saw more tough decisions as you set about converting the smallholdings of your nation and reclaiming land that was, frankly, in the wrong hands if you wanted to make your country count.

'As they say, every little bit helps.' Up on the screen popped a series of statistics, represented by a complex Argand diagram. Most of the assembled group were impressed, both by the clarity of the PowerPoint presentation and to see their work – their nation – featured so positively in a chart. The professor alone understood the methodology behind the diagram and tilted his head to try to interpret the mathematics. The numbers were seemingly nonsensical, expressed as they were by a vertical line of conjecture, but he nodded approval to hide what must surely be his own misinterpretation.

The American consultant, having built up his audience's confidence with praise, dashed it with a slow shake of his head. 'But you will recall that even those great efforts weren't enough.'

One by one, the assembled men hung their heads in shame, including the president, whose eyes filled at the memory of his nation's shortcomings.

The consultant broke his silence with a bark: 'But did we give up? Did we give up on you and turn our backs on a floundering client? No way, siree. When our clients are struggling, we're struggling. That's in the small print, remember! That was when our very brightest guys got together and strategized you out of your predicament. You had the benefit of some of the best thinkers in our organization. Blue sky? Forget it. We're talking about stratospheric thinkers. It was the best of the best, our alpha team, that came up with the final phase of Operation

Acorn. It was then that we asked you to gather your men and prepare for the final assault.'

Alix's sharp intake of breath could be heard around the table. The word 'assault' hung painfully in the air and the American consultant grasped it with both hands. Conscious of the power it had granted him, he wrestled metaphor from it with unbridled enthusiasm.

'From general to foot soldier, you rallied the troops, assembled at the front line and formed the ranks to make the final push. That great effort, the final full-scale attack, allowed momentum to gather. The conversion of gardens and domestic curtilage to full-scale crop production allowed us to break through that final frontier. Together, the effort made on behalf of your people has provided the additional land we needed and I am now delighted to announce that you have met your quota and, with some eighty-eight million tea plants now producing the finest Vallerosan tea, we have enough to sustain a viable export market.'

The most indiscernible of pauses was followed by hearty spontaneous applause and Sergio breathed a huge sigh of relief, as he mopped the sweat from his brow. Throughout the preamble he had been dreading a further postponement of good news and the timing of this delivery was perfect for the week's campaign plans. Without a note to rely upon, he leaped to his feet and delivered a heartfelt oration.

'Gentlemen, ministers, advisers, our American consultant. It is on occasions like this that I am able to remind myself of our duty as governors. We are here not simply to uphold law and order but to mould the country for the future. This is a living example of the beauty of Elective Dictatorship – Continuity for Sustainability! – and a perfect instance of the practicality of a government with longevity. We are not merely parliamentary officials, we are custodians! Caretakers of a land that, properly nurtured, we can pass on to our successors with pride. We are responsible not just for creating a legend but delivering that legend, and actually harvesting its crops! My predecessor, my father, instituted a change in policy and that was a brave, bold move, one that has taken more than a decade to implement. It has been implemented now, not without considerable sacrifice and hardship. A weaker leadership might have abandoned the policy much sooner, but because we have been entrusted with the safe-keeping of this nation for such a long time, we are able to see through these changes for a much brighter future. A government that is not hampered by the ever-changing direction of new leaders and the policy U-turns that are inevitable as adversaries take to the stage, pulling the country's people from left to right and back again. We are able to stick to our guns and make a real difference. I'm proud to be part of that change, proud to be part of such a defining moment of our history.

'Now, honoured guest, would you care to join us in a cup of our finest?' He raised an empty cup in mock salute. In a synchronized movement, the assembled group swirled the dregs in theirs and brought them to their lips, showing their respect not just to their leader but to the many men and women who had sacrificed their own small plots to meet the targets set by their visitor. The American consultant smiled blankly until he realized he was supposed to join them in their tea-sipping ceremony. He shrugged and twiddled a pencil. The men around him were expecting something more. He shrugged once more, by way of an apology.

'Guys, guys. I'm from the United States of America, don't forget that! Tea might be the most popular drink in most nations, and it's that global potential we're tapping into here, but I've got to tell you, in the great US of A, tea is just not that important. In fact, it trails behind soft drinks, milk, beer and coffee.' He let this fact sink in and, noting the assembled ministers' look of disbelief, added for emphasis, 'Actually, eighty per cent of the tea drunk in the US of A is served cold. I can't imagine that tea as you know it would feature in any ranking of preferred beverages.'

Enzo Civicchioni visibly paled and there was a low growl of disgust from the commandant. The rest of the men were trying to redefine that strange country, which appeared to be devoid of any good taste or culture. 'I'll drink your health at the bar later. Don't take it personally, guys. I'm just not a tea man.' With that, he closed his laptop decisively and shuffled his belongings into a neat pile.

CHAPTER 7

In Which the President Has Doubt

SERGIO WAS MEETING in his private chambers with the man formally known as Signor Angelo Bianconi, chief of staff to the president, but more comfortably known by Sergio as Angelo, good friend and occasional drinking partner. A decade the president's senior, he could easily be mistaken for the younger of the two. Lean, lanky and with an unruly fringe that refused to conform, his habitual lack of tie and jacket, and his blatant disregard for the hierarchical procedures that governed both Parliament and the country, Angelo's languid nature belied his seniority within the cabinet. He had known Sergio all his life and had been there to share the milestones, from the woefully early death of Sergio's mother, to the first breathtaking bicycle ride down the north-west run, from his ascendancy to president upon the sudden death of Sergio Senior, to his first non-elective election. As such, Angelo was the only cabinet member who really had the president's ear. He was confidant, special adviser, chess adversary, bridge partner and, in all but name, the president's deputy. He leaned forward, paper and pen at the ready, as Sergio paced backwards and forwards.

'A few thoughts from that session, Angelo. Vlad – find out whom he's fallen for. If she's remotely suitable, let's make sure her father finds out. That will hasten a marriage. And Cellini. He's making me nervous. Check his bank account, and make sure there's nothing to worry us. Too much or too little, either way I want to know. If we can rule out bad debt or blackmail, we can begin to work out what's making him sweat. A speech. I need a good speech on this agricultural policy. I felt I was really on to something earlier. Was there anything there we can work on?'

Angelo consulted his notes. 'Continuity for sustainability, I liked. And the legend bit, definitely something there. But this is a good-news speech, sir. Good news always takes at least seventy per cent fewer words to deliver than bad. I'll get going on something straight away.'

The president stood with his back to the room, looking beyond the balcony to the Piazza Rosa. 'Angelo. Something's troubling me. I'm relatively new to this game and I understand that Feraguzzi has been running the economy well for a long time, against considerable difficulties, many of which were not of his own making. And I understand, too, that in comparison to our neighbouring countries we have probably fared better than most. But I'm wondering, Angelo, if it all stacks up.'

'Stacks up how, sir?' Angelo came to stand by Sergio and joined him in his appraisal of the view below, understanding that the trickier conversations were always much easier to broach without eye contact.

'The numbers. Do they add up? If we're not importing anything, and we're going to sell everything we've got, and all we've got now is tea, what are our people actually going to live on?'

Angelo rifled through his mental store of justifications and rationale, supplied with such ease by their American consultant. 'I suppose, Sergio, it comes down to ambition and desire, whether those things exceed or fall short of our needs and expectations.'

Sergio wanted answers not conjecture: 'Our needs? But we've never needed anything. We've always had enough.'

'Enough?' probed Angelo.

'Yes – enough food, enough tea, enough of everything. We've always been able to satisfy our needs without help from anyone.'

Angelo thought about this and tried to remember the consultant's arguments, which had seemed so compelling, so urgent, at the time. 'It's not very fashionable, I mean on a global level, to simply sustain yourself. It seems that by trading and entering into import and export contracts with our neighbours our world standing might improve.'

'But do we need our world standing to improve? Our neighbours don't think ill of us – they don't think of us at all. And that's always been fine, hasn't it? Being ignored by the rest of the world has actually served us quite satisfactorily. And, anyway, why do we need more? Whom do we offend if we're satisfied with enough?'

'I don't know the answer to that, Sergio. I think we feel a duty to our people to aim higher, to be more ambitious for them.'

Sergio hesitated. Then: 'I've always been interested in the notion of trade, of commerce, Angelo. It seems that the obsession the world has is whether we can ever have enough money to spend. And if we haven't, how to get our hands on more. But it's surely no coincidence that the English verb "to spend" can only be applied to the using up of two resources. Money and time. And we can choose how to spend both of these, can't we? My concern, if I'm honest, is that we could find ourselves in pursuit of money to spend while finding that time is diminishing at an equal rate. We'll all be working so hard that we won't any longer have time to do anything else. We'll have spent it all on the acquisition of money. And as we know that money can buy you pretty much anything but time, is that what we want for our nation?'

Sergio thought quietly for a moment, the puzzle clear in his eyes. 'And I'm still left wondering, Angelo, what we're going to live on, if all we're growing is tea and we sell that to another country. What will we eat?'

Angelo paused. He had a fairly good idea, as he was no different from many of the people who lived in the valley. He had a mother and a brother under his one roof and a table to fill each evening and morning. But supposition in this scenario was not remotely appropriate. 'I'll make some enquiries, sir.'

Sergio nodded, giving the outward appearance of a man who had been appeased.

CHAPTER 8

In Which a Protestation Is Made

SERGIO WAS IN HIS PRIVATE CHAMBERS, writing quietly while the rest of Parliament Hall slumped in May's debilitating afternoon sun. With the hours of siesta well under way, all was quiet both inside and out and, apart from the rattles, creaks and groans provided by the state apartment, Sergio was able to enjoy something very close to silence. His breathing had begun to steady and he was forcing his mind to concentrate on the speech he was preparing for his State of the Nation address.

This speech, as Angelo had indicated, should have been easy. He had good news to deliver, the country had met the challenge made to it by the American consultant and, though he knew that many of the men, particularly those of the land, had always doubted the outcome, he felt that on the whole he had taken them with him, that this had been a cohesive effort of which the whole country could feel proud.

But concentrating on writing a positive speech was hard when your subconscious mind was gripped by grim dread. Whichever technique he employed, nothing could shake the feeling that he was teetering on the brink of unmitigated disaster. There was something amiss in the angle at which his minister of finance sat now at assembly meetings. The silence had continued too long after siesta when it should have been broken by children's laughter or the impromptu playing of music in the Piazza Rosa. Even the weather conspired to unsettle him. Vicious electrical storms and relentless rain showers were followed by the hottest, angriest sun that melted the mettle of everyone in the country. It was shining once again, and its long rays were making inroads into his chambers, picking out the faults and highlighting the dust at play in the air and the loose threads that threatened to unravel the carpet.

Sergio's large, mahogany desk reflected his mood. Sometimes it glowed, proud of the part it played in the presidency, and at others it was a tired piece of timber wearing the many scratches and scuffs that Sergio's own face bore as thanks for the responsibility he carried.

Now, his pen lid replaced with a deafening click, Sergio's head sank into his hands as the dark knot took hold deep in his belly. He could actually visualize it when he closed his eyes: something black and tumorous, always on the move. Growing and spreading to tighten its grasp on the arteries and veins that fought valiantly against its slippery, superior force. He sighed deeply, knowing that the words would never flow when he was fighting this kernel of anxiety, and rose to retrace the most worn path in the carpet to his favoured position at the window. Today he was looking for something definitive out there, a positive sign that hinted at even the tiniest glimmer of hope.

Instead, he had to blink a couple of times to try to banish the image below him. When the mirage persisted, he rubbed his eyes and even backed away from the window, then approached it again in the hope that what was, surely, a sunspot caused by the extremes of light and dark would have vanished. When it stubbornly remained beneath him, he edged shakily to the curtain to peer out at the apparition more closely.

Beneath him, not twenty feet from the Parliament Hall railings, and in full sight of the entire Piazza Rosa, should any of its sleepy occupants choose to glance out, stood a protester: a sole man clasping a placard in both hands. He wore charcoal grey flannel trousers with the white shirt and black tie of the educated. And while his sleeves were rolled up and his tie loosened to combat the heat of the early-afternoon sun, he had an air of respectability. Something about the tilt of his head, his proud stature, the shine of his shoes suggested a man of quality.

Sergio, palms sweating, his breath caught tightly in his throat, leaned forward as far as he dared to read the words on the placard.

'*Negotii indigeo. Quaeso.*' The use of Latin confirmed Sergio's immediate assumption. The language of education amplified by the manners of a gentleman.

Perhaps this was worse than any of the nightmares he had hitherto imagined, one in which the civilized should revolt. He could understand the country's few peasants and layabouts taking issue with recent policy, but should the educated decide to rise up, then the nation's stability was over and it would be his fault. During his jurisdiction, chaos would reign. While acting as caretaker he would be responsible for the country's first ever conflict and it would be this for which history would remember him.

Sergio checked his watch. It would be a while before the city awoke, which was a good thing, but the timing was poor in that most of his ministers, including Angelo, would have wandered home for a bite to eat and a sleep. There was absolutely nobody around that he could call upon. So, wiping his sweating palms on his dressing-gown and licking his dry lips, he braced himself for confrontation, something he feared more – if possible – than the humiliation that the alternative offered.

He slid the windows open and moved quietly onto the balcony. Obscuring himself in part behind one of the columns he signalled to the protester with as loud a hiss as he dared. The young man continued to look straight ahead, placard held aloft for the world to read and laugh at. Sergio stood out a little from the shadows and hissed again. This time the noise registered and the protester cocked his head, squinting towards the balcony. On a third signal he took the bait properly, moving one or two tentative steps forward to ensure that the shadowy man on the balcony was actually addressing him.

'Come, come closer – quickly, quickly!' Sergio beckoned with one hand while using the other to ensure that his dressing-gown stayed firmly closed.

The protester looked left and right to ensure that the soporific palace guards weren't going to stir themselves into action and came as far as he could, still holding the placard while straining to look up through the railings to the balcony above him.

'What on earth do you think you're doing?' hissed Sergio from the shadows.

'I'm making a peaceful protest.' The agitator stood firm, still sure of his actions.

'Against what are you protesting?' said Sergio, still in stage whisper.

'Against the governm—' At that moment the young man recognized the robed man on the balcony above him. 'Against you. Sir.'

'Well, that's no way to go about it. Make an appointment to see somebody. What about Signor Lubicic? Have you spoken to him about it?'

'Of course not,' the protester shouted. Sergio silenced him with a finger to his mouth. The young man dropped his voice once more. 'Of course not,' he repeated, in a hoarse whisper. 'Signor Lubicic is a government official. I am just a student.'

'Just a student? *Just* a student? Do you know how privileged you are to receive an education, provided by your government? What about the minister for education? Have you spoken to Professore Scota? He deals with all matters pertaining to education, satisfactory or otherwise. Make an appointment to see him if you're not satisfied with *just* being a student!'

'That is not an option that is open to me,' the student protester retorted. 'You don't just make appointments to speak to government officials. That's why I'm protesting.'

'Well,' said Sergio, sternly, 'quite frankly, I'd rather you didn't.'

The student protester became a little more agitated. 'But I want my voice to be heard. I have serious issues to raise and I need an audience – an audience equipped to listen and take action.'

'Well, speak now. You have an audience. I am your president and, as such, I am equipped both to listen and to take action. Get on with it – there's no time like the present. Speak to me now.' With this, Sergio thumped his hand on the balcony balustrade allowing his dressing-gown to fall open. He clasped it to him, now furious at the protester and his own less than professional attire.

'Well, sir, with all due respect, the points I have to make are worthy of a more formal recourse. Apart from anything else, I'm not sure I can keep this whisper up for very much longer.'

With a stamp of his foot, Sergio whispered, 'Oh, very well,' and disappeared back inside, sliding the doors behind him.

Below, in the square, the minutes ticked slowly by and the student was unsure whether to flee before imminent arrest and possible detention, or to wait obediently and possibly indefinitely. But soon the president reappeared at a small door almost immediately below the balcony. He opened it just a few inches and beckoned the student to join him.

'How do I get through the railings?' asked the student.

'Through the gate,' came the exasperated reply.

'The palace guards are at the gate. Will they let me in?'

'Not *that* gate.' Sergio was enraged at the suggestion that this wanton dissenter might drag his protest any more publicly through Piazza Rosa. 'Through *this* gate – my gate.' He pointed to a small gate that broke the otherwise continuous fence line. With nothing but the smallest catch to differentiate it, it was no wonder that the student had missed it on his first cursory inspection.

The young man laid his placard at his feet.

'Don't leave that *there*. Anyone could see it. Bring it with you.'

The student picked it up and tucked it under one arm. He tiptoed through the gate, closing it quietly behind him, and up the path to join the president, who was now wearing a casual pair of trousers and a shirt, his braces hanging down in loops at either side.

In silence, the two men traipsed upstairs, the president leading, too hot and bothered to consider any potential security threat, the student following, with the barest trace of a smile, born of his own audacity in taking on the government and finding himself in this most unlikely of pairings.

They entered Sergio's private chambers where the president ushered his visitor to one of the lion's-claw-footed chairs in front of the desk. The young man lowered himself, politely tweaking his trousers at the knees, a habit he had adopted to avoid creasing while at his studies.

'Name?' said Sergio, wresting authority out of the so-far-unsatisfactory exchange. He pulled a clean notepad towards him and dipped his pen into the ink with a flourish.

'Woolf.'

'Son of Renzo Woolf?'

'Nephew.'

'Hmm. Yes, yes, I think I know those Woolfs. Occupation? Yes, yes, of course. Student.' Sergio pushed the notepad away from him and leaned back in his chair, shaking his head slowly as though addressing a small child. 'And, young Mr Woolf, do you not think that before your rebellious and potentially inciteful protest, you might have found another less confrontational means to express your dissatisfaction with me?'

Sergio felt in control again. Perhaps he might not be the most skilled negotiator when dealing with dissidents but this was a Woolf and Woolfs he could deal with. He raised his eyes to meet the pale green pair gazing fearlessly back at him.

'I wrote to you first.'

Sergio shrugged to indicate that he had never received any correspondence. 'Perhaps it got lost in the post,' he countered.

'No. I delivered it myself. I handed it to the palace guards. And before writing to you I wrote to the ministers for employment and education. And before writing to

71

them I wrote to the head of the university, and before writing to him I requested a meeting with my tutor, who felt he was not in a position to take up my cause. When all my letters went unanswered, I chose to demonstrate my disquiet with a peaceful protest.'

'And to whom, exactly, have you spoken about your so-called peaceful protest? Am I dealing with a lone Woolf, or are there more protesters out there, waiting to attack the very fabric with which this society is woven?'

'Well, actually, I have spoken to nobody. It was – it was a spur-of-the-moment thing. It wasn't really until this afternoon that I decided to protest.'

Sergio leaned further forward, looking deeply into Woolf's eyes. 'And you're quite sure of this? There's no underground movement that I should know about, spreading malaise and unease among my people?'

Woolf shook his head.

'No secret late-night meetings, fuelled by unlicensed drink and Western song lyrics?'

'No, sir, none that I know of.' Still, Woolf continued to meet Sergio's gaze.

'And your dissatisfaction, Woolf, is with what exactly?' Once again, Sergio dipped his pen, ready to take notes.

'It's quite simple. As my placard says, I need a job. I'm looking for employment, sir.'

Sergio was partly disgusted, partly relieved. 'But you're a student! Surely you'll follow the course of all students and when you've finished your education you'll use the skills you have gained to find an appropriate position in the employment market.'

'But, sir,' Woolf cried, 'I'm thirty-two years old! I've been in full-time education since I was five! That's twenty-seven years! And for most of those years I've been continually promised an appropriate position once I've completed my studies.'

Genuinely baffled, Sergio probed deeper: 'But until you've graduated, you're still officially a student and therefore not available for employment.'

'Exactly,' said Woolf, in frustration. 'But when will that *be*? I've a master's. I've a PhD. I can speak Italian, French, English, Latin and Russian fluently. I'm ready to take a step into adult life but I have absolutely no prospects whatsoever. When I think I'm ready to graduate, I'm press-ganged into yet another few years of full-time education. When is it going to end?'

Sergio let out a low chuckle with what he hoped was a combination of contempt and ridicule. 'Well, really, as president you'd think I'd have heard it all. But of all the ungrateful whining adolescents I've ever heard ... Do you know what a privilege it is to be so educated? There are people around the world for whom access to even the most basic levels of literacy and numeracy would be considered a luxury yet you have the nerve to sit here and blame me for giving you *too much* free education? You should be grateful that your tutors consider you worthy of such great investment.'

Sergio scribbled wildly on his notepad while he contemplated his next move. Woolf was unable to decipher the notes upside-down, and when Sergio got a sense that he was trying to read them, he put a protective arm between them and his onlooker. Finally he stopped writing and carefully turned over the paper, away from prying eyes.

'So, you want a job,' he began. 'What sort of job? What do you want to achieve? Where do you live?'

'With my parents, of course, and my brothers.'

'Good, good. So you have no cause for complaint. You have a roof over your head and food on your table when you get home. Good food and a decent roof, if I remember the Woolfs correctly. Yes?'

'Yes, of course. I have a nice home and good food.'

'And you are intellectually stimulated every day. Your tutors continue to challenge you?'

'Yes, indeed. I have excellent tutors – they have much to offer.'

'And you think, with the wonderful arrogance of youth, that you have learned everything you can, that you know as much as those entrusted with your edification?'

Woolf lowered his eyes for the first time since the line of questioning began. 'No, no, of course not. There is much still for me to learn.'

'So, remind me. You have a comfortable home, food on the table, and are challenged every day intellectually. You protest against what, exactly? Which element of your human rights have I abused, would you suggest?'

'I – I have no complaints now to speak of. It's the future I'm most concerned about, my prospects. I've lost sight of where I'm going.'

Sergio threw back his head and laughed, while Woolf fiddled nervously with his fingers in his lap. 'Now I really have heard it all. I am the president of a great nation and my time is best spent offering counsel to young students. You have lost sight of where you're going? Well, my young friend, I suggest you do one of two things. You acquire a compass or you do what the wise have been doing for many thousands of years.' Sergio leaned forward to whisper this nugget of advice: 'You live for the moment! Enjoy your student years because, trust me, when you're an old man, worn small through hard toil, you will look back on them as the best of your life.'

He leaned back in his chair. 'Chess? I always find it clears the air.'

Woolf nodded and sat looking around the fine room while Sergio set up the board. The president glanced at his watch. 'Tea will arrive soon. Shall we?'

They played, barely exchanging a word as tea arrived, was strained and poured. The game continued briskly, silently, and, despite Woolf's very best undertaking, it called upon almost none of the many strategic outcomes Sergio had at his disposal.

As Sergio removed Woolf's queen with a flourish, he bowed his head in recognition of a battle nobly fought, but lost nevertheless.

'Your education, young man, will be complete when you can beat me at chess. And when that time arrives, come and see me and I will employ you myself.'

Woolf stood up, under no illusion that the meeting had drawn to a close.

'See yourself out, will you?' Sergio gave a dismissive wave. With that, he turned his attention back to the notes he had been working on earlier. Before Woolf had quietly left the room he was brandishing his pen, continuing his line of thinking with renewed fervour.

Sergio pushed the disputation to the furthest reaches of his mind as he worked late into the night. Though he was confident that he had effectively dealt with the infringement and banished the memory, his sleep was restless and interrupted by the relentless imagery of attack.

When he awoke suddenly the next morning, exhausted as if he had not slept at all, he sat bolt upright, the sweat running freely, gluing his pyjamas to his skin. He experienced a flood of relief as he became aware of his surroundings – his bed, his bedside table, his fireplace, his pile of books – but this was quickly replaced by a renewed and exaggerated sense of panic. He had not dreamed the noises after all. There was another bang and then another. Gunshots, some quite close, were filling the valley. He gripped the bedcovers tightly and, acutely aware that he had no intention of being overthrown in his pyjamas, swung his legs out of bed, his mind set upon dressing as quickly as possible. In those mid-air moments, when his feet had freed themselves from the twisted, clammy sheets but had not yet hit the floor, he became aware of other noises – dogs barking and the low, indecipherable shouts of men.

The animals' excitable squeals and their range, from faint yaps that suggested they were far up in the hills to the louder barks that intimated they were just above the town, sent slow signals to Sergio's sleep-fuddled brain. He lowered his feet to the carpet and listened intently. The leisurely 'Peee-eww' of a buzzard punctuated the frenzied cacophony on the ground, and this final contribution to Nature's orchestra allowed Sergio to place what had been the noises of a siege on Parliament Hall.

Saturday morning. An automatic lifting of the hunting ban. The men were out in full force, combing the hillsides and rooting out the wily wild boar that were now leading them and their dogs on a merry dance through woodland scrub and tea plantation. The desperate baying of the dogs closest to the town did not necessarily signal a sighting but that they had picked up the scent of other dogs belonging to another hunting party. In this way the men and their beasts could happily lose the first few hours of the weekend hot on the trail of each other. When guns were fired they were most likely being fired into the air to warn other hunting parties that the sound of crashing through scrubland was caused by them, not by a swine giving chase. Occasionally, through the clash of a boar's misfortune and a man's serendipity, contact between bullet and pig hide would be made and the happy hunters would return home with a tusked trophy on which to feast. Almost as often, though, it would be the shooter's foot that warranted attention. It was not unusual for the tired, dispirited men to return home with a wounded stalker slung between them on a makeshift stretcher.

As Sergio flopped back onto his bed, trying to decipher the different cries that echoed back and forth from either side of the valley, he put his hand to his heart and felt the beat gradually settle to a steadier pace. His panic had subsided, but the sleep that claimed him now was uneasy and his dreams provided him with no respite from the impending sense of doom that increasingly dominated his waking hours.

CHAPTER 9

In Which PEGASUS Has Her Wings Clipped

THE PEGASUS STEERING GROUP met with increased frequency as the early June deadline drew closer.

Sergio now oscillated between great optimism and unalloyed dread, and his men, guided by the lightest touch from Angelo, did their best to anticipate, interpret and respond appropriately to the increasingly frenetic swings in his mood.

The solitary protester's stand had unsettled the president more than he had at first realized, and the impact on his behaviour was immense. Where he had experienced moments of self-doubt before, he now lived almost perpetually in fear of imminent failure. And though Sergio Senior had been dead for some years, it was his father he most feared failing. When Woolf had appeared on that sultry afternoon, Sergio had been momentarily proud to have dealt with the matter singlehandedly. But the ramifications of acting alone now ran deep: the memory rattled around in his brain only, haunting him day and night.

There was nobody with whom to share the burden so the protester's significance was greatly magnified by memory.

It was hard to say who bore the brunt of his vacillations. There were moments when Feraguzzi's economic strategies seemed the root cause of Sergio's dissatisfaction. At other times, Alixandria Heliopolis Visparelli was to blame for either his lackadaisical border controls or his over-zealous military presence, which was clearly the underlying reason for the distinctly dour disposition of the citizens. Scota was simply confused when an accusatory finger pointed towards him, while Cellini, Mosconi and Pompili took turns to cower in the background, shuffling their colleagues into the limelight in an unlikely imitation of chivalry.

The one person who remained untouched by the preparations was Chuck Whylie: he kept to his own quarters, only venturing out to the university to catch up with his email, the purpose of which seemed to be to make snide and inappropriate comments at his hosts' expense. If the consultant had picked up on the increasing tensions in the city and among the ministers, he failed to show it. If anything, he appeared more self-satisfied than ever.

At the penultimate meeting of the PEGASUS steering group, as the days stretched out to show their true potential, Sergio assembled the quorum and made an unexpected announcement. 'I cannot risk a Big Celebration on the night of the arrival of our royal visitor. There is simply too much at stake.'

Twelve pairs of eyebrows shot up simultaneously. For the previous two and a half months the men's collective focus had been almost exclusively upon the impending Big Celebration. The food, the drink, the security, the protocol, the music, the dancing, each detail had been prescribed.

Angelo, the least cowed by his president's moods, spoke first. 'Sir, with respect, our main focus has been on the Big Celebration. Will it not be a considerable disappointment to the people if there is to be no party?'

'I did not suggest that there would be no party,' snapped Sergio, imperiously. 'What I cannot risk is a Big Celebration, planned by the government. If the party is not well attended, if the crowd attendance falls below expectation, if the music is sub-standard, if the atmosphere is dull, if the wine does not flow, if the food is not the tastiest that has ever been served, then the political ramifications will be enormous.' Sergio accompanied each scenario with a thump of his fist on the table and followed his inventory of potential pitfalls with a slow and deliberate appraisal of the assembled men, glaring at each in turn, sparing none. 'I don't think any of you has grasped the importance of this period in my political career. The date for my re-election is set for just after midsummer. There is absolutely no time for any political recovery between the Big Celebration and election day.'

Signor Posti piped up – somebody was clearly expected to respond to this challenge. 'With respect, sir, we're not anticipating any difficulty at re-election. The mood of the nation is good, we have positive news to report, we're expecting less than a handful of negative option returns, and I can probably tell you who will be responsible for those ...'

'Well,' countered Sergio slowly, fathomless contempt dripping from every syllable, 'I keep my ear a little closer to the political ground than you do, Signor Posti, and I think you overestimate the mood of the electorate.'

Rolando Posti examined his fingernails and waited for another voice to fill the considerable chasm the president's words had left in the air.

'So,' ventured Rossini, after a prolonged and painful silence, 'what are you suggesting? That we cancel the Big Celebration?'

'Cancel the—' spluttered Sergio. 'Are you mad? I hope you're substantially more skilled at healing the sick than you are at managing political unrest. No, I'm suggesting that we replace the Big Celebration with a spontaneous outpouring of jubilation.'

'Spontaneous?' echoed at least half of the gathered men.

'Yes, I want a party organized by the people, for the people, on the spur of the moment.' Sergio looked around him, as if this was the most obvious idea he had yet put forward. It was clear from a dozen blank stares, however, that he needed to enlighten them further. 'That way, if the party is a disaster, it will be the fault of the electorate. If it is a success, it will be our triumph for providing an atmosphere conducive to the flourishing of such impulsive festivity. I want our visitor to witness a nation that can literally burst into merrymaking.'

The men kept their eyes firmly on the president for fear that a shared glance between one and another might constitute betrayal.

'And,' ventured Civicchioni, tentatively, 'who would you like to, er, spearhead the spontaneity?'

Impatient at the stupidity of the question, Sergio responded, enunciating each word as if addressing a particularly stupid child, 'The committee, of course. Do you think I'd leave something as important as this to chance?' He snapped shut his notebook, pushed his chair back and, with exaggerated irascibility, flounced from the room.

Angelo turned to a clean page in his notebook. 'Right, gentlemen, you heard the boss. A spontaneous outpouring of jubilation it is.'

'And don't forget to schedule some merrymaking,' quipped Scota, but Angelo silenced him with a look, reminding them that merrymaking was no joking matter. The men continued to sit and talk, each individually wishing to honour his president's demands and to take the instruction seriously, but each also knowing that what had been asked of them was both illogical and impossible.

CHAPTER 10

In Which a Royal Visitor Arrives

THE VIP WAS DUE TO ARRIVE on the 05.05 freight train, the only one to stop in Vallerosa. The track actually serviced a major network that began in the French Alps to the south-west and ended in Austria to the north-east and managed, through the judicial placing of a mountainous outcrop, to carve a narrow route through the uppermost corner of the country. This meander across Vallerosan soil lasted less than three kilometres, but the government of the time, led by Sergio's canny grandfather, had been quick to recognize the opportunity: it had granted permission to the rail company to lay the track across a corner of its land. In return the rail company would provide, at their cost, a station and a generous annual stipend with which to manage it. At the time, the deal had been heralded as an international negotiation of unparalleled success, and many days of celebration and festivity had followed. Sergio's grandfather had earned himself the nickname 'the Deal Maker', and had justly garnered the praise of his fellow citizens, who now had access to and from other countries. The Deal Maker, however, was not blessed with the wisest of financial counsel, and while the fee paid by the rail company had seemed a grand gift from the heavens, the incumbent minister of finance had failed to negotiate an annual increase in line with inflation or any other monetary index. Over the intervening decades the annual income had been eroded by the ravages of economics, and today the stipend barely covered the wage of the part-time ticket collector.

Whether it was a reflection on the retrospective change of circumstances, or the genuine linguistic trickery that often takes place when a name is translated from one language to another, via Latin, and back again, Sergio's grandfather was remembered now in the history books as 'the Big Deal'; the ambiguity of the moniker suited those with a fond, ever-patriotic nostalgia for the previous regimes as well as those who remembered less kindly the deals with which the country was now lumbered in perpetuity.

Three times a day the diesel would roar through Vallerosa, accelerating as it drew towards the station. Curving dangerously as it sped past, the passengers on board might just glimpse the short platform and the black and red flag snapping in the train's draught. Since the mid-1940s, the passenger trains had no longer stopped in Vallerosa, and this arrangement suited the current administration. While civilization had mercifully ignored or forgotten the small country during two world wars, today's increasingly unstable climate would have required the opening up of rigorous border patrols, including a full-time Customs and Immigration Service.

Demand for travel to the country was negligible and as no one in the world had yet come up with any particular reason to visit Vallerosa, the current traffic was restricted to a single freight train stopping once a day. Upon this service, the occasional visitor might have negotiated a fare and, depending on the amount of currency that changed hands, take their chances with a seat among the parcels and packages in the mail carriages or secure a much comfier ride in the driver's cabin, where there were two springy fold-down chairs and copious amounts of tea from the seemingly bottomless urn. From there visitors would alight, crumpled, disoriented and in desperate need of the washrooms that waited, spotlessly clean, to service them.

The current stationmaster, Gabboni, relished his dual role as ticket and passport inspector. Indeed, he had one of the most enviable roles in the country. Admittedly he must be up early to greet the train each morning, but for most of the time he lived a relaxed and solitary life, tasked with keeping the station platform swept, the toilets and washrooms stocked with paper and towels, and ensuring there was always a glorious display of hanging baskets and window boxes to guarantee that one's very first sighting of Vallerosa was a positive experience.

Each year several intrepid travellers would deliberately set out to discover this most elusive of countries for themselves and Gabboni dedicated himself to welcoming them. On the whole, this group was made up of hikers and mountaineers, historians and students of General Isaak von Bunyan, explorers, cartographers and tea connoisseurs, who had heard talk of rare flavours and properties of the local brew. But there were many more whose visit was entirely accidental. Typically, these weary travellers would have embarked on a night train somewhere in the pretty hills of the north-east of Italy, or as far back as the south-eastern tip of France, and would have awoken suddenly, confused, to the screech of the diesel brakes and a neck-jerking deceleration. They would shake themselves awake to the incomprehensible realization that they were pulling into a station, although they had been told, in many multilingual announcements, that there were no further stops along the way. Leaping to their feet, hastily grabbing their luggage from the rack above their head, they would hurl themselves and their cases from the train on the false assumption that either they had slept through the country they were intending to visit or they had arrived at their destination slightly ahead of schedule.

While the statistics would almost certainly be excluded from the annual report issued by the minister for tourism, it is fair to guess that the majority of visitors to Vallerosa would have begun their unintentional visit with a glance at their watch, a quick but futile calculation of any number of time zones they might have crossed during their eastward journey, and a hurried exit from the train, tumbling to the platform alongside the mailbag, in the pre-dawn darkness. Internal panic rising, they would turn to see Vinsent Gabboni emerging from the shadows, smiling the knowing smile of a stationmaster who has seen it all before, many times.

Gabboni, so keen to protect that most coveted of positions, ensured that he did every aspect of his job with absolute diligence. And so, on the rare occasions when a visitor chose to stop at that crease of a country, he would draw himself up to his full five foot seven inches and guarantee that the visitor, American or otherwise, was treated with the unabridged Vallerosan welcome. Having allowed his visitor to alight, he would walk purposefully towards them to greet them. First he would place a friendly hand on each shoulder, and then, staring into the eyes of the often startled traveller, he would pronounce, syllable by syllable (always respectful of most foreigners' lack of learning), 'Your weary feet can find comfort here, your wandering soul can find answers, your heavy heart can find solace and your parched mouth can be quenched.' Then, before the visitor had had time to recover, he would draw them firmly to his chest, laying his head briefly on their right shoulder. With a slap on the back, they would be ushered into the waiting room to meet him in his official capacity as junior minister in charge of Customs and Immigration. While the visitor would reorient himself in the small, tidy waiting room, wondering if, perhaps, he had been mistaken for somebody else, Gabboni's head and shoulders would reappear alarmingly through the hitherto unnoticed hatch in the wall.

This very special morning, which had begun more than an hour before with the unruly clanging of the church bells, it had been decreed that Gabboni's special welcome alone was not enough for the expected VIP.

There had been much debate, both in Il Gallo Giallo, and in Parliament itself, as to who, or what, would be most appropriate to form a welcoming party. At the peak of the debate, it had been suggested that Sergio himself might be there to greet the visitor but Angelo had spelled out the danger of allowing the visitor to think that too much significance had been attached to the occasion. In the end, it was felt by all that Sergio must retain a healthy detachment and act with the standoffish dignity of a leader who was accustomed to (perhaps even bored by) state visits. Eventually, through a rigorous process of elimination, three ministers had been duly elected to form the welcoming party.

Settimio Mosconi, the minister for tourism, was an obvious choice, and with the addition of the ministers for recreation and leisure, it was felt that just the right level of gravitas without obsequiousness had been attained.

It was agreed by all that Vinsent Gabboni had excelled himself. The station gleamed, while the scents of geranium and rose made all three ministers proud to be Vallerosan. Mosconi's shoulders heaved and he was seen brushing the back of his hand across each eye, but whether this was because the moment was charged with emotion or because the air carried a little dust that dry morning was open to speculation. Gabboni had unrolled the red linoleum, reserved for just this type of occasion but which had only been called upon once before. On that occasion, Sergio had left the country for a week's visit to his neighbouring countries but returned just two days later, apparently because his work had been accomplished with unrivalled

89

efficiency; those closer to him wondered if he had been homesick.

With a full ten minutes to go before the scheduled arrival of the train, the three men took their place. Initially they ordered themselves tourism, recreation, leisure, but the gradually descending height differential added a comic dimension that was neither dignified nor intended and they quickly regrouped with tourism, the tallest, flanked on either side by recreation and leisure. On this solemn occasion, Gabboni had been relegated to the ticket office but he was proud and excited to be included and had, without either the knowledge or permission of Mosconi, agreed to head afterwards for Il Toro Rosso where he would hand an exclusive scoop to Edo Cannoni, a post-graduate English student who aspired to run the country's only independent newspaper, the *Vallerosan Reporter*. As this newspaper was still an idle dream, young Edo was resigned – apparently indefinitely – to running the student newspaper and it would be to the thundering photocopying machine in the basement of the university that he would turn once his copy was filed.

The sound of the diesel engine cut through the clear morning air and could be heard for some minutes before it eventually slowed to a screeching halt at the small station. A few moments later, two heads poked out of the driver's cabin door, which swung back fully on itself. A smallish sports bag, with a tennis racquet strapped to its spine, was thrown to the platform. This was soon followed by the unceremonious dumping of a large rucksack, which hit the ground heavily, raising a cloud of dust. Moments later, two tired visitors stepped down from the train and looked, first, at the line-up of smartly saluting men to their right, then to their left, where the end of the platform and the tracks curving into the distance offered no alternative exit route. The middle-aged man stepped forward, casually slinging his jacket over one shoulder and picking up the sports bag in his other hand.

The three ministers held their breath. There was, they admitted to themselves later, a degree of disappointment that this man, clearly a man in charge, had not thought to dress in official uniform and hadn't even deigned to sport a necktie. But, of course, they quickly rationalized, for security reasons it must be safer to travel incognito and, with no security men to accompany him, this precaution was probably very wise.

They shared, too, their simultaneous reaction to the second visitor, previously partly shielded by the man. Lagging behind, having taken a few seconds to heave her heavy rucksack to her back, she hurried forward to catch up with her travelling companion, falling into step silently beside him. The three ministers, in unison, dropped their saluting hands to their sides and stared, unprofessionally, unabashed and unashamed, at the tallest and most beautiful woman they had ever set eyes on. Not even the sum of their combined dreams had yielded anything quite as mouth-wateringly, tear-jerkingly heavenly as the vision that now walked towards them. Perhaps the equestrian habits of their forebears were behind their unanimous thoughts as they sized up (with the open admiration of

stockmen at market with a full purse to spend) her powerful legs, her wide but graceful shoulders, her magnificent
neck and incredibly strong, shiny white teeth. The sun had
not yet risen and still her pale hair glowed in a lumines-
cent halo, as if illuminated from within. The few short
seconds, as she strolled towards them, spiralled recklessly
into cinematic-quality slow-motion as each man
harboured unsolicited images, set to the music of harpsi-
chords and tumultuous cymbals, of tumbling naked limbs,
of the strong hindquarters of Arabian stud horses, of
Amazonian hunters, of peach-skinned necks, of open
mouths revealing rows and rows of pearlescent teeth, of
whips and jodhpurs and the palest, smoothest, roundest
buttocks.

The tall blonde woman approached the welcoming
party, first with a little trepidation and then with confidence, as she realized that these three uniformed gentlemen, each resplendent with shiny ribbons and glinting
medals, were there to meet her and her fellow traveller.
She towered over the man beside her as her generous
mouth spread into a wide smile and she stepped forward,
her right hand held out. The male visitor shuffled forward,
hand extended, with a puzzled smile. The two weary travellers were greeted with a moment's confusion followed
by three stiff salutes.

Mosconi was the first to gain control of his senses. He
wrestled the sports bag from the gentleman, falling
smartly into step beside him and only dropping back
when it was apparent that they could not both fit through
the turnstile at once. In an embarrassing moment of previ-

ously undefined protocol, the tall blonde woman was left alone behind the men. With her sunglasses now pushing her silky hair off her face, she waited to have her paperwork examined.

Gabboni's moment had arrived, but the agreed-upon procedure had disintegrated. On receipt of the required documents, he looked for leadership from Mosconi, who met his eye with a stern shake of the head. He grasped both lots of paperwork tightly to his chest, bowed low and returned it to the owners. With a small scuffle, the dignitaries and visitors shuffled themselves into order, passing through the turnstile one by one and stepping out to meet the rising sun.

The blonde had been delighted by the sweet-smelling station, enthralled by the formal greeting and enchanted by the warmth of Gabboni's cursory ticket inspection. But nothing had prepared her for the view that met her as she passed through the ticket office to the station forecourt. The sun was poking its head above the far valley wall, and its gentle light was starting to penetrate the vast crevasse below. The landscape of Vallerosa was unique, for virtually its entire landmass was dominated by the steep walls that rose dramatically from either side of the powerful river Florin. The country tilted, too, from north to south, which lent drama to the water, which tumbled and frothed as it made its way through the mountainous region. The only land that could properly be considered horizontal was the plain at the top of the valley, on which the passengers now stood. For as far as the eye could see, the land there was host to hundreds of hectares of tea plantations. To anyone visiting Vallerosa for the first time, this view was quite literally breathtaking. The elaborately whorled tea plants at the top of the valley, resembling acres and acres of tightly quilted velvet, gave way to the city, which clung precariously to the valley walls. Houses, built from a uniform red rock, seemed hewn from the cliffs. And now, as the sun began to play on the rapids below, the river Florin began to reveal its many hues.

'Oh, my gosh!' the tall blonde squealed, clapping her hands together in delight. 'It's absolutely gorgeous. I had no idea!' Despite her height, she skipped daintily forward, breathing deeply, then turned to face the ministers. 'It's really, really lovely! I can't believe I'm here at last!' She gambolled forward and ran her hands across the closest of the tea plants. The densely packed leaves gave under her touch and bounced back into place obediently as she marvelled at the plantation. A goat lifted its narrow head from beneath the leaves and stared unblinkingly at her. It bleated half-heartedly and disappeared again. Around the animal, the shrubs panned out, filling every spare inch between the station and the start of the city. The combination of dark, glossy leaf and the red town below stirred something in the visitor and she stared, open-mouthed, into the distance. Remembering herself at last, she returned to her small audience.

'Oh, you must think I'm completely barking. I'm so sorry. Is there a taxi available? I'm staying in the main town at the ...' She pulled a piece of paper from the net pocket of her rucksack and, fearing mispronunciation, pointed out the name of the hostel with a manicured fingernail.

Meanwhile, the gentleman visitor pulled his jacket a little closer around himself, and raised an enquiring eyebrow at the three ministers. They snapped to attention. Mosconi clapped his hands loudly, summoning from the side of the station a small pony trap, driven by Gabboni's flat-capped, toothless father. The three ministers huddled together for a moment and, though briefly thrown by the arrival of not one but two guests, quickly surmised that the tall woman must be the personal assistant of the British VIP. As such they were both ushered into the pony trap, to the tired acceptance of the man and the utter delight of the woman.

The dusty road quickly gave way to a narrow, cobbled drive, and before long the conveyance was slaloming its way through the red town, underneath lines of washing and pots of tumbling geraniums. The blonde clutched the side with one hand while snapping away at every opportunity with her digital camera, her pure joy apparent at every moment. Her gentleman companion allowed his eyes to rest for much of the bumpy journey.

THE NEWLY ARRIVED VISITOR, Lizzie Holmesworth, passed a handful of vehicles on her ride down the hill, but on the whole the cars were up on blocks, parked at an unfeasibly steep angle or, on one occasion, being used by a family of hens that had made a rusting old Trabant their home. As the angle of incline sharpened, and the twists and turns came more frequently, Lizzie realized how perfectly suitable the nimble pony and the small trap were for a precipitous commute.

MEANWHILE, the three ministers were cycling frantically downhill, in a perilous head-first descent reserved only for the most urgent trips. In this way, albeit breathless and sweaty, they arrived in plenty of time to form part of the formal welcoming committee that stood in readiness in the Piazza Rosa.

By the time the pony trap arrived, a dozen officials were there to greet the visitors while a small crowd of Vallerosans had gathered, cups of tea in hand, to watch their arrival. A large area in front of the Parliament Hall had been elaborately cordoned off, and Commandant Alixandria Heliopolis Visparelli himself now patrolled the boundary, checking the crowd for possible subversives and scanning the rooftops for would-be assassins.

Finally the pony trap clip-clopped across the piazza and came to a lurching halt.

Rolando Posti stepped forward to greet the occupants and, not trusting himself entirely with his memorized speech (even though he had practised it hundreds of times in the last few weeks), glanced down at his typed notes.

'Honoured guest. Guests. It is my humble privilege to welcome you. You both. To our homeland. Vallerosa is a small but proud nation, and while you are here, we open our hearts and our hearths to you. To you both. Please.'

He stepped back, calling them forward to be greeted personally by each of the assembled ministers. The gathered spectators, banned from being close enough to hear the dialogue, were nevertheless pleased with the show so far, threw their caps into the air and whistled appreciatively. As the two visitors stepped out onto their second stretch of red linoleum, a sharp cry of 'Paul!' was heard clearly above the rest of the adulation. Visparelli swung around, instinctively putting a steady hand to his gun, but it was quickly apparent that there was no threat. Instead, the American consultant, Chuck Whylie, awakened by the church bells' early call that morning, had decided to join the crowd to witness the event. To his obvious joy, he had recognized one of the visitors.

'Paul!' he called again. He ducked deftly under the twisted rope and shouted a string of enthusiastic greetings as he made his approach. 'Paul Fields, you made it!' As the two men met, they joined in a complex dance that involved some feigned right hooks and dives and a series of backslaps and high fives. 'Well, well, well, well, well! Look at you! I wasn't actually expecting you for another week or two. You should have emailed, I'd have met you at the station myself!'

Visparelli remained alert, his hand hovering a couple of centimetres from the handle of his weapon. His whole frame was poised in case this unscheduled salutation should turn nasty. Likewise, the assembled Vallerosan dignitaries stood back a little, out of natural deference to the American, but unsure whether to continue with their much rehearsed official duties. The overriding sense of pride in finishing the job satisfactorily jostled with the growing sense that they were possibly the fools in some ghastly misunderstanding. How on earth did their American consultant know their British VIP? Were the Americans and British really such close allies that they were all in cahoots? Were the Vallerosans, perhaps, the victims of something altogether more sinister, a conspiracy of sorts?

SIMILAR THOUGHTS were running through Sergio's mind. He had adopted his favourite position just behind the curtains in his private chambers and had been able to watch, undetected, as his trusted ministers had arrived, abandoning their bicycles just out of sight in the small alleyway that ran up the side of Parliament Hall. Then, as the sun rose, he had enjoyed watching the gathering of a substantial crowd. At this he had allowed his confidence to build a little: the number of spectators boded well for the evening's party. Finally Sergio had witnessed the arrival of the pony trap, conveying to his door not one but two visitors.

He had been confused by the addition of the towering woman and then by the arrival of Chuck Whylie, who had seemed to hijack the official proceedings. Now Angelo joined him at the window and, voices lowered even though there was no danger of being overheard, they speculated as the pantomime unfolded beneath them.

'What do you think of the American? I mean, off the record,' Angelo began, seizing a rare moment to chat openly, as friends.

'Off the record? He has skills we don't have. He has knowledge we cannot possibly accumulate. And, as I have always said, we can't ignore that. To stay looking inwards would be a mistake for us. We have to take the country forwards a little, and to do that we have to have the advice of somebody like the American, Whylie. He has a global vision, he's an American, he sees the whole world as his private backyard and we have to be able to turn that to our advantage. If we can play a little in his backyard, without compromising our integrity, then I think we're OK. I know he's arrogant, but he's incredibly well connected – look at him now! Is there anyone he doesn't know?'

They watched the earnest conversation between the Briton and the American, and as the two men, in their almost identical smart-casual uniforms, edged themselves away from the ceremony and took up their conversation in a head-to-head huddle, the blonde threw her head back in laughter, much to the obvious surprise and pleasure of the six small men who crowded around her.

As the act unfolded, realization dawned on Sergio and his adviser.

'Angelo, Angelo, Angelo,' Sergio begged. 'Please tell me she is our VIP's secretary. She is, isn't she? In a minute, Chuck will notice that he's holding up our ceremony and the duke will do what he's supposed to. Yes or no, Angelo?'

Angelo looked out from the opposite curtain, rubbing a hand over a worried face. The ministers were falling back into their intended positions, allowing the blonde to walk slowly down the aisle, greeting each with a generous handshake and a few well-considered niceties intended to placate, flatter and cajole each man.

'I don't know, Serge. She looks … I don't know how to describe it. Royal?'

'You're not wrong, Angelo. She's done this before. He,' with a cursory nod in the direction of the racqueted man, 'is a red herring. She's our VIP.'

Sergio and Angelo looked at their watches and calculated that they had just a few minutes' grace before the royal visitor joined them.

'I don't understand how we could have made a mistake. A duke is always a man, I tell you. There is absolutely no room for a misunderstanding. I have promised my country a visit from the Duke of Edinburgh and what do I have instead? I have a woman! A woman! What will the country think of this – of me? I will be a laughing stock!' Sergio paced up and down, getting redder and redder in the face. 'Our people will think this is an insult, sending a woman in place of a man. They've put up with a lot recently and they're not going to like this one little bit.'

Sergio moved to his desk and fell back into his chair, his arms dangling loosely beside him in utter despair. 'You know, Angelo, I've felt for a while now that I'm losing control. I see no tangible signs of it but, from the periphery of my vision, I can tell that, little by little, the things I have within my power are becoming more precarious. When my father died there was so much I wanted to address, so much I wanted to correct. We talked about it, didn't we? Redressing the balance, restoring a little more consensus to our people, governing with a lighter touch? But perhaps my father was right. He might have been firm, but it was his firm hand that kept the lid on this country.'

He continued, his voice rising, 'I've made a lot of promises, Angelo, and I mean to keep them, but there's unease in the air. I can smell it. I can see it in the eyes of the men out there. I wake up in the middle of the night sweating, fearing. Fearing what? I have nightmares of revolution, of men throwing petrol bombs through my window. When I wake in the morning I don't feel rested at all.' He rubbed his eyes, allowing a fresh wave of melancholy to wash over him.

Angelo squeezed his arm for attention. 'Look, Sergio, look out there. There must be a couple of thousand men and it's not even seven in the morning. They didn't have to come out, did they? The official reception isn't until this afternoon. They're here to support you, and to show off their country to a visitor. Look, they're smiling, laughing even. They're not looking like a revolutionary crowd to me.'

Sergio got up and crept to his eyrie at the window. He peered from around the curtain, a handful of the starched material clutched tightly in his fist. 'They might well be laughing now, but they're watching and waiting for me to deliver. And now I can't even deliver them a duke!'

THE BACKSLAPPING CONTINUED and Chuck, as he jostled and punched, was quick to notice his friend's tennis racquet. He made a backhand motion and, clicking his tongue against the roof of his mouth, imitated the hollow clunk of ball meeting strings. 'Good job! You remembered.' He lowered his voice a notch, to hint at discretion, but not enough to obscure his words completely. 'The courts here are decidedly third rate, I've seen better surfaces in *Iowa* but, I tell you, a game of tennis with an ally is just what my mental-health practitioner ordered! I was on my way to pick up a prescription for one dose of intellectual stimulation and a large serving of competent physical adversary!'

While they'd bantered, Remi the postman had, with the countenance of a man who should not be stopped, manoeuvred himself into as close a position as possible. Now he leaned over the rope barrier and craned his neck, scrutinizing the mannerisms of the newly arrived dignitary and trying to reconcile the visitor's somewhat ungainly gestures with that beautifully looped handwriting that he alone had been privileged to examine. As he observed them thoroughly, the two men laughed, and while the subtlety of the language might have been lost on Remi he was immediately suspicious – if not absolutely certain – that his country might just have been slandered among the raillery.

The blonde woman, meanwhile, had decided to take her own needs in hand, and stepped forward. 'I wonder if you can possibly help. I'm expected – I have a letter here that details my arrangements … Would you mind?'

Several pairs of hands reached out to grab the letter and a little tussle took place as the ministers fought to interpret her needs. But it was very soon apparent, even from those just leaning between the shoulders of other men, that the woman was holding a sheet of official government paper in her hand, bearing the proud crest of Vallerosa, and that the accommodation to which she referred was, indeed, the Parliament Hall.

The ministers grasped suddenly that the blonde vision was their VIP! Abandoning the man to their American consultant, they fell back into line, then ushered the woman down the reception line and under the crossed swords of the attendant Parliament Hall guards, who had been standing alert, awaiting this moment, since the pony trap had arrived.

As the woman passed down the line, salutes were abandoned, one by one, in favour of the firm handshakes suggested by the guest. Some lingered for a fraction of a second longer than the job properly deserved, and to onlookers, it might have been unclear as to who was welcoming whom. But the blonde took it all in her sizeable stride and made each minister feel as though he were tall enough to meet her oceanic blue eyes.

The crowd almost groaned in their disappointment as she was ushered through the doors into Parliament Hall, knowing they weren't going to get another glimpse of this remarkable woman for several hours. Some turned homewards, with chores to attend to and angry wives to fear, while many more headed for the bars to begin their day as they meant to continue, with beer, singing and a string of increasingly lewd jokes. But to a man, behind the macho jostle there was quiet anticipation. Something good had happened that morning in Vallerosa and, like a ray of sunshine on the greyest February day, a load had been lifted from their hearts.

CHAPTER 11

In Which Plan B Might Work

UPSTAIRS ANGELO CONSULTED the official programme for the day and insisted that the schedule should be adhered to as far as possible. Celebrations had been planned and if those celebrations were to involve a VIP of the female variety, instead of the promised duke, then so be it. Celebrations would continue. In the meantime, a private audience between Sergio and the visitor had been scheduled. Sergio was simply not comfortable in the presence of a lone woman, so Angelo, at the urgent bidding of his president, had agreed to stay in the room but to hover in the background. 'I'll be there if you need me, but I'll disappear if you don't. Trust me, you'll be absolutely fine.'

Less than half an hour later, the washed and brushed blonde was ushered into the study. Sergio rose grandly from his chair, walked around to the front of his desk and clasped her hand in both of his. Angelo rose just a few inches from his chair in the corner, out of respectful convention, but sat down quickly again to indicate that he formed no part of this conversation.

'Welcome to Vallerosa. I trust your journey was not too tiring. Here.' The president gestured to a pair of chairs in front of the desk.

The woman sat down, smiling still. Her knees neatly together, she tucked her feet to one side and beneath her. 'Oh, it was fine. Better than I expected – I love train journeys, really I do. So much more interesting than flying. You really get the feeling that you're travelling and leaving everything you know behind you. Sometimes I wonder if, when you fly, your body actually realizes it's left home behind. It can be so disorienting. Oh, I'm sorry, I'm gabbling again, aren't I?'

Sergio smiled graciously, nodding to indicate that he shared her misgivings about flight as a transport option. 'No, not at all, please continue.'

'Oh, I'm finished. I just wonder sometimes if the ease with which we all jump on and off aeroplanes makes us a little glib about travel.'

'Certainly that is a possibility.' Sergio's mind was suddenly clouded with images of people jumping from the sky, and he wondered whether he might be safer with a subject he knew more about. 'And what do you make of our country so far?'

'Well, I can't describe how excited I am.' She put a large, pale hand to her chest. 'It's too beautiful for words. I mean, I'd looked at it on the internet, but I didn't get any idea of how dramatic the landscape is – I mean, it's so deep, and so red, and so grand!'

Sergio straightened his back a little. Grand, yes, grand was good. 'And what, if I may ask, are you hoping to achieve here in an official capacity? I recall from your initial letter that you will be staying for a month.'

'Yes – I mean, that's my plan at the moment. In an official capacity? Well, I would like to demonstrate that I have integrated fully into a culture that is unlike my own.' Here she began to tick off her wish list on her fingers. 'I would like to make a real difference to the lives of the people here – maybe, I don't know, work in an orphanage or with the needy? And I'd like to learn to live more independently. I also want to go home ready to face the next challenge.'

Sergio nodded sagely. 'An ambitious programme. And, I take it, much of this must be recorded for the press?'

The British visitor nodded, but a little less surely. 'Well, I'll certainly be hosting a blog, maybe writing a few articles, and taking plenty of pictures,' she said, waving the ever-present digital camera in front of her. 'It would be nice to think I'll get a little coverage when I get back. I don't know, though – I hadn't really thought about it.'

'And there are obviously issues of protocol to be discussed. Security, for instance, a single woman travelling alone in a foreign country. I'm not sure that is advisable?'

'Oh, I'm sure I'll be quite safe here. The people seem incredibly friendly and there are so many police and military men around … I'm quite sure I shall feel secure. Anyway, I'm used to travelling on my own. Daddy says I'm as strong as an ox!'

'Nevertheless a single woman is vulnerable and I note that your arrival has already attracted much attention. Some of it might not be strictly – how shall I say? – honourable in intent. They're hot-blooded men, the Vallerosans. I shall assign you twenty-four-hour security cover. I think that would be safest. I'm surprised, quite frankly, that your own country felt it would be wise to send you without the company of a man.'

'Oh, don't get me started! Us Holmesworths are tough, you know. And we're quite used to looking after ourselves, thank you very much.' She giggled and in that moment her protestations counted for nothing and she looked both vulnerable and quite extraordinarily precious as she toyed with the strap of her camera.

Sergio worked hard to remain professional, while his instinct was to cradle her head in his lap and stroke her hair. 'As for the other protocol, it's best to get that sorted, for our own purposes, you understand. What title do you like to go by?'

'Miss is fine. I've toyed with the idea of being a Ms but Daddy always says it's reserved for lesbians and spinsters. I know, I know, he's absolutely rooted in the dark ages, but whenever I try to use it I see him standing in front of me, shaking his head in disappointment. But you don't need to call me by any title. Elizabeth is my name but Lizzie is fine. And you are?'

'Officially, I am President Sergio Scorpioni, Protector, Guardian and Elected Dictator of Vallerosa, her land, her boundaries and her people. But I am very happy for you to call me Mr President.'

Lizzie looked momentarily baffled, but a lifetime of good manners and the very best girls-only education that money could buy meant that decorum won. Bafflement was replaced seamlessly with polite enquiry that in turn became instinctively apologetic.

'Gosh, Mr President. You're the President of Vallerosa? I had no idea! I'm – I'm – Well, yes, of course you are. The palace, the guard of honour. Oh, golly, I think there's been some mistake. Am I in trouble?'

'Trouble? Heavens, no, you are here as our most honoured and welcome guest. When I received your letter, asking that you may be granted a permit to visit our country, I was extremely gratified and felt privileged to be able to open our humble doors to you. Our hearts and our hearths, as the old saying goes. I suspect what you refer to is the somewhat misleading communication, from which we might have deduced that we were to expect a visitor of the opposing gender. Well, I must say we were all a little taken aback, but trouble? No. You have caused not the slightest ripple of trouble, just – if I am being absolutely candid – your arrival might have been marred by the tiniest tinge of disappointment, but I expect we must all learn to overcome that. Expectation is a dangerous bedfellow.'

Sergio leaned forward and lowered his voice, glad to have an opportunity to contribute to this cultural ambassador's understanding of his country's customs. 'Remember, we are not quite as liberated as some of the other Western European countries and women here rarely achieve positions of power. Well, seldom.' Here he craned his neck to address his adviser, behind him. 'Angelo, remind me, when did a woman last achieve a position of power?' Angelo held up both hands, indicating an empty vessel. 'You see? As I thought. Never. But that is here, and you are from there, and if you are keen to make a study of the difference in our cultures then that is just one very interesting observation that you might like to undertake. After all, who better to examine the role that womankind has to play, or not, in our country than a woman?' Sergio smiled benevolently, and was only able through the exertion of the utmost willpower to stop himself pinching her rosy cheek between his thumb and index finger.

He exhaled slowly and steadied himself, reminding himself that, more than ever before, he must appear presidential.

'But, Miss Lizzie, I am an open-minded gentleman and am happy to entertain the so-called equalities to which you aspire, but while you are in my country, I must ask that you observe some of our conventions. We are a small country and have remained an independent nation throughout thousands of years of history while others have fallen prey to empire, to colonialism, and as victims of devastating warfare. Boundaries have blurred, cities have been retitled, passed from one owner to the next as chattels. Flags have been lowered one day and raised the next day bearing another insignia altogether. But we are still here, standing tall and proud. And you might well wonder how we have escaped the ravages of war over the millennia. How have we managed to attain this unparalleled autarchy? Clear communication with our people by

109

the dissemination of information through the proper channels. We aim not to oppress but to suggest. And one of the means we use, to indicate a hierarchy that can be both understood and respected, is clear delineation between different strata of our society. I can well understand that you may have chosen, through some sort of quasi-socialist pretension, to abandon your soubriquet, but while you are our guest, there is no place for such false modesty. I would like, while you are here, to refer to you always by your full title. What is the feminine version of "duke"? "Duchess"? Yes, of course, you are indeed the Duchess of Edinburgh and my English is simply not good enough to have correctly identified the subtle difference when you wrote.' Here he clasped both her hands in his. 'While you are here, we must present you to the government and to our people correctly. These things are very, very important to us.'

Lizzie gasped a little. 'Oh, I say, you don't think … Well, I'm not exactly … I have a horrible feeling that you might have … Oh, golly!' Wresting her hands free, she finally found the words to ask, 'Mr President, who exactly *were* you expecting?'

Sergio shook his head in slight irritation and spoke a little more slowly, for fear she was struggling to interpret his accent. 'As your letter clearly stated, I am expecting you. A visit beginning today, the fifth of June, from the Duke of Edinburgh. Or Duchess of Edinburgh. I forget exactly the words you used …'

His voice trailed off just as understanding struck Lizzie. A red blotchy mess spread from her upper chest to her throat and settled on her neck. Two symmetrical circles of pink coloured her cheekbones as the enormity of her fraudulence became clear.

'Oh, I am most terribly sorry but I think you must have made the most awful mistake. I'm here to undertake an exercise for the *Duke of Edinburgh Gold Award*. It's a programme in England that aims to further our citizenship, to allow us to cross that difficult bridge between adolescence and adulthood. What I'm actually trying to achieve is, um, a certificate.'

Sergio, unable to comprehend this explanation, awaited a fuller one.

'I'm not the Duke of Edinburgh! Well, of course I'm not the Duke of Edinburgh! I'm travelling – I'm taking a year out! Oh, Lordy, I'm a *student*!'

Sergio slumped again and, as if through a process of osmosis, the colour drained from his face as it rose in Lizzie's. His mouth fell slackly open, and somewhere in the deepest recess of his inner ear, the humming began.

He had managed to convince himself, as the conversation unfolded, that he could make this work, that a royal woman would be better than no royal at all. For a brief moment, his imagination had taken him one step forwards: perhaps he could use this as a platform from which to launch a radical new political agenda. Women might use this visit as a signal to take a more active role in the community. As Miss Lizzie had been talking, he had begun to see a huge political coup attached to the stunt. There was a grand gesture to be made for the President of Vallerosa to be seen in public actively accepting and promoting this woman's power. Sovereign or otherwise, she was still a woman of great importance and, by endorsing her position, he could demonstrate to his populace another, altogether more private, side of himself. But no sooner had this absolute jewel of a plan begun to harden in his mind, than it was all slipping through his fingers again, nothing more than coal dust. First a duke, then a duchess, now nothing. A student? He had plenty of students – he had a country full of students. He had more *students* than he knew what to do with.

Angelo, sensing the looming crisis, leaped up and came between them, leaning heavily on the desk. The president was pale and visibly panting – possibly on the verge of hyperventilation. Miss Lizzie, meanwhile, looked close to tears and – as both men knew all too well – tears must be avoided at all costs. 'Sergio,' he whispered, 'may I?' He bowed and excused himself to Miss Lizzie and propelled Sergio through a door behind them. It led to Sergio's private bathroom and, once inside, Angelo locked the door and ran both bath taps at full force to drown any possible leakage of conversation.

Sitting on the side of the tub, they addressed the situation. 'This is a major problem, Angelo. This is as big a crisis as I've ever faced. This is as big – no, bigger – as the agricultural quota failure. This is a catastrophe! She's not what we thought she was. At all.' Angelo tried to interrupt but was silenced with Sergio's raised hand. 'We have an official welcome planned for this afternoon, we have spent this year's entire annual domestic budget on the midsummer party and we are due to hold an election soon after.

We absolutely have to deliver, I can't face failure. Failure is not an option.'

Angelo nodded slowly. There was no point in denying that this was a major issue for the government and a potential political disaster. Even now the band would be warming up, the bunting would soon be raised and the whole town would be in the throes of preparation for the afternoon's event.

He began slowly, cautiously, as though testing the words out on himself as well as the president: 'Sergio. You're an intelligent man. You thought she was royalty. I am a reasonably intelligent man. I, too, was fooled. But did you see her out there? The crowd loved her, the ministers were practically dribbling. Do you see where I'm going with this? If we thought she was royal, then perhaps we can get away with it. She could still be royal! She's due to stay for one month. Only a month. We can do this for a month, surely?'

Sergio nodded slowly and then, as the idea took hold, with unabated enthusiasm. Understanding and relief flooded his features. 'Yes, yes, of course. She looks royal, she sounds royal. Of course she could still be royal. A month. Yes, a party this afternoon. Fine. And then a month. A few royal tours – just as we'd planned. A speech or two – just as we'd planned. And then home on the train. Yes. A month.'

Angelo looked at his watch. 'We have an hour before the ministerial gathering and three hours before the official ceremony starts.' He left the taps running, opened the door and beckoned the anxious woman towards him.

113

'Miss Lizzie, in here, if you don't mind. I have a proposition for you.'

Lizzie rose cautiously from her seat and tiptoed gingerly towards him.

CHAPTER 12

In Which the British Visitor Is Made to Feel at Home

IN THE BOARDROOM, the gathered ministers chattered excitedly in an undignified audible whisper. The space had taken on a new scent, one perhaps never smelt in Parliament Hall before. Brylcreem fought with aftershave, which, in turn, took issue with perspiration and testosterone. Toothpaste had been utilized more energetically than ever before, combs and brushes wielded with abandon. Even Signor Civicchioni had taken some trouble over his appearance: his shirt – while not exactly ironed – had been tucked in and, worn as a badge of wanton infidelity, he sported a tie for perhaps the first time since his wedding day.

The conversation strayed sometimes towards official duties, rotas, schedules and the upcoming non-elective elections, but soon bounced back to their visitor, the blonde. When words failed, hand signals stepped in, and there was much deep sighing and lip-licking. As the clock's hand nudged excruciatingly forward to ten minutes past the appointed hour, the conversation peaked and troughed with each suspicion of an imminent arrival. Finally, they were rewarded, and in came Sergio, alone, with the woman. Unusually, Angelo was nowhere to be seen and on this occasion it was left to Sergio himself to draw out a chair for his visitor and to arrange himself primly beside her. The men, who had risen to their feet in unison, took to their chairs once more and turned, unashamedly, towards the blonde.

'Gentlemen, ministers. It is my privilege and honour to introduce you to our venerated guest, the Duchess of Edinburgh, Miss Elizabeth Holmesworth. As you are all aware, we have been planning for her arrival with much anticipation, and she and I have managed to facilitate an open and honest exchange in which we have covered much ground.'

Sergio looked around the room, glad to see that, while they were listening to him, his important visitor had the full, studied attention of his men. He was aware, too, of a new tension. He continued, carefully scrutinizing each minister as he spoke: 'Her brief, on this visit, is to under-stand the cultural differences between her country and ours. These are not just the differences that are clear for all to see, the British monarchy with its fashionable democracy as opposed to our less-understood elected dictatorship. But we're hoping this cultural exchange will afford us all an opportunity to delve deeper into each other's being.'

Many pairs of eyebrows simultaneously shot up at the prospect of delving deeper, and each minister edged forward, hearing, but not listening to, every word while examining in all its perfect detail the rosy complexion, the shining golden hair, the quality of the cotton shirt and the way it opened, just one button more than a woman in Vallerosa might have dared, to reveal at least two inches of unencumbered cleavage. And what unknown riches did that bottomless crevasse promise? There was not a man present whose eyes had not roamed and lingered luxuriously there for a few pauses too many, who was not right now dreaming of burrowing a nose, a mouth, a whole head between those two beautiful pink cushions.

Miss Holmesworth did not respond by buttoning up or clasping her shirt more tightly to her. Neither did her expression scold. Instead, she sat up straight in her chair and looked at each man in turn, smiling, returning their gaze with benevolent kindness and reserved dignity. If she knew she was the object of impure thoughts, she did not let on. Instead, she listened intently, her head politely askance, to each word of the president's welcome.

'While she is here, I would invite you to make our visitor completely comfortable. If she has a need, I charge you with meeting it. If she is lonely, I urge you to offer companionship. If she is hungry, open your cupboard to her. If she is thirsty, it is up to you to see that her need is quenched.'

The men nodded, a chorus of gulps echoing around the table.

Sergio pulled himself up and cuffed his forehead with the flat of his hand. 'What a poor host I am! I must proffer my most sincere apologies for using words where actions would have spoken with greater eloquence. Your Royal Highness, may I offer you a cup of tea?'

Miss Holmesworth smiled broadly. 'Golly, absolutely. I could murder a cup of tea! I thought you'd never ask!'

A bell was rung, and in a few minutes the rattle of the tea trolley could be heard making its way down the long corridors. A few moments later Miss Holmesworth sat back politely as the ritual unfolded before her: the setting out of pots and cups, the distribution of strainers among the contingent party, the elaborate pouring. With grace and restraint, she awaited her cue from her host. When the time was ready, and the tea had made its journey from the darkest brown to its current amber, Sergio indicated with a small gesture that she should drink first.

Miss Holmesworth leaned forward and took the most delicate of sips, studying as she did so the twelve pairs of eyes fixed on her. She sucked in her lips a little, and returned the cup with great care to its saucer. 'Is there any honey available? Would you mind?' The men glanced nervously from one to another, while the lightest shadow of a frown glanced off Sergio's brow. He nodded his approval and Mosconi stepped briskly from the room. They waited, silent, while the honey was fetched. More nervous glances were exchanged as the clock marked the slow crawl of time. Eventually, Mosconi returned, stepped quietly across the room and placed the honey, with a saucer and teaspoon, in front of Miss Holmesworth.

'Thank you.' She smiled, unaware of the tension that was currently darting through the air. She scooped a generous spoonful of honey into her tea and stirred, eventually tapping the spoon on the side of the cup and replacing it on the saucer. Once again she lifted the cup to her mouth and this time she allowed herself to take a full mouthful. She swallowed. 'Beautiful. Just what I needed!' She returned the cup to her lips.

Sergio refused to meet the eye of any of his attendant ministers but instead followed suit, helping himself to a spoonful of honey, then passing the pot to his right. As he tentatively sipped, a look of surprised delight passed across his face. Then he swigged greedily from his cup. The honey went around the table and, for a few delicious minutes, the room was filled with the sound of stirring, tapping and gentle murmurs of appreciation.

'Beautiful,' Dottore Rossini agreed.

'Delicious,' added Civicchioni. 'So sweet.'

'Very different, quite, quite different. But I like it.'

The comments were addressed not to the table, but quietly to themselves, as each man was transported somewhere else – a full cup, a previously untasted nectar, and all in the company of a beautiful woman, who herself might have been dripping honey for the men to catch on their outstretched tongues.

As the cups were drained, it became clear that the lead now needed to come from their visitor. She pushed away her empty cup and, having turned pointedly to thank Mosconi for fetching the honey, she turned back to the room. 'Um, gentlemen. It is my real pleasure to be here with you today. Your president and I have agreed a form that this visit might take and it seems best, if you don't mind, that you treat me as one of yourselves.' She looked around the room for approval. They stared in unblinking incomprehension. 'Um, as you would treat your wives?' This elicited a more open response but the smirks and nudges were, Miss Holmesworth sensed, a little more lascivious than she had perhaps intended.

'What I mean to say is that, with the exception of the occasional ceremony, like this evening, I would like to be left to explore your beautiful country as though I were just an ordinary tourist. I'd like to be able to get to know you all a little better,' more smirks, more nudges, 'and, well, make myself at home for the duration of my stay. I think it's fair to say that much more effort has been put into my welcome than I perhaps intended,' she looked at Sergio, 'and while I'm delighted to take part in these formal ceremonies, and am at the disposal of your president when he specifically demands it, for the bulk of my visit, well, you can pretty much expect me to muck in.'

The men pretended that they had been listening to her every word instead of escaping into the elaborate fantasy concocted by their collective imagination. Being brought back to worldly matters, with the mention of 'muck', they paid attention. Relishing the feeling that she had control of her audience now, she continued with her address: 'There are some aspects of my visit with which I would like your help. It is my hope that during my visit I can accomplish some good work, something perhaps of a charitable nature.' She turned to Dottore Rossini. 'You're the doctor, aren't you? Is there perhaps an orphanage I might be able to visit while I'm here?'

Rossini frowned. 'An orphanage?' He looked around the table, seeking help from his peers. They seemed as confused as he felt.

Lizzie smiled gently, almost relieved to encounter an English word that they failed to understand. 'An orphanage is an institution that cares for unwanted babies or children with no other family …'

'Yes, yes, yes, I know what an orphan is. Harry Potter. Oliver. Annie. Yes, yes, an orphanage. But no. Not here.' He glanced around again, seeking permission to continue, and as no one seemed willing either to challenge him or to step in and help he pushed on bravely: 'You see, I think you'll find that an orphanage is necessary only where there are surplus children, or children with no parents. Here in Vallerosa, just maintaining our population numbers is one of our government's primary objectives. As for unwanted or parentless children, we simply don't have any. In the very unfortunate circumstances in which a baby is orphaned, at birth, for example – which you must understand happens very rarely under my watch – then the baby would automatically be raised by its extended family. I cannot remember an occasion when a baby wasn't embraced by the women here. Really, that is the function of our women, to nurture the children. That is what they *do* … I'm sorry …' He trailed off, disappointed that he hadn't been able to acquiesce to the very first request made.

'Oh, but that's marvellous. Absolutely fascinating. I'd be very interested to learn more about this. And perhaps see for myself your hospital and maternity ward. Might that be possible?'

'Well certainly. I'd be delighted. I'll ensure a full tour is built into your schedule.' The doctor grinned sheepishly, trying to disguise his delight.

Lizzie went on politely, 'And are there any other projects, of a charitable nature, in which I might involve myself? I would be happy to help the needy, wherever you feel there might be an opening for me. I'd very much like to feel that my time here hadn't been wasted.'

'Needy. Hmm.' Dottore Rossini thought for a moment.

'There's Franco. He's pretty needy,' suggested Signor Pompili. Everyone laughed but hushed themselves quickly at the insensitivity of their ridicule.

Sergio frowned at the immaturity of his men. 'Our approach to community is quite unorthodox and you'll find many things that you won't recognize from your own country. I hope you are able to embrace these differences, although you may think we are a poorer country for not having the wealth of facilities you have with which to scoop up the hungry, the poor or those who struggle to fit in with day-to-day living. We, of course, share many of the same issues, but our policies are different. Here, these are not issues of government but of family. If somebody is hungry, they will go next door and be fed. If a baby needs caring for, there is always a sister, an aunt, a grandmother … or, in the most desirable cases, a combination of all of these. My suggestion to you is that you keep an open mind and you look thoroughly at the way we live before passing judgement.'

Lizzie nodded, humbled.

'And there will be many detractors around the world who will be very happy to pass judgement. They will make uneducated assumptions about our political regime and will push us to exchange it for something else altogether, because it does not conform to the wishes of those so-called democratic leaders. Those leaders are pointing their weapons of democracy at us and at other dictatorships around the world. But,' he softened his tone, 'stay with us. Our discussions are transparent. We invite you to join us and witness our government at work as we implement policy. Sit in on the meetings. I have nothing to hide. Take notes – who cares? Not me. Then, and only then, you may judge.'

LIZZIE CHEWED HER LIP as she listened, smiling the smile that softened Sergio and the rest of the men around the table. Now there was little more to be said. The men were speechless, Sergio was cautious and Lizzie was hoping to say as little as possible while she tried to absorb the scale of her deceit – a duplicity she had agreed to only because she had found herself perched on the side of a bath next to a president who had been convincing on matters of national security.

The meeting drew to a close and Lizzie, with a conflicting sense of nervous excitement, was accompanied to her quarters.

CHAPTER 13

In Which the Visitor Goes Exploring

GLAD TO BE ALONE AT LAST, Lizzie was grateful for the short amount of time off she had been granted to settle into her surroundings and to unpack. Her journey had been exhausting but had been made even more so by her inability to engage her almost constant travelling companion. He had caught her attention during a couple of train changes early in her journey and again when they'd waited together before the final leg. Lizzie prided herself on her good manners and the ease with which she could find common ground with her elders but her travelling companion had remained obstinately aloof. When it became apparent that they were to share two tiny jump seats in the driver's quarters for the last long stretch, she had attempted once more to make conversation but he had rebuffed her. He had the countenance of a man who had a good idea of what lay ahead of him and was already weary of it.

Lizzie's bubbling enthusiasm was not, however, wasted on either the train guard or the driver and she was fed biscuits, with tea from a large urn, and given a blanket to tuck around herself for warmth in the night. None of these small luxuries had been afforded to her fellow traveller who, despite his air of entitlement, was apparently entitled to nothing. She had been a little disappointed to share the pony trap, perhaps the most thrilling adventure of her life, with such a negative personality but his lack of enthusiasm hadn't dented her own and she hadn't given him a second thought as she'd arrived at Parliament Hall.

After a brief morning snack of tea and bread, she had been allocated a spacious room on the west wing of the main parliament buildings. It was worn, but comfortable. ('A little more shabby than chic,' her mother would have commented.) There was no en-suite bathroom but there were totally passable facilities just down the corridor. Also, it seemed that she was the only guest using them, so her accommodation felt both generous and private. Her small balcony was on the corner of the Piazza Rosa, which afforded her a good view of the palatial square below. She drew the curtains, locked the door and made herself comfortable on the bed, quite exhausted and about as far away from anything she knew as she had ever been. She must have fallen asleep for, after a short while, she awoke with a start, suddenly aware of the presence of something or someone in the room with her. She lifted her head, momentarily alarmed, to discover that her companion was a bat, swishing from one side of the room to the other. It was the disturbance of air that she'd felt, rather than the creature itself, and once she'd reassured herself that the bat's superior guidance system meant it was unlikely to collide with her, she lay down and watched it for a while. Eventually it hooked itself neatly to a rafter, then shook out its leathery wings and tucked itself tidily away.

Lizzie rose, with renewed energy, to explore the piazza before the evening's ceremonies. After washing the grime of her train journey from her face and checking her mobile phone to see if it had picked up any signal, she left her bedroom, retraced her steps through the building and found herself on the cobbles of Piazza Rosa.

She decided to acclimatize by surveying the town as best she could. She had shaken off the offer of a guide, preferring instead to walk alone and ponder upon this morning's almost farcical outcome. Her rational self wanted to condemn the intended impersonation – after all, it went against the good manners that she had been reared to uphold – but her egotistical self rather liked the pretence. For the moment this personality won, convincing the other, better-behaved, Lizzie that sometimes one had to follow one's heart. Also, there seemed a real need on the part of the president, and who was she to turn down orders from such a high-ranking official?

Lizzie walked slowly around the edge of the Piazza Rosa, using the arched walkway for shade and glancing in through the many beaded curtains to take in the full array of wares on offer in the shops. She stopped in front of a shaded window, whose fading signage seemed to indicate a charcuterie, ignored the flies batting around the entrance, and pushed her way into the dim but pleasantly cool interior. Having barely eaten since a sandwich on the station of some small Italian province last night, she had suddenly felt quite weak and wondered whether a little ham or other local morsel might be available for a late lunch. As her eyes became accustomed to the dark room she found herself meeting the glare of a row of pig's heads, lined up on top of a long marble slab. Each offered an identical pair of pink waxy ears, a bristly forehead and a glistening nose for her inspection. Their glassy eyes stared accusingly at her, as if she had stepped in to deal one more humiliating blow to their already much diminished anatomies. Not daring to glance below to the chilled cabinets for fear of what genocide she might find there, and glad not to have come across a human hand with responsibility for such slaughter, she retreated, her need for food curiously revoked.

Shuddering, Lizzie continued her journey. She passed several more shops, most of which seemed only to service the most domestic of requirements. Just last year she had been touring Venice with her parents and in that city's great square, which, admittedly, had made much less impact on her than the Piazza Rosa, she had been able to find only goods specifically made for the tourist. Here, there was no such tat, no small ceramic reproductions of the Piazza Rosa, no lenticular renditions of Parliament Hall, gaudy religious icons or beer glasses emblazoned with Vallerosa's name. Instead, as she passed from shop to shop, she found many opportunities to purchase cooking implements and clothes pegs, unfeasibly large bags of grain, endless buckets and coils of rope in varying dimensions.

Sauntering along, with a pleasant afternoon to while away before the evening's celebrations began, she hesitated outside the empty façade of what appeared to have been a flower shop. Even with its shades half pulled down and mail gathering dust on the door mat, she was immediately transported to her mother's favourite florist in Fulham, where she could quite easily spend thirty pounds on cut flowers on a Saturday morning. In a laughable moment of self-projection, she saw herself serving customers here, in Vallerosa, with precious bunches of long-stemmed roses and bright arrangements of dahlias and gypsophila. With her hair tied back in a high ponytail she would smile and greet every customer by name, content to bring colour and scent into the homes of her many new friends. She walked on, laughing, dismissing the idea as nonsense, before her father's image had had a chance to creep in and scold her lack of ambition with a steely glare from beneath lowered eyebrows.

Eventually, she found herself heading for the welcome sight of a bar. Many of the tables were occupied and she was aware that her slow approach had attracted the attention of most of those sitting there. It was only as she got closer that she realized there were two bars on offer: the second group of tables around the corner belonged to a separate establishment. Now she hesitated, confronted with a dilemma. She could take a seat at the first table available in what appeared to be the more crowded bar, where the tables were shaded and she would have to sit shoulder to shoulder with some rather intimidating police and military men, or she could continue to the adjacent place, sit at one of the more spacious tables and bask in the afternoon sunshine. Therein lay the dilemma. If it were simply up to her, the second, sunnier, bar would be the obvious choice. However, she hesitated because she might cause offence by walking past the first to favour the second.

Knowing that in faltering she would make even more of a spectacle of herself, she silently resolved to visit both bars often and to be scrupulously fair in her patronage. With the diplomatic decision made, she took a seat in Il Gallo Giallo, among hordes of uniformed men who had not – as far as she could tell – uttered a single word since she had noticed they were staring at her. Gradually, as she settled in her chair, nodding and smiling in the general direction of their upturned faces, a small amount of noise returned to the bar.

The bar owner was soon standing before her, wiping his hands on his apron and asking what she would care to drink: 'Tea or beer?' For some reason, this seemed to be the root of much hilarity and she smiled gratefully at him, determined to demonstrate that *she* would not mock his good manners.

She deliberated for a moment. The tea here was awfully bitter, but beer might be a little unladylike, particularly quite early in the afternoon. Once again manners dictated her response and she turned her face up to the barman's, smiling brightly.

'Tea, please. Could you bring some honey, too? And I'm rather famished. Could I have a little bowl of crisps or nuts, do you think?' He failed to return the smile and backed away into the dark interior of the bar. Once again, this smallest of exchanges seemed to have created a minor furore among her fellow drinkers and she was painfully aware that they were now slapping their palms on their knees as they laughed, openly and – Lizzie wondered – somewhat cruelly.

She replayed the conversation slowly in her mind. It might, of course, be a language thing, but she had already been so amazed by the almost perfect English used in the country that she couldn't imagine she might have been misunderstood. While she pondered any possible unintended insult or double entendre, she looked out at the Piazza Rosa, marvelling once again at the splendour of the architecture and the vision of its creators. As the city crept up the valley sides on either side of the river, there were tiny discrepancies in colour of stone and style of building, but the piazza and its surrounding buildings had been dealt an incredibly even hand. Granted, the piazza was a little tired, but the scale on which it had been built was grand and the attention to detail stunning. From the profile of the clock tower to the elegant lines of Parliament Hall, its symmetry and graceful proportions suggested a master plan executed with care and pride.

While Lizzie contemplated the scene before her she was tempted to snap away with her camera but was aware that, in her duplicitous position, such behaviour might not be altogether suitable.

MEANWHILE THE BAR OWNER was scrabbling around at the back of the bar, pulling out boxes and crates until he found a couple of packets of peanuts. Anxious that his royal visitor might notice that the use-by date had been exceeded by a number of years, Dario decided instead to decant them into a beer glass, which, though not exactly classy, was certainly an act of unprecedented hospitality.

He carried a small tin tray towards Lizzie's table and, with something that might have resembled a flourish, set out the glass of nuts, a teapot, cup and small jar of honey. The latter he had fetched from his own quarters above the bar, confident that it was perfectly acceptable, after the judicious removal of some breadcrumbs from his breakfast.

The honey, though crystallized, smelt of rosemary and Lizzie stirred a couple of generous spoonfuls into the tea. Absently she groped for a handful of peanuts, tipped her head back and dropped them one by one into her mouth, still stirring. The onlookers, silenced again by this blatant display of sensuality, stared with unbridled lust, occasionally wiping their mouths with the backs of their hands.

THE PRECEDING TEN MINUTES had attracted the attention of another onlooker. Not even when the American consultant had come into town had Dario deigned to bring tea to the table. As for the nuts, well …

'He's certainly been keeping those provisions up his sleeve,' fumed Piper, to nobody in particular, as he surveyed the scene. He leaned at the doorway of his bar, silently furious that the important visitor had chosen his rival's for her first drink. Arms crossed, he observed the customers' childish behaviour as they swapped open-mouthed drooling for childish giggles. It was hard to imagine that those men represented the highest echelons of Vallerosan society. Piper shook his head in disgust, the taste of jealousy bitter in his mouth. Retiring inside, he half-heartedly wiped down his tables.

'One amazing-looking woman! No?' said Elio, the potter. 'I could do justice to those curves.' He chortled, imitating with his hands the fluidity of clay on wheel.

Piper dismissed the coarse gesture with a glare. 'She, Elio, is exactly what I've been waiting for.'

'Uh-oh! She's exactly what we've all been waiting for, my friend, so get to the back of the queue!' Elio laughed some more, delighted that young Piper might have set his sights on such a lofty prize.

'No, you don't understand. Not her, exactly, and it's not even her royal status that interests me particularly. But somebody like her, a tourist, somebody who isn't going to settle for the same old *shit* every day!' Piper used his hand to take in his whole bar and his scattering of customers, who now looked up to see what had excited the usually gentle host. 'I'm in the service industry. That's what you all fail to understand. But what's the point of serving anyone here if you don't really care what you get? And most of you,' he fired this point directly at Elio, 'don't even pay. Why should I bother to deliver anything other than the absolute basics?'

Elio stood up. He might be an artist but he still had his integrity and he certainly wasn't going to take insults from a barman. 'I do pay! I might run up a bit of a tab from time to time, but you just say the word and I'll clear it. I won't have a word said about my credit. My honour's at stake here.' Elio puffed out his chest, ready to fight if necessary.

Piper defused the situation with the flicker of a smile. 'I know, I know. I meant no offence. I'm very happy to continue serving you and grateful for whatever you throw my way from time to time,' he said, with a nod in the direction of the earthenware pots that lined a shelf above the bar, all proof of debts settled in the past. 'But don't you see? This is a real opportunity for me – for all of us. Here, at last, a discerning customer. Not even the American consultant counts. We all know his game, importing crates of his weak American beer and bringing in bottles of Jack Daniel's. How many times has he graced us with his custom over the years? Once? Twice? And then only when he's been currying favour with the toadies next door.'

Piper carried on wiping tables distractedly but his eyes were soon drawn back to the other bar. 'But there, look at her!' His voice softened. 'Finally. A customer who deserves the very best.'

The two men stopped what they were doing to stare unabashedly at Lizzie. She brushed her sunlit hair off her face as she leaned forward to sip her tea. Then, realizing she had attracted the attention of the men at the bar next door, she gave a little wave and busied herself with the contents of her handbag.

CHAPTER 14

In Which Tourism and Recreation Go into Battle

AFTER TWO OR THREE cups of tea, Lizzie was beginning to get a taste for the dark brew. Just as she was wondering whether she should complete her circuit of the Piazza Rosa, then head back to her room for a nap before dinner, Remi the postman came rushing towards her, clutching a manila folder to his chest. He folded himself into a deep bow upon reaching her table. 'Your Royal Highness,' he gasped, 'I have an important presentation to make.' But as he scrabbled among the paperwork to pull out the relevant papers, two uniformed men shuffled forwards and swept him out of their way with a stern shake of their heads. Remi coloured as he resealed the folder, then retreated. The uniformed men sighed apologetically and indicated the empty chairs beside her. 'May we?' they chorused, in unison.

'Be my guests!' Lizzie gushed.

'It is a great honour to introduce ourselves to you personally. We met this morning at the station and again with the president.'

Lizzie pushed up her sunglasses. 'Oh, yes, of course, how rude of me. It was all a bit of a blur this morning and I've been up for what seems like days, so forgive me for not recognizing you immediately.'

'Of course, of course, Your Royal Highness. Let me introduce us. I am Settimio Mosconi, senior minister for tourism, and this is Signor Marcello Pompili, the senior minister for recreation. We are part of Sergio's inner circle. He absolutely depends on us to help our wonderful country continue to thrive.'

'How marvellous. The ministers for tourism and recreation! What an amazing job you two must have, looking after such interesting aspects of Vallerosa. Tourism and recreation. So what is the difference? Who does what?'

Pompili and Mosconi shared a puzzled look. It was Mosconi who attempted a reply as they took their seats and pulled their chairs into the table, scraping them as noisily as they could to ensure there was not a man in either bar who hadn't noticed whom they were taking their tea with.

'The difference? Chalk and cheese! Tourism and recreation are two very, very different things. Completely and utterly different. There is no way that anyone could confuse tourism with recreation.' Mosconi smiled generously to demonstrate the endless patience he would devote to explaining the complex workings of government. 'I look after tourism. That is to say, I look after the outward-pointing aspects of our country. It is my job to ensure that we attract foreign visitors and that, once they are here, they have a completely satisfying time.'

'And I,' piped up Pompili, 'am tasked with ensuring that everyone, citizens and visitors, has plenty to do while they are actively engaged in leisure time. For a tourist to enjoy recreational activity, he must first make himself at home. Once that has been established, I can ensure that his leisure is well spent.'

'Without stepping on Signor Cellini's toes, of course,' Mosconi interjected, with a quick frown.

Pompili reddened a little and corrected himself: 'Well, that goes without saying. I must not step on Signor Cellini's toes. It is important to ensure the delineation between my role and his. Yes, indeed. I am the minister for recreation. Signor Cellini is the minister for leisure.'

'Two completely different things,' reiterated Mosconi.

'Yes! Very different!' agreed Pompili, still anxious that he might unintentionally have taken some credit for the role of the absent Cellini.

'And the differences are?' Lizzie enquired, now a little confused.

'Well, it is not entirely my job to explain the role of Signor Cellini. I am sure he would be much happier to undertake the elucidation of his mantle himself. But, to put it simply, recreation is the action you take within leisure time. While leisure itself is really quite inactive.'

'Resting?' proffered Lizzie, hoping she was helping.

'Oh, I think that might oversimplify the matter. There is probably much more to leisure than simply resting. But that is not my job, or my special interest, although I did once, as a much younger man, consider going into the leisure end of the business. But I believe, as it happens, that Cellini is much better suited to leisure and I have certainly found my niche in recreation.'

'So I suppose the three of you work closely together? Tourism, leisure and recreation?'

'Oh, very, very closely,' agreed Mosconi. 'Although of the three of us, I probably have the greatest fiscal responsibility so I will also work very closely with Feraguzzi. I have a budget. Recreation has no budget.'

Pompili drew himself tall in his chair, offended by the subtle but deliberate barb. 'That's not true at all. I would go so far as to describe it as a gross fabrication. I indeed have a budget, a substantial one. What you mean is that I have no *income* responsibility. Having an income agenda within a recreational framework would be counterintuitive. It is my government's wish – and, indeed, my own – that recreation is something that should be free, accessible to all.'

Mosconi considered the distinction for a moment. 'Yes, very true. I will give you that, and it is a valid differentiation between our two roles. As minister for tourism, I am keen that foreigners visit our country with an agenda that reaches beyond noticing that our country is attractive. I must also ensure that while our tourists are here they spend money that will remain within the country. My colleague here is intent on ensuring that there are recreational activities available to everyone, whether they are just visiting or not, and that many of those are free.'

Pompili, having sat quietly awaiting the restoration of his honour, now slapped both palms on the table in quick succession. 'Tell Her Royal Highness about the bridge that

137

is a perfect example of our different approaches to our ministerial roles!'

Mosconi nodded. 'That is indeed a very good example.' He leaned forward to be sure he had his visitor's complete attention, then began his tale. 'Once, Vallerosa had just one bridge to connect the south and the north banks of the river Florin. We debated in Parliament for years whether to make this a free or toll bridge. I argued on the side of the toll bridge, on the basis that a small contribution from the purse of each visitor was a good way to raise vital funds. I examined case studies from around the world and charging a toll seemed a very legitimate taxation.'

Pompili interjected: 'Meanwhile, I felt that this would be too great a burden on the citizens of the country and might indeed have a negative effect on the pursuit of recreational activity. Perhaps this small charge might impinge upon a resident's freedom to roam.'

Lizzie had been concentrating hard on each argument, as they took it in turns to speak. 'So how did you resolve this?'

Pompili answered, pride and joy in his voice. 'We built a second bridge. At one bridge you pay a toll, the second is free.'

Mosconi was a little more measured in his tone but the pride was evident in his voice too, and his eyes shone. 'Yes, indeed, a very healthy collaborative resolution. Government working at its pinnacle, I would say.'

'Although the toll bridge only charges in one direction,' added Pompili, conscious that the facts must be clear and that his own delight shouldn't cloud the underlying truth.

'It does?' Lizzie felt a little doubt creeping into her voice and resolved to concentrate even harder.

Mosconi sighed a little. 'After the free bridge had been completed, it was felt that the toll bridge discriminated a little too heavily against those on the south side of the river as many of the vital functions of the city take place on the north side. These good citizens didn't want to pay to walk across, and after a period of thorough consultation we concurred.'

'But couldn't they have just walked across the free bridge?'

The weight of political debate rested heavily on the shoulders of the minister for tourism. His shrug, though not pronounced enough to dismiss the burden, conveyed the gravity of political process and consensual reform. 'Well, yes, that option was discussed at length, but the issue wasn't that there was an alternative bridge for access, more that there was now a charge imposed on the toll bridge, which had been there for a very long time and had, up until the time of the toll, been entirely free.'

Pompili lightened the atmosphere, reminding his colleague and reassuring their guest that this sensitive issue had, after all, been resolved to the satisfaction of all. 'Everyone seems very happy that a toll is charged from north to south, but not in the other direction. And the free bridge remains free in both directions, which makes it a very attractive alternative.'

Lizzie pondered this for a while but dismissed the prospect of challenging the logic any further. 'Well, it's great that you listen to the needs of your people and I also think it's fantastic that your government places such emphasis on the more enjoyable aspects of life. I was a little concerned before I came here that you hadn't really taken the tourism potential of your country on board. I mean, when I first tried to research your country, it was hard to find out anything at all!'

Mosconi swallowed. 'We view tourism very much as a growth opportunity, Your Royal Highness. It is fair to say that we aren't quite open for business yet, if you understand me.'

'Oh, please stop the "Your Royal Highness" bit. To tell you the truth, it makes me rather uncomfortable. Call me Lizzie.' She stuck out a hand to be shaken in friendship but both men knew that to transgress with the formalities might be misinterpreted as lack of respect, which might consequently undermine diplomatic relations between their two countries.

Mosconi shook his head vehemently. 'Oh, we couldn't. I'm afraid it is not in our culture to be so casual.'

Lizzie folded her arms as she sized the men up. 'Well, how about "Miss Holmesworth"? Would that suit you?' She unfolded her arms and this time held out her right hand with greater determination.

'Fine. Perfectly fine, thank you,' they mumbled. They took it in turns to shake.

'Well,' said Lizzie, picking up where they'd left off, 'if you're not exactly open for business yet then you jolly well should be, I think your country's absolutely beautiful – or what I've seen of it so far. And the people are so friendly! Honestly, I've travelled a lot – my father has always insisted that it's a vital part of my education – and I'm totally impressed. Really!'

Mosconi blushed in gratitude. 'You are very generous. Thank you.'

'So, if you're head of tourism and it sounds like you've got big plans for the future, sell it to me. Go on! I've got plenty of time here and I don't want to miss a single thing. Sell it – tell me what I should do and what I should avoid. I want to know every single attraction.'

'Attraction? You mean like a theme park?' Anxiety clouded the minister's features once more.

'Well, of course, if you have any – but, you know, the stuff you'll put on your website when you get to build one, or that you'd put in a brochure if you were making one for tourists to look at. Sights to see, landmarks, museums, you know the sort of thing.'

A deep grin broke out over Mosconi's face. 'A museum! Yes, of course we have a museum. We are very proud of it. But to *sell* it to you, as though I am merely a cheap copywriter? No, I don't think so. What I would like to do, with your permission, is to show it to you myself. Might I do that?'

Lizzie smiled gratefully. 'I'd like that very much. I'm free, um, well, I'm free full stop, I think. Unless there's any official duty for me to do, I can pretty much fit in a museum trip any time soon. You name the day!'

'Tuesday. Of course it must be a Tuesday. Our museum is only open on a Tuesday,' scolded Mosconi, as though even the newcomer should know such essential information.

'Well, Tuesday it is. Is that a date?'

'Yes.' He beamed. 'It is a date.'

Marcello Pompili, whose idea it had been in the first place to approach the guest, sat back in his chair, ignored and fuming. While Settimio might be in charge of tourism and Miss Holmesworth might have arrived as a tourist, should he not be responsible for her recreation? And what about Cellini? He was definitely going to have something to say about Settimio's very aggressive stance. A stance that looked likely to impinge on the tourist's leisure time.

While Pompili sulked, Lizzie relaxed in her chair, unaware of the several diplomatic spats that were springing up around her. While they were only suggestions of arguments now, they had the potential to build into something much larger. More than a century of friendly bar rivalry was suddenly overshadowed by menace that threatened to develop into an unprecedented war, while the two comrades, Marcello and Settimio, firm friends since childhood, now eyed each other with suspicion. One seemed to have grasped the prize and was already living in fear of it being wrested from his hands, while the other was feeling the stirrings of an unfamiliar blend of jealousy and determination. As they all stared forward, the two men pretending to admire the view that the visitor was enjoying, Settimio Mosconi had already resolved that the prize would indeed be his, whatever that acquisition took.

CHAPTER 15

In Which the President Loses His Cool

WHILE LIZZIE MIGHT HAVE IGNITED the fuse that could trigger any number of altercations, Sergio was already anticipating the worst scenarios that might result from the spark's connection with a hoard of highly combustible explosives.

His intention that afternoon had been to practise his address for the welcoming party but when he looked at the words on the typed sheet in front of him they swam away. He swallowed hard and drew the curtains. Then he lay down with a wet flannel draped over his face.

'Breathe,' he said to himself. 'Breathe.'

He replayed the morning's events in his mind. Either he had set in train a catastrophic series of disasters or had saved himself from impending calamity. It was hard to tell which, so early on, but his instinct was to assume the worst. That Angelo was in on the deception gave him a degree of comfort – to have a co-conspirator gave him an advantage, he was sure. Unless he had presented his chief of staff with an opportunity to undermine Sergio's power at some future point. That, of course, was unlikely: Angelo was his greatest friend, his confidant, a brother almost. But politics were dangerous, and leaving yourself open to blackmail was perhaps the most fundamental of all misjudgements.

'Breathe.'

The VIP was certainly impressive. She had handled herself well in front of the ministers at her first official appearance. There had been no trace of nervousness in her demeanour – in fact, she seemed to have taken to that part with uncanny ease. And surely now she, too, was implicated in the deceit, she would have to continue or admit, in public, to the fraud.

'Breathe.'

But had she defrauded anybody? She had merely said she wanted to be treated as a normal person. She hadn't even hinted that she might be of royal descent. Hadn't she done quite the reverse? She had publicly declared she was the same as everyone else. Was she playing him already at this game? Perhaps she was more conniving than he had given her credit for. Perhaps she was already plotting to use his chicanery to depose his government.

'Breathe.'

Perhaps she and Angelo were already in cahoots.

'Breathe.'

He was going to have to tread very, very carefully. From now until the moment she was on that train in a month's time, he had to watch every move she made. And he would have to be careful with Angelo, also. He had always had the appearance of an honest man, but it was possible that a chink in the presidential armour could give his hitherto ally an opportunity to further his own political career.

'Breathe.'

Nevertheless, he needed Angelo. Now his mind was so fuzzy, he wouldn't be able to read his own speech. He was going to have to resort to memorizing the words, a tactic that had always served him well in times of stress. Sergio stood up, threw the facecloth in the general direction of the bathroom and called for Angelo.

CHAPTER 16

In Which the Dancing Begins

THE SMELL OF SLOWLY ROASTING PORK had been gently infiltrating the nooks and crannies of Vallerosa since shortly after the arrival of the special guest early that morning. Several beasts were being turned by hand over flaming logs of cedar, and the combined scent of meat and wood had been more effective in bringing the people of Vallerosa out to Piazza Rosa than any official decree.

Angelo and the rest of the PEGASUS committee hovered around the periphery of the piazza. After some discussion they had decided to disperse themselves among the crowd rather than to huddle as a collective. This, it had been agreed, was the most accurate interpretation of Sergio's wish for something less contrived than the original Big Celebration.

It was easy to engineer unbidden music. Music just happened in Vallerosa, and of its many associations, none was so natural and instinctive a trigger as the smell of roasting pig. As the crackling began to spit, hiss and turn golden brown, the men of Il Toro Rosso reached for their accordions and violins and struck up an impromptu ensemble, in just the note of impetuous merrymaking that Sergio had been so keen to achieve.

Angelo quietly punched the air and smiled from the sidelines as the people of the town arrived in Piazza Rosa to dance up an appetite. He went in search of Sergio to congratulate him on his foresight. Sergio, now the crowds had amassed, was keen to deliver a rousing speech from the balcony but Angelo convinced him of the merits of keeping the evening low-key. The crowds were happy, the VIP was enjoying warm Vallerosan hospitality in the company of some senior ministers, and the atmosphere was as joyous as anyone could remember. 'This way,' Angelo reminded his boss, 'the VIP can make her own acquaintance with our people and you will not publicly have introduced her as one thing or another.'

Sergio acknowledged the wisdom in this but a nagging voice in his mind suggested he might just have been robbed of a personal political opportunity.

Lizzie had been fetched from her lodgings by a very proud and incredibly nervous Tersilio Cellini, who now felt unable to let her drift more than a couple of feet from him. She was grateful, as it happened, for his attentiveness because she was already fretting that she might be required to dance. As she watched the men and women take to the floor she knew she had neither the skill nor the practice to join them.

The men and women moved together in dignified pair-ings, the seriousness of the undertaking evident in the

147

men's upright movements as they glided around in uniform circuits, their left hands stiffly out in support of their partners' marginally more relaxed gait. As each song drew to a close the dancers waited a few moments, listening with deep concentration to the opening bars of the next, then swept into the steps that matched it. In that way, the pairs worked in harmony as they made their way around the dance floor in sweeping circles.

Lizzie watched in admiration. A combination of lanterns swinging from the archways of the piazza's perimeter and the moon's great arc lent an enchanting lambency to the scene, which had a charm that made Lizzie's heart swell, but it was the dancing that captured her imagination. She had never before witnessed such efficiency of movement and ease of footwork. No rehearsed moves of the many barn dances and Scottish reels she had joined had had this fluid grace and decorum. She blushed at the memory of her own ungainly leaping and bopping at a party just before she had left on her travels.

She followed the footwork, trying to identify a pattern she might be able to imitate but each dance varied, and though the dancers were unfazed by any change in tempo, she became quite flustered as she watched until she was led to a chair on the sidelines where she could admire the spectacle without the fear of being pushed out to make a fool of herself.

She was flanked by Pompili and Cellini, her devoted companions for the evening, but Mosconi was never far away and was the first to ferry platefuls of fatty hog, crusty bread and tart apple sauce to the guest.

As the momentum built and it was obvious to all that food and drink was being generously shared, and that the citizens had entered into the spirit of the event with enthusiastic abandonment, the ministers relaxed a little, assured of a triumph. Lizzie sat swaying to the music, delighted by her companions and by the city.

Despite the undeniably convivial atmosphere, Cellini released an exaggerated sigh.

It had the desired effect on Lizzie who turned immediately to him with a worried frown. 'Whatever is the matter? This is such a wonderful party, but you seem so desperately sad.'

'Exactly. Like sunlight picking out the dust in a newly swept room, there is nothing like the happiness of others to amplify the tragedy of one's own life.' Cellini smiled sadly, conveying the impression that he was quite capable of suffering with stoicism.

'Tragedy? I'm so sorry. Is there anything you feel you can talk to me about? I find that sharing a burden often helps.' Lizzie patted his arm while he, dramatically, framed his response.

'It is nothing that I cannot bear alone, which I must get used to, I suppose. The great sadness of my life is that I am in my prime with no prospect whatsoever of finding a woman with whom I can share the fruits of my labour and lessen the loneliness of a long winter.' Cellini shook his head and sighed again. After a brief pause he drew himself up tall in his chair. Pointing disgustedly at the dancers, he exclaimed, 'Look at Vlad! Could he dance with any greater degree of self-congratulation?'

Lizzie peered at the dancers, trying to work out whom Cellini might have meant. 'Him?' she asked, as a couple twirled slowly past. 'Vlad, the minister for employment?'

Vlad was currently picking a careful route around the dance floor. He held his partner lightly, as if she might break, should he clasp her any closer. An anxious frown of concentration played across his face and he bit his lip to disguise the counting he was trying to suppress as he measured his steps. The minister studied his feet, and only occasionally met his partner's gaze.

Lizzie couldn't detect a trace of complacency in Vlad's gait but Cellini was unrelenting in his critical appraisal. 'Without a partner in life, what is the point in working hard to achieve success? I am without purpose. I am simply resigned to my fate as a bitter elder statesman.'

'But you're still a young man!' Lizzie exclaimed. 'I'm sure you'll find somebody to share your life with. Take a look around you – perhaps there's a young woman you could dance with here. Besides, moping certainly won't help you meet the woman of your dreams.'

But the minister had set his heart on self-pity. 'Trust me, there are no spare women. I have investigated any possible leads and Liliana there, the woman dancing now in the arms of my comrade, was one candidate I had only recently identified as a possibility. But I suppose I have met my match. I am minister for leisure. He is minister for employment. Leisure or employment? Hardly a fair contest. Without employment, leisure is not noble. It is simply unemployment.'

Signor Pompili had been similarly entranced by the dancers but now, sensing that Cellini had taken liberties in conversation with their guest, using the occasion to indulge in melancholic reflection, he tapped Lizzie sharply on the shoulder. 'Look closely, Miss Holmesworth. What do you see?'

'I see a beautiful piazza in the centre of a gorgeous city. I see many happy people, drinking and eating. I see musicians playing and dancers ...' She trailed off, wondering suddenly if this minister, too, was being obtuse and in search of a murkier perspective than her own.

'You see these things indeed, but they are superficial. Examine the scene with a little more scrutiny and you'll notice many other things too. You see government in action. You see the manifestation of utilitarianism, the consequence of a collective working at the pinnacle of its power. You see spontaneous merriment of the type that can only flourish among a truly content populace.' Signor Pompili spoke loudly, then dropped his voice to a hoarse whisper for his dénouement. 'And, Miss Holmesworth, should you find yourself asked in any formal capacity what you witnessed tonight, it is important to remember that you are seeing a nation that accesses recreation with the effortless ease of the well practised.' He paused. 'Please understand the distinction between "well practised" and "rehearsed". I would not like you to mislead an enquiry with the suggestion of conspiracy or collaboration.'

Lizzie laughed lightly. 'I've got it. Effortless and well-practised recreation. I think I can remember that.' She turned her attention back to the dance floor. Remi the postman twirled past her at that moment with a much older woman held tightly in his arms. He caught Lizzie's gaze and took the opportunity to propel his partner towards a chair, exclaiming, as he seated her firmly, 'Mother, you tire so easily!' His natural momentum from this movement landed him precisely at Lizzie's side, where he now rustled in his inner pocket for a piece of paper he had taken to carrying with him wherever he went.

'Your Royal Highness, I have a proposal to make that will greatly enhance the standing of our country in the eyes of our international peers, while simultaneously furthering the perception of its most diligent civil servants.' He bowed elaborately, scraping one knuckle on the ground at Lizzie's feet.

'Oh, really! You must stop that!' squealed Lizzie, who was unsure whether to be alarmed or amused by the man's genuflection to her.

Mosconi, hovering nearby, had tuned in, with uncanny instinct, to the potential of his country's standing being enhanced in the eyes of foreigners, which was something he felt uniquely qualified to care about. He appeared immediately and filled the limited amount of space between Lizzie and the postman.

'Remi-Post, if you are aware of a matter that is of significance to the minister for tourism or are in possession of information that might or might not impact on the country's standing then I implore you to follow procedure and make an appointment with my under-secretary who will arrange for you to consult with me as a matter of urgency. With all due respect to our visiting dignitary, I cannot imagine a scenario whereby a direct approach by yourself to her could possibly bear fruit of a material nature.'

'But, Settimio – Signor Mosconi, sir, my proposal directly involves our royal dignitary and I think it behoves her and you, sir, to grant me an audience.' Remi glanced nervously behind him as if to check his escape route, should a rapid exit become necessary.

Mosconi turned to Lizzie for approval. She nodded, and in that shared moment, the minister and his visitor had quite clearly collaborated on matters of importance. Mosconi dismissed the postman with a shake of his head, and urged him to follow protocol and pursue a formal audience, immensely pleased with himself and the outcome of the evening.

Lizzie, on the other hand, was suddenly aware of the magnitude of the day's events and the weight that now lay on her shoulders. As the dancers swayed in front of her, turning their hypnotic circles tirelessly, she felt her eyes begin to close. When she had yawned into her hand several times, she was eventually given permission to retire. She excused herself politely, blaming her exhaustion on her early arrival, and walked slowly back to her room, with the sound of the accordions accompanying her. She hugged the memory of the evening tightly to her and felt a renewed confidence that she could certainly rise to the task Sergio and Angelo had set for her.

On reaching her room, she undressed and fell into a deep, untroubled sleep to the sound of the music playing in the piazza below.

CHAPTER 17

In Which the Visitor Gets a Lesson in Timekeeping

THE FOLLOWING DAY, after a leisurely morning of reading, updating her journal and steadfastly putting off the moment when she would have to make human contact again, Lizzie stepped out of her cool lodgings into the afternoon sun. Deliberately she set off in an anticlockwise direction around the Piazza Rosa to avoid the accusation that she might have snubbed the kind patron of Il Gallo Giallo in favour of the neighbouring Il Toro Rosso. Once again stealing glimpses of the domestic necessities available to the citizens of Vallerosa she made slow progress, stopping every now and then to admire the sheer banality of household wares occupying what was surely the country's finest retail space. In any other she might have reached for her camera to record the precariously stacked oilcans or rows of unidentifiable brown pickles and preserves. But to turn a tourist's amused eye on what appeared to be a practical and entirely satisfactory lifestyle seemed cynical and, given the generous courtesies that had been lavished upon her since her arrival, ungrateful.

Today there was activity in the piazza. Scaffolding had been erected on the face of the clock tower and several men were working up high, apparently on the clock mechanism. A dozen uniformed men hovered below, waving their arms and shouting vague instructions or words of encouragement, while twenty feet away a smallish crowd had gathered to watch the progress and to alternate pessimistic shakes of the head with nods of cautious approval.

As Lizzie approached to their right, the now inevitable silence descended upon all three groups of men, onlookers, overseers and workers. Tools, while not downed, were lowered and the unabashed appraisal as the young woman walked by seemed to put the piazza's very atmosphere into abeyance. Time decelerated and, with it, Lizzie's pace slowed to an unintended crawl as the air, thick with the complex language of the unspoken, fought to hold her back. Determined to break the pattern that seemed to follow her wherever she went, she raised a hand in a cheery wave, smiling broadly as her eyes swept across all of her admirers, even those peering down from above. That had the desired effect: the men nodded in response and turned back to each other.

Lizzie's hair swung as she gathered speed. She cut the final corner of the piazza, went towards the scaffolding and then in the direction of the two bars.

The barmen had adopted symmetrical poses. Dario leaned to the left-hand side of his doorway. He watched Lizzie's approach nervously, compulsively wiping his hands upon his apron from time to time, conscious that a handshake might even be *de rigueur* on a second visit and anxious that his visitor might find his palm disagreeably clammy. Meanwhile, Piper leaned to the right-hand doorpost of his establishment. His face was stony and, as yet, unwelcoming but his thoughts rested purely on his prospective customer. Had his prayer been broadcast over the piazza's extensive loudspeaker system, the townsfolk would have heard, 'Please come to my bar. Please come to my bar. Please come to my bar.'

As the young woman cut a path to the corner of the piazza, she seemed to Piper to be heading, by a clear degree or two, for Il Toro Rosso. His mantra increased in ferocity and he rearranged his face to accommodate the smile that would be his trump card. Lizzie, her mind set firmly on the younger man's bar, had barely noticed her host in the doorway but now she met his eye and indicated a chair with an unspoken 'May I?'

Piper stepped out of the shadows and moved quickly to attend to his guest. He could not suppress a quick glance to his right to ensure that his rival had witnessed the decision but caught only a glimpse of Dario as he went back into the depths of his own bar. There was, however, a sizeable audience at the outside tables and many observers, even those with decoration on their epaulettes, were now eyeing his two spare tables. Had one made the leap, many more might have scrambled after him, but no one was prepared to risk undoing hundreds of years of tradition in one hastily calculated moment. So, with the subtlest of shifts, they readjusted their angles to enjoy the view.

Piper was now at Lizzie's side, a tea-towel folded neatly over his arm, paper and pencil clutched at the ready. 'Good afternoon. It is a beautiful afternoon, is it not? And what might I fetch you today?'

'Tea and honey would be perfect, thank you. And perhaps a glass of water?'

'Certainly. I shall be right with you.'

The simple exchange rang in Piper's head as he bustled back into his bar. It had shone with authenticity and he was delighted with its flawless execution. He had practised the greeting so many times, then worried that either the words might sound insincere or, worse, he would fluff them altogether. He had awoken that morning with sweat pouring off his forehead and the sound of Dario's laughter ringing in his ears.

He returned to Lizzie and set about straining her tea with an efficient flourish. Then, before setting the cup finally in front of her he whipped out from under the knotted tie of his apron a paper doily, which he flicked into the air, with a superfluous snap of his wrist, then laid in front of her. He placed upon it her cup and saucer and a second saucer bearing teaspoon and honey pot, lid askance.

If he was concerned that his masterful effort had gone unnoticed, he needn't have worried. While Lizzie was pleasantly surprised by the light colour of her tea and the attentiveness of her waiter, the real object of Piper's efforts was also watching every movement. Dario turned to his bar and contemplated the large box of shining peanut packets in front of him. Shaking, he lifted it down behind the bar and pulled a couple of bottles of pickles in front of it, then returned to his position at the doorway. While his faithful customers heckled him for more drinks and jostled each other at the bar, he continued his vigil with narrowed eyes. 'A paper doily!' he replied, to a baffled Professore Giuseppe Scota, who had politely asked for a beer. 'Now I've seen everything!'

Piper, his confidence building by the second, found time to joke with his other customers while nimbly stepping between the suddenly crowded tables to attend once more to the young lady. 'Is your tea to your liking, Miss?'

'Delicious. I'm really getting a taste for it. I found it a little bitter when I first arrived, but it's incredibly refreshing.'

'And might I fetch you something to accompany your tea? Some peanuts or potato crisps, perhaps?'

She wrinkled her nose, remembering the aftertaste of yesterday's stale peanuts, and opted for the crisps.

Soon, Piper was back at her table brandishing a china bowl, hastily borrowed from his kitchen that morning, piled dangerously high with crisps. He placed it in front of her and backed away – a customer had a right to some personal space while paying for the pleasure of drinking and eating.

As Lizzie's gaze drifted around her, the other patrons nodded and smiled – one or two even tipped their hats. She had been brought up to be a confident, self-assured woman and the solid application of good manners in her upbringing had taught her to make people feel comfortable in her presence. That, though, was being undermined by the constant scrutiny she was under. While she was fairly sure that her own fraud had created the gulf that now prevented her chatting amiably, as she might otherwise have done, she felt that something else, something other than her elevated position, was keeping them from reaching out to her with the warmth she had no doubt they harboured behind their nervous smiles.

An uncharacteristic self-consciousness had invaded and she focused intently on the clock repairs while she sipped her tea.

'Are you interested?' asked a man at the table nearest to hers, but he spoke so quietly that she wasn't sure he had addressed her.

'I beg your pardon?' She leaned a little towards him.

'In clocks. Are you interested?'

'Well, I really don't know anything about them, but it's a beautiful thing, isn't it? It's a shame that it doesn't seem to work, but perhaps they're fixing it.'

Her neighbour nudged his chair very slightly in her direction and tipped his body forwards so that he could talk to her without raising his voice. He was rendered a little self-conscious by his brazen intrusion but confident on his subject. 'They are. At least they're trying to. The men in uniform are in charge, and they're using some of the palace workmen to do the job. Give them another half an hour and they'll come over here to ask if there's a clockmaker around. The answer will be no. They'll fiddle around a bit more, then probably take the scaffolding down. They do this in the run-up to every election. The president issues a demand that the clock be fixed. They scamper around like headless chickens. The clock doesn't get fixed. End of story.'

Lizzie turned to examine the speaker more carefully. He was young and attractive. Too young and attractive, in fact, for the weight of irritation and bitterness that she had detected in his voice. 'Well, that's a great shame. It seems such a waste that it doesn't work. Will it ever be fixed, do you think?'

'Not if I have anything to do with it.'

Lizzie picked up her cup, put it on his table and shuffled her chair across so that she could continue the conversation without having to strain to hear him.

The two other men at the table were clearly embarrassed by the exchange and examined their fingernails with an intensity that, though a little grubby, they probably didn't deserve.

'Let me introduce myself. I'm Miss Lizzie Holmesworth. I'm here on ... on official business. But for the next few weeks I'm just taking in some of your beautiful scenery – seeing the sights, meeting the locals. And you are?'

'I'm Pavel. And this is Elio, the potter, and his apprentice, Armando. Pleased to meet you.' Elio and Armando smiled, then continued to study their fingernails.

'So come on. Spill the beans. You said that the clock wouldn't get fixed if you had anything to do with it. What's it done to upset you?'

Pavel looked up at the tower. From where they were sitting it was impossible to see the clock face, but they could easily see the complex mechanism and the profile of the small door through which four effigies should emerge to announce the hour. Right now, a workman was crouched down and peering through the doorway. 'And again?' His words rang out but the clock remained stubbornly silent.

Pavel took a swig of beer and spoke into the space in front of him. 'My great-grandfather built that clock. Not alone, of course, he had quite a big team under him. My grandfather looked after it all his life and the other city clocks too. But by the time my father inherited the business, the team had dwindled to just himself. He was up and down ladders each and every day, working really hard to keep everything ticking, just right. He was a real perfectionist, more so perhaps than his father or grandfather. If all the clocks in the city didn't chime exactly together, it drove him wild.' Pavel smiled at the memory. 'They cancelled his contract. I don't know why. He'd been in and out of Parliament Hall every day of his life but they didn't even tell him in person. He got a letter from the minister of finance saying they were reviewing all the service contracts granted by the government and his position was now duplicated by the workmen responsible for other palace maintenance. Clocks were the same as boilers, apparently, so the plumbers got the work.'

'That's terrible – after such a long history of being involved with the clock and everything. How sad.' Lizzie was genuinely shocked by this callous treatment and raised a hand to her chest, leaving her fingertips resting lightly on her heart.

Pavel nodded. 'It gets sadder. It killed him.'

Elio interjected: 'They might be tyrants but I think it would be hard to pin your father's death on the government. He lived for, what, another twenty-five years? And there never was a happier man in all of Vallerosa.'

'He dropped dead twenty-five years *to the day* after receiving that letter. Do you not think the ignominy played on his mind throughout his adult life? He was devastated, a shadow of his former self after his humiliating sacking. They might as well have put a gun to his head. Regardless of all of that, he was getting on in years but he had an apprentice, and that apprentice should have carried on with the contracts – that's the way it should have happened.'

As if on cue, the workmen began to climb down the ladders. The military man clearly in charge of the operation approached the bar with a confidence that ensured many of the drinkers sank lower in their chairs and pulled their caps further over their eyes.

'I'm looking for a clockmaker. Is there a clockmaker around here? You!' He indicated Elio. 'You know everyone around here. Where can I find a clockmaker?'

Elio shrugged and took a slow, insolent drink of his beer. Armando, beside him, stood up slowly, put his cap on his head and left the bar while the official stood and watched. The military man swung back, his eyes trained on the potter, whom he watched through narrowed eyes as the young man smacked his lips and had another swig. Impatient, the official wandered on, scanning the occupants of remaining tables, then going off to enquire of the shopkeepers.

Lizzie wasn't sure why the exchange had discomfited her. When she had made her pact with the president she had feared she might, inadvertently and irrevocably, have aligned herself with his government. She wondered now whether she would be able to distance herself sufficiently from the regime to befriend some of these men, the people who, by dint of age alone, she was probably more naturally akin to.

She leaned towards Pavel, removing her sunglasses to look at him properly. 'I'm really sorry to hear your story. You must miss your father terribly. What happened to the apprentice? Did he stop making clocks?'

'No. Some say he's better than the clockmaker before him. I doubt there's a watch in the whole of Vallerosa that he hasn't repaired.'

'Others say,' said Elio, 'that without him, the country simply wouldn't keep running!' He and Pavel laughed together, revealing twin sets of startlingly white teeth.

'I hear,' said Pavel, in a conspiratorial tone, 'that he is extremely good with his hands. And it isn't just the country's clocks that get the benefit of his fine tuning.'

'That's not quite what I've heard!' said Elio, looking earnestly at Lizzie but unable to disguise the humour in his eyes. 'I've been told that his own mechanism runs a little fast.'

Lizzie looked from one to the other and joined in with their laughter. She met Pavel in the eye. '*You*'re the clockmaker, aren't you?' She paused. 'But I don't understand. They need you – why don't you just help them? Wouldn't it be so much better just to fix the clock?'

Pavel grew serious. He didn't answer while he meticulously rolled two cigarettes and chucked one across the table to Elio. Elio immediately lit his, while Pavel tucked his own behind his ear. He breathed out his response. 'They insulted my father and our profession. I'll fix their clocks for them when they make appropriate amends. But not a moment before.'

The mood was serious but Lizzie, anxious to return to the lightness they'd been sharing before, broke the ice by unclasping the cheap Timex she always wore when travelling and handing it to Pavel. 'It's running a little slow. I'm not absolutely sure it's worth mending but …'

Pavel ran a thumb over its face and weighed the watch gently in his hand. 'Of course it's worth fixing. It's a perfectly good watch and will carry on working long after your internal clock has packed it in for good. There is no reason at all that a good, solid timepiece like this shouldn't work for ever, provided it's looked after. Bring it to my shop any morning. I'll be happy to sort it out while you wait.'

'So why …' Lizzie didn't want to drag the mood down again, but she needed to understand the feud '… why doesn't one of the ministers simply come and find you at your shop? It makes no sense.'

'Because then they'd be admitting that they were wrong to fire my father. Stupid pride, I guess. They know I'm the clockmaker, they just don't want to ask me directly. They're hoping that if they pull this stunt enough times then one of these days I'll jump up and offer to fix their clock for them. But they'll be waiting a long time.'

As the mood darkened again, Pavel brightened at the sight of two young women emerging from the alley between the two bars. He tried to beckon them towards him, but they glanced quickly around the tables as if looking for someone else and disappeared back into the shadows. Lizzie watched his face crumple. 'Friends of yours?' she asked kindly.

'My cousin, Maria, and her friend Claudia,' he said, with a noncommittal shrug.

'Claudia was here?' Elio, looking quickly around him, was more animated than he had been all afternoon.

'She was, but she left immediately.'

'Oh, that hurts, Pavel! After you danced all night together!'

'Perhaps she's shy?' suggested Lizzie, recognizing Pavel's crestfallen expression and wanting to ease his disappointment.

'She's not shy. She is incredibly well connected – or, at least, her father is. She's used to mixing in governmental circles so I doubt very much she'd be shy around you or me. But Maria's in charge now. Claudia might not know it but she's appointed the toughest chaperone in the whole of Vallerosa.'

'And your cousin might not want you to see more of Claudia?'

Both men laughed at the easy mistake. 'No, no,' protested Elio, quickly. 'Cousin Maria will want Pavel seeing much, much more of Claudia. But it's out of his hands now. There is a way that these things have to happen and Maria won't want to leave the romance between her best friend and her favourite cousin to things like mutual attraction. Heavens, no!'

Pavel laughed, acknowledging the truth in this and that, of course, things must now evolve at a pace he couldn't possibly dictate.

Lizzie called for another round of drinks and the three sat in easy companionship. She did her best to stick to neutral topics of conversation and avoided any mention of the clock or the government contracts. There was a history here that she daren't unravel, but as the afternoon sun paled in the sky, and the swifts emerged to dip and dance in the cool evening air, their banter skipped comfortably from one subject to another, so mindlessly enjoyable, that she didn't press the point.

CHAPTER 18

In Which Lizzie Makes a Bedside Visit

THE FOLLOWING MORNING, Lizzie had scheduled a visit to the hospital with Dottore Rossini. She rose, bathed and wandered out to the square but was unable to find something that resembled breakfast. Eventually she went to Dario's bar, the decision made for her by the closed shutters on Piper's door. Dario was busily sweeping around the chairs and tables and, despite the lack of obvious competition, ignored her approach, trying instead to look nonchalant. He was holding his breath, nonetheless, and only exhaled as she stepped up and motioned towards a chair.

'Do you mind? Is it too early? It's just that I'm rather hungry and can't seem to find anywhere for breakfast. Do you serve breakfast? I don't need much – a bit of bread and jam would be fine. Or a pastry …' The idea of a pastry lingered in the air between them while Dario recomposed his face. He beamed his response.

'Bread and jam? Of course! It is breakfast time. What else would you do for breakfast than come to my bar to eat bread and jam and to drink tea? Yes, yes, bread and jam. Certainly. And tomorrow, if you're here at the same time, there will most certainly be pastries!' He announced the last promise with a flourish of his arm that conjured high stacks of pastries and sweet breads studded with nuts and dripping with honey. That was not his to promise yet, but he had managed, in one deft movement, to buy himself twenty-four hours to deliver pastries and he had arranged for her to return to his bar at the same time tomorrow. For the moment, however, he had to busy himself with his first ever breakfast guest. He dashed up to his quarters, rummaged around in his fridge, cut a small piece of butter, wiped a knife on his apron, balanced several jams of dubious content on a tray and delivered it to Lizzie's table. He then rushed up the alley in the direction of the bakery.

'Lanfranco! Lanfranco! I need bread for breakfast!' Dario yelled breathlessly, as he barged past the empty counter into the warmth of the kitchens beyond.

Lanfranco, the dough-faced baker, was rinsing his hands under a tap and shrugged, barely turning to acknowledge the intruder. 'Well, it's late! It's almost eight o'clock and I don't keep my doors open all day, you know.'

'But it's urgent! I need the finest bread quickly.' He scanned the empty wooden trays and feasted his eyes on two remaining ciabatta. He reached over and grabbed them both, smelling each in turn, then discarding the poorer example. 'I will come back later today and we must make an arrangement, an *exclusive* arrangement, about bread,' he whispered.

Lanfranco sighed heavily, his big sad eyes suggesting that this was perhaps the worst news he had heard for a very long time. 'Bread, yes, I suppose that is what I do, so that is certainly what I must arrange for you. I will look forward to hearing the details of your proposal later on.' He sighed again.

'And pastries,' Dario added, whispering directly into Lanfranco's ear.

Lanfranco froze. His shoulders stiffened and, though the tap continued to run, he stopped rubbing his hands under the water but chose instead to stare into the middle distance. That word had not been spoken in his bakery for many a year. 'Pastries, you say? You want pastries?' Immediately his thoughts turned to the sweet treats that so often invaded his dreams at night. Recipes danced in front of his eyes, interspersed with snippets of received wisdom that concerned the plumping of raisins, the crisping and layering of the finest filo, the melting of butter, the glazes of syrup and honey. Fearful that the words he had heard just a moment ago were the delusion of a sad old baker, he turned slowly to greet the man who had delivered the mouthwatering mirage. But Dario was already hurtling back to his bar to slice the loaf and arrange it in a basket. This he presented to Lizzie with another flourish.

'Bread, Madame, to go with your butter and jam. And you tell me what else your heart desires each day for breakfast and your wish shall be my command.' He retired to the bar to prepare the tea while Lizzie experimented with one jam after another, smiling to herself at Dario's exuberance. None of the jams looked wonderful – one was even covered with a thin layer of mould, but she was able to peel this away with the waxed paper disc that was there to protect the jam beneath. And, to her delight, each was uniquely delicious, tasting of the warmest summers, the freshest autumn breezes and the promises that the passing of winter could hold. Spreading them liberally in turn, she ploughed her way through the bread basket and had finished most of the loaf by the time Dottore Rossini had arrived to escort her on her tour.

Better still, Dario was able to remove all trace of Lizzie's visit before Piper had even unlocked his doors for the day. 'What a triumph!' he marvelled, as he washed the dishes. 'This morning I have cornered the breakfast market in Vallerosa and by tomorrow I will have created such a vast chasm of difference between myself and my closest rival that no amount of pastry will ever allow him to catch up! He might well be using paper doilies, but who is it that has the pastry market wrapped up? Oh, yes, oh, yes! That will wipe the lime-stinking smile off your face!' With that, he went to visit the baker, who had remained motionless in front of the sink, now eyeing the empty wooden trays stacked up against the wall and imagining them brimming with sweet morsels.

Dario surprised them both by spinning the baker around to face him and planting a big fat kiss on Lanfranco's lips.

MEANWHILE, Lizzie and Dottore Rossini were beginning their tour by climbing slowly up to the north-west quadrant, arriving eventually at the big square building that provided all the medical care for the entire population of Vallerosa. The hospital was housed in a beautiful solid building, built of the ubiquitous red stone. The shutters were painted an unusual shade of green, which matched perfectly the corrosion of the copper gutters and the moss-strewn roof tiles. Inside, it was light and airy, with windows thrown open to welcome a breeze that swept through from north to south, casting out the germ-strewn air and replacing it with a cleaner, fresher variety.

Lizzie and the doctor washed their hands before beginning the tour. They set off at a leisurely amble, heading up the grand marble staircase to visit the wards. As they ascended their footsteps rang out, echoing into the hall beneath them. The doctor spoke softly to Lizzie and she had to strain to hear him.

'I have studied all my life for this job. Elementary, primary, secondary and tertiary education, followed by a degree, a post-graduate degree, a PhD and two specialist degrees to qualify for surgery and for cancer care. My father before me had this job. He was a respected physician until his retirement twenty years ago. At that point, I stopped my education and stepped into his shoes. Physically.' He gestured towards his shoes. 'These were my father's. Ironic, I know.' He smiled. 'The doctor's education is extremely important – the textbooks, the demonstrations, the expansion of understanding of medical terms and treatments. I can honestly say, with my hand on my heart, that I am the most accomplished and experienced doctor in the land!' Lizzie looked for a trace of a smile, but there was none.

He opened the double doors to the first ward where women, young and old, recovered from their ailments. Even to her untrained eyes, Lizzie could tell that the women suffered in varying degrees, from a minor injury borne stoically by a chirpy young mother to the stillness of a dying woman in the far corner. Her sickness was grave, and she had reached the point where she could only swivel her eyes in greeting; moving the rest of her body was just too painful. At either side of her bed sat other women, her family. One was holding her hand while another was fussing around, tidying, sorting and bustling as people bustle when they're comfortable in their own homes.

'How are we?' Dottore Rossini asked, in a gentle tone.

'We're good, aren't we, Mother?' said the woman holding the dying woman's hand. 'We're doing what you told us to do, just being quiet now.'

The doctor squeezed her shoulder while smiling warmly at his patient. 'Yes, my dear. Slowing down for a bit of peace and quiet is just the right thing at this stage. You're doing a wonderful job.' And he left them to it.

At another bedside a woman was dishing out what looked like stew onto a plate. She sprinkled some chopped herbs on top, then gave it a quick stir.

'Mmm,' said Dottore Rossini, appreciatively. 'It smells delicious. That will put the colour back in your cheeks!'

The patient's eyes sparkled as the tray was set up in front of her.

'We don't have any catering facilities in the hospital,' the doctor explained. 'Our patients are served the food that their families are eating at home. They'll take it in turns to come and eat with their relative at mealtimes. That way, the patients get what they like, with the people they like most. The quickest way to recovery, of that I'm certain.'

'Well, that makes sense. But is it hygienic, bringing food into a hospital?' Lizzie wondered. How odd it was for the smell of boar stew to be stronger than that of disinfectant.

'Well, who is most likely to be careful about ensuring your food is free of germs? Your loved ones, or a caterer you're never likely to meet in a kitchen that you're never likely to inspect? Think of it this way. Each meal is prepared to the exact specifications of the patient and served at a time to suit them. Can any of your big London hospitals boast that?'

'No, I suppose not. Not when you put it like that.'

They went into the men's ward. Here, Lizzie's arrival had greater impact than it had had on the female ward. A group of men were gathered around one bed and their game of dominoes was immediately halted by her entrance. To a man they stopped play and examined every inch of their visitor with their eyes.

The doctor laughed. 'Look at you, Paolo, I do believe some colour is returning to your cheeks. Would that be the effect of the dominoes ... or something else?'

The patient coloured further. 'I feel fine, thank you, much, much better.' He nodded at Lizzie. 'I'm sorry if we were rude. We don't get many women, or, rather, we don't get many women like you, around here.'

Lizzie dismissed his apology with a wave of her hand. 'Well, if you tire of dominoes, I'd be happy to come and read to you, if you thought that might aid your recovery.'

A visitor at the sick man's bedside spluttered, and the others joined in with a big display of nudging and winking. The patient, however, remained focused on Lizzie. He coughed weakly into his hand. 'Well, thinking about it, that might indeed make me more comfortable.' He bit his lip, shocked by his own audacity, while his friends stifled their laughter.

One turned to the doctor: 'Come to think of it, I'm not feeling so well myself. There's a couple of spare beds over there – perhaps I could have a little lie-down and partake of some of your special treatments, Doctor?'

'You're a fool,' the doctor admonished him. 'But, nevertheless, you're very good to your brother. If Miss Holmesworth wishes to come and read to him, I think that would be an excellent idea, but I shall make very sure none of you is here to share in his good fortune.'

He moved on to the next bed where a man lay dozing, his wife knitting beside him and two children playing quietly at her feet.

'Oh, Doctor, I can't thank you enough. He's made a remarkable recovery. We've had him up and walking around today – worn him out as you can see. We'll have him home in no time at all.' She smiled shyly at the doctor, clearly awed by him.

The doctor and Lizzie continued their rounds, encountering similar scenes of familial comfort as they made their way around the hospital. 'In the same way that the best food to prescribe is home-cooked, I believe that the best nursing care is given by those who care most for you. Families, this is what they are for. To care for each other.'

The two continued their walk, the doctor proud of the hospital and Lizzie quietly thoughtful. They walked downstairs together, passing busy nurses on the way. 'So, if the nursing is being done by the families, what are the nurses tasked with?'

'Strictly speaking, the nursing isn't done by the families, the caring is. That is not to say our nurses aren't caring, don't misunderstand me. Our nurses are trained here, at the hospital, to a very high standard. They administer medication, assist with operations and work alongside the junior doctors. What they are not here to do is to clean, to feed, to wipe up after the patients. Families do that better. And it's a fair exchange. If you are sick, your family looks after you. If they are sick, you look after them. To bathe a sick person in a bed, surely that is the role of a mother or daughter, son or father. The families bring their own bed linen in because patients, particularly really sick patients, respond better to having familiar things around them. When the linen needs changing, it goes home to be washed.' The doctor paused for a moment. 'And there is another important benefit, too. When somebody becomes sick within a family, the whole family suffers. They are all contaminated with that same sickness, a sickness of the heart through empathy. Keeping busy is vital in everyone's recovery. If you know your mother is dying here, do you want to suffer at home while she lies lonely among strangers? Absolutely not. What a ridiculous notion! Your role is to be busy caring, cooking, wiping up after her, holding her hand. And through your busyness you will feel stronger and more useful, so more able to care for her. You follow me?'

Lizzie nodded slowly, her head lowered. She thought of her own grandmother's slow demise back in a London nursing home. She had been put there because it was the best place, everyone had agreed. But now she was wondering who had made that decision. Her mother had rationalized it before the transition had taken place: 'I'm just too busy to give her the care she needs,' she had said, signing the paperwork and grimacing at the vast sums she must commit to that care. But what had her mother been busy doing? Lizzie couldn't remember. Good works, she supposed. Her committees, her charities, and she was a school governor, depended upon by so many people, strangers all.

The doctor was striding down a long, cool corridor. He pointed through round glass windows at the three operating theatres. Two lay idle, bathed under a cool blue light, with the glint of stainless steel winking at the onlookers. The third was being washed down by a young doctor and nurse who were slowly wiping instruments and laughing together as they worked. Rossini and Lizzie watched them, enchanted by the intimacy of the moment.

'We have incredible care here. Our junior doctors are very well qualified, and among them we have specialists to cover the broad spectrum of medical requirements. We have an oncologist, cardiologist, two paediatricians, two geriatricians, our own orthopaedist ... There is little room for them to be promoted, however, as the structure here doesn't allow it. For one of them to reach a more senior role, I or one of my fellow doctors must retire, and none of us is ready to hand over yet. I fear for them sometimes, wondering if a better opportunity lies elsewhere, outside our borders, but so far I can ease their frustration by offering them further educational opportunities. We have a generous allowance here for students. Our government is very proud of it – and the beauty of medicine is that it is never fully understood. There is always so much more to learn.

'I learned a great deal from my tutors and from watching my father work. I stood by his side as he removed a cyst the size of a football from a young woman who thought she was carrying a child. I held his tools for him as he cut away cancers, sewed up boar wounds and mended broken bones.' He shook his head. 'I studied for twenty-four years in total. But so much of what I learned, as perhaps you can tell when you walk around my hospital with me, I learned from my mother.'

Together they walked outside into the bright afternoon sunlight. Lizzie shielded her eyes, temporarily blinded by the glare after the cool, dim hospital interior. 'I understand a little better why my offer of charitable work was laughed at now, but I'm happy to help. Even if they don't need me to read to them or to cook or to clean, or to do any of the few things I thought I might be able to help with.'

Rossini laughed. 'Do you honestly think I would turn down your offer of help? I'd be lynched if word got out that I had. My only concern is that others will hear of your hospital visits and we will have a run of some mysterious, hard-to-diagnose illness on our hands. But come back, please. Reading sounds like a good prescription, and I can think of a number of patients who might benefit. Late evening would be good – that is always the hardest time, when families remember they have homes to go back to. Saying goodbye each night is always difficult.'

Together they wound their way back down the hill, picking their route through the darkest, coolest alleys and keeping to the shadows when forced to cross the wide-open spaces. Lizzie was surprised by the amount of time she had spent at the hospital and, as it neared lunchtime, might have been tempted to find something to eat at one of the two bars. But even the thought of choosing between them made her anxious so instead she shook the hand of Decio Rossini just before they entered the Piazza Rosa and made her way back to her own quiet room in the palace.

CHAPTER 19

In Which the Curiosities Are Examined

TUESDAY MORNING DAWNED, and no sooner had the sun hauled itself over the eastern hills to light the valley below than the mercury began to rise and bubble in thermometers across the country and the citizens prepared themselves for a mercilessly hot day. Shutters remained resolutely shut, and even Sergio, working in his rooms above the piazza, drew his curtains across the windows to try to keep the interior temperature down by a few essential degrees.

Below, Lizzie awaited her tour guide. Standing by the palace railings and shading her eyes with one hand while scanning the piazza for a familiar face, she made circles with her shoulders, loving the feel of the sun on her face and enjoying, after a fabulous night's sleep, being a tourist on holiday.

She was dressed appropriately for the weather: cool linen trousers, open-toed sandals, a long, coral linen shirt and, tucked into the top of her handbag, a wide-brimmed cotton sun hat. She had packed the outfit as a last-minute addition, just in case she needed to look smart, and now she was hugely glad of it, given her recent promotion from lowly student to royal dignitary.

Keeping well into the shadows of the western façade, Mosconi made his way to meet her. Lizzie smiled inwardly. How could she have thought she might not recognize him? He was walking towards her in full military uniform, carrying the bright pink brolly that was the emblem of tour guides around the world. He raised it to her in acknowledgement, and she skipped towards him, thrilled by the pomposity of the uniform and the seriousness with which senior Vallerosans applied themselves.

She fell into step with him as they headed off towards the museum. 'I'm afraid it's a bit of a walk,' he said, 'and the day is one of the hottest of the year so far. Will you manage?'

'Oh, yes. I'm certainly up for a bit of exercise and, to tell you the truth, I absolutely love the sunshine. We don't get enough of it at home, and you know how it is – we always want what we can't have.'

Mosconi blushed sheepishly, as if she had read his thoughts.

They wandered over to the far corner of Piazza Rosa, to the left of Parliament Hall, and ducked into a dark, cool alley.

'We'll walk along here, if you don't mind. There's a prettier route by following the river Florin, but it would be too hot this morning and I don't want to wear you out before we even get to the business at hand.'

Lizzie was pleased to be in the cool of the immaculate passageway. On their left were the tall, solid walls that formed the back of the main buildings that surrounded the piazza. The few windows tended to be higher up and barred with sometimes quite elaborate metalwork. An occasional open door atop a short flight of steps suggested a hint of life beyond, but peeps inside were rare. The detail to the right was marginally more interesting as the alley was lined with the first of several rows of houses that led gently down to the riverbank. These dwellings, enjoying a prestigious position close to the piazza, were a little grander than some of the houses Lizzie had passed on her initial journey down to Parliament Hall and she examined them closely for clues of domestic life as she wandered by. Although they would never suffer from sun exposure, most were still shuttered, as if the whole city had decided to take cover for the morning.

'These, on the whole, are homes of ministers and senior ministers. Some have been in the same families for many generations.'

'Which implies,' said Lizzie, somewhat cautiously, 'that the senior government posts have been in the same families for many generations?'

'But of course.'

They turned a corner and descended a flight of steps.

'And is that a problem?' enquired Lizzie, politely.

'How do you mean, a problem?' countered Mosconi, unaware of the political slant of the question.

'Well, that the big jobs go to the sons of the most senior politicians.'

Mosconi seemed to grope for words. Perhaps he himself was the son of the previous minister for tourism and had assumed that his own son would probably one day fill his shoes. He paused and put a tentative hand on Lizzie's arm.

She stopped, too, with one foot already on the step below. The unscheduled freeze-frame allowed them to face each other eye to eye.

'I think you misunderstand, Miss Holmesworth. The "big jobs" do not automatically pass to the sons of senior politicians. They go to those most *qualified* to take them on. A combination of education, history and genetics will quite often conspire to make the son of a senior politician, a young man who has probably been steeped in politics since the cradle, most qualified for the job. It's a case of linear evolution, Miss Holmesworth, not a conspiracy.'

Lizzie was satisfied with his answer although, in reality, she neither understood nor cared enough to challenge him further.

They continued down the steps, passing on their right three more alleys that stretched off into the distance. The houses seemed, from an initial glance, to get smaller until they reached the very bottom row where they sprang up again in height, just a few feet from the grey-blue water that rushed past them.

'Golly, it's loud!' Lizzie said, clutching her ears to demonstrate that she couldn't hear Mosconi now they were so close to the raging river. 'Does it ever flood?'

'Several times a year. Always when the ice melts upstream, and occasionally exceptional conditions lead to flooding at other times. But the city was built to withstand the seasonal fluctuations of the river so we've never had any problems.' As they walked across the bridge, Lizzie stopped to look at the beautiful red houses that lined the riverbank. On first glance, she wondered if they were flats. They appeared to be double-storey houses, with doors at the ground and upper levels, with wrought iron or stone steps climbing to each of the upper doors. On closer examination, however, it was apparent that the ground floor was home to nobody: an empty shell designed to absorb the river's swelling waters. Domestic activity began on the first floors, with their cheery balconies and pots of tumbling geraniums. Even the laundry hung at the higher levels.

They began to cross the bridge and now, exposed to the strong sun, Lizzie reached into her bag for a bottle of water. 'Is it much further? I might have to put on some sun block,' she said, feeling the back of her neck.

'The same again. We're exactly halfway, but don't worry, we'll walk in the residential area as we head south again. You'll be out of the sun just as soon as we're over the bridge.' Lizzie looked downstream to the point Mosconi had roughly indicated with a flick of his hand. She looked back to where she had begun her journey and calculated that, unless she was very much mistaken, the museum was on exactly the same line as Parliament Hall and, unless she was very much mistaken again, there was another bridge – an even bigger, grander bridge – over which they could have walked thus avoiding the long trudge they had taken through the town and which they were now about to repeat as they wound their way back down the far side of the river.

Clearly, Mosconi was taking his role as tour guide seriously and wanted her to see as much of the town as possible. She hurried towards the welcoming darkness that beckoned her in the form of another alley on the east bank.

Their journey south was similar. Having climbed a flight of steps, they wove their way along a passage with Lizzie peering into the occasional open door or through unfettered windows. What struck her, not for the first time, were the immaculate floors with neither litter nor animal waste to step around. And she could not have judged the social status of the inhabitants from the quality of the houses they had passed, the shine of the door furniture: each one, regardless of size, was pristine. The air smelt sweet, despite the enclosed nature of the alleys, and the walk was pleasant.

After fifteen minutes of ducking in and out of seemingly endless paths, only distinguishable, perhaps, by the height of the buildings and the width of the doors, they emerged into a piazza, a miniature rendition of Piazza Rosa.

'Piazza Verde!' announced Mosconi, allowing Lizzie to stand and admire the architecture. The name could only have been taken from the dull green of the copper used for drainpipes and gutters on the surrounding buildings and perhaps from the large mossy statue that occupied the centre of the square. It was hard to tell whose memory was being honoured beneath the sprawling greenery, but it made a striking image and Lizzie whipped out her camera. She took a few quick shots, then, having confirmed that there was nobody to act as official photographer, beckoned to Mosconi to stand close to her and snapped them at the foot of the statue. As they continued their path across the piazza, she checked the quality of the images to make sure the strong sunlight hadn't silhouetted her subjects. On the contrary, the camera had made the appropriate adjustments and the images were sharp and bright. There she was, smiling, her hand on Mosconi's shoulder, pulling him in towards her. From the unintended juxtaposition of his eyebrows to her cleavage, he seemed to be considering taking refuge in her loosely fitting shirt.

Lizzie reminded herself that she ought to be a little more restrained physically. Grabbing her guide like that would be inappropriate even for a tourist, but for royalty? Allowing a guide such a close-up view of her underwear would surely be frowned upon.

'We're here,' said Mosconi, at the foot of a flight of wide steps that led to imposing double doors. He climbed them, Lizzie following. At the top, he crouched at the museum's door, ear to the wood, then knocked sharply.

Nobody answered.

After rapping loudly again a couple of times, Mosconi muttered, 'Typical,' and unclipped the huge bunch of keys secured to his belt buckle.

He inserted a key and turned it, then a second and a third, and finally pushed the door inwards. Inside, after the strong light of the piazza, Lizzie could make out nothing but a series of oppressively large display cases that ran around the perimeter of the cavernous room and a series of glass-topped display tables that ran down the central gangway.

At the far end a green-glassed lamp stood on a desk, throwing artificially yellow light onto some papers. In the otherwise orderly layout, it looked as if it had only recently been abandoned.

'Typical, typical,' repeated Mosconi, as he grabbed a long-handled pole with a brass hook and manipulated it to push up the wooden slatted blinds that hung heavily at each high window. Gradually, with each shove upwards, light began to flood into the room and Lizzie moved forward to examine the first of the display cases.

It stood some twenty feet tall, a glass-fronted cabinet that housed bottles – as many as forty or fifty on each shelf, each one beautifully labelled in a neat print. The bottles were not, as one might have expected, early hand-blown glass, or even the crude ceramics that might depict the passing of centuries. Instead, they featured the bold, bright graphics typified by modern consumerism. There, tucked towards the back of the third shelf up, was a large white bleach bottle, with the dazzling typeface that signified zinging cleanliness. Higher, near to the top third of shelves, a bulky bottle with a handle had once contained liquid floor polish.

On the whole the graphics were indecipherable to Lizzie, but each bottle or canister, glass or plastic, shouted its contents and its origin. Below, the labels spelled it out. Apple cider from Bosnia. Liquid paraffin from Greece. Fresh milk from Croatia. Olive oil from Turkey.

Lizzie moved on to the next cabinet, which offered a quite different display. The bottom shelf housed a selection of umbrellas. The next shelf up held magazines and books, the one above an attractively arranged selection of spectacles – strikingly, a glass eyeball took pride of place in the centre. As the shelves continued upwards, Lizzie tried to find a common theme or logic behind the displays. Eventually, unable to contain her curiosity any longer, she turned to Mosconi, who was admiring not the contents of the room but the shape of Lizzie's legs. A shaft of sunlight was travelling straight through the fabric of her trousers, leaving little to the imagination.

'Excuse me, you spoke, Miss Holmesworth?'

'I've never really seen a museum like this before. What is it, exactly?'

'Thank you. We like to think of it as unique. It is called the Museum of Things Left Behind. You'd be amazed at what careless people abandon, like so much unwanted baggage. Come here! Look at this!' He beckoned her towards the table on which he was leaning and swung round to show her its curiosities. There, pinned with tiny nails at each corner, were banknotes of all denominations and currencies, each one captured, preserved and displayed with the same love and attention that a butterfly collector might apply to his rarest species. 'And this, look,' he moved on to show her, with obvious pride, coins, beautifully arranged in size and colour, including a pre-2001 British 50p piece.

'This symbolizes to me so many different things. The beauty and diversity of the man-made world, of course …' with an elaborate wave of the hand '… but something darker, deeper too.' With a sad shake of the head, he continued, 'The wastage and blatant disregard for the world's riches deserve to be recorded for posterity, don't you agree? Look at all these coins, abandoned down the backs of chairs, dropped out of overflowing pockets – priceless!'

He walked her slowly past each display case, pointing out his personal favourites and chuckling from time to time as he recounted the story of its origin. 'A prosthetic limb! It was left on the train by a man apparently in too much of a hurry to remember his own leg! A Vallerosan picked it up, with what intention I don't know as we had no idea how to return it to its rightful owner. It made its way here, and here it will rest. Who knows? One day its owner may return to these parts, and what a delighted reunion we will have constructed!'

He moved on.

'So people can collect their items – I mean, they can have them back should they find them here?'

'Well, of course. None of these goods has been *impounded*. We should like very much to reunite people with their possessions. It would complete a cycle very poetically, don't you think?'

'Like – like a lost-property office?' faltered Lizzie.

'I suppose so. I hadn't really thought of it like that. But "lost" sounds so final. I like to think of these items as more found than lost. It gives them back their purpose.' Mosconi hurried on to the next display, anxious not to dwell too deeply on the great philosophical divide that underpinned the purpose of his country's most ambitious attraction. 'And this I love. An unopened packet of biscuits, left in the hostel. Well, there was somebody with money to burn.' Judging by the neat printed label, 'Biscuits 1998', they were long past their sell-by date.

As they passed shelf after shelf of abandoned hair-brushes and lipsticks, scarves and mittens, rulers, pens, pencils and compasses, Lizzie found enough words of encouragement and surprise to satisfy her host. Gradually, they edged back towards the initial cabinet, the one housing the bottles.

'Ah, now, this is something quite different altogether. None of these bottles was lost, as such. They were almost all empty when discarded, so more thrown out than lost. But can you guess, Miss Holmesworth, at the common bond that ties each and every one of these four hundred and thirty-eight bottles?'

Lizzie examined the display again and shook her head, sad to disappoint the expectant face but anxious not to blunder into a tactless answer.

'Each and every bottle has been delivered to us by our own stretch of the river Florin! While, strictly speaking, the river belongs to Nature, it is in our care and under our jurisdiction for nearly eight kilometres! And on its shores it spills out, from time to time, its treasures. I like these particularly because they signify to me the vast earth we inhabit. The Florin passes through our country, of course, but think where else she has travelled, not just under her own name but as her tributaries, the streams and brooks that feed her from far distant lands. And as proof of her boundless strength and global origins, she brings us these gifts to remind us of where she has come from and where she is going to. Look at the languages – Circassian, Cushitic,

189

Czech, Austric, Hindi, Icelandic and Latvian, to just name a few!' Mosconi fell silent as he contemplated the riches before him and, apparently overawed, took a cotton handkerchief from his pocket and blew his nose loudly.

They stood silently, gazing at the artwork in front of them and dwelling on their own interpretation: Mosconi, dreaming of lands and faraway shores he would never visit, and Lizzie recalling the average wheelie-bin full of rubbish that was routinely carted away from her gate.

Their reverie was interrupted by the ostentatious shuffling of paperwork at the far end of the room and a series of polite coughs and throat clearings. The curator had returned. 'Sir, madam, you honour me with your visit. I am glad that you were able to make yourselves at home in my absence.'

'I am surprised that I had to. The museum opens at ten a.m. on Tuesdays, I believe?' Mosconi approached the desk, his face much darker than his voice portrayed.

'Unless the thermometer displays a temperature in excess of thirty degrees, sir. The constant opening and closing of the main doors allows too much light and heat to penetrate the museum, and I fear some of our more vulnerable exhibits are at risk. We are, of course, available by appointment at any time so no visitor would ever be denied access.'

Lizzie, sensing tension, interrupted with a breezy 'Postcards. I understand that you have postcards.'

'Postcards? Most certainly. Please, this way.'

Lizzie followed him, her hand already reaching into her bag for her purse.

'A very fine selection, do you not think?' The curator gestured towards a display cabinet where a host of postcards from around the world was displayed, some with their photographs turned away to reveal the handwritten scrawls of holidaymakers and the bright stamps of foreign countries. 'Are you a collector?'

Dropping her purse back into her bag, she smiled pleasantly. 'No, just interested. Thank you. They're perfectly lovely.' She examined the cards for as long as she could feign interest, then thanked the curator formally for the delightful visit and turned to her guide to signal that they could leave whenever he was ready. It was clear that Mosconi could have lost himself in the delights of the museum for many more hours, but he respected his visitor's need to leave, aware that it was a huge amount to digest in a first visit and certain she'd return for a more leisurely look.

LIZZIE AND MOSCONI enjoyed some easy conversation as they reversed their morning's journey. They bade each other farewell as they entered the Piazza Rosa. As she walked across it, Lizzie admired the grandeur of the façade and marvelled at the sheer beauty of the architecture. The only thing that marred it was the scaffolding that shrouded the clock tower. Ugly green mesh, intended to restrict the view of the work, hung limply from the metal poles but had no purpose: there was nothing to hide. No work was being undertaken, though the scaffolding remained stubbornly in place. This blot on the landscape irritated Lizzie who, in a flash of impatience, resolved to convince Pavel to set aside his differences with the government. This was something she could fix, in the otherwise perfect city, and she set her heart on making it happen.

CHAPTER 20

In Which Lizzie Exerts Some Power

LIZZIE SLEPT WELL, dreamed intensely and awoke with purpose. As she'd drifted off the night before she'd realized that she'd never had to make a single decision in her life. She had felt adult, independent, even, but she knew with absolute clarity that until she had arrived in Vallerosa and, most notably, until she'd got to know Pavel, she had been a child pretending to be an adult. Pavel was a man who acted on his principles. He had a deep sense of right and wrong, and was prepared to live by the guidelines that he had determined. He wasn't much older than Lizzie but there he was, already a man with a past and a passion. Lizzie's father had made a pretence of allowing her to think she was growing up but he had simply cast her in his own mould. Her thoughts, her beliefs, her ambitions, even, were all his. Her mother, too, had somehow allowed her own character to be subsumed entirely by her husband's, so she and Lizzie were simply poor copies of his design.

Here she had a role. A role that was hers to define and develop. She knew that she must make something happen while she was visiting this beautiful country. If she didn't, what was the point of her?

It was with renewed vigour that she shot out of bed to talk to as many ministers as she could find in an attempt to get the clock repaired. But in two hours of knocking on doors, hanging around in Il Gallo Giallo and asking for help wherever she went, she found that every man she wanted to pin down had suddenly become elusive. It was with growing determination that she marched towards the president's quarters, motivated not by a sense of entitlement but of *royal* entitlement, the type of power that should open doors.

She rapped decisively on the president's door. Angelo answered. He would have liked, Lizzie thought, to show no surprise at the unannounced arrival of a visitor, but his raised eyebrows betrayed him.

'Miss Holmesworth, how may we be of service?'

'I'd like to come in, if I may?'

'I don't think that is possible, Miss Holmesworth. The president is otherwise occupied and was not expecting your visit. Perhaps another time, with an appointment?'

'No. That won't do. I want to see Sergio now.'

If Angelo's eyebrows could have climbed any further up his forehead, they would have. Not only had Miss Holmesworth's voice increased in volume, she was now pouting and had seemed to plant herself more firmly, perhaps immovably, on the president's threshold.

'What is it?' called Sergio, somewhat faintly – from within his bedroom, perhaps.

'We have a visitor, sir. Miss Holmesworth is presenting herself for an audience.'

Silence lingered until Sergio's voice could be heard again, this time much closer.

'Send her in. I am always happy to welcome my special guest, regardless of how inconvenient it might be.'

Lizzie pushed past Angelo and made straight for the president's desk. She faltered for a barely perceptible beat when she saw that the president was sitting at his desk in his bathrobe. A few seconds later a pretty young woman in a white apron left Sergio's bedroom and shuffled past them, eyes averted, as if trying to make herself invisible. Lizzie swung around to watch the girl's undignified exit.

'Busy, were you?' Lizzie said, barely masking her disgust.

'I was having my back waxed.'

'Your back waxed ...' Lizzie's tone didn't suggest agreement.

'I was having my back waxed!' Sergio insisted, drawing his bathrobe a little closer to himself.

'With the help of Angelo here?' Lizzie asked, sarcasm dripping from every syllable.

'Well, with Angelo present, Miss Holmesworth, I am more likely to have been having my back waxed than indulging in any impropriety you may be suggesting. Would you like to examine my back for proof? I think you'll find there's a somewhat unbecoming patch that will now have to await further attention.' Sergio began to part his bathrobe for inspection.

'No. I really don't want to see your back, thank you. And sorry.' She lowered her eyes.

'Sorry for coming up unannounced? Sorry for accusing me of something you have absolutely no business accusing me of? Sorry for what exactly, Miss Holmesworth?'

'Sorry for coming up unannounced. But, one, there is very easy access through a gate in the railings and, two, I've been trying to get an appointment to see your people all day. I'm only here for a month and, thanks to your deceit, I'm here on official duty. As such, I'd like to get on with some of that duty without further obstruction. Do I make myself clear?'

Sergio blanched. 'Very clear, Miss Holmesworth. May I ask the nature of your official duty, as you see it? It might just pave the way for an easier passage if my men and I can be clear about the motive behind your investigations. It is an extremely busy time in our political calendar and I am hearing reports that the line of questioning you are taking is hinting at unwelcome criticism of our country. You must understand, Miss Holmesworth, we are a very proud nation and criticism of any aspect of our land is criticism of the whole.'

Lizzie's hand shot to her mouth. 'Criticism? From me? Absolutely not! I have nothing but respect for you and your country, Mr President, except perhaps for your passing me off as a royal visitor, and even that I can justify in my own mind for the sake of the government and all that. But, for the first time in my life, I have a sense of purpose.

When I set out to come here, I had some grand notion of making a difference but I hadn't any idea what that meant or whether that was even a realistic goal. The improvement I could make to my CV was my end-game and I had no notion of how I would do that. I just wanted to tick a box. But now I'm here I've fallen a bit in love with your country, and I can see very, very, very small areas that I really might be able to help with – but trying to get anything done here is incredibly frustrating. I'm helping you out, so let me get on with something I want to do, Mr President.' She slammed her palm down on the table, a little half-heartedly.

Sergio correctly interpreted her anger as the action of a passionate woman, rather than an angry one. 'Who do you want to see? Who is proving difficult?'

'I want to see Roberto Feraguzzi for a start.' She met the president in the eye, the challenge evident.

'You want to see my finance minister?'

'Yup.'

'So, the thing you want to make a difference with is my finances? You're going to help run the economy, Miss Holmesworth?'

'Of course not. But he is the key to unlocking some of the frustration of this place and I might need to speak to him before I can speak to Giuseppe Scota.'

'You want to speak to Giuseppe Scota also? You want an audience with my minister for education?'

'Yup. I need to speak to Giuseppe Scota before I can speak to Settimio Mosconi. I need to talk to them if I'm going to get things done.'

'And these things, they involve finance, education and tourism.'

'Well, I probably need to see Rolando Posti, too.'

'And Commandant Alixandria Heliopolis Visparelli? You need to see my defence minister?'

Lizzie frowned and looked up at the ceiling, seriously contemplating the offer. 'No … I don't think so.'

'Well,' sighed Sergio, 'I suppose that is a blessing.'

He picked up his pen and scrawled some illegible instructions. 'Angelo, see that Miss Holmesworth has an appointment with each of the ministers she needs to see, beginning tomorrow. She has a difference to make, and this mission must not be interfered with.'

Angelo smiled and opened the door for her. Lizzie shook the extended hand of the president, and breezed out. Angelo stopped her as she passed him with a soft touch to her shoulder. He dropped his voice to a register she could barely hear. 'Let me give you some advice, Miss Holmesworth. Hierarchy is valued here by those who are the beneficiaries of its rewards and those who stand to benefit in the future from its successful continuation. If you want to access a minister, don't approach him directly. For every minister there is an ambitious under-secretary. Make him your friend. And another thing, next time you want to see the president, you will make an appointment through me. A man, even a president, is allowed a little down-time. Understand?'

Lizzie smiled as she skipped out of the room.

CHAPTER 21

In Which the Americans Play Ball

IN SERGIO'S OFFICE, the atmosphere was tense. The president had chosen a smaller, more formal setting in which to conduct the interview. The room was clad with warm cherry-wood panels and the furniture was ornate, though sparse. An oil portrait of Sergio's grandfather adorned one wall while opposite a watercolour painted by a junior minister provided the Big Deal with the eternally consistent view of an over-coloured river Florin at sunset. The room was used only on very rare occasions: with no external windows and just one entrance leading off a long, dark corridor, it was dank and airless. Sergio and Angelo occupied two seats at the far side of the table while Chuck Whylie and his tennis-playing colleague, Paul, sat opposite, nearest to the door.

Whylie was relaxed, certainly more so than he had been on any of the occasions on which he had made formal representations to the ministers. He had already nudged his chair backwards by a foot or two, allowing him to slouch lower in his seat, his right ankle resting just above his left knee and his airborne foot wagging up and down in a playful rhythm that, despite the unchallenging reputation of the Hush Puppy, seemed menacing to the two Vallerosans. A smile played on his lips, and while the formalities of tea pouring were enacted, he leaned over every now and then to whisper a word or two in the ear of his colleague. On a couple of occasions Paul laughed more uproariously than a mere short phrase could justify and this, coupled with the almost tangible unveiling of a passive-aggressive game plan, contributed to the discomfiture of the two Vallerosan hosts.

Paul quickly identified himself as another consultant from the Boston office of Whylie's firm. 'My visit,' he reiterated, for the third or fourth time, 'is purely speculative. Chuck's been telling me about your beautiful country and some of the great ground you've covered together. I figured, why not chance it? You know what they say, you must speculate to accumulate. And, hey, if nothing comes of it, I go back with a great tan and a few good stories to dine out on.'

Whylie stepped in seamlessly. 'You see, guys, we've got a great relationship going and we've built some solid mutual understanding here. But Client Opted Inc. is not *just* about agriculture. We cover the whole gamut of specialisms from fiscal strategy to exit strategy, and we've rescued many, many small countries from some greater predicaments than yours ...'

'And some pretty sizeable ones, too.' Paul, receiving the shot, lobbed it gently back to Whylie.

'You're gonna need some top-drawer coaching as you square up to face the hard balls you guys are going to be up against when you step up to the line for your first game outside of Little League.' Whylie volleyed to Paul.

'And let's look at the field. There are some big hitters out there.'

The current game had started more than an hour ago and, at an uncomfortable stalemate, they had broken for tea. In the preceding set, no amount of protestation on the part of Sergio had drawn the conversation to a close. Even when Angelo had painstakingly spelled out the government's recent resolution on a cautious approach – they had unanimously agreed to see how the agricultural policy panned out over a number of years before entering into any other commitment – the consulting duo were determined that their audience should receive them and give them the attention they felt they were due.

And while Sergio and Angelo had steadfastly refused to enter into a conversation that they were fairly sure was being forced upon them, they were also uncomfortably aware that they were the weaker side. The Americans were looking less like two men with a hard sell ahead and more like men who already knew the end-game.

Impatient to bring the unscheduled tea break to a close and to resume the discussion at a pace they'd worked hard to establish, Whylie broke the silence first.

'Guys, guys, guys. You need to hear us out. We've got something to offer that your country needs. And if you don't think you need it now, well, you can bet your bottom dollar, you're going to need it soon.' He continued, the bit between his teeth: 'You've managed to carry on pretty much unnoticed for a good time here and your survival instinct is impressive, granted. And I know that you're justly proud of the neutral stand you've taken over the years. But, guys, just between these four walls, tell me something off the record. Can you put your hands on your hearts and say that over the last eight hundred years you actively sought to avoid war, or would it be closer to the truth to suggest that war has avoided you?'

Both Sergio and Angelo remained steadfastly impassive even though Whylie was now broaching territory that Sergio would be compelled to defend most vocally. Eight centuries of peace was an achievement that nobody could take from them, but there was the hint of a suggestion from the American that it was about to be undermined in one hour of tea drinking.

'My guess is that I've hit the nail on the head. War has avoided you, hasn't it? Why is that? Why do you think you, of all the nations that surround you, have been so successful in evading conflict? I can tell you the answer to that, too. It's because, up until now, you've had nothing that anybody wants. Diddly squat.' He shrugged expansively and eyeballed his opponents, daring them to come up with a more plausible explanation.

'But that's all changed, guys. The political landscape has changed around you and you yourselves have changed your back-story in recent years. You are sitting pretty on a tidy export crop and a potential GDP that your neighbours would kill for, literally. I've got to look you in the eye and tell you I'm just not sure it's going to be possible to stay under the radar for too much longer.'

Sergio and Angelo, in tandem, ran a finger under a damp collar, wishing they'd chosen a cooler room for their chat.

'And what happens when you're finally noticed? How do you think your neighbours are going to react? Let's face it, you've been living next door to them *for ever* without so much as a shared cup of sugar to show for it. What are they going to do? Come knocking on your door with a casserole and introduce themselves? Hell, no. I've worked with these guys before. They're going to march straight in here and take what they want.'

Both Sergio and Angelo, still acting in perfect unison, sat up and shook their heads. Sergio opened his mouth to respond, but Whylie was too quick.

'You don't believe me or you don't want to believe me? There's a big difference between the two. Wake up and smell the coffee, guys! You're sitting pretty in the middle of one of the most unstable landmasses *in the world*. Let's put the two world wars aside for a moment. Since 1950, if you take into consideration both military and civilian casualties, you're talking about two million dead as a direct result of relatively unimportant and, in global terms, smallish skirmishes fought in the direct vicinity of your country!

'And what are they fighting for? Something you haven't got? Don't underestimate yourselves, and please, please, please – like I've been telling you for at least a decade – please don't sell yourselves short. What are they fighting for? You answer me!' He used his whole right fist to pull back the thumb on his left hand. 'There's religion, first of all. And that's the mother of all reasons. It's lose-lose whichever way you look at it. If you don't offend the guys to the east then you're sure as hell going to piss off the guys to the west.'

He moved swiftly on, pulling back his index finger and swinging his leg down at the same time, planting both feet squarely on the carpet. 'There's oil. You haven't got any? Maybe not, but there are pipelines going in at the moment that make the New York Metro look like child's play, and pretty soon somebody's going to realize that the most direct route to get what they want from A to B means carving a path directly through your backyard.' He pulled back his middle finger. 'And if you need a third reason, there's power. Europe's gotten a lot bigger recently and the rest of the guys out here are going to want some strength in numbers. You might be small but, strategically, you could be huge to them.'

Sergio rolled his pen back and forth between thumb and index finger. 'So what are you suggesting?'

At the first positive bite, Whylie resumed his relaxed pose. 'Well, we need to examine all your options. You know, you might be proud of escaping a few wars over the years, but do you think the United States of America has seen much bloodshed on her soil? We're talking about going back a hundred and fifty years to find a dead American soldier that didn't have to be shipped home by airfreight. How do you think we maintain that stance? By ignoring the rest of the world? Hell, no, by defending ourselves. No one's going to take a pop at us because the first guys that do?' He gestured with a line drawn from one side of his throat to the other. He enjoyed the effect his hand signal had had on his audience's eyebrows. 'We're talking about defence, guys, a little deterrent that's going to make your neighbours think twice about taking a pop at *you*.'

Angelo, though there strictly as adviser, stepped in, unable to sit through the American's rant any longer. 'We have defence. We have a strong police force and a highly skilled military unit. We feel confident that we are appropriately equipped should the need ever arise, but we are equally confident that, given our track record, these measures will not be necessary.'

Whylie nodded enthusiastically, and even offered a warm smile of encouragement. 'As I would have been, my friend, *before* you put your head above the parapet and started waving your big expectations around. Two years ago, most people wouldn't have been able to point to you on a map, but I'll tell you something for nothing, you're going to find yourselves on the map now, guys.'

Sergio, growing impatient, jumped back in: 'What sort of defence are you talking about, over and above our immediate resources?'

'Well, that's where my friend Paul Fields comes in. He happens to be our resident expert on these matters. Over to you, Paul.'

Paul smiled his thanks at his colleague and took a deep, theatrical breath while he captured the attention of his target. 'I'll cut straight to the chase, guys. The world's moved on. A tank here, a fleet of F1s there, that's nothing, these days. There are kids on the streets of New York City who have more modern weaponry than you can lay claim to. You want to do the right thing by your citizens? You want to sleep at night? We're talking about nuclear deterrents.'

Sergio stifled an automatic laugh. 'That's crazy … We're not in the game … We have no such designs …' Words to express his horror had fled, allowing Paul to step straight back in.

'The entry level into the market is much, much lower, these days. You don't even have to have homegrown nuclear capability. You're our friend, our ally! Sometimes it pays to have friends in high places. You know what we do for our friends? We share our knowledge.'

'Let me get this straight. You're talking about developing nuclear capability, here, in Vallerosa?' Sergio said, with a trace of a smile. The idea was so risible that a response other than ridicule would have given the suggestion too much credibility.

'No, no, that wasn't on my agenda. But if that's the way you guys are thinking, then let's talk. We'll entertain any suggestions you want us to consider. But, no, I'm not talking about you taking such a big step. I was thinking you might want to dip your toes into the nuclear waters as a first move. We're thinking we can hook you up with some guys who should be able to provide you with just what you need off the shelf. There's a market in repurposed weaponry and I'm pretty sure that we'll find something out there to suit your requirements.'

'But this is preposterous! We're talking about billions of dollars!'

'Not billions. Millions. As I say, the entry level has lowered significantly. Obviously all the work I undertake is strictly confidential and I couldn't possibly betray those confidences, but you would be pretty surprised to learn of some of the smaller countries that have already taken the step. And I don't want to alarm you, but it wouldn't surprise me if one or two of those weapons were pointed in this direction.'

Sergio and Angelo exchanged a look. Alarmed.

'OK, OK, they may not be pointed at you, but who's to say they're not pointed at an area just beyond you? Are you going to risk your entire country being obliterated by a bad aim?' Paul allowed the idea to drift in the air before Whylie stepped in.

'Do you think I want that on my conscience? Sure, you'd have got there on your own, but I've got to take my share of the responsibility here. The very fact that you're more visible is partly thanks to me. Do you think, after the things we've been through together, I'd walk away and not at least help you to prepare for any potential ramifications? Hey, I want to sleep at night. Look at it this way, me introducing you to Paul is the very least I can do for you after all the great hospitality you've shown me over the years. And you're on our books. Let's face it, we're practically partners in this!'

Exasperation clear on his face, Sergio wanted to end the conversation, to dismiss the Americans from his office, attend to the needs of his country and get back to a world he understood. But, as hard as he tried, the vocabulary to do so failed him. 'Even millions are beyond our means. Our country is tiny! We run a small economy. Our defence budget is minuscule. We just don't have millions of dollars to play with.'

Paul gave the polite smile of a patient teacher coaxing a reluctant child in the most rudimentary of lessons. 'Don't worry about the millions. While you've been burying your head in the sand, a phenomenon you might not have heard of has been established to look after these very matters. Ever heard of the World Bank? It is currently sitting on a fat purse and each year it lends tens of billions of dollars to developing and impoverished countries like yours. That funding is there for the taking.'

Whylie cut in: 'Guys. Access to credit is a basic human right. You're going to deny your people that opportunity? You want that on your conscience?'

'A basic human right?' Sergio counted them off on his fingers. 'Food, shelter, education, clean water ...' He hesitated. 'Tea.'

'You and I are not working off the same page here. Since when was tea a basic human right?' Whylie sneered, incredulous at his opponent's ignorance.

Sergio didn't acknowledge this as rhetoric. Instead, he decided to take the question literally and answer it as best he could. 'Well, what is tea? It is the leaf of a plant, grown locally, infused slowly in potable water.' Sergio's eyes became misty and he looked up at the Big Deal as he picked his way around the argument in his head. 'The water must be boiling, of course, which serves a dual purpose. It greatly aids the alchemy that allows the release of the healing benefits of the leaf, but the act of boiling the water itself removes any impurities, which ensures a safe and thirst-quenching drink. Something healing and safe can be a great medicine in a poor country.'

Whylie moved to interrupt but Sergio silenced him with a raised hand, still keen to follow his train of thought through to its proper conclusion.

'If you have no access to a cup of tea – that is, some leaf, some water, some method of heating and purifying the water – you have nothing. If you cannot share a cup of tea with a friend, or indeed a stranger in need, you have nothing. So perhaps I would further justify my proclamation that tea is a basic human right by suggesting that the ability to offer a cup of tea to a stranger is a basic human right.'

Sergio thought for a moment, pleased with this rationale, and as he continued to lock eyes with the Big Deal, he was already wondering whether his tea-sharing rights should perhaps be written into the constitution of his country. Angelo cleared his throat noisily, bringing Sergio back from his reverie. 'So, I will grant you that food, shelter, education and sharing a cup of tea with a stranger all constitute basic human rights. But, debt? I don't think so.'

Whylie tutted, irritated now at Sergio's obtuseness. 'Credit, I said. Not debt.'

'But the minute you give me credit, I am in debt to you, is that not correct?'

'Credit allows a level playing field and there are people throughout the free world for whom credit makes the difference between poverty and subsistence.'

'But the minute you are in debt, you have less than nothing. You are then truly impoverished.'

'Listen. There is not a man in the developed world who will disagree with me on this one. Credit is a leveller and I'm telling you that you're entitled to it. It's there for the taking and the terms are so damned attractive that not to take advantage of it would be criminal. This is something I can do for you. The paperwork is not pretty – you need a degree just to address the envelope – but that's where I come in. Client Opted Inc. has a successful track record in helping small to medium-sized nations apply for what is rightfully theirs. And you might as well get in line because if you're not going to grab some of this cheap money the next country will. That's what the money's there for, to even out the playing field. To ensure that Little League guys can play ball in the Nationals.'

Imploring now, Sergio took another tactic, one that had worked a thousand times before with his own ministers. 'I don't know. I've got to be led by my heart, and in my heart, this doesn't feel right. It doesn't even feel particularly honest.'

'Well, guys, let me let you in on a secret.' Whylie beckoned the Vallerosans to come closer. They leaned across the table until all four men were in a huddle. Then he took one of each Vallerosan's hands in his own, bouncing them gently against the table surface in time with his words. 'In my heart, it doesn't feel quite right to pretend you've got a British royal staying with you when you and I know she's a two-bit debutante from Sloane Square who's never going to get closer to the royal family than the queue in the beer tent at a polo match. The deception of your people on such a great scale is not particularly honest … Sometimes, guys, you've got to ignore what your heart says and follow your head instead.'

Sergio sat back heavily in his chair while Angelo moved in closer, taking a more aggressive pose. After a few moments, he felt his president's sagging, defeated posture beside him and, reluctantly, he, too, fell back into his chair. Their united retreat suggested that the opposition had won the first round.

Paul scrabbled in his satchel, feigning a spontaneity that both his hosts doubted. Sergio, resigned to his fate, muttered, 'If you want us to sign something, it's impossible. We pass no statute without a full quorum and, in this country, all twelve of my men must be present when issues of national importance are motioned.'

'Go easy,' said Paul, not looking up from his satchel, whose flap he held open with his chin. 'I'm not talking about signing you up to anything. I'm merely here to offer my services as your consultant, on an exclusive basis, for a term of, say, five years while we establish your needs and come up with an appropriate solution for a position that we have already established is at best vulnerable, at worst, precarious.

'I'd like to say the terms are the same on which you employ my colleague here but, as I'm sure guys like you are only too aware, when it comes to serious issues like defence, particularly when we're using the N-word, then not only are the bangs bigger, but so are the bucks.' Paul smoothed out a single A4 sheet of paper.

'Don't fret, it's not a contract. You won't need your quorum to sit for this old thing. Just the Ts and Cs, a heads of agreement that'll let the guys back home get the ball rolling.' He slid the document across the table, one proprietorial hand upon it until, reluctantly, Sergio dragged it the last few inches towards him. He turned to Angelo and their eyes met. Sergio paused, but not for long enough to let Angelo's evident fury cloud his own judgement.

Sergio brushed his hair back off his forehead and focused on the paper in front of him. He was barely able to make sense of the small type as it swam and danced before his eyes. 'Where do I sign?' More sad than bitter, he exhaled the words and made his mark.

CHAPTER 22

In Which the Visitor Gets Down to Business

LIZZIE HAD ARRANGED for a meeting with Signor Rolando Posti, the minister for the interior. It would take place in his offices and she had been allocated a ten-minute slot. This had been bewilderingly difficult to organize, even though she had been given *carte blanche* by the most senior officer in the country and an access-all-areas pass. It had taken considerably more time to arrange her short meeting with Signor Posti than the amount an under-secretary had allocated to her.

Carlo was a young man with great ambition. His youth was a source of great frustration to him. Although he found himself in a very favourable position, with great career prospects ahead, the dogged determination of the senior minister, whose job he hoped one day to inherit, meant there was no end in sight to the period – most likely decades – during which he would serve in this junior role. To ease the endlessness, he enacted every task allotted him with mind-numbing precision. By stretching a job that might ordinarily take just a few minutes into something that took days, or even weeks, he hoped to trick time and to make it work at a pace more sympathetic to his requirements. In this way, he believed, he might be able to manipulate and warp time so that he would soon find himself a middle-aged man with a desk in the centre of the room. His current desk, made of metal and tucked tightly against a pale beige wall, filled him with shame. Above it hung a watercolour of the Piazza Rosa, executed in the 1950s (you could tell this by the absence of any white plastic chairs outside the bar). He could help dissipate some of the humiliation by the knowledge that one day he would commission and hang an oil rendition of Signor Rolando Posti, his mentor and role model. 'This man,' he imagined announcing, as he invited an important visitor to pull up a chair to his desk in the centre of the room, 'this is the man who taught me everything I know. Sadly he passed away a *very* long time ago.' At the moment, however, Signor Rolando Posti was a belligerent though healthy seventy-something, and Carlo had to content himself with the punctilious filling in of forms.

Before Lizzie could have her allocated time with Signor Posti, she had been instructed to visit Carlo in order to make an appointment to see Carlo in an official capacity at which time they could discuss scheduling a time that might be convenient for her to see the minister. Naturally she tried charm and impatience to consolidate the first two meetings into one.

'But, Carlo, I'm here now, and you have Posti's diary in front of you. Could we please just make an appointment?'

He shook his head. 'You must understand, that is simply not possible. There is a protocol to follow, and protocol dictates that I must get the meeting cleared in advance of making it.'

'Who do you have to clear it with?'

'With my boss, Signor Rolando Posti.'

'So perhaps at the same time as clearing the meeting with him, you could tell him the time that we've scheduled.'

'That is simply not possible. Protocol dictates that I must follow the exact procedure for this set of circumstances. You need to make an appointment with me in order to make an appointment with the minister. There is much paperwork to complete and I cannot possibly prepare it all on the spur of the moment.'

'Fine.' Lizzie resigned herself to the fact that her access-all-areas pass had limited powers. 'When might it be convenient to see you?'

'Let me look.' Carlo flipped through the diary, running his finger down page after page and shaking his head. Occasionally he would stop and nod, only to see something else that prohibited him making a time available. Tutting loudly, he continued to flick laboriously through the pages. Lizzie's heart began to race when she realized she was now looking through dates towards the end of November. She started to speak but was hushed as he continued to scan his diary.

'You understand, don't you, that I am only here for one month, Signor Carlo?'

215

'Yes, yes, of course, but *you* must understand that I am an extremely busy man and the diary of my boss, Signor Rolando Posti, is even busier.'

'And you understand, don't you, that I am due to see your president this afternoon and report on the co-operation I have received from his staff?'

'And at what time would that be?'

'I have a meeting scheduled with him at two.'

Carlo flipped slowly backwards through the pages, feigning disinterest at this latest development. 'Well, it is a great shame. I have absolutely no time in my diary to meet with you. Most inconvenient, most inconvenient. Except, I suppose, I could squeeze you in in thirty minutes' time. I see I have a cancellation then.'

Lizzie looked at her watch. Thirty minutes' time. Half past eleven. 'Lovely, so I'll be back in thirty minutes to see you about scheduling an appointment with Signor Rolando Posti.'

'That is my understanding of your agenda. But I think it is an excellent precaution to be specific about your intentions as no one likes to be surprised, Miss Holmesworth.'

'Quite. Would you mind if I wait here until the meeting begins?'

Carlo looked alarmed. 'Wait here? In my office? That surely would constitute an unscheduled appointment within the confines of the government buildings and as such would be in breach of countless regulations. No, absolutely not – and, besides, I have an enormous workload to prepare for our meeting. I must insist that you leave now, but I will look forward to welcoming you back here in ...' he glanced at the clock on the wall '... twenty-eight minutes' time.'

Lizzie backed out of the room, thanking him. Rather than wander around outside in the heat she chose to wait on a wooden chair just outside his office. She heard the harsh grating of his chair as he pushed it back, and before she had even seated herself comfortably, he had put his head around the door.

'Miss Holmesworth, I thought we had a clear under-standing. You must leave now, and I must ensure you leave the building or I will have to make a call to security.'

She rolled her eyes, pushed herself upright and walked along the few metres of corridor. She opened the door and stepped out, closing it firmly behind her. She paused for a moment, giving Carlo time to take his seat once more, then opened the door and walked back down the corridor with deliberately certain footsteps.

She knocked on Carlo's open door and he looked up from his desk impatiently.

'Good morning, Signor Carlo. I'm early for our eleven-thirty meeting. Shall I take a seat in Reception?'

'Of course, take a seat outside. I admire punctuality and particularly admire early arrival to meetings. It allows everyone to be better prepared. Excellent.'

Lizzie sat on the wooden chair she had just vacated and listened contentedly to a few papers being shuffled around a desk for twenty-six minutes. Every now and then the near silence would be broken with a perfunctory staple.

Her second meeting with Carlo passed with relative ease, in that it was an exact repetition of the earlier performance. This time, however, she had to provide information for a form that was to be completed in triplicate.

'Reason for meeting?'

'Er, to discuss matters of the state?'

'I need to be more specific, Miss Holmesworth. It is my job to prepare my boss and he does not like to be surprised.'

'How about to discuss matters of the interior of the state?'

'Good, good. Interiors, yes. Very relevant to Signor Rolando Posti. His speciality, one might say.'

'Excellent.'

The honing of the finer detail involved plenty more audible perplexity and the turning of many more diary pages. More minutes ticked by as Carlo hesitated, then continued to flick slowly forward. Eventually they settled on ten past three that afternoon. Carlo made it clear that the meeting was to last for no longer than ten minutes. If she needed to extend it, for any reason at all, he would need at least three weeks' notice. 'In writing.'

'I'm sure ten minutes will be fine. Thank you.' Lizzie left with a big grin on her face and an inordinate feeling of satisfaction that she had managed this simple task. She had official government business planned for that afternoon. Now she just had to think carefully about her tactics.

CHAPTER 23

In Which the Purpose of Education Is Questioned

THE MINISTERS WERE MEETING once more and there was a dark mood in the air. Sergio was impatient, Angelo was clearly fuming, and there was an almost tangible tension between the two men, who were usually so at ease with each other. The assembled senior ministers shifted uncomfortably in their seats as the president rushed through the preliminary proceedings, barely able to contain his frustration as tea was strained and served.

'I would like, if I may, to begin with an update from our minister for employment, Signor Lubicic.'

Vlad Lubicic jumped. He had not been expecting to make a contribution that afternoon as, during the run-up to the election, there tended to be more pressing matters at hand. He glanced nervously around the room for clues from his colleagues and leaped impetuously to the conclusion that the bad feeling emanating from the president and his aide was a direct consequence of something he had done or had failed to do. 'Mr President?'

'An update, please.'

'On employment matters?'

'Clearly. When I ask you to speak on matters that don't concern you, I shall give you ample warning.'

Lubicic cleared his throat. Sergio governed the country with a lightness that was a direct result of his ease with his advisers. His gentle touch had made the very act of governing a pleasure, a marked contrast to the more didactic approach that Sergio Senior had taken. Today, though, even the president's perspiration was dripping with sarcasm and he wasn't sure how to react.

'The numbers remain static, Mr President. We have zero unemployment. Or one unemployed, if you consider Franco, but he has not taken up any of the offers that have so far been presented to him.'

'And of the sixteen thousand eight hundred adult men or so that we have in this country, how many are actually gainfully employed?'

'I don't quite follow you, sir. As I just stated, all of them.'

'Clearly not all of them, Signor Lubicic. I think you'll find that at least half of those men are in full-time education.'

'But, sir, those men do not qualify for employment. Of those that qualify for employment, all of them are actively employed, sir.'

'And how many men of over twenty-four are in full-time education and as such are not qualified to work?'

'I couldn't say, sir. That would be a question for Professore Scota. With respect, sir.'

Giuseppe Scota made a noise to indicate that he was about to speak, but Sergio silenced him with a raised hand and continued to look at his minister for employment.

'But you should know the answer to that, surely. Aren't these men prospective employees for the country? Aren't they the workforce of the future? And they'll need jobs, at some future point, so are you making plans to accommodate them?'

Lubicic was now visibly uncomfortable. 'But, sir, the men are released from full-time education when they are required for work. In the meantime they continue to increase their skills and their relevance to the workforce. We have some of the most educated men in the world here, and that is the result of the brilliant policy you yourself made several years ago.'

'But what are the prospects for these men? It is all very well making this fine education available to everyone, but what are they going to do with it when they've finished?'

'Finished what, sir?'

'Their education.'

'But you yourself said, sir, an education is a process of evolution that begins the day you are born and ends, if you are lucky, on the day you die.'

There was silence in the room.

'I did?' Sergio looked uncharacteristically baffled. Not only did he appear to have no recollection of this groundbreaking policy he had apparently masterminded, he had the countenance of a man who couldn't remember what he was doing in the room. He looked startled now and stared beseechingly at Lubicic for further illumination.

'Yes, and when we implemented the policy of extended education for all, it was met with great enthusiasm by the whole country. That was a landslide year. We received half a dozen spoiled ballots at most. You predicted it, remember? You told us that education was always a crowd-pleaser.'

'I did, did I?'

Sergio's uncharacteristic vagueness was as perplexing to Lubicic as it was to the other senior ministers.

Angelo was still quietly fuming in the corner, his foot tapping nervously, his arms folded firmly across his chest. He was so busy assuming this stance that he was barely picking up on Sergio's gentle slide from righteous leader to the befuddled led.

'Yes, you did,' soothed Lubicic, sensing that the worst of the storm had passed and understanding finally that this attack wasn't personal, and if it had been to begin with, it probably wasn't any more. 'Yes, you predicted it and, of course, you were absolutely right.'

'And do we have anything else on the agenda?' Sergio was somewhat contrite. He couldn't sit and be accused of undermining his own policy, a policy everyone had admired only recently. While not entirely satisfied with the answers before him, he made a mental note to park the problem somewhere else and examine it afresh later, in private.

Now he looked expectantly at Lubicic, who in turn looked around the room, seeking with narrowed eyes and pursed lips some help from his colleagues. The professor, feeling that he was the beneficiary of an extremely narrow escape and that he, somehow, had Lubicic to thank for it, stepped in.

'Sir? There is no agenda today. You called the meeting.'

'I did? Yes, I did.' Sergio shrugged, somehow suggesting in that slight movement that a bunch of idiots was assembled before him. 'That will be all. You're dismissed,' he barked, then leaned back in his chair to drink his tea quietly.

The men filed out, baffled and uneasy, walking in monk-like silence. If they were to risk speculation, it would be within the stone walls of their own homes. To analyse today's proceedings without pointing a finger at the mental stability of their president was challenging but, even as they left the building, the memory of his aggression as the meeting had started was softening, and that of his conviction at the end had strengthened until barely a trace of the uncertainty they might have detected remained. By the time they had walked through their front doors, hung up their hats and gone in search of food, they were already rewriting the meeting as an unqualified success.

CHAPTER 24

In Which Lizzie Beats the System

LIZZIE WAITED PATIENTLY outside the offices of the minister for the interior. When her allotted time came, she was led through the offices of the minister for the exterior, who was buried behind a huge pile of paperwork. Mario Lucaccia barely raised his head to acknowledge her, but as soon as she had settled into Rolando Posti's domain, he chose to busy himself in the filing cupboard immediately outside Posti's office. From this position he could easily hear the conversation as it unfolded.

'So, how are you enjoying your visit so far, Your Royal Honourableness?' the minister began, with the intention of allowing his esteemed visitor to feel relaxed in his company.

'Oh, please, I'm much more comfortable with Miss Holmesworth,' Lizzie implored.

'As you like.' He nodded, giving her permission to continue.

Lizzie smiled at the old man, warming immediately to his twinkling eyes, which smiled despite his frowning eyebrows. 'I like your country very much. People here are very kind.'

Immediately his eyebrows frowned a notch more. 'And you expected something else, perhaps? That our people might be unkind or inhospitable? Barbarians, even?'

Unsure whether this was a gentle tease or something more sinister, Lizzie stiffened a little, cautioning herself to tread carefully. 'Heavens, nothing of the sort. I had no preconceptions. I knew very little of your country, which perhaps is why it is even more surprising to find such a perfect place.'

'Aha, that is not my job!' Posti exclaimed, slapping his palm on his desk.

'Excuse me?' Lizzie was alarmed at the sudden shift in the minister's manner.

'It is not my job to make a good outward impression on potential visitors. We have two men whose job that is. If you would like to make a complaint about the lack of information about our country, I suggest you raise it with—'

There was a loud cough from outside the room.

'Settimio Mosconi. He is minister for tourism and if he were doing his job in completeness you would have been given much more information on which to base some preconceptions and then you would not have had to be surprised. No one likes surprises, Miss Holmesworth.'

'Well, no one likes bad surprises, like no one likes bad news. This was a good surprise – I mean I was pleasantly surprised. Sometimes it's rather wonderful to discover something entirely by yourself. I've got student friends who have been travelling in Asia only to find they bump into friends from school or their neighbours.'

'Amazing. That would indeed be a good surprise,' agreed the minister, relaxing once again.

'Well, sort of. But it's more because they're all following the same guide books, you know, *Rough Guide* to this or that. They all end up taking exactly the same route, meeting the same people, and I'm not sure they will have set out to do that.'

'But the importance of a journey is to discover things that you didn't set out to do, as you quite rightly stated yourself not a moment ago.'

'Yes, well.' Lizzie faltered. She could battle this one out but she had been allocated only ten minutes, several of which must already have been used up. She glanced uncomfortably at her watch.

Posti was immediately admonished. 'Yes, indeed, we must move on, I understand you are a very busy woman and I apologize most profusely for allowing the conversation to drift from the one stated on your paperwork.' Here he glanced at a purple-hued copy of the form she had watched Carlo complete just hours before.

'I see you would like to talk about matters of the interior. And here are we discussing matters of the exterior! For that conversation you would probably have been better off making an appointment with my esteemed colleague, Mario Lucaccia.'

Another loud cough from outside the room.

'And I don't believe he is available this afternoon for consultation. So perhaps, if you don't mind, we could stick to the prepared subject? That will save an awful lot of paperwork and will make our lives much, much easier. Shall we continue?'

Lizzie swallowed noisily and steeled herself to be clear. 'Er, yes, indeed. I wanted to talk to you about how the government works here. I mean, what I really want to know is, if I wanted to make something happen, make a difference to something, how would I set about doing so?'

'Well, that is a very intelligent question and one that deserves a full and honest answer. And clarity, yes. It deserves a clear and straightforward answer that foreigners, unused to our ways and our culture, can follow clearly.' He paused until he was certain that Lizzie had felt the weight of his hesitation. 'I'm sorry I can't help you.'

'You can't?'

'Well, the machinations of our government, like any other, are varied and complex. I can't possibly give you the answer you deserve. I would have to understand exactly what you want to achieve. If, for example, you wanted to return home and wage war on us, then that would require an interview with the person most able to advise you. In this case, Commandant Alixandria Heliopolis Visparelli.'

'Well, of course I don't want to wage war on you!' Lizzie squeaked.

'Ssh,' Posti warned. 'It is inadvisable to talk loudly about war in this building. It is liable to make people a little nervous.'

'But that's not what I want to talk about.' Lizzie's frustration was mounting: she was unable to grasp this conversation and send it in any sort of direction.

'Well, you must be clearer. If you want a full and honest answer, a clear and straightforward answer, you must honour me with a full and honest question.'

Lizzie inhaled deeply and exhaled slowly. 'OK. I would like to talk to you specifically about the town clock.'

'Oh, so it's like that,' Posti growled, his frown so deep in his forehead that the twinkling eyes were no longer visible beneath his brows.

'Like what?'

'You visit our country and, despite the warmth and hospitality of our fine people and our beautiful and splendid scenery, you have decided to focus on the negative.'

'Well, not really. I just was interested – I certainly didn't mean to cause any offence.'

'Of course not. They never do, do they?'

Lizzie floundered, still rattled by the suggestion she might want to wage war on Vallerosa. 'I'm just interested in a country that seems to have such a clear grip on its infrastructure—'

'*Seems* to! You imply that what we present here is a façade? A sham? That we are not what we say we are?' Posti now folded his arms across his chest in a stance that suggested a barrier of insurmountable heft.

'No, no, no. I mean, there is so little wrong I wondered why you would allow the clock to remain broken for so long.'

Posti sighed and echoed the phrase: 'That we *allow* it to remain broken. Interesting choice of words, Miss Holmesworth. You imply that we are somehow complicit. Are you suggesting that this is my conspiracy or one that is enacted by the entire government?'

'I'm suggesting no such thing. I'm merely asking why you don't fix it.'

'Aha, now we get to the very crux of the matter. The clear and straightforward question I was seeking in the first place. If you had come in here and asked, as you sat down, "Your Excellency, why don't you fix the clock?" I would have been able to answer you immediately. Instead, after all the game playing we've been trying to pick through for the last ten minutes, you're out of time.'

Lizzie slumped in her seat. Despair washed over her and she looked at her watch.

'No. I have at least another minute – see?' She showed him her slow-running watch. 'Quickly, while we have a minute. Tell me, please, why don't you fix the clock?'

'The clock,' Posti snapped, quite unpleasantly, 'is not my problem. The clock is the fault of –' a third loud cough from just outside the door '– it is the fault of Roberto Feraguzzi, minister of finance. If you want to understand the innermost workings of our government with respect to things that don't work, then I suggest you make an appointment with him. Good day.'

As Lizzie left the room she heard him mutter, 'Meeting closed satisfactorily at three twenty p.m.'

Lizzie left Posti's office blinking back tears of frustration. She wandered slowly to the bars and, barely cognizant of the choice that usually plagued her, she slumped heavily into a seat at Il Toro Rosso. Clouded by weariness, she felt unable to take in the scenery around her. She pulled her sunglasses down from the top of her head, happy to hide behind them while she pondered this latest encounter and wondered whether it was possible to make anything at all work in Vallerosa. Letting her eyelids close for a few seconds, she tipped her face in the direction of the sun, allowing its warmth to restore her. After approximately twenty seconds the coolness of a shadow fell across her. She opened her eyes and squinted at the smiling face of Piper.

'Tea, beer, a little something to cheer you up?' he asked, with the perfect balance of warmth and subservience.

Lizzie sighed heavily and allowed a little of the despair she was feeling to creep into her voice. 'Oh, right now if I was at home, I would probably ask for a large vodka tonic, but that's clearly not the done thing around here. What do you suggest?'

'Let me diagnose. You feel a little down? Sluggish, perhaps? Maybe even a bit homesick?'

'All of the above. Yes, you've hit the nail on the head.'

'I have just the thing!' Piper snapped his tea-towel in the air and hurried off.

Lizzie wondered what he might be prescribing. Truthfully she felt better already to have found somebody who was pleased to see her.

Before long, Piper returned. He carried a small tin tray, on which stood a tall glass of pale sparkling liquid, the colour of good champagne.

'Gosh, if that's alcoholic I won't be able to stand up!' gushed Lizzie, reaching thirstily for the glass.

'No alcohol. More effective than that.' He took a step back the better to observe her reaction as she took a small sip from the cold glass.

'Interesting, certainly.' She couldn't put a finger on the flavour, on the multitude of flavours. There was something floral that hit her nostrils as she leaned in to sip, but something decidedly herbal or medicinal on her tongue. She sipped again, more deeply.

'I like it, but have absolutely no idea what it is. I don't think I've ever tasted this combination of flavours before.' As she pondered, and smiled generally in Piper's direction, it hit her. Not recognition, but a response. A healing warmth had begun in her stomach and was working its way into her every nook and cranny. Never had she been so conscious of the connectors and pathways that made her body work. Veins, arteries, neurones and synapses were all being switched on as the effect spread, gathering momentum as it travelled. And then she felt better. Astonishingly awake, astonishingly alive. Altogether better.

'Aha, I see from your eyes that my tea tonic has worked its magical powers upon you!' said Piper, beaming.

'Wow, gosh, that really is something special.' She picked up the glass and drained it, then handed it back for an immediate refill.

'You won't be requiring any more. That will do the trick. Even for a woman of your, er, stature. Unless you want to be awake still tomorrow morning!'

'Is it really that powerful?'

'Indeed it is. My tea tonic has unique properties. It is designed to keep you alert, regardless of how physically tired you might be. The students here swear by it, and the night shift at the hospital too. It is made to my own secret recipe!'

'Well, guard it with your life. You don't want it falling into the wrong hands,' Lizzie quipped, gesturing at Il Gallo Giallo.

Piper shrugged. 'It's probably a little late for that.'

'Dario has a similar recipe?'

'Not Dario, no, but he might as well have. I gave the recipe to the American.' Piper hung his head in shame.

'Why on earth would you do that?'

'He was particularly interested in it when he first came here. He even hinted that he had contacts in the drinks industry in the United States of America, so I wrote it down for him. Nothing seemed to come of it, though. Now I have to trust that he doesn't share it further, but ever since I gave it to him he's avoided me. If he deigns to drink in the piazza at all, it's always next door.'

'Well, I think we'd know if the ministers were drinking your tea tonic. They'd be bouncing off walls, wouldn't they?'

They both looked at the other bar, where several ministers sat dozing in the cool shade, barely finding the strength to lift their teacups to their lips.

As her gaze travelled round the other bar, Lizzie caught Feraguzzi's eye, and she jumped up. Suddenly she had the energy to deal with these infuriating ministers.

'Hi, Roberto, can I join you?' she shouted, and rushed towards him.

Desolate, Piper was left alone again. He watched Lizzie weave her way through the chairs to join the minister. At least, he thought, he had been able to give her something that lay outside the reach of his rival. He resolved next time to keep her for longer if he could possibly engineer it.

LIZZIE DRAGGED A SPARE CHAIR towards Roberto Feraguzzi who, caught off guard, couldn't decide whether to be affronted by the interruption to his little rest or thrilled that she had singled him out of the many men she might have chosen. After a short deliberation he decided to be thrilled and pulled himself up to his full height.

'So, Signor Feraguzzi, I have just had a very interesting conversation with Rolando Posti. We were talking about the clock.'

'Which clock would that be, Miss Holmesworth?'

'The clock tower clock. I am very interested in clocks, always have been. I rather assumed that fixing it might be an issue for the interior minister, but I assumed wrongly. According to Rolando Posti, it falls out of his remit – and is one of the many areas under your management.' Lizzie blinked slowly a couple of times while trying to disarm him with a steady stare.

Feraguzzi craned his neck as if to scrutinize the clock from where he was sitting but, of course, it was out of view, being almost directly above Il Toro Rosso. He could see its profile, though, and allowing his eyes to train on its outline appeared to help him frame an answer.

'The issue of clocks does indeed fall under the jurisdiction of the interior minister.' Lizzie was about to protest, but Feraguzzi held up a silencing hand. 'However, the distribution of contracts for the proper care and maintenance of said feature would fall under the jurisdiction of the finance department, my own.'

Lizzie was relieved that she was closing in on this seemingly endless wild-goose chase. 'And may I ask, in a completely unofficial, off-the-record, just-sitting-in-the-bar-with-a-friend sort of way, why can't you fix it?'

'Because I do not have a suitable contractor on my list of government contractors.'

'And if one could be found?'

'One can't be found. There is only one person with the capability of fixing the clock but unfortunately he fails to meet the appropriate criteria to be an official government contractor.'

'But isn't that ridiculous? On what grounds does he fail?'

'Well, in an unofficial, off-the-record, just-sitting-in-the-bar-with-a-friend sort of way ...' the minister reached for exactly the right words '... Rolando Posti doesn't like him.'

'Why? What on earth could Pavel—' Lizzie caught herself a moment too late. Having named the contractor, she had revealed her agenda too openly.

Feraguzzi was shocked. 'You understand, don't you, that you have absolutely no business talking so brazenly about official government business while in a public place? No pre-meeting has been arranged. No meeting has been arranged. There's no one to minute the business between us and, as such, we are already in breach of countless regulations.'

'I'm so sorry. But I want to continue the conversation if I may. Hypothetically.' Lizzie chewed her lip and held her breath, desperate that any progress had been stymied by her blunder.

'Hypothetically.' He considered the proposition. 'You are sure this is strictly hypothetical?'

'Yes, of course. What I meant to say was, why on earth would Posti take a dislike to any young man in the country? I cannot imagine the path of a senior government official would cross very often with the path of a tradesman of, I assume, very little consequence.'

'Well, that might well be the case. But imagine that the young tradesman of very little consequence had been born to a woman of very great beauty. And imagine, if you will, that the then young minister for the interior, before he was even in such a lofty position, had been spurned by such a woman of very great beauty, who instead chose a simple clockmaker – a man of little more consequence than a peasant. Imagine what that would mean to a man with all the makings of greatness mapped out ahead of him. What a slur that would be.'

'Well, I can see that, ego-wise, it would be pretty painful.'

'And there is very little place to redirect that pain, I would imagine, other than at those satisfactory bedfellows: vindictiveness and revenge.'

'So, the young minister, hypothetically, might have arranged to have the contracts revoked and to ensure that the successful clockmaker was suddenly less successful?'

'One might be able to envisage such an outcome in those circumstances. Though, of course, it wouldn't be the position of the minister to make or break such contracts. He would have to use his powers of persuasion to convince a minister such as myself not to invoke any contracts by, perhaps, bringing the reputation of the clockmaker into disrepute.'

'And this, hypothetically, would be achieved how?'

'With difficulty. It would probably take decades of work on the part of a bitter old man to exact his revenge and finish the career of a clockmaker who was probably very close to retiring anyway. But cross old men can be stubborn and it is difficult to undo the past.'

'And young, vibrant ministers, can they be persuaded to change their minds?' Lizzie asked, a smile playing on her lips.

Feraguzzi's eyes twinkled. 'Young and vibrant?'

Lizzie took a deep breath. The tea tonic was still coursing around her body and pieces of the jigsaw were falling into place. 'You're a married man, Signor Feraguzzi?'

'I am indeed, happily married for these last twenty-five years.' He sighed with a note of disappointment, as he looked into the pale blue eyes of the pretty girl opposite him.

'And you have a daughter of about my age?'

With a start, Feraguzzi pulled himself out of his daydream. Yes, of course, he had a daughter of about Lizzie's age.

'And, hypothetically speaking, what if your daughter had fallen in love?'

'Well, I suppose I would be very happy. It is certainly the age to be married, as her mother was before her, but good men are few and far between. It wouldn't get my blessing unless it was a very good match.'

'Of course, but what if the match were good? What if she had fallen in love with a young man who hadn't yet noticed her but probably would quite soon? Wouldn't you want that man to have every opportunity ahead of him, so that he could provide well for that daughter?'

'Hypothetically speaking, of course. Love is very important, but a poor bedfellow without a down mattress.'

Lizzie struggled for a moment with the analogy, but carried on fuelled by the tea tonic and anxious that its magical properties might desert her soon.

'And what if, as the father of such a girl, you had it in your power not only to increase the prospects of the young man in question, but to help bring the daughter to his notice at the same time?'

'Well, that would be an admirable piece of matchmaking, I have no doubt, and I imagine the mother of the daughter in question would be very, very glad to know that the father had played such a key role in a romantic story with a satisfactory outcome.'

'Well, come on. There's somebody you must meet.'

Lizzie scraped her chair noisily back and tugged Feraguzzi to his feet. As she marched him out of the bar she stopped to wave cheerily to Piper, who caught her broad smile and returned his own, forgiving her for her earlier desertion.

CHAPTER 25

In Which Love Is the Answer

LIZZIE LEFT THE BAR with Feraguzzi in tow while Dario was still busying himself preparing a tray of delectable morsels with which to tempt his special guest. By the time he returned to the table, it was empty. This was witnessed, with much amusement, by Piper, who was suddenly very pleased to have had the patronage of Miss Holmesworth for as long as she had graced his bar. Though perhaps, he wondered, if he were to continue plying her with his tea tonic, she wouldn't sit still anywhere for long enough to be called a customer.

In the meantime, Lizzie was weaving her way through the back-streets of the north-east quadrant heading for the small shop kept by the young clockmaker.

The metal shutters were still pulled down from the siesta, but not to the ground, suggesting that Pavel was in or around.

She stooped and called into the shop through the gap. Feraguzzi looked around nervously, anxious that a passerby might notice a senior government official in the midst of such undignified practice.

There was a clatter from within and the shutter was soon being heaved up and out of the way, allowing Lizzie and Feraguzzi to enter. It wasn't an impressive showroom, just a small space with a faded linoleum floor and a number of glass cabinets displaying clocks and watches, an assortment of straps and general timekeeping curiosities.

Pavel bristled when he saw that Lizzie had company and retreated behind a glass-topped cabinet, assuming the position of shopkeeper rather than friend. He stood to attention and addressed Lizzie, ignoring her companion. 'Good afternoon, Miss Holmesworth. I am glad that you have found the time to bring me your timepiece for correction.' He motioned to her wrist and she undid the strap for him.

'Absolutely, I've been meaning to do this for a while. Thank you – it works, just runs a little slow.'

'No problem, happy to oblige,' he said, removing the back cover to inspect the inner workings.

'But that can wait, Pavel. I'm here to introduce you to Roberto Feraguzzi. He is the minister of finance and he's come to have a word with you, if you have the time.'

FERAGUZZI WAS LOOKING around the small room and wondering whether his daughter could do better. It was not much of a living, after all, fixing a watch here and there. And most watches lasted a lifetime, so it wasn't likely the business would expand. He watched Pavel as he busied himself. On the other hand, he thought, as he contemplated him, he was a fine-looking man, and who was he to stand in his daughter's way?

'I believe you know my daughter.'

Pavel stopped what he was doing and frowned. 'Do I? No, I don't think I do.' Genuinely confused, he looked to Lizzie for guidance.

'Claudia?'

'Claudia! Claudia is your daughter?' His delight at the memory of her name, her face, her eyes as they had danced briefly together on the night of the spontaneous party, clouded with this new piece of information. 'I knew she was a daughter of a government official. But I had no idea she was the daughter of a minister. Pity.'

But Feraguzzi had seen the young man's eyes light up and was not immune to the magic of young love. He also understood instinctively that if he were to be complicit in his daughter's courtship and subsequent marriage, his wife would be extremely pleased with him.

'She's a very fine woman. Of marrying age. She'll be looking for a partner at the Spousal Waltz, I imagine.'

'The Spousal Waltz is an outdated tradition, one that demeans the men and patronizes the women. Nowadays, young men and women like to get together through less barbaric practices.'

Pavel was not making a good impression.

'Nevertheless, even if traditions change, a young man will still need the blessing of a young woman's father. That, I assume, is not outdated.'

Pavel met Feraguzzi's eye. His shoulders relaxed a fraction. 'I apologize if I was rude, sir. I am not used to the company of government officials in my shop. I forgot my manners.'

'Your shop is a little humbler than I remember it under your father's care. Times are tough, perhaps?'

'Times are just different. I've diversified a little.' He laid Lizzie's watch gently on a piece of soft cloth and spoke as he searched for an eyepiece in a drawer. 'I mend a few watches, but that isn't really a business any more. Timepieces are funny things, these days. They're built either to last or to throw away. Nothing much in between. My father's business existed on fixing watches and running the government contracts. My business would have gone under if I'd relied on either of those as an income stream.'

'So you have diversified how?'

'I build clocks. Come.'

He went through a door behind him into a cavernous workshop. Hefty wooden benches lined the walls and clocks of all sizes filled every space. The floor was littered with coils of metal shavings. Shelves hosted glass jars of every size, all immaculately labelled. There were sheets of glass taped and stacked in one pile, and heaps of timber in various stages of polish in another. To the far right a large object was covered with a dustsheet. The workshop smelt of an amalgamation of raw materials: the acrid sting of metal, the sweet odour of wood recently cut, the honeyed tones of wax.

'This is what I'm working on at the moment,' said Pavel, and whisked away the dustsheet to reveal the clock beneath it.

It was unfinished, uncased, just the intricate workings of a huge mechanism. It was balanced on a workbench designed to allow the pendulums to hang free. With a gentle touch, Pavel swung them and immediately the clock sprang to life.

Both Lizzie and Feraguzzi started to speak, but Pavel silenced them with a finger to his lips.

They listened. The dulcet tick filled the room, and the audience listened in admiration. The sound was pure and certain, yet left a hint of unfinished business in the air at each second.

'I'm pleased with this one. The sound, at least, is very good. I have absolutely no idea what it might look like yet, but time will tell.'

Feraguzzi stared at the clock in open admiration and looked closely at Pavel's hands. They were strong, but the fingers were long, thin and straight. An artist's hands.

'Is this a full-time occupation, Pavel, or might you have some time in your schedule to take on some other work?'

'Government business? Not interested.'

'It's a good contract.'

'I don't mind how good the contract is. I don't want something that can be whisked away from me at the first sign of displeasure. I don't want to be your servant the way my father was. I value my own craft more highly than you will and I'm not prepared to be destroyed. So no, but thank you.'

He stopped the pendulum and, once he was sure it was completely steady, began to cover the clock again.

'That is a very fine clock you're building. You're obviously very talented,' offered Feraguzzi, suddenly more interested in this man than he had planned to be.

'Thank you,' said Pavel, a note of pride creeping into his voice.

'But you got your skill from your father, there's no doubt about it, and his finest work was the clock in the square. It must pain you a little to see it silenced. Surely, out of filial duty, you'd like to see it restored?'

'It's filial duty that allows me to keep it silent,' Pavel countered, with a half-laugh. 'You know, every day I pass it, I itch to get my hands on it. Anyway, you're wrong, my father didn't build it – his grandfather did. My father merely maintained it. So sentimentally it was very important to him but he and I both agreed that it was a good clock but never a great one. Of course, in my dreams I would very much like an opportunity to bring it to its full potential. The face is quite attractive and the bells and whistles are fun, although a little frivolous and rather a distraction from its true purpose. But the mechanism behind it is only adequate. I could fix it tomorrow but what I'd really like to do is to work on it properly. But, as I said, out of filial duty I shall never touch it. I owe that, at least, to my father.'

'Do you know why his contract was cancelled, Pavel?'

'Because our government is an autocracy prepared to put its own needs ahead of its people's?'

Feraguzzi, who had been polite and contrite until that moment, was not prepared to stand and listen to the slander of his government by this stubborn upstart. 'That is an outrage! Autocracy had nothing to do with it. This was all about love!'

'Love?'

'Yes. Rolando Posti was in love with your mother. Your mother chose your father. He was heartbroken. But once the heartbreak wore off he was angry and hurt. It took Posti a good twenty-five years to amass the power needed to revoke the contract. And once he had the power, that was what he did. He fired your father.'

'Did my father know this?'

'I have absolutely no idea.'

Pavel frowned and thought for a moment. 'Did my mother know this?'

'I have absolutely no idea.'

Pavel was silent, thinking of his mother all alone in the house and trying to imagine whether she would be horrified and insulted or amused to hear of this latest development. Or perhaps she had known all along. He was intrigued, though, to discover an explanation that made sense on a human level of his father's sudden dismissal. His palms were tingling with excitement: there were so many different strands that this conversation might follow. Feeling that this was a moment to heed his heart, and ignore any of a dozen rational reasons against taking action, Pavel decided to defer his response. There was more at stake than the mere matter of a contract to fix the clock.

'I'll meet you in the piazza for breakfast tomorrow morning. But I want Signor Posti there too.' He spoke with a level of decisiveness that Feraguzzi respected. He agreed with a nod and shook Pavel's outstretched hand firmly.

Lizzie wanted to linger and admire the clocks, but the meeting felt closed and Pavel's expression was hard to read so instead she made her exit with Feraguzzi. As they walked back in the direction of the bars, she turned to the finance minister.

'Well, that wasn't a disaster, was it?'

'No. I agree, that wasn't a disaster at all.' He smiled at her and together they headed into the evening. 'But I think in order to avert any potential calamity, you'd better join the meeting tomorrow. Something tells me we're in this together.'

CHAPTER 26

In Which a
Deal Is Done

THE FOLLOWING MORNING Lizzie made the familiar journey across the piazza with her eye firmly on Piper's bar. She could see Pavel and the woman she assumed to be his mother, and there was Feraguzzi with Rolando Posti. The ministers' progress under the arches was a little slower than her own as the two men were deep in conversation and sometimes stopped walking altogether as they talked. It was difficult to tell from their body language whether they were arguing or discussing, or even debating and laughing, but their slow pace meant she had soon overtaken them and reached their shared destination first.

Equally, it was difficult to tell from the expression on Pavel's face whether he was happy, excited, nervous or vexed. But he was kind to Lizzie, standing up to pull out a chair for her and introducing her to his mother.

Pavel's mother nodded curtly. 'Amalia Berlardi. Pleased to meet you.' She looked less than pleased, however, as she appraised the young woman. 'You are very tall.'

Lizzie smiled and bowed her head in agreement.

'And very pale.'

'Mother!' interjected Pavel, but with a suggestion of patience, which hinted that his mother's direct approach wasn't a surprise.

'Well, it is true. Too pale and too tall to be good for you, I should think.'

'Mother, please! You are going to behave, aren't you?'

'It is not my business to behave. It is the business of these young so-called women you waste your time with to behave. I see absolutely no point in you spending quite so much time with this so-called woman when you clearly have no interest in marrying her.' Amalia brushed imaginary crumbs off her chest and pulled a little at her blouse and skirt to avoid having to look at Lizzie while she insulted her.

'Mother, really, you're embarrassing me!' Pavel shook his head, but was still grinning broadly.

'Well, really, wasting the best years of your life tinkering about with bits of metal when you should be settling down and starting a family.' She frowned at Lizzie. 'Not with the likes of this so-called young woman. Too tall, too pale for my taste.'

Lizzie laughed loudly and reached out to squeeze Amalia's hand. 'Don't you worry, Signora Berlardi. Sadly for me, I'm too tall and too pale for Pavel's taste as well. But I do happen to know he has his eye on an extremely delightful young woman who is just about the right height and just about the right colouring to do justice to your handsome son.' This she said in an exaggerated whisper, with the express purpose of allowing Pavel to hear.

'You be careful what you tell my mother. She'll be quizzing every young woman in Vallerosa and they'll all be running for miles. You can see why I can't take a woman home to meet her, can't you? If I do ever find one to put up with me, I shan't be letting her near my mother until after the wedding day. She'll never walk up the aisle with me if she's met her first.'

It became clear, as he chatted, that Signora Berlardi was no longer listening. Instead, she was scowling at Feraguzzi and Posti, who now stood half in the shadows, half in the sunlight, still in deep discourse but now only a few metres away, just at the far reach of Dario's bar.

Lizzie and Pavel turned their heads to follow the direction of Amalia's glare.

The men, too, felt its power as, in unison, they turned to face her. That they were steeling themselves was evident, and after a prolonged pause they emerged out of the shadows and walked, in step, across the corner of the piazza to join the rest of the party at the table.

Both men attempted to shake Amalia's hand, but she kept her arms folded firmly across her chest. She looked them each in the eye, in turn, but there was no softening in her expression.

Pavel's mouth twitched at the corners. He was delighted to see his mother's fire restored, for perhaps the first time since her husband's death. And restored it was.

'So, Signor Posti, you look very much older. The years have been unkind to you.'

Rolando Posti bowed his head and absorbed the insult with no discernible trace of hurt. 'In contrast, you are every bit as beautiful as I remember.' He allowed his eyes to travel across the face of Amalia Berlardi, luxuriating in the journey, taking in and evidently admiring every feature.

Pavel squinted at his mother, and looked closely at Posti. Was he being facetious? He was not going to allow his mother to be insulted, regardless of any history between them. But Posti's face bore no trace of derision. Instead, he gazed at her with such adoration that Pavel and Lizzie immediately felt superfluous. Feraguzzi seemed enchanted by the exchange.

Pavel and Lizzie busied themselves ordering tea from Piper and tried hard not to appraise either Posti or the object of his affection too closely.

'I am surprised an old man like you can go that far back in his memory.'

'I remember every detail, as if it were yesterday.'

'You remember it with the twisted recall of a senile man in that case.'

'No, my mind has not let me down. And when I look at you now, it is still as though you are plunging a dagger through my heart.'

'Well, clearly I didn't plunge it deeply enough if you are still making moon eyes at me.'

'The pain you inflicted could not have been greater. The wound could not have been more severe. That I lived at all was only so that I could see you again, and make you smile at me once more.'

'Smile at you? Why should I ever do that? I made my choice when I married my Luciano. And there was never a better man in the whole of Vallerosa.'

'You made your choice, and it nearly killed me. You chose a mechanic over a future government minister! Think what you missed out on! A life of power? Of luxury? My pension alone is a greater dowry than your clockmaker could ever have delivered.'

'My Luciano could dance like a prince.'

'But I was a man on the way up!'

'My Luciano could recite poetry from his head. And he did, almost every night of our married lives.'

'But I was to amount to something!'

'My Luciano was very good with his hands.'

Posti looked down at his own hands and paused, tracing the liver spots on his left hand with the thumb of his right. 'I am still very good with my hands,' he said softly.

Lizzie could feel her colour rising. She was aghast at bearing witness to this exchange. Pavel was stirring spoonful after spoonful of honey into his tea, even though usually he drank it without. Feraguzzi, meanwhile, continued to enjoy the exchange, nodding and smiling with each insult and compliment.

'You might be good with your hands. But your mind is rotten through and through.'

'My mind is good and sharp.'

'If your mind were good or sharp, you would not have fired my Luciano. That was very, very low.'

'He had it coming! He had been sneering at me for too many years. That man! I despaired, eventually. You know,

251

he would insist on coming to collect his contract from me personally each year, when he could easily have had my under-secretary deliver it. But, oh, no, he liked to see me squirm. And he would always mention you. He couldn't just come, like a decent man, sign his contract and leave with dignity. No, no. It was "I must hurry, my wife is waiting for me"; "I must run, my wife doesn't like me to be away from her for too long"; "I must be quick – it is siesta time and you know what that means for me and my wife." I tell you, he was a cruel man.'

'My Luciano was not a cruel man. He was probably just telling the truth. I didn't like to wait for him. I never liked him to be away from me for too long. And siesta time always was our favourite time together.'

'He was being sadistic. He knew it and I knew it. Anyway, he might have won you in the battle, but I won justice in the war.'

'You fired him. That must have made you feel like a big man.'

'No, I never fired him. This man fired him.'

Feraguzzi, who had been smiling benevolently up until this moment, realized he had just been drawn into the argument. 'I only fired him because you told me to. I was quite happy with the clocks and the way the contracts were handled. I fired him because you said it was a matter of honour, and I never question honour.'

'Honour, pooh! It was a matter of spite!' spat Amalia.

'You are so incredibly beautiful, Amalia. You make my heart melt.'

'You know, Posti, my Luciano has only been gone for two years.'

'You still set the table for him at night?'

'Of course. He must have somewhere to return if he feels lost. It is only two years.'

'But you are still a beautiful young woman. You must have needs.'

Amalia glowered. Her arms were still staunchly folded against her chest. Pavel stirred another spoonful of honey into his now cold tea, watching the whorls and patterns with increased concentration. Lizzie examined her fingernails in minute detail and wondered whether it might be considered rude to leave. Feraguzzi kept his eyes on Amalia, awaiting her response.

'I expect my son here to work for the government once again. I expect him to have the contracts renewed in his favour. I expect him to earn enough money to employ an apprentice and I expect you to look after him as though he were gold dust.'

'And what may I expect in return?'

'You may expect to dance with me at midsummer.'

Amalia scraped her chair back, stood up and beckoned to Pavel to accompany her. Pavel got to his feet, extended his arm for her to hold and, together, mother and son left the bar and walked slowly into the alley between the two bars.

Rolando Posti never took his eyes off her until she had disappeared altogether.

He sighed loudly and mopped his brow with a handkerchief. 'What a woman!' he exclaimed, to nobody in particular.

'What a woman indeed!' echoed Feraguzzi, nodding enthusiastically.

Lizzie was incredulous. 'So that's it? That's the government in action? You take a contract away because you're broken-hearted and you give it back on the promise of a dance?'

'Not just a dance, a dance at midsummer – that is altogether more promising. I do believe I will win back the affection of the love of my life.'

'But this is outrageous! You can't act like that – you just can't. Surely there must be some procurement process! How do you know that Pavel will charge the right amount? How do you know the government will get a fair deal? How do you know Pavel can even do it? I mean, he's great, don't get me wrong, but don't you have a responsibility to the rest of the ministers and to the people of the country to be more thorough?' Lizzie's colour had risen and her eyes burned with anger. She looked from one minister to the other, unable to believe the exchange she had just witnessed.

'And you,' she spluttered, 'Roberto, you're the finance minister! Is that how you work all the time? With absolutely no integrity whatsoever? I thought our politicians were bad, but this is completely atrocious!'

Feraguzzi looked at her quizzically. 'I have no idea what you're getting upset about.' He beckoned to Piper for a fresh round of tea.

'Whatever I just sat through is what upset me. I thought you had more about you than that.'

He took his time to answer, prepared his tea, loosened his collar, smiled at other people as they came and went, complimented Piper on the quality of the tea, commended him on the little sweet biscuits that had been sent out to accompany it and eventually looked Lizzie squarely in the face. 'You wanted the clock fixed?'

'Yes – I mean, we all did, didn't we?'

'And it seems to me that this is now very much more likely to happen than at any time in decades.'

'But surely there must be a process.'

'You wanted the clock fixed. The clock is going to be fixed. Posti wanted a second chance at courting the love of his life. It looks like he's going to get it. And Amalia? All Amalia wants is to dance in the arms of a man who adores her.' Feraguzzi nodded at Posti, who was still looking at the entrance to the alley into which Amalia had disappeared, as if her essence were still lingering there, awaiting his arms. His eyes held a dreamy, faraway look and it was clear that none of this talk of clocks was making an impression upon him at all.

'And that's it?'

'It would appear so. And we should thank you.'

'You should?'

'Yes, you have brokered a peace deal that looked unlikely, if not impossible. I think, Miss Holmesworth, you have the makings of a great diplomat. But I don't believe our work here is done. Perhaps we can extract just a little more fun from this clock business …'

'Fun?'

'I have the inkling of a rather fine idea, but we must find Angelo and enlist his help. And we must move to the other bar. The biscuits are pleasant, but drinking with the peasants is beginning to make me feel a little queasy.'

Lizzie laughed, signalled to Piper that she needed to settle up and took her leave, chasing after the minister.

CHAPTER 27

In Which the Piece Fits

AFTER A ROUND OF TEA that seamlessly became a round of beer, the very vaguest outline of a plan had been agreed upon. In order to get it into action, it was imperative that Pavel was happy to co-operate. The scheme was exciting, Lizzie was sure, so it was with a degree of trepidation that she set off to enlist the support of the young clockmaker.

She approached his shop anxiously, rubbing her wrist where her watch normally lay and wondering whether the scheme she had just engineered was a good thing or a bad thing. She could hear him whistling before she had even reached the shop-front and, at this, her heart sang just a little bit. 'Pavel?'

No sooner had she ducked through the doorway than Pavel pounced on her, kissing her cheek noisily and lifting her off the ground, albeit by just a few centimetres.

'Put me down, you'll hurt yourself!' she squealed.

Elio, who had been busy in the workshop, rushed out to perform a similar ritual, kissing Lizzie's other cheek. 'You did it! We are fixing the clock!'

'And can you do it? I mean, it's an enormous task, isn't it?'

Pavel disappeared into his workshop, Elio and Lizzie trailing after him. With surprising agility, the clockmaker used one hand to vault onto his workbench and, using the shelves on the wall to steady himself, walked slowly along, examining jar after jar of unlabelled contents. Eventually, just as he was running out of workbench he reached up on tiptoe and wrestled a small glass jar from behind a cluster of larger containers. Holding it to his chest, he leaped to the floor.

Lizzie smiled at his enthusiasm, with absolutely no idea of whether he had heard her question.

Pavel shook the jar, forcing the smaller items to jiggle their way to the top. 'Aha!' he cried. Using his thumb and forefinger as pincers, he prised out a very small copper-coloured object. This he held up to the light for both wide-eyed onlookers to inspect. 'Sometimes, my friends, to make even the biggest things happen, all it takes is one very small cog.'

Leaving Elio to mind the shop, Lizzie and Pavel headed back to the bar to discuss the clock repairs and to allow Pavel to consider the added layers of complication that the newly hatched plan would inevitably bring.

AS PAVEL POURED A BEER and ate a handful of crisps, Lizzie chatted excitedly, thrilled by the progress they were making.

'You,' Pavel said, 'deserve thanks of the very highest order. I will go to church on Sunday and your name will be whispered in the ear of the Boss. Of that you can be sure.'

'Church? You're religious? I've heard the bells ring and I've often spied a priest in the bar next door but I hadn't got the impression that religion figures too highly here.'

'I go to church for the same reasons that everyone goes to church,' said Pavel, with a dismissive wave of his hand. 'When I feel guilty, when I feel grateful and when it is important to have my devotion witnessed. But other than the guilt or the gratitude, the births, deaths and marriages that, of course, must be honoured, I feel no need to remind God of my existence. And I don't need any further reminder of His existence than to breathe the Vallerosan air. Look around you. This piazza is the altar of a very holy place. When we step out into it each day, it's impossible not to give thanks.'

Lizzie frowned a little, wanting a label to help her understand the doctrine and perhaps the people a little more. 'But you do believe in God? What God? What religion do you practise?'

'Does He need a name? To have faith that tomorrow the sun will rise over the mountains is to have faith in God. To know unconditionally that there is a higher purpose.'

Lizzie smiled. 'Surely knowing that the sun will rise tomorrow is just believing in science.'

Pavel ignored her playful rebuttal. 'No, Lizzie. Believing in science is to know that one day the sun won't rise. Believing in God is to trust that it will.' He removed the cigarette from behind his ear, contemplated it for a moment, then replaced it with exaggerated resignation. 'Enough of God, the attention will go to His head. Let's show our thanks with another beer, shall we?'

They clinked their empty bottles, and as Piper hurried over to take their order, God was once again held responsible for the town's recent good fortune. The barman muttered some thanks of his own under his breath.

CHAPTER 28

In Which There's Education in Moderation

SERGIO HAD RETIRED ONCE MORE to his study where he sat at his desk, the fingers of both hands woven together and propping up his chin. He faced forward, the notebook beneath him winking its blankness at him in accusation. The humming was intense and he was experiencing a new sensation, a prickling in his back and neck that seemed to foretell of some other, rarer, strain of impending disaster.

Angelo burst into the room. 'We're just going to let them walk all over us, are we?'

'The students?'

'Students? No. Of course not the students. The Americans.'

Sergio continued to stare steadfastly ahead. 'Angelo. Please do something for me. Go and look out of the window.'

The chief of staff opened his mouth to speak but, sensing a cooling down after the previous row and, perhaps, a better opportunity to talk about the Americans rationally, he walked up to the window. He looked out.

'What do you see?

'I see the Piazza Rosa. The clock tower is in scaffolding again, the bars look reasonably busy—'

'I mean do you see anything *ominous*?'

'Well, there's a preternaturally large crowd around our rent-a-royal but I wouldn't say that's particularly ominous. Depends if she's kept her word and, being British, I suspect she has. But nothing else, no.'

'Good. Good.' Sergio's shoulders relaxed a little and he allowed himself to roll them and, in doing so, lose the prickling feeling that had spelled doom.

Angelo took the more convivial atmosphere as an opportunity to begin again, this time on a lighter note. 'What was that all about, in there?' He nodded his head in the direction of the conference room.

'My policy, Angelo. You helped me draft it, didn't you? What did I call it? Education through Saturation, wasn't it? Surely that can't have been it.'

'Hmm. I know what you mean. Sounds a bit on the wet side now, doesn't it? Education through a good dunking, held securely by the scruff of the neck.'

Sergio allowed himself the smallest of laughs.

'I sense a U-turn, Sergio. Are we not liking the education policy any more?'

'No, I don't think we are. These are grown men, Angelo. They deserve better. I mean, what are their prospects?'

'Their prospects? Well, realistically, their prospects are to replace their fathers. That's all any of us can really hope to do. And, on the basis that our population doesn't seem to be expanding, that's a sustainable policy.'

'And just replacing your father. Is that a good prospect, do you think?'

'Depends on who your father is. If he's the President of Vallerosa, yes, I'd suggest your prospects would be pretty fine. If he's Franco, maybe things are a bit gloomy in the opportunity stakes.'

'I suppose you're right. A U-turn might be a bit strong. I was thinking that perhaps a subtle change of direction might be beneficial. Our men deserve a little more than Education through Suffocation.'

'Education in Moderation?'

'Exactly. Education in Moderation. Opportunity in Profusion.'

'Tea in Infusion?' suggested Angelo, glad to have his sparring partner back.

'I think so. Just a smidgeon of something in mine, thank you.'

Sergio replaced Angelo at the window as his aide went to pour the tea. 'Looks like the scaffolding's coming down again. That blasted clock, every time I look out of the window it seems to jeer at me.'

'I know what you mean. But fixing it is a pretty small point on the agenda when you consider the other things you need to deal with. What, for instance, are we going to do about our American friends? I thought that was the purpose of the meeting today.'

'It was, it was. But I was distracted. We'll do it tomorrow. I'll call a meeting, tell them I'm concerned about

263

security issues and suggest we employ the services of our friends at Client Opted Inc. to investigate the possibilities. Just that. I'm not going to scare anyone rigid about nuclear deterrents and whatnot. It's not like we've signed up to anything as such. Just a bit of consultancy.'

'Like the last bit of consultancy that's still ongoing all these years later?'

'Granted. But we got somewhere eventually, didn't we? Our country is, apparently, in better shape. We've pulled a farming industry out of the hat. There are plenty of job opportunities there now, opportunities that didn't exist before. And we'll have some cash coming into our economy …'

'Which we can spend on more consultancy.'

Sergio peered keenly out of the window once more. 'Do you sense unrest in the country? Is there any thought in your mind that there might be a movement towards revolution?'

'A revolution, no.' Angelo smiled. 'A small amount of belligerence from a few disgruntled citizens, perhaps, but what do you imagine they're going to revolt for, exactly?'

'Jobs? Opportunities? Prospects?'

'I don't sense we're on the eve of revolution, but if you lose the plot completely and put the money that ought to be going to help create jobs, widen opportunities and increase prospects into a second-hand gun, you might just have a revolution on your hands and I might be the one who starts it.'

Sergio looked round sharply, and relaxed on seeing his friend's face, which hinted at none of the animosity his words had suggested.

'You're doing fine. We're doing fine,' urged Angelo. 'And if something's spooked you that you're not sharing with me, then take it as a sign. A kick up the backside from the anti-complacency police.'

'Mm. Complacency's no good.'

'How about No Vacancies for Complacency at next week's rally?' suggested Angelo.

'Yes, that might …' He saw Angelo's face. 'Oh, I see, you jest.'

'Yes, Sergio. I jest. But, seriously, we need something up our sleeve for the election, even if it's just to give you the confidence to stop feeling sorry for yourself and start thinking like a president again. Something that will make people take note.'

'How about the girl? Could we use her, do you think?'

Angelo dropped into an accent that he had absorbed while chatting to their English visitor. He had studied languages voraciously for much of his life, but more recently he had been paying particular attention to the little nuances that differentiated her use of the language compared to, say, their American visitors'. 'Yes, absolutely we should. I mean, to have a royal condescend to visit us all the way from Queen Elizabeth's Great Britain, it would seem almost impolite not to use her, would it not?'

'Indecent,' quipped Sergio, a willing partner in the game.

'Quite,' finished Angelo.

CHAPTER 29

In Which the Chief of Staff Plots

WHEN LIZZIE NEXT MADE A VISIT to the Piazza Rosa in search of a drink, she now faced an even greater quandary. Her initial plan, to frequent each bar equally, had seemed fine as a theoretical exercise but now, having befriended Pavel and Elio at Il Toro Rosso, she feared that to return to Il Gallo Giallo would snub Piper and her new friends. The alternative, to visit Piper's bar again, might run a greater risk still: that she would offend Dario, and possibly the upper echelons of the country's hierarchy, with whom she felt she was beginning to make real headway.

The problem, seemingly insurmountable, forced her usually sprightly step to a crawl, and it was while she was nudging forward in the direction of both bars, still with no clear destination in mind, that she heard hurried footsteps behind her.

'Might I join you?' It was a dishevelled Angelo, who decelerated abruptly to fall in with her impossibly slow pace.

'Lovely. I was heading out for a drink. A few days here and I've already fallen into a routine.'

'We all do here. Routine is part of our very essence. Come on, let me buy you one.'

So the problem was solved. Angelo made his way unreservedly towards Il Gallo Giallo, and while the bar was unusually busy for a mid-week afternoon, a few drinkers seemed mysteriously to evaporate, vacating a prime central table by the time the two visitors had arrived at their destination.

They sat down and Angelo frowned. 'Something's different,' he said, looking around him.

'The tablecloths, perhaps? I don't remember seeing them yesterday.'

'Of course! Tablecloths. How very …' he surveyed the bar once again and noted that a white cloth was draped on every table '… unusual. And pleasant.'

He smiled up at Dario, who now stood nervously at the ready, notepad in hand and an anxious smile on his face. 'Marvellous, Dario, very nice indeed. I must say I think the tablecloths are a good addition. It looks classier somehow.'

'Thank you, sir. May I get you a drink? Tea? Beer?'

'And table service! This is an honour indeed.'

As they placed their orders and exchanged pleasantries, Lizzie stole a glance at Il Toro Rosso, keen to see if her friends were sitting there, and if they were, whether they seemed perturbed by her not joining them. Her view was blocked by the glowering figure of Piper who, even when she raised a hand in greeting, held fast his stance, which radiated disgust and disappointment in equal measure. And just in case there had been any room for misinterpretation he turned, with a dramatic toss of his head, and busied himself wiping tables, regardless of whether they were occupied or not.

Next to her, Angelo was speaking and she turned back to hear him repeat his question. 'I was saying, how have you found your stay so far?'

'Well, I like it very much. This is certainly one of the most beautiful countries I've ever been to. I can't get over the valley and the houses, this gorgeous piazza and the government buildings. It's all so, so perfect, really.'

'And what about the citizens? Have you been treated well?'

'Oh, absolutely. Everyone has been very kind. Mosconi took me on a tour across to the east side of the river to see your Museum of Things Left Behind, which was …'

'Curious?'

'Yes. And charming. I'm almost tempted to leave something behind deliberately so that it will find its way into the collection!'

'Of course that might be possible, but there is a very different quality between the things that are genuinely misplaced and those that are not. There is an air of the forlorn about abandoned articles. I cannot go into the museum without feeling very, very sad. It moves me.'

Lizzie checked that Angelo was being serious but there was no trace of irony. Aware that the conversation was turning, she asked brightly, 'Why do you always come to this bar, not the other?'

'I have never thought about it. Tradition? Habit? Heritage, even? I had my very first drink here with my father and I have never stopped coming. It was such a deeply ingrained habit for him too, that I suspect that – even after death – he probably pops in for his afternoon tea or a late-evening drink. If that's the case, then I think he would be happy to see me here, drinking still with his friends and the sons of his friends. He's left his imprint and I fit into it very comfortably. He was a man of habit, my father. I don't know what he would make of this, though …' He trailed off as Dario placed the tea on the table, followed by a small selection of china bowls containing nuts, crisps and olives on sticks. 'Sometimes I think the world has gone mad.' Angelo glanced around him: the men with whom he had drunk every day of his adult life were chatting amiably and dipping their hands into similar dishes of snacks or waving olives at the end of sticks to emphasize a point.

'And your mother? Is she still alive?'

'Very much so.'

'And what does she do?'

'Do? Well, she does what mothers do, of course.'

'Which is?'

'Oh, you know, the usual. You must meet her one day – she'd like that very much. Come for dinner.'

'I'd love to. What about the rest of your family? Brothers, sisters?'

'A younger brother, a student at the moment. I would have loved to have a sister. Wouldn't we all?' he said wistfully. 'But it was not to be. And I consider myself as having two brothers. Sergio and I grew up together so he is a brother to me really. Younger in years, but he had to do so much growing up when his own father died that he somehow overtook me. He has the weight of the world on his shoulders.'

'He certainly has the air of a man with worries. And what about Sergio? Is he married?'

'Not yet, no. His schedule hasn't really allowed it, but I am hopeful that after the elections are out of the way he might turn his attention to this matter. A wife would be excellent news for Sergio personally and, of course, a wedding is always good for the country.'

'And you? Is your schedule too busy to make room for wife hunting?'

'Well, it's a matter of priorities. Sergio's needs are greater than mine at the moment, so we will look for him first. When he's happily wed, I suspect I might be tempted to settle down myself. But I must be realistic …'

'Well, you're a young man still. You're good-looking and you've got a great job. You'd make a fabulous catch for some lucky woman. They should be queuing up for you!'

Angelo shook his head sadly. 'That certainly won't be happening. But,' he said, brightening, 'we'll see, shall we? Enough of me. What about you? You have a couple of days yet before your big performance at the weekend's festivities. Have you thought about what you might want to say?'

'Say?'

'Oh, didn't Sergio mention it? We thought it might be appropriate for you to make a speech at the midsummer *festa.*' The laboured innocence in Angelo's voice hinted that he knew very well this would be news to Lizzie.

'No, he didn't mention it.' Lizzie pouted, and leaned forward to whisper, 'In fact, he promised that the very most I would have to do to reinforce my so-called royal status was parade in front of his people at state occasions. I don't equate parading with speaking.'

'But you might consider it?' questioned Angelo, with a teasing smile, and speaking at a normal volume to entice Lizzie to do the same.

But, still whispering, Lizzie was resolute. 'Absolutely not. As long as I'm here, just visiting, then if people want to mistake me for somebody they think they would like me to be, that's their problem. If your president chooses to mislead them deliberately, that's his prerogative. But as soon as I actively engage in the deceit, don't you see I'd be lying to them? Impersonating a member of the royal family – there are laws against that in my country. It's probably treasonous. I could be beheaded for it!'

'My dear, I had no idea.' Angelo put a comforting hand on her arm. 'Your country still practises the death penalty? That is indeed a terrible and barbaric thing.'

'Well, not exactly. I'm not sure that the beheading thing is accurate. But I wasn't joking about the treason. I can't do that. And even without the law prohibiting it, well, I'd feel guilty. Embarrassed. Disloyal. The people I've met so far are taking me into their confidence and I'd feel like I was betraying them.' Lizzie glanced at the room around her, aware that other conversations had dropped to a whisper or dissolved altogether.

Now Angelo leaned in and spoke quietly into her ear. 'Don't you think that the betrayal might be greater the other way around? They are taking you into their confidence because of who they think you are. If you were then to reveal yourself to be somebody quite different, they might feel much more cheated. Hierarchy in this country is incredibly important. The different strata are not enforced but naturally sustain themselves, and we have learned through many centuries of peaceful existence that to remain among your own is a way of perpetuating that peace. Envy is a very destructive force. If you can learn to live without resenting the lifestyle that others lead, you will be much happier. As such, those from the higher-ranking echelons are naturally respected as people of power. If people are befriending you, it is because it is the respectful thing to do. I wouldn't be surprised if the tablecloths have come out for your benefit. You are an important visitor to them. Don't deny them that little pleasure.'

'I don't intend to – and I'm certainly not going to break the promise I made to you. But to ask me to promote the lie, that's going a step too far, isn't it?'

'I don't think so. Imagine that the power you have, the real power, is to give pleasure to the people of this country. If you are blessed with this gift, don't you have a duty to exercise it as completely as possible? If you have it within you to make a few more people even happier by your words, I think that would be a very noble thing to do. Not at all deceitful.'

'But I'm not a speechwriter. I wouldn't know what to say.'

'Come for supper tomorrow, meet my mother. She'll inspire you. Then we'll sit down somewhere quietly and prepare something that you'll feel proud to say and the people here will feel happy to hear.'

'You'll help me?'

'Absolutely. It would be my pleasure.' Angelo raised his glass in Lizzie's direction and took a long, cooling slug of his beer.

CHAPTER 30

In Which the Troubles Escalate

SERGIO AWOKE AN HOUR BEFORE his alarm was due to ring after a restless night's sleep full of disturbing dreams packed with ominous symbols and portentous imagery. There wasn't a broken ladder or a flooding river into which he couldn't read the impending uprising of his people and subsequent collapse of his government. As if his troubled thoughts weren't painful enough, he had also to contend with the relentless scolding and the wagging finger of his father. That crooked digit, stained nicotine yellow, persisted in its disapproval throughout his sleeping and waking hours. He groaned and stumbled, bleary-eyed, out of bed in search of tea, limping into the gloom of his study and rubbing his eyes as he tried to dispel his nightmares. Shying away from the unwelcome glare that the electric lighting would undoubtedly bring, he instead drew his curtains to allow the first glimpses of dawn to herald his day. He froze. Before he had even examined the piazza properly, the silhouette jumped out at him. Still with one hand gripping a fistful of curtain, the other raised in some unfinished task, he stood and stared.

From the gloom beneath him, the silhouettes quickly took form as his eyes got used to the dull morning light. Not one but two protesters, each armed with a placard. As yet, they did not appear to be fully committed to action because they were chatting quietly to each other. Aware that any further movement might rouse them, Sergio lowered his left hand and gradually helped the curtain fall back into place. He took a step back and swung around, his back to the window. He exhaled slowly, then counted his breaths to restore calm. Then he peeped nervously around the edge of the curtain again but it was still too dark and the placards were not quite at the right angle for him to read the words that inevitably accused him of some heinous shortcoming. He looked at his watch. Not yet six o'clock. If one idle protester during the hallucinogenic heat of the siesta sun had not spelled disaster, then two before dawn certainly did. And what if it wasn't just two? What if these men were the early risers, the advance guard, and were planning to assemble a whole piazza full of angry young men, all baying for their president's blood?

His chest hurt. He put a hand to his heart and wondered if it might oblige him by stopping altogether. That would certainly allow him to avoid the humiliation he was about to face. He waited for a few moments, to be sure that death wasn't about to come to his rescue, then shed his pyjamas and deftly slipped into yesterday's trousers, shirt and braces. On the way to the door, he remembered socks and shoes. 'Must retain some sort of dignity,' he muttered to himself, feeling far from dignified.

The two men in the piazza, arguing softly over the time that their protest should begin in order to attract the appropriate attention, were not aware of the downstairs door opening or of their leader tiptoeing gingerly down the path to open the gate. It was only when they heard, 'You two, here now,' hissed from the shadows that they simultaneously dropped their placards with a clatter.

The president slapped his forehead with the palm of his hand to indicate their complete stupidity and signalled that they should follow him. 'Quietly, please, and bring your things with you,' he commanded, aware that, if he continued with such superb efficiency, he'd have them out of harm's way in no time at all.

The two men followed him on the same journey that Woolf had recently made and the passage was exactly as he had described it. Up the stairs, down the corridor, and then they were being ushered into the president's expansive private chambers.

Pointing them each to a chair, Sergio set about boiling the kettle and making himself a cup of tea. He had the beginnings of a crushing headache and he needed to be able to think clearly. 'Tea?'

'Yes, we're here about the tea.'

'You're here about the … No, no, I mean would you like a cup of tea with me?'

The men eyed each other, unsure of the protocol. They settled on a mumbled 'No, thank you,' and sat up straight in their chairs, mustering a confrontational pose, made fractionally harder by the hospitality they were now being offered.

'Jobs, I suppose. You're concerned about your prospects, are you?'

One of the men picked his placard from the floor, raising it just high enough to be read. The president picked out the carefully painted words. '*Servate theam nostram!*' said one.

The other raised his. '*Reddite nobis nostros hortos!*' said the other.

Sergio rubbed his eyes tiredly. 'Students?'

'No, farmers,' muttered one protester, a note of indignation betraying the insult he felt at the error.

'But your sign is written in Latin. Latin tends to be the domain of the educated.'

'We had help.'

'Woolf, I presume.' Sergio rolled his eyes to indicate his disdain for his adversary.

The man on the right, the owner of the 'Save our tea' placard, nodded, just as the second shook his head. They looked sharply at each other, glaring.

Sergio tutted. 'Oh, don't worry about protecting him. I wasn't born yesterday. Woolf got his way by protesting and put you up to this. What's he trying to do? Right the world's wrongs through bill boards?'

Both protesters stared sullenly at their dirty fingernails.

'Well, who are you?' the president said and, in a weary repetition of the routine he'd adopted with Woolf, he reached for his pen.

'Stefano,' mumbled one.

'Salvatore,' mumbled the second.

Sergio eyed them carefully, taking in their utilitarian work clothes, their workers' hands and strong frames, rendered weak and unassuming by the splendid surroundings they now found themselves in. 'Come on, then. Out with it. What exactly are you after?'

Stefano muttered, 'We want to save our tea, sir,' unable to meet his president's eye.

'And what makes you think your tea needs saving? It's never been better. In fact,' the president said, dropping his voice to a loud whisper and leaning in to share a secret, 'I can tell you in complete confidence, and well ahead of the official announcement next week, that our tea quota has been met and that our tea industry is burgeoning.' He relaxed in his chair, triumphantly.

Now Stefano looked his president in the eye. 'We want you to save *our* tea. We've heard rumours, terrible rumours, that the tea is all to be sold. Without tea we have nothing.'

'Well, I think you're being a little dramatic. Without tea you have less tea. What you have in its place is an income and you can buy anything you want.'

The men were clearly confused.

Sergio smiled patiently. 'I must say, it's a little early in the morning for a lesson in economics but I can see I'm going to have to deliver one. The requisitioning of the tea is for your own good. We are entering a global market and, as a responsible government, we are ensuring that we are positioned as a country with something to offer. You want prospects, don't you?'

The men nodded.

'And opportunities?'

They nodded again.

'Well, that's what I'm giving you. A better future! We're entering a supply chain and, as with any supply chain, the person with the goods to offer is in a very strong negotiating position. We sell our tea and with that we can buy anything we want. I can understand that you might have become sentimentally attached to the crops you grow, but you must trust your government and understand that cash is, arguably, the best crop of all.'

'Will we still have tea to drink?'

Sergio chuckled. 'Of course you'll have tea to drink. We will only sell what is surplus to our requirements. And you will have enough money to buy all the tea you could dream of! Of that you have my word. Does that make you feel better?'

Stefano frowned but nodded, and continued the examination of his fingernails.

'And you? What's your concern?' asked Sergio of Salvatore, more gently now he knew he had the upper hand.

Salvatore raised his eyes shyly upwards to meet the good-natured enquiry of his president. 'We want to save our gardens. They're being taken from us. We no longer have our own land.'

'Don't be ridiculous! Of course you still have your gardens. We simply issued an instruction to plant them with tea to ensure we meet our collective targets. The gardens are still yours. They belong to your families. Nobody is going to take them away from you.'

Salvatore looked at Sergio more combatively now, wriggling his bulky body into a more commanding stance in his chair. 'They are no longer our gardens if we are not free to choose what we plant. They become the government's gardens then.'

Sergio weighed this up in his mind, giving it proper consideration. 'You were not coerced into tea growing, we merely asked for a pulling together of the nation's efforts and were glad and heartened by the enthusiastic response. If you feel we were being heavy-handed, then forgive me. That was not my intention. Where do you live?'

'Upper north-west. Eleven hundred metres.'

'Ah, yes, the start of the prime tea-growing land. Well, young man, if you're lucky enough to be blessed with a garden big enough to grow tea you are fortunate indeed. And if I had been born with such luck I would feel very guilty if I complained about it, particularly if I did so in public. How do you think that will make those at the lower levels feel, those who can't grow tea at all or who haven't even got a garden? They would think you were a very selfish creature.'

Salvatore bit his lip, knowing full well that the circumstances of his birth were, indeed, all that separated him from his less fortunate peers.

'And if they got wind of the idea that you were dissatisfied with your beautiful big garden, do you not think they might ask to swap with you? What would you feel then, if you sat in, say, the lower south-west with no garden at all, just a window box full of tomatoes? Would you feel better then?'

A frown played across Salvatore's forehead, but he'd lost his argument before he'd ever started. And suddenly, amid the splendour of his president's furniture, he couldn't quite remember what his argument was. There would be tea to drink, his president said. There would be money, too. He could grow whatever he wanted, provided they met their quota. And he was a lucky man to have a garden. He felt light-headed.

Sergio, whose spirits were rising in direct proportion to the sinking of his opponents', felt cheery enough to try to perk his visitors up a little. 'Now, gentlemen, what you probably require is a cup of tea yourselves. Am I right?'

They nodded.

'Imagine,' said the president, with a benevolent smile, as he poured the brew, 'this tea we are drinking might well be the very tea you grew. That should make you very, very proud!'

The men beamed, and with the lip-smacking, grimacing, puckering that always accompanied the first swig of the day the three sat and slurped the reviving liquid from the president's dainty china cups.

After they had left, without their placards, the president locked the door. Leaning against it, he breathed deeply. That had been incredibly close. He had pacified them, he felt sure, but somewhere out there somebody was stirring them to revolt. Not Woolf: Woolf was a pawn. And certainly not those two – they had barely put up a fight. But his feelings of impending disaster were now beginning to ring true. He crossed the room and opened the cupboard where he had put the first placard. Now he stacked the two new ones with it. He had to address the root cause of these grievances before they escalated out of control. He would have liked to speak to his ministers about it but they might sense weakness in him. And who knew? It was not out of the question that one was involved in the plot. Cellini had been uncharacteristically anxious. Yes, a plot to overthrow him! One of them was taking confidential information, state secrets, deliberately misleading the people, and now they were being stirred to revolt.

Angelo. He could talk it through with Angelo, perhaps. But, no, he should trust nobody at the moment. If there was indeed a widespread conspiracy to overthrow him he mustn't take any chances. It could be one man, it could be two. It could be all twelve under the guidance of Angelo himself. No, if he was going to defeat this evil, he had to act alone until he was very sure of himself.

CHAPTER 31

In Which Lizzie
Shares a Secret

TO ENTER ANGELO'S HOUSE, Lizzie had to bend almost double to fit through the small door. If she had felt tall next to the men she had so far befriended, then beside Angelo's mother she felt like a behemoth.

Nonna Ada was naturally diminutive but had also lost a good few inches through the rounding of her upper back. She was perfectly proportioned within her home, which, two or three streets above the Piazza Rosa, was still central enough to be considered a good address while perhaps lacking the grandeur of the lower levels. It appeared to have been built around her, with her stature in mind, and as such Lizzie felt uncomfortably tall and clumsy – even the teacup she was handed upon arrival struck her as smaller and daintier than necessary. She felt as if she had stumbled into the home of the Seven Dwarfs and might, at any moment, be chased out by an apple-bearing witch.

Angelo, by contrast, seemed to benefit from the change of scale. His low voice reverberated fetchingly and his frame, as he hugged his mother, seemed manlier than Lizzie had previously appreciated. She now sat perched on the front of her chair, trying to redirect some weight to her feet and away from the seat's wooden frame for fear of entering the realm of another fairy-tale and having to flee, leaving a broken chair and a bowl of uneaten porridge.

Upon arrival, Nonna Ada had spoken in faltering English as she had fussed around preparing tea and making her guest comfortable. But as soon as Angelo had removed himself from earshot, perhaps from the house altogether in response to some barked command from his mother, she fell into the much more accomplished form of the language, adopting the structured grammar used so widely among the Vallerosans.

'So. What have you learned about my country?'

Lizzie blushed a little, wrong-footed by her physical size. 'I like it very much. It's absolutely beautiful—'

Ada interrupted with a dismissive wave of her hand. 'Yes, yes, of course. But what have you *learned*?' She leaned forward in her chair expectantly.

Lizzie pondered the question. She'd thought she had learned quite a lot, but now, put on the spot, she wasn't sure that she had. She knew that there was a complex political system that involved an unelected dictator, the sort she had been taught to fear, but since her whispered conversation with him in his bathroom and the many cups of tea they had shared, she wasn't sure he was that sort of dictator after all.

'Perhaps I know less now than when I first arrived. I seem to be relearning all sorts of things at the moment.'

Ada nodded, enthused. 'You mean you are having to undo some of the assumptions you had already made about our country before you had arrived?'

'Yes. Quite. And now I'm not even quite sure on what grounds I had made those assumptions. There's so little written about your country that it should have been a blank canvas. Somehow I was expecting a bit more misery and subjugation.'

Again, Ada was pleased with her response, her face creasing into a tangled web of lines etched into her face through a lifetime of smiling. 'And that would have suited you, I presume?'

Lizzie sat forward in her chair as she forced herself to delve more deeply into her feelings for Vallerosa and her relationship to it. 'In a funny way, yes. I was very much hoping to do some charity work while I was here. The British are brought up to believe that everywhere they go the people they meet will be somehow inferior – financially, emotionally, culturally, religiously – and, as such, in need of our help. It's help we give generously and unstintingly but, here, in the context of Vallerosa, I'm rather embarrassed by the notion that I thought I might have something to offer you. Your country seems well organized, its people well looked after, and there's a lightness in your footsteps that I don't think I've ever encountered at home.'

Ada smiled kindly and gazed across the room at a space just beyond Lizzie. She cocked her head, as if listening to another conversation that only she could hear. 'A lightness, yes. That is a good observation.'

'And I suppose the biggest surprise to me is that this country has such a strong military and governmental presence – it hits you as soon as you arrive – but it doesn't seem to have a negative effect on the quality of life. I don't think I've ever encountered such a peaceful or welcoming place.'

Ada probed further: 'And why do you suppose that is?'

Lizzie thought for a few quiet beats. 'Until you asked, I hadn't really thought about it. It's hard to put my finger on it.'

Ada probed again: 'So what else have you learned about my country? Is there anything you've noticed particularly?'

'I feel … at ease. Which is a surprise, of course, because I must look like a freak to the people here. I tower over the men and I haven't seen another blonde since I arrived …' She trailed off as realization dawned.

'Go on …'

'Well, now I come to think of it, I've met just a couple of women since I've been here. I think you're only the third I've actually spoken to. On the whole everyone I've met since the moment I arrived has been a man. I've only come across men in the government, the bars, the shop-keepers, the students … all men. And yet – it's odd – it doesn't seem to feel oppressively masculine.'

Ada touched her heart with both hands, an expression of gratitude or relief fleetingly conveyed. 'So it seems you have grasped quite a lot about my country, more perhaps than you'd understood.'

Lizzie was now intrigued. 'So where are all the women? What do they do?'

Ada shrugged and looked down at her lap, unable now to meet Lizzie's eye with the same honest gaze she had unleashed when Lizzie had sat down. 'Oh, this and that. They do what women do.'

'That's funny – that's just what your son said. But what exactly do they do?'

Ada dropped her voice into a hoarse, theatrical whisper. 'Can I trust you?'

'Of course.' Lizzie leaned forward, too, until their foreheads were nearly touching.

'While the men play, the women run the country,' Ada said, with a conspiratorial smile.

'But … I saw no women in the parliament buildings, and the meetings I've sat in on so far have been attended only by men. Even the domestic roles seem to be played by men, from what I've seen.'

'Of course, but who says a country should be run by its government? The more a government has to do with running a country, the less well it will probably succeed. The women in this country make things happen that no amount of statute-writing can achieve. We keep the wheels greased.'

Lizzie was reminded of her own mother, who used to protest that her job of running the home, of keeping her father in order, was more important than his and that he couldn't even get himself to work on time without her help. She wondered if the behind-every-strong-man myth was perpetuated even here as a means for women to justify their supporting roles.

'You mean, by keeping the domestic side of life running smoothly, that enables the country to run smoothly?'

Lizzie posed, troubled by the feel of the argument on her lips.

'No. Not at all. The domestic side of life runs smoothly because we have it organized to do so, but we control all aspects of this country. Our secret? Our secret is to let the men think they run it. But look at it realistically. Do you think they could actually run a country from a bar?' She gauged Lizzie's response. 'No. I don't think so either.'

Lizzie laughed, uncertain of how seriously she should take the matriarch's words. But as she was relaxing into the evening, and even as she could hear the footsteps that suggested Angelo had returned, Ada leaned forward once again. 'And I'll let you into another secret. The reason we are heading for disaster?'

Lizzie's eyes widened, now ready to accept the poisoned apple.

'Because we're running out of women.'

At that moment, Angelo re-entered the room and, like a ray of sunshine, seemed to light it up, breaking the spell. Lizzie smiled gratefully at him, confused by the conversation and unsure of what she had heard or even understood.

'Time to eat. Come through.'

The two women stood up, Lizzie crooking her head to avoid the low beams. They filed down a tiled corridor and into a simple dining room where a table was set for five. Despite the empty chairs, they sat down. Angelo and Ada started pulling the lids off the pots and pans that filled the table.

Until that moment, Lizzie had lived on a staple of pasta accompanied by a simple meat or tomato sauce, with an occasional treat from Dario or Piper. Here, they feasted. Thin slivers of dry cured ham. Jar upon jar of sweet preserves and spicy pickles. A rich stew of wild boar enhanced with the strong, perfumed flavour of juniper. A rabbit pie with the lightest, flakiest pastry and the most delicate, tender filling. The predominantly brown palette of the spread disguised a range of exotic and delicious flavours, covering the full spectrum of tastes, from the earthiest, richest porcini to the lightest, sweetest accompaniments that captured the very essence of summer.

They ate heartily and talked rarely between plate after plate of the choicest morsels. Ada seemed to have lapsed into a more stilted version of English and Lizzie made no reference to their earlier conversation, restricting her comments instead to gushing enthusiasm in praise of a new flavour discovered or polite interest in the ingredients and their origin.

Angelo seemed uninterested in the food. He ate hungrily but with little deference. A few minutes after they had started the meal, his brother, Marco, joined them at the table. Having kissed the top of his mother's head, he nodded politely to Lizzie and took his place. Once he had piled his plate high, he leaned heavily on his left forearm while shovelling forkful after forkful into his mouth with his right hand. Every now and then he would use a finger to help load the fork even more ambitiously and, with virtually no conversation at all, he ate greedily while stealing furtive glances at Lizzie. When he had finished, he excused himself briskly, picked up his plate, fork and glass, then left the room.

The fifth table setting remained unused.

Once the table had been cleared, Angelo made his excuses to his mother and apologized, explaining that he and their guest had work to do. This was a signal for Ada to leave the room and now, the two of them alone, Angelo fetched paper and pencils.

'Angelo, I can't possibly think about this speech thingy. I'm absolutely stuffed. All I want to do is sleep now.'

He smiled but continued to scribble. 'Stately, commanding and – above all – positive. That's what we're after. How did you find my mother? Inspirational?'

'Yes. Absolutely.'

'Thought you might. Right, anything you feel like talking about in particular? Your reaction to the country? It would help us enormously if you could be very upbeat about your impressions and especially about the president. We need an ebullient reference to his hospitality and maybe a bit about how much you like some of the specifics. The museum – we're very proud of our museum so that would go down well. And the tea? Of course the tea. It's our national drink, obviously, so perhaps a mention of how delicious you find it and how much you wish you could get something similar at home ... That would serve a double purpose. You'll flatter the people and reiterate that there is a market for Vallerosan tea elsewhere.'

'There is?'

'Well, we're waiting to find out. Got a meeting with the American again tomorrow. He is supposed to tell us then exactly what sort of market he's found for us. Keep your fingers crossed. And don't forget the delicious pig. But don't favour an individual pig. There are several from each quadrant and it wouldn't do to offend some of the producers.'

'Angelo?'

'And the tipple. Perhaps you could take a glass with you to the podium and raise it. But don't drink it on stage. It wouldn't be good to see you choking. It's strong stuff. In fact, don't drink it at all. It would probably just about finish you off. Can't have that. Better still, take a glass of water to the stage and pretend to drink it. That way you won't offend anyone and you'll live to tell the tale, too.'

'Angelo?'

This time he paused and looked up.

'Why don't you just write my speech? I'm happy providing you're happy, and you've got a much better idea of what it should contain. If I think of anything specific, I'll just add it, shall I?'

Angelo, who was, after all, used to speech-writing in a non-collaborative way, was relieved. 'Excellent idea. Leave it to me. I'll make sure you get a final draft twenty-four hours in advance. That will give you plenty of time to practise your delivery. How long are you comfortable speaking for? Ten minutes? Fifteen? The crowd will feel they're getting better value if you can last that long.'

'Five minutes absolute tops.' She glared at him sternly. She wanted him to understand that she meant what she said. She underlined the finality of her stance by pushing her chair back and excusing herself from the table. Head held high, she walked off in search of Nonna Ada. But Angelo's mother had already disappeared: the small sitting room was empty, the fire in the grate had died to a few glowing embers and there was no sound coming from the kitchen. She called softly, but when there was no response she left by the front door and closed it quietly behind her. Stepping onto the cool, dark cobblestones of the alley she unwound herself gratefully to her full height and headed home.

CHAPTER 32

In Which the Ministers Measure Up

THE TWELVE MEN sat at the conference table, which was empty of everything but a scattering of pencils – though heavily laden with nervous expectation. They had, by silent consensus, decided to forgo the usual pre-meeting banter in favour of anxious throat-clearing, nervous pencil-twiddling and the occasional furtive exchange of worried frowns. The president's increasingly irrational behaviour had set them all on edge.

When, eventually, the president entered, all twelve sets of shoulders quickly slumped. It was immediately apparent that their leader's good humour had not returned and that they were in for another dark, disturbing episode of haphazard governance.

Before he had even sat down, Sergio barked his first question in the general direction of the table but intended for his minister of finance.

'I'd like a recap on spending. Divisionally.'

Roberto Feraguzzi responded immediately. He was an efficient man, frugal with words and sparing with small-talk. A direct question aimed at him with no preamble, while unfamiliar, was not an anathema, and he responded with an appropriate measure of forthright information combined with patient explanation to ensure that all present followed him.

'We have ten days left of our annual budget and would expect all figures to be close to a hundred per cent. In this context that means we have spent the full sum allocated one year ago. A lower figure suggests we are ahead of budget and will carry reserves forward to the next fiscal year. By contrast, a higher figure suggests we have over-spent and will have to cut next year's budget or borrow from those departments that have some money left.'

'Yes, yes. I think we're all very well aware of how an economy runs by now. The details.' Sergio was curt, his lip curled.

Feraguzzi was unperturbed. As he launched into his summary, the ministers sat up a little straighter, aware that they were about to receive the latest figures that demonstrated how effectively they had run their depart-ments. Each felt as if he was getting back a marked assign-ment and, just as within any classroom environment, there were the quietly smug ones clamouring to have their results publicized while others shied away from exposure, sending out silent prayers for a more favourable outcome than they could realistically expect. Accordingly, the ministers sat forward, smiling encouragingly, or back, more warily, depending on how they felt they would fare.

'Health. Sixty per cent.' The verdict on Rossini's year was delivered loudly and clanged to the table, ringing painfully in the ears of all present.

'How do you explain that, Dottore Rossini?' barked Sergio, before the doctor had even registered the figure as his.

He answered thoughtfully, considering an honest but diplomatic response: 'I'd like to put it down to good management, sir, but I'm afraid it's more likely to be as a direct result of lower than forecast birth rates.'

'So, no good news there,' Sergio stated, with a trace of accusation in his voice.

'None, I'm afraid. I would like to ensure that the surplus is reinvested back into my health service, though, as I would hope to engineer some more proactive initiatives to deal with our current situation.'

'You're suggesting that we *buy* a larger population?' sneered the president.

'Not in so many words, but I believe there are some things we might be able to do to persuade our citizens to have larger families.'

'We'll come back to that,' Sergio said firmly, then turned back to Feraguzzi. 'Carry on.'

'Tourism. Thirty per cent. The spend remains in line with the previous fiscal period, but you will recall that we budgeted for a significant increase in spending as we had some ambitious plans to exploit our tourism opportunities,' Feraguzzi offered, on the minister's behalf, aware that Mosconi might need some friendly support.

'Mosconi. Your comments, please.' Sergio glared at him.

The minister cleared his throat noisily. 'I still have my ambitious plans, sir. They are just harder to execute than I had imagined.'

'Exactly what have you achieved this year? Tell me some good news. Are tourism figures up? Are visitors returning? Are they staying for longer?'

Mosconi's colour had risen alarmingly and he forced a smile to disguise his anxiety as he scrabbled for some positive spin with which to gloss over his evident inadequacies. 'I think our recent esteemed guest might have a beneficial effect on numbers. She has friends, is well connected, and I know she is enjoying her stay immensely. I had the good fortune personally to escort her to—'

'Mosconi. One visitor does not make a tourism industry. What have you actually achieved? Perhaps you think we should not be flaunting our country's attributes abroad. Perhaps you are ashamed of Vallerosa and think it doesn't deserve visitors. Is that closer to the truth?'

At this Mosconi spluttered and fought not to dissolve into tears. To have his own loyalty questioned, and by none other than his president, without doubt represented the very worst moment of his life and nothing, thus far, had prepared him for it. He looked wildly around the room, seeking help or endorsement from his colleagues.

'Vallerosa is everything to me, sir,' he said. 'It is the sweetest air to breathe, and if I never breathe any other I shall die a happy man. Vallerosa is my first love, my childhood sweetheart and my betrothed. Vallerosa is the one I have chosen as my lifelong partner, and it is in her warm soil that I will make my final resting place. I shall be proud to be enclosed by her, as I have been to live here, to walk upon her.'

'Lovely,' the president spat, pouring contempt into the word. 'But I want action. I'm giving you forty-eight hours to come up with a plan and it needs to be convincing.'

'Recreation,' Feraguzzi continued.

CHAPTER 33

In Which Tourism Is Boosted

LIZZIE AND MOSCONI sat in Il Gallo Giallo, drinking tea. Mosconi had now dried his eyes but sniffed occasionally as he attempted to explain his overwhelming despair. 'For the president to doubt me is the biggest tragedy of all. If he wants to call me an incompetent fool, I shall accept it. If he wants to tell me I have failed at my task, then I must bow to his better understanding of the requirements of the job. But to question my love of my country, my loyalty to the nation? It is preposterous and a slander of the highest order.' The sniffing began again in earnest, and Lizzie dug around in her handbag for a tissue to hand to him.

'But you tell me the president has not been himself. Perhaps this isn't a personal attack on you at all. Perhaps he has other worries on his mind that you aren't privy to and he is just taking his frustration out on you,' she suggested brightly.

'You are a very wise woman. I think this is exactly what has happened. But the knowledge does not lessen the humiliation, and my predicament remains the same. I must convince him I am worthy of my job or I will be removed from my post. The shame! The humiliation! It does not bear thinking about. My life certainly would not be worth living.'

Lizzie assumed her most practical and businesslike air, the one she had watched her father employ to great effect over the years. 'Well, let's think about your task. You need to come up with a convincing plan to show that you intend to bring tourists in, yes? Well, it might just be that you've come to the right person. My father has always suggested that marketing is a good career for me but, for the first time ever, I'm actually interested in it – now I can see there's a real purpose for it, a real problem to solve. Much of it must be common sense, surely, so let's brain-storm.' She chewed one arm of her sunglasses thought-fully. 'First, you need a marketing strategy. Maybe a catchy line that will sum up your entire campaign.' She reached into her handbag for a notebook and pencil.

At the thought of such decisive action, manifested by the practical utilization of executive tools, Mosconi became animated. 'Oh, yes. That's very good. The president is very keen on sound-bites, particularly those that are alliterative or rhyme. If I can come up with one it would certainly show I mean business.'

Together they thought for a while. Mosconi stared off into the distance, mouthing words and shaking his head impatiently. Lizzie, in the meantime, repeatedly doodled on her notepad and scribbled out her musings.

'How about "Vallerosa, a forgotten Paradise"?'

'No!' squealed Mosconi, his voice rising by an octave to highlight his vehemence. 'No alliteration, no rhyme, and to be forgotten is the worst thing that can possibly happen to you.' He became glum once more.

In an effort to distract their attention from the long silence, Lizzie summoned more tea and, as she slowly stirred honey into hers, she began to smile. 'I have it, I think. "Vallerosa knows the secret of time …"'

For a few moments, Mosconi allowed the phrase to swill around in his head as he tested it from every angle. Lizzie bit her lip anxiously as he processed the idea, narrowing his eyes to bring its full effect into focus, tilting his head, allowing the sound of the words to ring true and clear. Eventually a slow smile spread across his face, splitting it in two. 'That's completely marvellous, undeniably original. There is no alliteration, no rhyme, and yet, and yet … I love it. It is the most perfect phrase I think I have ever heard. It is poetic and lyrical. It summons up our heritage and our glorious future and perfectly presents the unique selling point of our great nation.' He thought for a few moments, then exclaimed, 'We could have posters!' This time the tears in his eyes sprang from happiness, not despair.

Lizzie was delighted by his enthusiasm. 'And you must print postcards with that strapline. People can send them home to show their friends where they've been!' She was happy to have played such an important part in the minister's transformation.

Remi the postman was sitting two tables away. With his dark glasses over his eyes, he had remained as inconspicuous as possible while straining to listen to as much of the conversation as he could decipher. At the mention of post-cards, he was unable to feign disinterest any longer. He leaped to his feet and dragged a chair next to the minister without waiting for an invitation. 'Your Highness. Sir.' Nodding politely to each in turn. 'You talk freely of postcards.'

Mosconi sighed impatiently. 'Did I not ask you to make an appointment to see me, Remi-Post?'

'You did indeed, but getting an appointment with you has proved harder than I had imagined. I have tried several different approaches and the goalposts have frequently changed. The most recent instruction I have received is to write a letter that I suppose I must then personally hand-deliver to your under-secretary before he will entertain the idea of an appointment. While I am much in favour of the full exploitation of the postal service, and the value of a handwritten letter, it is my fear that our guest will have left this land long before my idea is allowed to reach frui-tion. You, Your Highness,' he said, turning his attention boldly to Lizzie, 'are vital to its success.'

Mosconi looked at his watch, anxious that this intru-sion would erode the special time he was sharing with Miss Holmesworth but conscious, too, that he must show himself in a favourable light in front of his guest. 'And your idea is what exactly, Remi-Post?'

'Your Highness,' Remi said, still with his eyes firmly fixed on Lizzie, 'in my remit as postmaster, as well as the humble postman, I have been monitoring outward-bound mail very closely and it appears to me that you have not yet written a letter home. It seems rather sad to me that your arrival in this country was facilitated through the dependence on a number of national postal services throughout Europe and yet you have chosen to eschew the service that would see a missive from yourself take the return journey. I do not wish to intrude, but wonder whether you might be able to explain this oversight.'

'Well, I've telephoned, of course, and I certainly plan to send a message home, but I suspect I will email as soon as I can access the internet. Not out of disrespect for your service, but out of convenience and speed.'

'Convenience? Could a letter be any more convenient? And speed? When has speed ever added to the quality of a letter sent or received? Your Highness, do you know how much an airmail stamp costs?'

Lizzie tried to remember what it had cost her at home. 'I'm sorry, I can't quite recall.'

'No, no, you probably can't. Why would a person of your position ever stop to consider the value attributed to the manual labour of a mere civil servant? Well, let me tell you. An airmail stamp costs less than a cup of tea. And for that you receive a hand-delivered bespoke service! If you were to choose to send a letter to the United Kingdom from Vallerosa, it would be these very hands that would process your letter and it would be granted onward safe passage using a number of methods of transport – most certainly train, and perhaps road, too. It would cross the sea by boat or perhaps by air. And all of this for less than the cost of the tea you are drinking!'

'Well, I agree it is enormously good value. But I come from a generation that likes the immediacy of email. I press send and my family immediately know what I'm up to – it feels like a miracle.'

'A miracle you say! Your Majesty!' he admonished her, with a disappointed shake of his head. He paused for a moment, searching for exactly the right analogy. After a while he asked earnestly, 'Do you watch the night sky?'

Lizzie considered the question seriously. 'Yes, I do. I often find myself looking at the stars. Particularly here where the sky is so clear and the stars are so bright. It's extraordinary.'

'You talk of a miracle. But think of the miracle of starlight. Some of the light that reaches your eyes was emitted by stars that have long since died. Stars that might have actually extinguished tens or hundreds of thousands of years ago! When you look upon that star, you are looking directly at the past and with this you are defying time. That is a miracle.'

'I find it hard to get my head around that sometimes.'

'Well,' said Remi, in the voice of a man who had already won his argument, 'a letter is just the same. Just as miraculous.'

'It is?'

'Of course. Post a letter now. Don't affix an airmail stamp, just a regular overland stamp. It will probably arrive after you return home. But when it arrives, it will carry all the magic of the moment you wrote it. The scent in the air, perhaps even the moisture in your skin. When you open it, Vallerosan air will spill from the envelope and it will be exactly as it was when you were here. A time capsule. And not only will it carry the essence of the moment. Something else will have been added to it. Other ingredients that cannot be included in an immediately delivered email. Nostalgia, interpretation, reflection and context. It is a different you who will receive the letter.'

'What a lovely thought! I suppose I've grown to value immediate gratification over the romanticism of the post but, now you put it that way, I'm very tempted to send a letter to myself, perhaps to my family as well. In fact, I shall! I shall tell myself exactly what I'm feeling now, today, and I'll write it among the tea plants and send some of that dusty air with it! What a joy!'

'I'm so glad you seem to understand. That makes me feel very proud.'

Excluded from the exchange, Mosconi interrupted: 'And this is going to further tourism how exactly?'

'Oh, forgive me, the sending of the letter itself won't further tourism. I have a much bigger idea. But it needs the approval of Her Royal Highness and of our government.'

'And your idea is?'

'A stamp!' Remi was unable to contain his excitement. 'A series of stamps. A series of stamps that commemorate the arrival of our royal guest to Vallerosa.' He turned back to Lizzie. 'Your Eminence, you are delighted by the thought of sending a letter, but can you imagine how proud you will be if the envelope of that letter is adorned by a stamp that specifically celebrates your stay here?'

Mosconi mulled over the postman's idea and liked it immediately. Certainly a combination of a carefully orchestrated marketing campaign backed up with themed postcards and stamps might encourage a large amount of outward-bound marketing of the viral nature that everyone had seemed so excited about lately, however poisonous it sounded.

'And you envisage the stamps looking like what exactly?'

Remi produced a piece of paper that had clearly been refolded on many occasions and now bore the stains of regular handling. He smoothed it out, stammering, 'I – I have only commissioned the f-first in the series. Y-you understand it would be an expensive undertaking to c-commission further images purely speculatively but you will warm to the m-motif, I hope, and your imagination will allow you to see how this series might d-d-develop.'

Mosconi and Lizzie looked at the drawing. The pencil lines were deftly executed and portrayed a man on a bicycle, wearing a peaked cap and bicycle clips, waving a disproportionately large envelope above his head. The cyclist was undoubtedly the postman himself.

'This, you understand, is the first in the series, representing the arrival of the news, the heralding of glad tidings, if you like. The first inkling that our lives would soon be irrevocably changed ...'

Mosconi admired the drawing and enthused without reservation: 'This is a first-class idea. Yes, the arrival of the letter, then perhaps an image of Gabboni at the railway station. And perhaps some of the official tours, too, could be represented. A senior minister outside one of our greatest tourist attractions, having just shown our visitor around. Perhaps with the suggestion that she is still inside,

305

browsing. What a marvellous idea. I think this might be a very good concept indeed, Remi-Post, and one that I shall propose to our president and my government colleagues at the very first opportunity. I can imagine a good deal of enthusiasm from across the board.'

Remi beamed with relief and exhaustion. His idea had kept him awake for several nights, and that it had received such a positive response from one of the most senior ministers in the land was sweet.

Lizzie patted Remi's arm. 'Well done, and I will certainly be paying a visit to your post office, you can count on that. But I might have to wait until we've printed some postcards and commissioned your stamps. What an excellent afternoon's work!'

Hardly able to believe his luck, and unwilling to risk it by outstaying his welcome, Remi left the bar in search of some citizens with whom he could share it.

Mosconi remained at the table, staring at Lizzie. He was now beginning to believe she was not only the most beautiful woman he had ever set eyes on but that she was clearly a marketing genius as well.

'But, Settimio, this is not enough,' said Lizzie, placing a steadying hand on his own. 'A strapline and some special-edition stamps will give you a hook to hang your marketing campaign on, but you're going to need some concrete plans to present if you're to convince the president that you're the right man for the job.' She thought for a moment, once again chewing her lip in deep contemplation. Mosconi sat absolutely still, trying not to remind her that her hand still rested lightly on his.

'What about a website?' she exclaimed, gripping his hand more tightly in excitement. 'A website would have been really useful when I was trying to find out about Vallerosa and, honestly, there's nothing very helpful when you Google it.'

Mosconi shook his head sadly, but placed his other hand on hers, now sandwiching it between his. To a casual onlooker they might look like lovers, an impression Mosconi was happy to encourage. Lizzie, suddenly aware that her hand had become trapped, wondered whether she might be able to release it casually, but as she began to experiment with the manoeuvre, Mosconi simply strengthened his grip. 'We're beyond a website now. That's not thinking big enough. That was my revolutionary idea for last year, and if I mention it again I will simply remind them that I haven't yet achieved my ambitious goal. They'll just laugh me out of the room. They might even laugh me out of the country.' He hung his head in shame. 'I am a failure, it is true. Perhaps I don't even deserve the job.' His body slumped in despair but his grip on Lizzie's hand tightened again. He was refusing to relinquish his prize.

Quiet for a moment, Lizzie brightened. 'A website isn't actually that difficult to build – it needn't take months and months. How about if I enlist the help of a couple of students? We could probably have something to look at in time for your meeting. You say you've got some money to spend? Well, let's pay the students to do the work – they'll certainly get on to it if you chuck a few *lire* at them.'

Mosconi considered this, but slumped again. 'This is all very kind, and I appreciate your great efforts, but still I need a bigger idea.'

Lizzie used her next thought to free her hand and used both to gesticulate expansively. 'Well, it's obvious, isn't it?'

'It is?' Mosconi said, sadder to lose the warmth of the pale pink hand than he could have believed possible.

'Yes. You want to attract tourists, but the single biggest issue that prevents people coming is transport. I cannot tell you how difficult it was to get here by train – it's a miracle anyone finds their way here at all. How about you begin conversations with one of the budget airlines and offer it the opportunity to be the first airline to fly to your country? They're operating all over Europe now, flying to the most outrageous places, cities you've never even heard of. They're amazingly cheap – you can get to the most unlikely places for, like, a pound or something. I'm sure you could get them interested.'

'An airline? But we have no airport! We have no runway! Where is an aeroplane meant to land in our country?'

'Even better. If you haven't got an airport, you build one. That'll create loads of jobs and opportunities. The country will know you're serious about expanding your horizons.'

Mosconi felt a prickle of excitement but the biggest obstacle was insurmountable. 'But we have no room for a runway.'

'With all due respect, you seem to have an awful lot of tea plants. I mean, I'm sure it's a very important crop to you, but every square inch seems to be devoted to the damn stuff. I'm sure you could spare a few acres to get a runway in. I have no idea how much land you'd need, but I'm sure I could find out.'

Mosconi's imagination stretched upwards to the high plains of the Alta Mesa, seeing for a moment a vision of endless possibility. 'An airport. A runway. Aeroplanes coming and going. People arriving and departing. Tourists, lots of them. Arriving to stay in our country and all because of me and my marketing strategy.'

'Exactly. You wanted a big idea. That's the biggest you can have. And if we get to work on it right away, you can make a huge presentation on Tuesday. I can help you, if you want, with timelines and budgets and ... We wouldn't have to go into a massive amount of detail, just outline the plan and say you'll work closely with the Department of Finance to come up with the figures.' Lizzie was now acutely aware that already she was substantially out of her depth. She hoped that the answers she would need to seek would be readily available somewhere within the university.

Mosconi, however, was sold, and where doubt had plagued him before, absolute certainty had swept in to replace it. 'This really is amazing – absolutely amazing. I have a big idea. I have the biggest idea of all the big ideas you could possibly have when considering the finer aspects of tourism. Yes, I can see it now. An airport with a departure lounge and an arrivals lounge. We'd need Customs officers and baggage handlers and ticket staff. We'd probably need airport police and many more pony traps. Think of all the jobs we'll create!'

Then reality stopped his dreaming in its tracks. 'But how do we pay for them all? I cannot pay all of these people out of my tourism budget. It won't stretch much beyond some posters.'

Lizzie answered, with a confidence she had no right to wield: 'I suppose you get the airline to pay for it. I assume they have to pay for the right to land here and for all the services you provide. On top of that most countries can tax every single person coming in or when they leave.'

'People would pay a tax to visit my country?' Mosconi asked, his eyes widening at the thought.

'Oh, absolutely. You sort of expect it. Particularly when you're visiting countries that are a bit off the beaten path. You can't charge a huge amount, maybe a thousand *lire* or something when they leave.'

'You would charge them to leave the country? This is most unlikely. I am sure there are many countries that a visitor will happily pay to leave, perhaps even yours. America, I suppose, you might pay a lot to leave. And Switzerland, I imagine. But here? Vallerosa? I think they would want to pay to stay.'

'Well, either way, there's a tax to pay on arrival or departure.'

'On arrival, most certainly.'

'Of course.' Lizzie dismissed Mosconi's concerns with a wave of her hand. 'Either way, it would be fine. So, if an average Ryanair flight brings something like a hundred and twenty people, you'd get a hundred and twenty thousand *lire* per planeload. And on top of that you'd charge the airline itself a fortune, just for the pleasure of landing here.'

'All that for each plane …' Mosconi was no mathematician, but already the sums sounded beyond his wildest dreams. For the third time that day, he had tears in his eyes. He looked up at the flags flying proudly above Parliament Hall and counted his blessings. This woman, this stranger who had arrived out of the night, was like a goddess, some sort of miracle worker who had arrived to brighten his life. She radiated goodness and now she had saved his job too.

'You are a wonderful woman. I cannot begin to thank you. You have saved my life,' he proclaimed, sliding his hand across the table, hoping she might grasp it once more.

'Oh, don't be silly!' she replied. 'But, goodness, we've got a huge amount of work to do. I need to enlist the help of your students and get access to the internet. I'm sure I'll find plenty of help at the university, won't I? I mean … you do have access to the internet, don't you?' Suddenly her plans looked like they might disappear in a puff of smoke.

Mosconi stiffened, his feathers ruffled. 'I don't know what you think this country is. Of course we have access to the internet. We are not an outpost here. We are teetering very close to the cutting edge of modern society.'

Lizzie grinned. 'Absolutely you are. Now, let's have a beer to celebrate.' She barely had to raise her glass to attract the attention of the hovering patron. Dario whisked towards her to take the order and quickly returned with two ice-cold glasses and a small spinning cake stand, featuring an eclectic assortment of pretzels, crisps, nuts and beautifully prepared raw vegetables. There were little pots to dip into as well.

'Mmm, lovely,' murmured Lizzie, as she poked a carrot into a peppery sauce, barely acknowledging the fanfare with which it had arrived. Dario stood to attention nearby, listening closely to the comments and fiddling with his tea-towel until he was quite sure his guest was pleased with the service. The way she lunged at the crudités suggested she was very content indeed. Nevertheless, he couldn't avoid an occasional surreptitious glance at Il Toro Rosso, where Piper wasn't even trying to hide the incredulity in his open-mouthed stare.

The young man shook his head with a wry smile. Tablecloths were one thing, but beer in iced glasses and chopped vegetables? Dario might be prepared to raise the stakes but Piper saw this not as a threat but a challenge. A challenge he would relish. He conveyed all of this with a sneer towards Dario, wiped his hands on his apron decisively and headed inside to prepare his campaign.

As Lizzie stood up to pay and leave, she wove her way to Piper's bar, smiling broadly at the glowering barman, who was now leaning against the doorframe. Lizzie spotted Pavel sitting there and greeted him warmly, pulling up a chair to join him.

Flustered at her unexpected defection, Piper rushed into the gloom of his bar and busied himself there. She had left Dario – not only had she left him, he had watched her go! Gleefully he prepared a laden tray, whistling quietly under his breath as he worked.

LIZZIE WAS MAKING FRIENDS FAST. She'd been introduced to a charming young student called Woolf, who felt sure he could help her with her research and website. They tossed ideas back and forth, talking them through and making plans for a session at the university the next day. A couple of other students came over to them and soon they were busy talking through the proposition. When Lizzie mentioned they'd be paid for their time, the men raised a cheer and immediately committed their future earnings to another round of drinks, assuring Piper with shouts across the room that he would almost certainly be paid in the very near future.

With impeccable timing, Piper appeared beside the table, understanding now just how crucial it was to make a really good impression. Cold glasses, beer, wedges of lime to squeeze into it. Bowls of delicious pickles, usually reserved for the grandest of festivities, were laid out alongside a vast bowl of hand-cut crisps.

The men ate hungrily and Lizzie joined in enthusiastically. Beer glasses were clinked in celebration and orders called for more of this and more of that. Sensing an occasion, passers-by stopped to watch the festivities and were soon called upon to grab a chair and join them. Piper ran backwards and forwards from the bar, fetching beer and spooning out bowl after bowl of delicacies. As if by osmosis, more revellers leaked from the shadows of the piazza, and when the tables and chairs were all fully occupied they stood in clusters on the fringe of the activity that emanated from Lizzie but somehow embraced by it, too. Rushed off his feet, Piper barely had time to glance across at Dario, whose bar suddenly looked quiet in comparison. True, his rival might have cornered the military but it was he, Piper, who had the youth market, and anyone would tell you that where the youth came, growth followed. Excitement and energy pulsed from the bar. If it carries on like this, I'm going to need staff, thought Piper, already imagining the pride in sticking a 'Help Wanted' notice to his window.

The bar filled, students and artisans appearing from the alleys in droves to join the late-evening surge. They queued two or three deep at the bar, laughing and shouting.

At each laugh and exclamation, Dario, at Il Gallo Giallo, flinched. He'd laid his cards out. He'd gone upmarket with tablecloths and the fanciest dips but what was she doing now? She was revelling! Her behaviour was nothing more than that of a rowdy commoner. How on earth was he to cater to that market? Where were all the people coming from? He had never seen his rival's bar so busy. With each new arrival, his heart seemed to shrivel. True, he had plenty of custom, too, but what good was that if the main attraction was over there, squeezing fresh lime juice into her beer? Fine! If it was lime juice she wanted, lime juice she would get. Now was the time to enlist help. It might pain him to do so, but he would speak to his wife. He wiped his hands on his apron and headed upstairs.

CHAPTER 34

In Which Laughter Spells Trouble

FROM HIS POSITION ON THE BALCONY, Sergio strained his ears. Shouts had alerted him and his heart had begun to race. But now, as he stood still and listened, he realized it was laughter he could hear. At the far side of the piazza he could see the crowded bars, both as busy as he could remember. People were standing to either side, holding beers. This was not a sight he had ever witnessed before and he wondered where the danger lurked in this new, unforeseen phenomenon. Would it present itself as a manifestation of the students, their requests educated and eloquent? Or would the farmers lead the revolution with their implements of the land raised in anger? Placards or pitchforks, either spelled doom for the president and he knew not which to fear most.

The instinct of a leader prepared him for the worst. He knew what to look for. An underground movement of students was probably the most likely source of a revolution, and wasn't a bar the most likely place for the revolutionaries to gather? It all made perfect sense to him now. And it wasn't just the students, was it? Dario's bar, Il Gallo Giallo, was crowded, too, and he couldn't discern a line where one crowd started and the next finished. Were they merging? This was perhaps the most dangerous signal he had received so far. His military men were being influenced by students and alcohol – what heady cocktail would be stirred by this combination? How many leaders had sat and witnessed a revolt begin before their very eyes? Had his people so little respect that they hadn't even the decency to hide away in some seedy, smoke-filled room to discuss his downfall? No: their confidence was such that they would flaunt it in front of him, in the very shadow of the building that they were, no doubt, planning to lay siege to at any moment. He trembled inside. But the biggest insult of all was the laughter. They drank, they plotted, they cheered their approaching victory and, most of all, they laughed in his face.

Sergio sank to his knees and gave in to some unfathomable feeling. A deep, deep fear shrouded by resignation. He put his face into his hands and wept.

CHAPTER 35

In Which Lizzie Supposes

THE MINISTER FOR EDUCATION was busy when Lizzie arrived for her appointment. She glanced at her watch from time to time and tapped her foot impatiently but soon found herself listening to one side of a conversation escaping through the gaps around his office door. Giuseppe Scota appeared to be engaged in a genuine debate, with a bona-fide political conundrum at its heart.

'Yes, my friend. I understand entirely. But they're either on my books or they're on yours ...'

'Yes, yes, indeed. But while I understand your dilemma, the timing is bad. Nevertheless, I'm tempted to do something to break the deadlock.'

There was a long pause, in which Lizzie imagined the professor holding the telephone away from his ear.

'Or at your peril, Vlad. I've been carrying this for a while, and time is running out. Not for me or for my department but for these individuals. I think they deserve more, don't you?'

Another lengthy silence, and Lizzie watched the second hand on the old municipal clock click forward. How was it that institutional seconds were so much bigger and surer of themselves than seconds at home? she wondered.

'Well, I'll give you the benefit of the doubt until after the election, but beyond that, I cannot promise anything. I must be going soon. I have an appointment with You Know Who.' At this thought, or at the response from the other end of the telephone, Scota roared with laughter, for far longer than Lizzie felt appropriate. A couple of times she stood, thinking he had finished his conversation, but each time he bellowed another round of laughter. Finally she heard the heavy receiver click back into place and, though he continued to chuckle to himself, she ventured to rap on his door.

'Good. A little late, but come in, my dear.'

'I was here on time, but you were talking. I didn't want to disturb you.'

'Anyway, you're here now. How may I assist?'

'Well, I'm on a fact-finding mission so I'm here to enquire about various aspects of your department. My understanding is that I have full clearance from the president.'

'And in your fact-finding mission, you're after what exactly?'

'I don't know. Answers.'

'Answers to what questions?'

'None specifically. I just thought we might be able to chat and I'd get to the bottom of the things that continue to mystify me.'

The professor scraped his chair back, swung his feet onto the desk, crossed one over the other at the ankle, then folded his arms languidly behind his head. 'You're an educated woman, Miss Holmesworth.'

This was a statement so Lizzie remained impassive.

'As such, you must have been taught the basic principles of enquiry. But let me remind you. An unspecific line of questioning is reserved for small children and the uneducated. "Mama, why is the sky blue?", "Papa, why does the river never change direction?", "Teacher, may I be excused for the toilet?"

'Those are questions asked with a right answer, a wrong answer or a judgement to be given. That is a reasonable exchange that enriches the questioner's knowledge, either educationally or morally.'

Scota seemed in no hurry with his preamble. If anything, he looked as if he might be settling down for a comfortable afternoon.

'A little later in life, the line of questioning must change. But to enrich knowledge, the student is no longer equipped to ask questions because the student does not know the framework. It is outside his knowledge base and, as such, he is unable to make further enquiry. At this point in a young person's development, the teacher must pre-empt and answer the questions that the student does not know to ask. "This is how you solve a simultaneous equation", "These arc the fundamental differences in the philosophies taught by Aristotle and Socrates", "This is the thinking behind quantum physics."'

Lizzie nodded, hoping she wasn't to be tested in any of these areas.

'And then you begin to reach maturity – the stage that you yourself have reached, Miss Holmesworth.' He swung his legs down, opened the bottom drawer of his desk and removed a pipe. Standing at the window, he noisily tapped it, blew into it, filled it, tapped it again and lit it, sucking heavily until the smoke billowed around him. He opened the window a few inches, then returned to his former position, feet on his desk.

'You have reached that stage I assume, Miss Holmesworth?'

Lizzie tried to nod with as little commitment as possible, in case her acquiescence should betray a lie later, under cross-examination.

'The final stage of education is to work on the basis of a thesis. Now it is time to hypothesize, to postulate, to surmise and suppose. You set out with a statement of fact that you wish to prove, then ask the right questions of the right people in order to do so. What I am trying to understand from you now is, what is your contention? Once I understand this, I might be able to help you ask the right questions.'

'You're saying that I must come up with the answer and then you'll provide the question?'

'Yes, indeed. That is exactly the right way for you to pursue your enquiries at this stage in your career.'

As Lizzie pondered, he took the opportunity to swing his feet to the floor once more, to open the second to bottom drawer, to remove a small flask and two glasses and to pour them each a measure of honey-coloured liquid.

'I don't think I should,' Lizzie said, a little anxiety revealing itself in the pitch of her voice, which was higher than she had intended.

'You don't know that you shouldn't,' he said, an eyebrow raised in challenge as he held a glass out to her.

Lizzie shrugged and they clinked glasses. She sipped the strong liquor, recalling the cough mixture her mother had administered, which had had the soothing effect of removing the tickle in her throat and putting her to sleep. This liquid, however, appeared permanently to remove any future tickle in her throat while also hinting that clarity and enlightenment might soon be within her reach.

Lizzie sipped twice more, then drained the small glass, returning it to the desk with a satisfying thud. 'Who taught Sergio at school?'

'That, my dear, is an elementary question rather than a disquisition. As a matter of discipline, I must insist that you begin with your assumption if you wish me to help you with your enquiries.'

'My assumption is that Sergio struggles a bit with written English. Perhaps all writing. My assumption is that he might even be dyslexic.'

The word hovered heavily in the air, and for a few painful moments, Lizzie seriously regretted her boldness. Scota's eyes had narrowed but he wasn't staring at her in an accusatory way: rather, he was looking right through her, into the past.

'That, young lady, is a very interesting proposition. But now I must understand something further from you. When a serious student makes a controversial hypothesis, it helps her credibility if the motive is understood. For if she is to have access to the sort of information that will support the premise, those who help her must be very sure there is no malice aforethought that might have unpremeditated ramifications.'

'You mean that helping me might get you into trouble?'

'No, not at all. That is a simple moral dilemma for the educator. I mean that the ethical standpoint behind the assumption must be understood in order to protect the questioner from making a complete ass of herself.'

Lizzie smiled the smile with the deliquescent properties that had long before melted the heart of the professor. 'I mean your president absolutely no harm. But certain things have troubled me since my arrival. If I can understand these problems, then perhaps I can help in a number of ways. Or it might be that highlighting this as a potential problem will be enough.' Lizzie looked him in the eye and waited.

When he spoke, it was with a softer, kinder inflection. 'Sergio was not educated in any of our formal institutions. It is not entirely surprising. He was the only son of the president and as such it was entirely natural that he would be protected from mainstream schooling. There is absolutely no doubt that our president is a very clever man – I myself have conversed with him in a number of languages. He grasps most of what various specialists tell him, although that in itself is often a case of the blind leading the blind.

'But as to whether he has any such disorder? I really don't know. I think much of his education was probably at the hands of his father, though no doubt there were plenty of governors and governesses around to help in the detail. Angelo would be able to shed further light, I expect, but tread carefully. Sometimes when a student comes to me with a hypothesis I will advise him to choose another. Not because it can't be proven, but because it needn't be proven.'

'I understand it is a very sensitive issue, but it would clarify a few things. The finer details of my visit, for instance. There was a little confusion about my arrival ...'

'Well, Miss Holmesworth, I would beseech you to continue your research without solipsism as your beacon for discovery. I submit that it would clarify some issues of a very much greater significance than the basis of your visit. It might well explain our esteemed leader's obsession with formal education, for a start. And that is in-teresting.'

Scota thought a little more as he sucked on his pipe.

'Miss Holmesworth. Our president has had a double dose of misfortune in his life. Often in parenting there is darkness and light, and these opposing forces are quite compatible providing they are treated as two different approaches to the same goal – the steering of a child through the labyrinthine choices that lead, when the correct path is chosen at each opportunity, to it emerging as an adult with integrity and a lack of blame for or anger with his own shortcomings. Those are the qualities that are needed to make you or me a useful member of society but they are even more essential in a position of leadership. Our president's mother had the softness and natural goodness that would steer Sergio into using his instinct in making the right decisions. She set his moral compass early, but she died before Sergio had taken full control of his own destiny, his own choices.

'After his mother's death, Sergio Senior jerked the controls with a much heavier hand. He was a man of integrity and wanted the best for his son, but was full of pride and also wanted his boy to be a reflection of himself – to act in a way that would portray him in a good light as both a father and a president. That looks, to the outsider, like successful management of parental responsibility but it leaves the child less able to feel his way to the right decisions. When Sergio Senior died, it was a very great shock to his only son, who had learned only to keep his father happy – I think that without his father's guidance he felt lost. It was a tragedy that his mother did not live for longer. She would have encouraged Sergio to trust implicitly that he was doing the right thing, without looking for external reassurance. You will understand, Miss Holmesworth, that honest reassurance is hard to come by when you are in a position of power and surrounded by people whose own positions are furthered by agreeing with you.'

His words, Lizzie thought, applied in some small way to her own upbringing. Her parents were both alive, but had her father really done anything other than try to perpetuate his own beliefs through her? Had she ever had an original thought that he hadn't seized, examined, rejected and replaced with a superior version? She tucked the thought away as the professor returned abruptly from his own reverie.

'Your conjecture is indeed very interesting. Perhaps I myself have been too distracted by the part I have to play in this country's management. It has always been my assumption that my students are forced to stay in education to keep them from having a negative impact on the unemployment figures. It wouldn't be the first time in political history, you know.'

He poured them another glass of liquor, and drank his own immediately. Lizzie left hers to catch the sunlight in front of her.

'I assume you know that the US government invented the concept of retirement and have since imposed it upon the rest of the world? Until this came along it was considered usual for men to continue working until they dropped. Not a bad thing, either. We're programmed to work. That's why our opposable thumbs evolved in the first place. Sitting down for twenty or thirty years towards the end of life was never the goal for a normal, healthy adult male. But in the USA, the unemployment figures were a bit scary and the government came up with an audacious plan. They invented retirement, insisted it was a basic human right, and thus lopped off a large chunk of the work force. Once everyone over the age of sixty was no longer expected or entitled to work, that freed up an awful lot of jobs for the younger folk.

'The really clever bit was the psychology, selling it to the people as part of the great American dream. Hey, you're worth it! You've worked hard, now it's time to sit on your backside and do nothing for a few years until you die! It didn't take long to catch on, either. Golf probably had something to do with it. That and the brainwashing.'

He poured himself yet another slug of liquor and again drained the glass in one.

'I always assumed that our prolonged education system was part of that same myth. Let young people feel it's theirs by right and they won't even notice they've been excluded from the job market for an extra few years.

'But now I'm wondering. I might have underestimated Sergio. Perhaps he does feel it's a basic right, which he was denied by his own father. Perhaps he's even felt that the exclusion has held him back. Perhaps in insisting his people access education for as long as they wish, he is merely fulfilling his own desire vicariously.'

'Perhaps?' offered Lizzie tentatively.

The professor filled and drained his glass again. 'Psychology is just one of my degrees and I like to exercise it from time to time. Come, time's up. Let's go to the bar.' He slammed the glass down.

Lizzie scraped her chair back, feeling curiously light-headed as she got to her feet. It might have been the effect of the extremely strong drink or perhaps the discovery that she had an ally, a minister who hadn't tied her up in knots and left her less sure than when she'd begun. It was with renewed vigour that she took his proffered arm and walked with him towards the bars.

CHAPTER 36

In Which Lizzie Dines Out

THE FOLLOWING DAY Lizzie was making her way back to her room, having spent the morning at the university, finishing only when siesta was officially declared. She was learning her way around the campus and making friends as she went. She had found that the more she collaborated with those she met, the easier it was to navigate the otherwise unfathomable by-laws that governed day-to-day living. The American she had failed to charm on her train journey was her frequent companion among the students and, most particularly, in those areas that offered internet access. Unlike Lizzie, he had chosen to traverse a less co-operative route and quite often found his internet access slow, interrupted or denied. Lizzie had long since stopped offering him help and had this morning left him alone, muttering over a dusty terminal, and headed back to her room and the daytime nap to which she was fast becoming accustomed.

As she neared Parliament Hall's gates, a figure lurched out of a doorway. Emitting a squeal, she put her hand to her heart, then laughed when she saw who it was.

'Mr Whylie! I didn't see you there – you startled me!' She smiled at the American.

'No, your head was well and truly in the clouds. And you appear to be skulking yourself, Miss Holmesworth, I've been watching your progress. Surely the quickest route would have been across the piazza.'

'Oh, I wasn't skulking exactly, just heading back for a rest. I wasn't quite in the mood for lunch at the bar, so thought I'd avoid it altogether.'

'You're tired of the folk here already, and you've been here a matter of days. I've been spending time in this goddam outpost on and off for years!'

'Oh, that's not at all what I meant. I'm not tired of them, just needed a bit of time to myself.'

'I understand completely. Come, have lunch with me – that will give you the rest you need.'

Thinking it might be rude to protest, Lizzie fell into step with the American consultant and followed him to his quarters. He, too, had been allocated lodgings within the palace walls, but on the far back corner of the building. His separate little house had its own private access from the alley that ran down the far right-hand wall, leading directly to the corner of the Piazza Rosa.

'Wow, this is great, more like an apartment, really. They treat you well here obviously!'

Chuck Whylie had a comfortable sitting room, with a door opening onto a small kitchen and another to his bedroom. The sitting room was ornately decorated with long silk hangings at either side of the floor-to-ceiling windows, which opened on to the dark rose stone of the building opposite. A sliver of blue sky above afforded some natural daylight but otherwise the room was dark and cool. 'Beer?' he asked, appearing from the kitchen with a Budweiser.

'Not for me, thanks. I'd sleep all afternoon,' said Lizzie, standing a little awkwardly by the window and feeling uncomfortable in the intimacy of the surroundings. She could see his bed through the open door and felt vulnerable.

Whylie flopped down onto the sofa, patting the space beside him for Lizzie to join him. He gulped his beer greedily. 'They have to treat me well. Their future is pretty much in my hands.'

'Whose future? The government's?' asked Lizzie, taking the offered seat but instinctively leaving as much space as possible between herself and the American.

'Yes, and for "government" read "the whole damn country". The two are inseparable as you'll come to learn – government, country, people, all one and the same. Whether you're talking about the guys in their brocade or the un-intelligentsia down at the bar, you'll find no more than a group of uneducated, undeveloped, unruly peasants. The guys in charge pretend to offer some sort of structure and stability but in reality they're no better than the rest of them. You want my honest opinion? They're barbarians, and back home I wouldn't employ any of them to pack my groceries.'

Lizzie had been studying the stonework of the alley wall, her cheeks pink with embarrassment at the disloyalty she was showing by listening to the man. She turned now, with a forced smile. 'That's harsh. They seem incredibly well educated to me.'

'Educated! You call them educated? They might be book-learned to a degree, but nothing that's going to stand up to Western scrutiny. Tenth-grade kids back home would give them a run for their money. Anyway, if you're going to get on in the real world it's not about what you learn from books. Latin! Where's that going to get you in the cut and thrust of modern business? No. It's about what you've got up here.' He gestured to his temple. 'This country is permanently on the brink of financial ruin and, hell, I don't want to be a scaremonger but, without my help, I don't think they'll come through.' He shook his head sadly.

Lizzie was torn between irritation at his condescension and genuine concern at the nation's plight. 'Gosh, how do you mean?'

Whylie reached to pat her thigh as he framed his answer. 'Oh, it's complex, but they're a small, underfunded nation with big, powerful neighbours, and I don't think I'd be exaggerating if I told you they're vulnerable to takeover.' He took another long pull on his beer and used the hand that had been patting Lizzie's thigh to wipe his mouth.

Lizzie gasped. 'War? Do you mean somebody is likely to attack them? That sounds terrifying.'

This elicited something between a sneer and a snort from the American. 'I don't think war would be necessary.

You could walk in here and have this country for the taking. First one to fly the flag would have it, in my opinion. Of course,' he said, and had another swig, 'they're actually pretty safe. No one would want this place. Mac cheese?'

'Who?'

'Mac 'n' cheese. Years of travelling here have forced me to prepare well. My office ships me enough ready meals and American beer to keep me going for every trip.' He stood up and went to the kitchen, throwing open a cupboard door to reveal row upon row of cardboard-wrapped food. 'These are great – long shelf life, microwaveable and tastes just like home. When I first came here I wasn't so fussy but now I insist that I have Budweiser brewed in America. I wouldn't touch the stuff brewed in Eastern Europe. Plays havoc with my guts.'

He pulled a couple of packages off the shelf and peered at them, reading out the labels as he sifted through. 'Mac 'n' cheese, tomato pasta bake, lasagne, take your pick – it'll be the best meal you've had since you got here!'

'Oh, no, thank you. I'm really not hungry. A glass of tap water is fine, thanks.'

'Tap water? Are you mad? It'll be full of all sorts of crap. Sewage, for sure. And, Jesus Christ, the pipes are rusty and probably full of rats. I've got some decent bottled water here. I don't ship it, I'm not entirely crazy, but the guards stock my fridge every week. I consider it part of my rider.'

Lizzie watched him as he punched buttons on the microwave and laid himself a knife, fork and plate on a tray. After a minute and thirty seconds he tipped the white mush onto the plate and brought it back to the sofa where he hungrily dug into it. 'Sure I can't tempt you? Smells good, no?'

Lizzie's nose wrinkled as she did her very best not to inhale the strange sweetness radiating from the forkfuls of gloop he was shovelling into himself. He would barely swallow a mouthful before loading in the next. She looked around the room, marvelling at the grand charm, the solid furniture and lavish soft furnishings. 'You're very lucky, you know,' she offered.

'Lucky? You're joking. The guys back home laugh at me. They think I did something to piss off the CEO to get this gig. Other guys are chucking fine wine down their necks and dining in the best restaurants around the world. And you know the really lucky ones? The guys who get the small African states. OK, their accommodation is probably crap compared to this but the big bucks are all there. You can smell it. Know what money smells like, Lizzie?'

'Yes, no, probably. I don't know.' She thought of her pink ceramic piggy bank at home and the memory of the sweet smell of her childhood bedroom filled her nostrils.

'Oil. But there's nothing like that here. First thing I checked out when I got here. Got the guys to run some pretty extensive geological reports on the sub-structure. Do you know what this country runs on?'

Lizzie shook her head.

'No? Water. Rock and water, that's all they've got. Probably just as well. If they'd got anything else I'd have been pulled off this job a long time ago and it would have been handed to one of the big shots in the office. It's how it works. But I'm doing my time, you know, slow and steady, and I'm bringing in a decent hourly rate here. Plus a good per diem. Few more years I'll make partner – sooner, perhaps, if I land a really big contract.'

'What exactly do you do for your firm?' Lizzie asked, more out of habitual good manners than genuine interest.

'I'm a consultant. I consult. I look at the big picture and try to monetize the obstacles. It's technical stuff. I don't want to bore you.' He went on, pausing only to swig at his beer: 'Imagine this country is a company. I look at its balance sheet, its statement of income, and try to help them balance the books. Some of it's just good old-fashioned accountancy but I like to think I can do a bit more for them than that. Sometimes when you're very close to a problem you can't see the wood for the trees. I look at the issues with a fresh pair of eyes and they pay me to help them come up with strategies for growth and improvement. I've earned my keep too.'

'I'm sure you have.'

'And it's not been without its hardships and frustrations. But I've got in place a sizeable deal for this country that will genuinely lift them out of poverty and take them on to bigger things.'

Lizzie looked at her watch and feigned surprise. 'Whoops! I'd really better be going.'

Whylie put down his beer bottle, swung around to face her and continued, without missing a beat: 'Stick with me.

333

This country might look backward, but you've got to play the game to get on here. You can move with the big boys, or with the losers. I know my way around and if you want to maximize your return here, sooner or later you're going to need my help.'

'I don't think I want to maximize my return. I just want to spend some time getting to know the people.'

'Bullshit!' He slapped his thigh. 'Don't give me that bullshit. I know who you are and I know where you've come from. I also know who you're pretending to be. So don't come over all innocent with me. You're in the middle of a potentially volatile situation, dangerous for you and dangerous for the government. You're going to have to tread a very delicate line.' He paused to search for an analogy that would illustrate his train of thought. 'You ever watch any of those PBS documentaries they run for charities? They show them from time to time about the land-mine clearing operations in war-torn Bongo-Bongo Land. You know the ones, where they're using rats and dogs and all sorts of clever technology to find out where these bombs are buried. The bombs are small, they're homemade, or they're small and sold to poor countries by rich countries. Whatever, they're pretty small but, despite the rats and dogs and other stuff they use, the bombs carry on going off, legs and arms flying everywhere. People get killed all the time. Even the good guys. Hell, especially the good guys. Well, imagine here, the paths you tread. They're littered with potential land-mines. You can try to tread carefully, you can alter your route from time to time, you can cover your tracks – but make one false move, and don't be surprised if they're your limbs that are blown clean off.' He wiped his plate clean and scraped noisily at his fork, licking the last remnants of cheese sauce off each prong.

Lizzie had paled visibly.

'Look, I'm not meaning to scare you, but you're playing with the big boys now and you're up to here in it.' He waved his fork somewhere near his Adam's apple. 'All I'm saying is, I'm here to help. It's what I do. I seek solutions and I consider myself a diplomat, a people person. So, if you need help, I'm here. You understand?'

Lizzie nodded. 'Thank you. That's really kind. Now I think I'd better be going.'

He shrugged and picked up his tray to tidy it away but made no move to stop her.

She let herself out, trembling inside. She had been violated in some way, but was unsure how. He had seemed to be offering his help yet the threats were barely veiled. Feeling tearful and out of her depth for the first time since arriving in Vallerosa, perhaps for the first time ever, she walked quickly back to her room where she lay down on her bed and stabbed at her mobile phone, trying again and again to find a signal that would deliver the healing tones of her mother. The American had touched a nerve with his land-mine analogy: nothing had moved her as greatly as the story of Princess Diana's foray into Angola. Her mother had been greatly affected by the princess's charitable work and had thought her the epitome of goodness and good breeding. 'The more you have,' her mother insisted, 'the more you must give. Duty comes with wealth,' she'd admonish, as she raced off to yet another charity auction.

Lizzie lay on her bed, frustrated, lonely and a little bit scared. Eventually she sobbed herself into a fitful sleep.

CHAPTER 37

In Which Tea Is Taken

THE NEXT DAY DAWNED brightly and the sun leaked into Lizzie's bedroom through the gaps between the curtains. As she dressed she made a number of resolutions, and to seal them, she muttered to herself as she walked around her room. 'I will not speak to the American. I will not speak to either of the Americans ever again. Who needs Americans anyway?' And she marched out of her room and down the stairs, with the sure-footedness that was hers by birthright. It was with that renewed confidence and vigour that she made a beeline for Il Gallo Giallo, confident that this was now her breakfast spot and happy that, for now at least, her loyalty would not be tested or torn.

As she reached the bar she was rewarded by the scent of freshly baked bread, the heady, yeasty aroma reaching her before she had even stepped onto the bar's apron. No sooner had she pulled out a chair than Dario manifested by her side, a clean white cloth around his waist and a broad smile cutting his face in two.

'Good morning, Miss Holmesworth. Tea and honey to begin with? And perhaps a little fresh juice to accompany your breakfast this morning?'

'That would be lovely, and there's a delicious smell of baking. Could I order some bread and jam, perhaps?'

'Well, of course, bread and jam is a possibility, but if I may be so bold as to trouble you to step inside the bar, I have a variety of breakfast choices at your disposal.'

Lizzie smiled and pushed back her chair, happy to be led inside the cool darkness. On the bar counter she found an impressive array of glass domes, offering protection to an amazing display of baked pastries and breads.

'Honey and almond ... honey and pistachio ... walnut and syrup ... apple tart ... pear tart ... fig tart ... fresh custard pastry ... fresh breads baked with pine nuts, with caraway seeds, with poppy seeds, with cheese and tomato ... Or perhaps something more substantial. I can offer you our special homemade pastries of wild boar and sun-dried tomato ... or wild boar sausage and juniper berry or perhaps ham and sheep's cheese.' The list tripped off his tongue so comfortably that anyone might have thought he was bored by the selection and almost a little apologetic for the lack of variety.

'Gosh! They all look and smell absolutely amazing.' She pondered and debated, giving each pastry proper consideration before plumping for one savoury and one sweet and returning the prizes to her table. As she sat down a shadow fell across the table, cast by the tall and gangly figure of Signor Enzo Civicchioni who wondered politely if he might join her.

He might have been about to launch straight into conversation but his eyes were drawn to the pastries in front of her and his stomach growled jealously.

'Breakfast here? I never even knew they served it! I think perhaps it would be rude to allow you to eat on your own.' He scampered off to the bar and soon returned with a plate laden with breads and pastries. He fell on them and it was a while before he wiped the crumbs off his moustache and turned his attention to his breakfast companion.

'I would like, if I may, to talk to you about tea.'

'But we've barely finished breakfast,' said Lizzie, her eyes laughing at the idea of another meal already.

'No, no!' He jumped in quickly. 'Tea to drink. Our Vallerosan tea.' He pointed to the amber liquid in front of her and scolded, 'You are not drinking it.'

'Only because I've been concentrating on the food. I actually like it very much.' She reached forward to spoon in a generous teaspoon of honey, then sipped.

Civicchioni leaned in, looking and sounding serious. 'I have a number of worries about tea, Miss Holmesworth, and I would be honoured if I might voice them to you on a strictly confidential basis. Would that be a burden?'

'Heavens, no. I'm not an expert, though of course I'm a big tea drinker. My family all are. Has to be Earl Grey in the morning, Lady Grey in the afternoon, and fine bone china any time of the day!'

He frowned a little, not entirely sure where the grand people to whom she had referred fitted in, but he pushed on: 'The honey. It is necessary for your palate?'

'For me, absolutely, because the tea here is much more bitter than I am used to.'

He winced a little. 'Bitter is not good presumably.'

'Well, it's not what I'm accustomed to, certainly, but it has other qualities that I find hard to describe. I've only got into a routine very recently but already I look forward to my first cup of the day ... It might be a little addictive but I'm not altogether sure why. It's not – and please don't take this the wrong way – it's certainly not the flavour I crave. It must be the effect it has on me.'

'Which is what, exactly?' Civicchioni was leaning forward, a little more animated.

'It seems to clear my head. I feel more awake. That's what it is. And later on in the morning, if I feel myself flagging a little, I'm thinking I need my next cup.'

'This is a good quality of our tea. Its wakeful properties.'

'I mean, all tea has natural caffeine in it, doesn't it, which is why we all drink tea and coffee? But perhaps this tea has more caffeine than others.'

'Perhaps. It is possible. Miss Holmesworth, might I ask you a very pertinent question, please?'

'By all means. Of course.'

'Do you think there is a market for Vallerosan tea in the United Kingdom?'

Lizzie swilled the dregs of the amber liquid around her cup and watched it, as if she would find the answer there. 'To be honest, I don't know. It's a crowded market. The British love their tea – we're a nation of tea drinkers – but we're sticklers for our traditional favourites. I mean, I'm not sure people are going to switch their brand – particularly to one that tastes so very different.' His face was falling as she spoke, so she tried to redress the balance. 'But, of course, if you could get people drinking it, they might find the benefits so overwhelming that they switch. It's just difficult to know how you would get them to try something so unfamiliar. Not impossible, just difficult.'

Civicchioni's admiration for her fought for space in his features with disappointment. After a short battle it gave way to resignation. 'You are a tea expert,' he declared, defeated.

'I'm not. That's just common sense, and a burgeoning interest in marketing.'

'You are more of an expert than our American consultant, and we pay him for his expertise. He's lectured us for more than ten years on the importance of exporting our tea crop and I'm not sure he has thought through who is going to drink it. Why would anyone exchange his or her brand of tea for another? It is a very perplexing conundrum and I think we must understand these issues much more before we make a terrible, terrible mistake. And perhaps we have already made one.' He started the process of straining another cup for himself.

'I really am no expert, but I was very surprised to see the tea plants here. I mean, isn't tea usually imported either from India or China? I don't think I've ever seen tea grown so close to home.'

'You are absolutely right, and very knowledgeable on matters of tea, as you are on matters of marketing, Miss Holmesworth. We are a very surprising and inventive nation. But we also rely very much on our own traditions and there is nothing, not one thing, that is more traditional than tea. Tea goes to the very core of our nation. I would go so far as to say that without tea we might not even be here. That is the truth.'

'Well, it's the first noticeable thing about your country, and it's so beautiful, the lovely glossy tea leaves against the red of your soil. It took my breath away when I arrived.'

'Thank you. You are very, very kind. And perhaps now I might give you the history of the plant, the heritage of the very leaves you are now straining. Perhaps when you understand the nature of our tea, you will understand something more about the nature of our people.'

He stirred his tea, leaned back in his chair and, oblivious to the world around him, to the waking up of the city and to the gradual filling of the bar with people who had been drawn to Il Gallo Giallo by the fine scent of the pastries wafting through the alleys, he began his story.

'Legend has it that our founding fathers were Cathars, chased here by those who were intent on persecuting them for their religious beliefs. They escaped from the Pyrenees in the south-west of France, journeyed across the southernmost coast of France, traversed the Alps, made the difficult and dangerous journey through the conflict-stricken region of northern Italy and then the unfeasibly difficult trek up into the Carpathian mountain range. When they left the Pyrenees, they would have been a band of some two or three hundred travellers, holy men in the main, but each leg of the journey would have depleted their numbers, and by the time they reached this beautiful valley there were just twenty-four weary travellers. They had been chased, hunted, starved. They had lost their families, their loved ones and their children. But they arrived here in this hidden valley and could journey no further. Perhaps because they could not face another mountain range.' Here, Civicchioni gestured to the east vaguely. 'Or perhaps because they knew they were home.

'Those who had pursued them so vigorously for a thousand miles gave up at the last dangerous peaks, and our valiant forefathers were left in peace to build a small community of religious people, committed to living in harmony with the land. They were tired of fighting for their lives and their beliefs, and they were certainly tired of running. So they settled. What, Miss Holmesworth, would you say typified the landscape of civilization in all the areas through which our forefathers travelled?'

Lizzie thought for a while, recreating in her mind her school trip to Carcassonne where she had learned about the Albigensian Crusades. She also thought about the family holidays in the South of France, the pretty scenery and the thrilling drives they had taken up into the mountains. She thought, too, about the skiing holidays in the Alps and the various Italian villas they had hired throughout her childhood. The scenery all came flooding back to her, but in truth, one holiday was probably indistinguishable from another.

'Well, scenically, I suppose, it's the hilltop citadels that I'm most familiar with. The little mountaintop villages with their medieval churches and crumbling brick walls.

Come to think of it, they've dominated the landscape in all of the areas I've been to in both France and Italy.'

'And what do you see when you look around here?' he probed.

She frowned, unable to follow his line of thought.

'The inverse, Miss Holmesworth. The inverse of what springs to mind when you imagine a town designed to fortify itself, to protect itself from its enemies. Vallerosa is built in a dip, a great big valley, and if you can imagine the worst place to build a town to protect itself, it is here. And yet we have survived. Not only have we survived, we have thrived. We are one of only a handful of nations in the world never to have entered into any conflict at all. I wonder, and this is a conversation that you probably need to have with Commandant Alixandria Heliopolis Visparelli, but I wonder if our forefathers were tired of defending themselves, so tired of fighting that they chose to do the exact opposite. By building themselves into this dip, perhaps they were making a statement of peace. A quiet surrender to their fate. Of course, what they were also doing was quite clever, because nobody ever found them here and they were able to develop this great nation with no threat from any neighbour at any time in our long and extraordinary history. But I digress. Let me continue with my story.'

He cleared his throat and went on, conscious now that the other customers had paused in their breakfast to listen openly to the conversation. They were nodding in agreement, shaking their heads from time to time, but attending to every word. Even Dario, who had been busily wiping tables, replenishing pots of jam and butter, or pouring more tea, had found himself a comfortable pillar to lean against and was now listening to the story.

'Our forefathers were not the only travellers to find this haven. You must remember that the twelfth century was a time of great conflict around the world. Education and religion were destroying dynasties, and for every intrepid explorer setting sail to further their understanding of the planet, many more were fleeing their enemies. As our forefathers settled here, other travellers were coming from the distant lands of the east. Legend has it that, at the time of the fall of the Yuan dynasty, land was being concentrated in the hands of Mongolian aristocrats and Han landlords. The people's livelihoods were also suffering from a series of natural disasters that made farming all but impossible. A small group of travellers fled their homeland, leaving their families, who were living in dire poverty, in search of fertile valleys to farm peacefully. They, too, made an incredibly dangerous journey, their numbers dwindling by murder or illness as they made their way from mountain range to mountain range, from the Tien Shan and on to the Zagros mountains. Their route would have taken them, the scholars believe, north of the Black Sea until they, too, found their way into the Carpathian mountains. Just a small handful arrived here, in this forgotten valley. Their journey was similarly perilous and the fact that they had arrived here at all was a small miracle. They were given respite – roofs under which to shelter, food and wine to heal them. They were very grateful for the hospitality shown to them by the early Vallerosan settlers, and by way of a gift, they planted a few straggly tea plants they had brought with them, carefully wrapped in hessian and preserved – another miracle – throughout their terrible journey. The plants were nurtured and survived. The altitude, you know, is similar to that of Darjeeling as are the growing conditions. But the climate is very different and the winters are so very harsh here, which is perhaps why the tea tastes a little less sweet. But it is holy tea, you must agree. Every plant you see here has come from those first few straggly plants, given to us by the wise men of the east. And as such it must have magical properties, do you not think?'

Lizzie sipped again, suddenly awed by the sacrifices and journeys that had been made to bring that bitter tonic to her lips. 'And what happened to the travellers from the east? Did they settle here too? Are you their descendants?'

'Only the tea remains. Legend has it they were so terrified that they ensured their plants were going to live and then took off, heading further into the mountains, never to be heard of again. They were not tired of running. They were not tired of fighting for their beliefs. Perhaps they had just not found their home yet.'

Lizzie sipped her tea, and looked around the bar at the men gathered there. Their eyes were misted and their minds were travelling in the direction of the steep cliffs above them to where the tea plants flourished. She was bothered, not by the tale, but by the effect of the tale upon her. This tea was important. It was important to the city and to the people and it was possibly their salvation. But

346

she didn't understand how. 'That really is a fascinating story. I can see that your tea is very significant to you, and you're right to be proud of its part in your heritage. I would like to talk to you more about tea, if you would like. Perhaps we could meet again, a little later. At what in England we refer to as teatime – four o'clock?' Lizzie ventured, the glimmer of an idea beginning to steep in her mind.

'Teatime!' exclaimed Civicchioni, delighted. The phrase rippled around the bar, the customers trying it out on their lips and enjoying the flavour it left behind. 'Teatime!' he exclaimed again. 'Yes, let's meet again then.' He raised his cup in Lizzie's direction and sipped slowly, savouring the taste and counting his many very good fortunes.

CHAPTER 38

In Which Dancing Spells Doom

LIZZIE WAS QUIETLY PLEASED with the progress she had begun to make. She'd had a very satisfactory meeting in which she'd introduced Civicchioni to a number of the talented young students who were now working closely with Mosconi on Vallerosa's new website and marketing campaign. Far from being divisive, the arrival of another figure of authority, a passionate advocate of the nation's favourite commodity, had served to increase the commitment devoted to the scheme and a tangible sense of change was in the air.

Much later that evening, Pavel had picked up a violin and was now holding court with one foot raised on a chair, tapping out the rhythm, as he entertained the gathered crowd. As the melody picked up pace, the audience clapped and laughed. Lizzie contented herself by watching the performance, smiling and nodding but steadfastly refusing to make any eye contact that might be construed as an invitation to dance. As the sun began to set over the piazza, yet more people began to snake out of the shadows, drawn by the sound of the fiddle. The nation's women emerged from their homes, alone or in small groups, peering cautiously out of the heads of the alleys, wiping their hands on their aprons – or removing their aprons and flinging them over their shoulders as they came. The young women of Vallerosa were striking: raven black hair shining down their backs, high cheekbones, straight noses and complexions the colour of honey. And all small. Not one would come up to Lizzie's shoulders, and their sandalled feet afforded them no pretence of greater stature. Lizzie found herself a chair and remained seated, terrified of overshadowing the newcomers and sending them scuttling back into the darkness of the town. In fact, she visibly shrank down in her chair, rounding her shoulders, making herself as small as possible.

The womenfolk had an immediate effect on the men. They all sat up a little straighter and were quick to offer up their chairs, even to brush away imaginary crumbs before the women sat. Some were obviously wives of the men there, and waved or smiled at their husbands, but preferred to seat themselves separately, heads huddled towards the centre of the table, laughing and gossiping among themselves. Other, younger, women were more watchful, twirling their hair in their fingers and standing a little to the edge of the proceedings, waiting to be invited to sit down or to join a group. Pavel beckoned his cousin Maria over. She smiled and called to a group of three young women, all Lizzie's age or younger. They sat and gave their orders to a beaming Piper in turn. 'This is good,' the barman kept repeating. 'So very good.' He bustled away to load yet another tray with teas and beers, flourishing doilies as he went and filling plates with crackers and homemade pickles. At one point, replenishing Lizzie's beer, he bent down and whispered in her ear, 'You are just what we needed here, the contrast we all seek to remind us of what ties us!' Lizzie laughed, flustered and flattered. These people, so warm and kind and generous, needed nothing from her. But she would find a way to make a contribution, if she could.

DANCING BEGAN A LITTLE LATER, under the cautiously watchful eyes of Dario and his uniformed guests at the adjacent bar. Some of the officers leaned forward, their eyes on the young couples and their feet gently tapping to the tunes. The thought of dancing, of joining in, was tantalizing, but that would not be appropriate, they knew. But more than that, this was a party to which they were not invited. The young men and women of Vallerosa were laughing, singing, dancing together, and there was no uniformed presence either insisting that they join in or insisting that they stop. This was a rare example of unscheduled merrymaking and, as alien as it felt, not one of the officers doubted its importance.

Not least Mosconi, who looked across and marvelled, watching the delight on Lizzie's face and recognizing in that smile the feeling of success. A happy tourist. A happy royal tourist. His heart raced as he began to dwell on the personal ramifications of this triumph. He knew it was a lot to ask, but he hoped from the bottom of his heart that the music would carry to Sergio and that he would be moved enough to look out upon the scene beneath him.

SERGIO WAS INDEED WATCHING. He had edged cautiously onto the balcony and sat on the floor, hugging his knees. He peered between the balustrades trying to make out the individuals, but the men and women were simply silhouettes against the light of the adjacent bars. Each swaying, sashaying shadow mocked him as it moved.

The whispering had started. The laughter had pre-empted it, laughter that echoed across the piazza, rippling in and out of the porticos and ricocheting from fascia to fascia to double in size and quadruple in exaggerated hilarity by the time it reached Sergio's ears. Increasingly the president left his curtains closed during day and night to eliminate any chance of seeing something unsavoury below him, but when he dared to peer from behind the safety of the curtain, once the sun had set, he could make out flickering candlelight in the bars in the far corner. Candlelight! There had never been candlelight before – in fact, the bars would traditionally have shut their doors before additional light became necessary. People would have drifted home to their families, to make polite, un-mutinous conversation with each other, of the crops reaped, not to sow the seeds of the malcontent. Candles spelled trouble. For what other purpose would his voters require candles, other than to pore over the blueprints of revolution? You didn't need candlelight to talk, to drink, to smoke. But most certainly you needed it to plot.

And, following fast behind the laughter there was the whispering.

CHAPTER 39

In Which a Walk Is Planned

THE DANCERS CONTINUED TO WALTZ in the flickering candlelight, and other musicians joined Pavel as the music picked up its pace. Lizzie, so set against joining in, had suddenly found herself pulled to her feet by Elio and swept along with the many other couples. Eventually she had fallen into a chair exhausted, having been passed from one partner to another, finally submitting to the music and allowing her body to eschew the forced moves of dancing at home, replacing them with the graceful turning that the music insisted upon.

Pavel's cousin Maria had struck up a conversation with her, a faltering, anxious conversation that warmed once they had found some common ground. As they laughed at Pavel's Vallerosan male pride, the young clockmaker sensed ridicule and came to join them, wiping beads of sweat from his forehead and collapsing into a chair next to them. 'What's the joke?' he asked, searching both women's faces.

'You!' they chorused, and burst into a renewed duet of mirth, but Lizzie reassured him with a squeeze of his hand before his prickly temperament undid the convivial atmosphere.

'There's no joke, really. Maria and I have arranged to go for a walk in the morning. The destination is all very clandestine, but I'm looking forward to it.'

Pavel gave his cousin a sideways glance. 'A walk, Maria? I trust your secret destination is not going to betray anything too sensitive?'

Maria shrugged and turned away.

Pavel turned with a small frown to Lizzie. 'Lizzie, you must understand that not many people get to drink in both bars. We have issues here that are not always for the ears of government officials, and we must respect that you are a guest of our president. As such, perhaps your first duty is to them.'

Lizzie now reached for Maria's and Pavel's hands. 'I don't know where my duty lies. With them? With you? Can't my duty be to Vallerosa? In which case it should serve the interest of both groups. Or am I being naïve?'

Pavel took a swig of his beer. 'It is in our blood to distrust the government. That is our role in life, and if you take it away from us, you take away the structure on which our country operates very successfully. Our leaders aren't bad men, they're not even particularly self-serving, but they are neither intellectuals nor visionaries and, as such, I don't see how they can make a proper contribution to our society. They are just administrators. Nothing more, nothing less. But not everything here is perfect, and when there is a serious threat to our society, we must take the matter into our own hands. If you see something, anything, that is perhaps not directly the wish of the government, you must understand that it might well reflect the greater wish of the people.'

Lizzie considered this for a moment, unsure where the conversation might lead. 'I have absolutely no idea what you're referring to, but I come with an open mind and would do nothing to undermine the friendship you have already shown me. You must trust me, if you can.'

'I trust you but, more importantly, Maria trusts you. Here, the women know about these things and we men must bow to their superior judgement.' He bowed his head to Maria.

Maria threw Lizzie a smile and reached out a hand to squeeze Lizzie's. 'So, Lizzie, we meet for a walk tomorrow morning, and you bring nothing but your open mind.'

Lizzie agreed and the three stepped out for a final turn of the makeshift dance floor before the fiddlers retired to bed.

CHAPTER 40

In Which Lizzie Begins to Understand

LIZZIE AND MARIA MET, as planned, under the clock tower at dawn. Both women felt nervous and Lizzie felt duplicitous, for which a lifetime of good manners and clear-cut moral guidance from her father, a nanny and a number of first-class teachers had ill-prepared her. That she might be drawn into something that would compromise the trust that Rossini, Posti, Angelo and Sergio had already placed in her made her regret the readiness with which she had agreed to the expedition. Her anxiety was amplified by Maria's furtive glances and her insistence that they talk in whispers and walk in the shadows.

In the cool of the morning shade they wound their way down the hill. They used the free bridge to cross the Florin, then began their slow ascent up the steep hill of the south side. Lizzie recognized much of the journey, but this time, rather than taking the circuitous route down the far bank of the river and up to the Museum of Things Left Behind, they cut straight up the south side of the gully, rapidly leaving the awakening town below them.

Eventually they reached a small opening leading into a pretty piazza featuring a crumbling old fountain, beautifully laced with brickwork. Here they stopped to catch their breath and to look back at the path they had taken. Now they were a little higher than the Piazza Rosa on the opposite face, approximately at the same height as the top of the clock tower. Lizzie imagined the bells ringing out to grace the whole valley, excited that somewhere in this complex town men were overcoming their pride to restore the sound. But right now it wasn't bells that enchanted her ears but, rather, the sweet song of the birds that darted to and from the fountain, bathing in the shallow pool and lining up on the branches of an acacia tree to sing about it.

'Come on. Let's keep going before it gets too hot,' instructed Maria. She led the way up some steps, through an arch and into yet another dark alley, climbing ever higher.

After another fifteen minutes, the houses began to thin, the spaces between them became more generous and a morning breeze fanned Lizzie's face, bringing with it a whole host of strange yet utterly familiar fragrances that she had not encountered before in Vallerosa.

As she quickened her pace, suddenly attracted by the quality of light at the end of the alley, Maria put out a hand to stop her.

'Lizzie, what you see here is a secret. It is not something known to our government or to many men.' Here Maria reconsidered. 'That is to say, it is a Vallerosan type of secret. Plenty of men probably know it in their hearts but none wants to acknowledge it, for fear of what it might mean to them. I need to trust completely that what you see will remain between us. Can I?'

'Of course,' whispered Lizzie, swallowing hard, suddenly a little afraid as she had absolutely no idea what she was agreeing to.

As they stepped towards the opening, the narrow view gave way to a sight that took Lizzie's breath away. Until that moment she had been so totally unprepared that she took a few moments to focus on the spectacle that unfolded in front of her – she had to lean against the wall to steady herself while she took it all in.

'My God. It's absolutely beautiful!' she breathed.

For as far as the eye could see, the mesa on that side of the valley was a hive of activity. Some areas appeared to be divided into small allotments, women busy tilling the soil, weeding, planting and watering. Other sections appeared to support larger areas of crops. There was an enormous patch of maize, swaying in the breeze, and beyond that trees were planted in regimented rows, suggesting orchards. Goats grazed among the ordered planting, apparently untethered, and a pile of shining milk cans lay glinting in the sunshine, waiting to be filled that evening. Everywhere Lizzie looked, women worked, and between them the air was filled not only with chat and laughter but the flitting of butterflies and the humming of insect life.

'Almonds and walnuts mainly over there, and fruit in that direction – apricots, peaches, plums.' Maria waved her hand towards the orchards. 'Here, on the lower levels, are people's private gardens where they tend vegetables, salad leaves, tomatoes. Anything that needs to be planted to scale for fertilization, such as sweetcorn, is planted in the larger plots and maintained collectively.'

All the femininity that was so lacking in the city centre was here, brimming with life in the fecund soil. The air was dripping with fertility.

'I don't understand why something so positive and natural has to be illicit. Am I missing something?'

'Come,' said Maria. She led Lizzie by the hand to the first of the fruit trees and reached up to feel the ripeness of the apples. Two that were ready for eating fell away in her hand and she motioned to Lizzie to sit with her in the shade. She crunched into her apple, noisily and happily, and Lizzie followed suit. It was a while before Maria spoke, and when she did she searched carefully for her words.

'A long time ago, more than ten years, I suppose, the previous president, Sergio Senior, hired an American consultant. Have you seen him around?'

'I have. I arrived in Vallerosa with his colleague Paul. I'm afraid when I did get to meet Mr Whylie, we didn't exactly hit it off.'

'Well, he comes from a very different world. But Sergio Senior seemed to place great trust in him to turn what we have here into a commodity. It was the tea that caught his eye, and he focused his attention on that. His problem appeared to be that we didn't have enough to make it worth his while selling it to another country so he made a plan to expand our capacity. Don't misunderstand me, we're very proud of our tea in Vallerosa. It is almost a national symbol and it is certainly the crop to which we attach the most importance. It also has special properties.'

Maria allowed her voice to fall away, leaving this thought trailing through the air as she sat in silence for a moment.

Lizzie's eyes widened. 'Special how? Like magical?'

Maria giggled, slapping Lizzie's arm lightly. 'No, silly, not magical. But it has a very high caffeine content, higher than the tea grown elsewhere, which is why it energizes you when you drink it. This country runs on tea. Honestly, if we stopped drinking it we'd probably all fall into a stupor and never get anything done.'

Lizzie thought of the effect the tea had on her: since arriving in Vallerosa she had been particularly alert in the mornings. 'You're right. It certainly clears your head. And I think I might be a little addicted – it's the first thing I think of when I wake up.'

Maria laughed, a mixture of joyful glee and national pride dancing in her eyes. 'Yes, it has that effect on you, I'm afraid, but everyone here is equally addicted. They say it is why our scholars can read for hours and hours without falling asleep.'

She was thoughtful for a minute. 'The American consultant, he became very interested at one point in these specific qualities. There's a very refreshing drink that Piper makes for people that need a bit of a pick-me-up – a tea tonic. You should try it. It is like drinking all the tea you need for a day in one glass.'

Lizzie acknowledged that she'd had first-hand experience of its properties. Maria smiled and continued, 'The American became interested in this and even got the recipe from Piper but nothing ever came of it. I think Piper was very disappointed, but then Piper so frequently is.' She frowned at the memory but dragged herself back to the present.

'Anyway, I'm wandering off the track a little. The government started to issue quotas that had to be met. We had to produce a certain amount of tea and it was a matter of national pride that we achieved this. At first we complied, taking out many of the orchards on the north mesa to accommodate the new plantations. The first few years provided a very good yield, a happy benefit from the high-density planting the consultant had insisted upon. The closer the plants are, the more effectively they use the sunlight available to them. But such high-density planting can't easily be picked by hand and this country doesn't have the infrastructure or equipment to automate any part of the process. It became very apparent within the next couple of harvests that the quality of the tea was not so good.' The two women watched a butterfly dance lazily past them, following its path until it disappeared into some long grass.

'Did you know tea, on the whole, is naturally sterile? It relies on bees and other insects to pollinate it. We think the lack of variety in the planting quickly made the tea less appetizing to the insects. But it wasn't just that. The government's plan was flawed for other reasons.'

Maria paused. She was taking a terrible risk in talking to a stranger. She watched Lizzie intently. The young woman had her head tipped back against the tree and was looking up at the leaves above her, enjoying the interplay of leaf and light in the completely new environment in which she found herself. 'Carry on, I'm listening,' Lizzie urged.

Maria took a deep breath. 'If all we grew was tea, what were we going to eat? And while we were waiting for this non-existent customer for our tea to materialize, what on earth were we going to do with the excess?

'It was Ada's idea, I think. Hers and a number of the other women in the city. Most of them are married to men quite high up in office so they were close to the policies that were being formed. And it was never really a concrete idea, nothing that was ever spoken about as such. It just sort of developed. Up here were the oldest plantations, and they were the first ones to be counted by the American. He came up once, barely made it to the mesa, scribbled down a few numbers and returned quickly to the sanctity of the north side of the river. He and his colleagues have never been back.

'First of all we took out some of the oldest tea bushes and planted instead an orchard – that's what you see there, the fruit of many years' labour. And then, as the government insisted on more and more intensive planting on the north side to fill the quota, we simply replaced the missing crops over here.'

Maria smiled at their own audacity. 'If anything, we have an improved infrastructure for farming now. It is less haphazard, more collaborative, and prevents us growing an excess of any one crop. But none of this was deliberate. It came about out of necessity. In the final phase, in the greatest insult of all, some families were told they must turn their own private gardens over to tea. Of course it made no sense, either commercially or agriculturally, but nobody wanted to oppose the order. It was made much more palatable because these secret gardens were by then flourishing and productive. We were able to take quick and decisive action by allocating to each affected family a similar-sized allotment here on the south mesa, allowing them to tend their own land without losing out.

'Nothing happens quickly in farming. The more time and effort you invest in the land, the better the results, and we were able to rely on the wisdom of Ada, her sister Evelina and others who knew the cycles, recognized the dangers and were able to respond to the potential threat to our livelihoods. This has been hard work and has taken a huge amount of commitment and personal sacrifice on the part of the women, but we have created something that in the end has become both essential and joyful.

'The advantage, a happy accident, really, is that you get the individuality of gardening coming through, the mix of vegetables and flavours that comes from personal taste rather than the bigger scale of the co-operative.

'Most people take just what they need from their own plots and the rest goes to the market to be distributed through the normal channels. It was never intended to reach such an industrial scale, but it worked. The crops have all thrived up here.'

Lizzie looked around her, understanding now the enormity of the work the women had undertaken. 'It's amazing. It feels like Eden up here!'

Maria looked at Lizzie's shining eyes and began to relax about her decision to confide in her. 'A good comparison, of course, because there is no doubt that this is Eve's garden.'

'And the men really don't know at all? Is that possible?'

'Oh, they most probably do – they must wonder where the food comes from that graces their tables each night. They just don't seem to think too deeply about it. What they're missing, though, is having their womenfolk around and that is the aspect that is likely to cause a revolution. The women hide themselves up here all day, from first light to dusk, and they're physically exhausted when they get home. It takes a lot of strength to feed a nation, you know.'

'Yes, yes, I can see that, of course. But, surely, some of the men must understand what is going on.'

'It's a complex matter. Nobody wants to be complicit, do they? Nor do they want to be the first to suggest to the government that their policies are pure madness. And it's all working now. The government quotas appear to be met and there's food on the table at the end of each day. Who is going to rock the boat? The time will come, I suppose, when the consultant delivers a big fat contract and we have to sell our tea. When it comes to harvest time we'll have less than half the amount we need to deliver and then the truth will come out, I suppose. But there's

364

any number of things we can blame for the deficit ... a poor harvest, bad weather ... Who's going to question our authority on the matter of tea? Will the consultant have a clue? No. Will the minister for agricultural development have any better answers? Well, that's a different matter altogether.'

'But that's Enzo Civicchioni, isn't it? He seems like a good guy ... Would he be so hard to reason with?'

'In Civicchioni's heart of hearts he knows. But he's doing what every other member of that government does. He's telling Sergio what he wants to hear and hoping it doesn't all come home to roost on his watch.'

'How much do you think he knows, really?'

'Well, his mother was Evelina Civicchioni – she died recently. But she was Ada's sister, so aunt to Angelo Bianconi, the president's chief of staff. That's the way it all works here – everyone is related, everyone knows everyone, so it's hard to keep a secret. But Evelina was one of the first women to instigate this. She saw what her son was allowing to happen and immediately set about coming up with a counter-plan. As he took crops out on the north side, she replaced them on the south. Plant for plant. And it didn't take her very long to recruit a whole army of women to help her.'

Together they sat in silence and admired the hordes of women at work. The sun was already high enough to beat down on them directly but they never slowed their pace. As it gathered in force, they kept at work, not allowing anything to break their rhythm as they toiled. Occasionally somebody would say something funny, or irreverent or both, and a ripple of laughter would break out but on the whole they worked in silence.

Maria threw her apple core into the long grass to her right. 'Nature is a funny thing, Lizzie. It has a way of righting itself despite man's intent to conquer it, harness it and bring it under control. You know why this land is so fertile, so special, so very productive?'

Lizzie shrugged, unable to guess.

'Because we used the excess tea from the early abundant years to make a very high-grade fertilizer. It's astonishing stuff – it appears that other plants respond to a good dose of tea tonic too. There's little wastage in nature and it's humbling to remember we must always work with it, for it, perhaps. Certainly never against it.'

'I'm amazed and touched that you shared this with me, Maria. But …' Lizzie hesitated. 'But I'm not stupid. There was no way I would have stumbled upon this on my own – I thought I'd already discovered everything there was to discover in Vallerosa. There was no real reason for you to show me. We're friends, that's true, but what you're sharing with me here goes beyond friendship. I have a feeling you want me to do something with this information, and if I'm going to honour our friendship, then you'll need to spell that out very carefully so that I get it right.'

'Perhaps that is so. But I can't spell it out because I don't fully know what it is I'm asking of you. But you're here with us for a reason. A woman in government, however temporary, is an asset the rest of us women cannot afford to waste. While you're here we must hope that your intuition will work, and together we will find our way through this. We have successfully introduced a solution that offers us some respite from any damage that government policy might inflict. But we must not continue to grow our crops in secret because they will soon begin to taste bitter.'

The two women rose to their feet and walked towards some shaded trestle tables where a number of women were filling in charts tacked to large pinboards that leaned against the trees. Colour-coded columns, in neat hand-writing, detailed rotas and schedules, yields and rotations. Another gave today's market prices for key crops and yet another detailed a complex flow chart of product exchange rates. 'Oh, you'll like this,' exclaimed Maria, as she noticed Lizzie frowning at the symbols. 'This was worked out a long time ago, our way of cutting out the middle man.' She went on to explain, 'Each crop has a designated unit size and each unit has an exchange rate. That way you don't have to sell your corn to buy tomatoes. You simply swap your produce unit for unit. It actually gets a little more complex than this as units can appreciate in value through additional labour. One jar of sun-dried tomatoes becomes three times as valuable as the equivalent number of fresh tomatoes. Under this system women can go on to increase their own productivity and ensure that their labour is fairly valued.'

'So, you barter?' asked Lizzie, delighted.

'Exactly. That's the name we use for this process! You're familiar with our system? I thought it might be unique. I had no idea that bartering was employed elsewhere.' Disappointment had crept into Maria's voice.

367

'Well, I'm quite familiar with the concept, but I've never seen it in action. Believe me, Maria, you're light years ahead of us.'

Maria smiled proudly, and they wandered on towards the allotments. The women didn't down tools, but they smiled shyly as they continued with their work. Their silent prayers, had they been spoken aloud, were shared by all. There wasn't a woman there, working on the land, who didn't secretly pray that Lizzie's visit might herald a solution.

CHAPTER 41

In Which a Meeting Is Tabled

WHILE LIZZIE AND MARIA had been taking their long walk up to the far north mesa, Sergio had called an emergency meeting. Not one of his ministers had been forewarned, not even Angelo. He wanted his men caught off guard, in the hope that an element of surprise would work in his favour and to the disadvantage of any potential dissenters. He had called the meeting for eleven o'clock and intended to be there a few minutes early to look for patterns of collaboration within the sequence in which his men arrived. However, at ten fifty, as he entered the room, the twelve men were gathered, already pouring tea and talking in low voices. Too late to retreat and listen, Sergio could only stumble blindly in, trying to catch the last words of the hushed conversation. As the mumbled discussion evaporated into silence, it was only 'tonight' he caught, an affirmation from Signor Posti that was quickly bitten back into the suggestion of the word as soon as the president joined them.

Sergio swallowed and took his seat. He dropped his papers to the table and fixed the silence with a long hard look at each man. He nodded to himself as he scoured the room and the men looked back at him quizzically, half smiling, waiting.

'I've called the meeting today to talk to you most seriously. This room,' he said, encompassing its four walls with a hand, 'has served us well. It is the room in which we have steered this country together. United. As one. And the table. This table,' he said, banging the flat of his hand upon the mahogany to the shock of the assembled ministers, 'has served us well. It is the table that has lent us support through many hours of deliberation together. United. As one. Together we lean upon it and it shares our burden, taking one equal part of each of us and spreading the load. It is a table crafted by some very skilled artisans, who understood the symbiotic relevance of form and function. And imagine, if you will, what would happen if one leg should be crooked, if even the slightest alteration were to take place that should see one leg shortened, say, by one inch.' He let the image linger in the air. 'The balance of the table would be lost. Things would slip and slide. Our tea!' Sergio suppressed a sob. 'The very symbol of our nation might turn from healer to hurter as a pot unloaded its burning contents into one of our laps.'

While he spoke, fleshing out the imagery as he went on, he scanned the room for latent unease. His stare was met with polite nods, half-smiles, encouraging murmurs, but with none of the sweat beads or furrowed foreheads that he was hoping to flush out. Decio Rossini was doodling, but not in a particularly offensive way. Commandant Alixandria Heliopolis Visparelli was sitting upright, arms folded in what might be perceived as an aggressive fighting stance, but his face was set in what appeared to be a generally interested expression and he looked as if he was both enjoying and following the analogical preamble. And, if anything, Settimio Mosconi seemed keener, brighter, more excited than usual.

Sergio swallowed loudly. 'Among us today is a crooked leg.' He folded his own arms, a mirror image of the stance Alix had assumed. He let the words sink in and, for the first time since the meeting had been called, the gathered men appeared to pull themselves upright into a more concerned, alert group.

'And the table will not function with a crooked leg. If one leg is crooked, all might as well be crooked. Because the table is no longer a table that can be depended upon to serve its function.' He chewed the inside of his cheek and nodded slowly, allowing the underlying threat to settle.

'And for me? As your leader? I would rather have no table than a table with a crooked leg. So I am going to leave the room, and you men are going to discuss the implications of this among yourselves. When we reconvene, there will be one leg fewer to support the table. The crooked leg will have removed itself. It will have limped and hobbled from the room and as such we will then be allowed to find a new, straighter leg to support our table. Do we all understand?'

371

Their bafflement was almost palpable. Roberto Feraguzzi pushed his chair a little back from the table to get a clearer view of the support mechanism beneath the gleaming tabletop. Up until today, this was something he had taken for granted, but it was clear now that further examination was necessary. He peered beneath him but his line of vision granted him a view of only one table leg, immediately to his left; though it was bowed, and therefore not exactly straight, it appeared to be deliberately so shaped and not, then, technically crooked. He looked up at his peers with a shrug. Sergio was already leaving the room, his head held high, but his men were deflated.

The president walked a few steps down the corridor, then darted inside the first door to his right, a utility cupboard that housed an assortment of mops and brooms and the best tea trolley, reserved for visiting dignitaries. Sergio squeezed himself in and pulled the door behind him. The slats that kept the cupboard aired gave him a disjointed but reasonable view of the boardroom's door. He held his breath, steadied his nerves and waited to see who might be expelled from the room. He stood still, his heart hammering, for a few anxious minutes before he was rewarded with the sight of the boardroom door opening. Through the slats Sergio could clearly see slivers of Angelo as he emerged, peered down the corridor, then held the door open to allow his comrades to exit.

'Thank you, gentlemen,' he said, in a hushed but firm voice. 'We are all in agreement that this small fly in the ointment changes nothing. We proceed, as planned, tomorrow. Agreed?' Each of Sergio's hitherto loyal band of men filed past Angelo and nodded or spoke their assent. Mario, Settimio, Decio, Vlad, Roberto, Enzo, Alix, Rolando, Giuseppe, Tersilio. The affirmative noises bounced ominously around the corridor, each one delivering a further blow to Sergio's crumbling nervous system. Marcello, the last to leave, stood for a moment and put his hand on Angelo's shoulder, looking him squarely in the eyes. 'We're with you, boss,' he said, and followed his colleagues down the corridor.

Sergio grasped the handle of the tea trolley with both hands to prevent his trembling knees failing him altogether. He squeezed his eyes tightly shut to banish the image of the betrayers but still the words reverberated in his mind. Sweat poured into his closed eyes and he let it run in rivulets down the crevasses of his face. Eventually tears joined the sweat, until he could no longer distinguish between the two.

CHAPTER 42

In Which Sergio
Faces the Music

MIDSUMMER'S EVE: it was so close now to a measurable dose of balance and equitability. The period in which a man could enjoy the greatest share of daylight of the year, and traditionally a time to celebrate the summer with carefree abandon. But Sergio was moping: the sickness in his stomach had spread, his limbs were heavy and his forehead leaked an oily sweat that stank of something rotten. By five thirty a.m. the sun was already hoisting itself over the eastern range, spilling its happiness into the crease below, but Sergio was pacing up and down, twisting the cord of his dressing-gown between his thumbs and fingers, working the silken knots like worry beads. His head ached and a dull numbness secreted by exhaustion was seeping through his body. His eyelids fluttered in half-wakefulness as he muttered his angst-ridden pleas to furniture unable to care.

The anxieties that were plaguing the president had reached their pinnacle. His beloved country depended on him to make the right decisions but now he felt sure he had let his people down. All of the conviction with which he had guided his ministers had dissipated and he wondered now whether entering into this Faustian pact with the non-royal from the United Kingdom of Great Britain had prompted a higher force to punish him. He would lose this election, of that he was certain. But before that, he would lose every ounce of credibility that had carried him thus far. They would laugh at him tomorrow, when it came to the speeches. He had nothing to give them, no promises to make, no assurances for the future. Instead, he would stand before a rebellious crowd incensed by dissatisfaction. If they didn't assassinate him, they would certainly overthrow him and leave him languishing in the city jail.

For a moment Sergio entertained the notion of imprisonment. Where would they make him wait while they cleared the cell of the filing cabinets that had gradually monopolized the space? One whole wall of the small room had been turned over to wine storage – the jail boasted ideal conditions for putting down the best reds. They'd have to empty that out, certainly, unless he was to become an inmate with a steady supply of claret. Perhaps with this, and a desk at which to write, he could be a happy convict.

He shook his head to clear his brain of the increasing flow of rambling nonsense and, with a growing sense of urgency, set to work, prompted by his reverie to submit to his increasing compulsion to transcribe his innermost thoughts.

He spent the morning at his desk, drinking tea and scribbling furiously into his notebook.

If these are my last words, then let them speak the final truth. Power for power's sake has no value. The only power that a man can accrue is power he doesn't unleash, for the moment it is put to influence, its currency is depleted. To wield power, therefore, it is better to be unaware of it. And, as such, the truly powerful man is the man with none. Conversely, the man with acknowledged, spoken power is so quickly feared that he is at once the enemy of himself and of his servants. To hold power in one hand, and friendship in another, is not an equation that balances, and therefore a man with power cannot use it to benefit his friends or his servants, only himself. This is why there is no such thing as a noble or true leader.

He replaced the lid on the pen and took a break, quietly confident that he was on the brink of a thought of startling importance. To find clarity, he took to his regular position behind the curtain at his window. Not far from the balcony, just a third of the way up the piazza, he saw a small group of men. He recognized Woolf immediately – the man's features haunted his dreams so it was no surprise to see him jump out from the shadows into the blazing sunlight of reality. And who was he huddled with? Pavel, yes. He knew him too. A bolshie desperado in the making. That was an obvious pairing, certainly. The two men were talking head to head but made way to include a third stepping from the dark catacombs under the arches. It was the burly form of Giuseppe Scota, capped and uniformed with his distinctive medals and gold brocade, mocking his leader from afar. The two young men, rather than shying away from the uniformed minister, welcomed him into their huddle and continued the conversation between them. Once they looked up towards the balcony, and Sergio shrank back into the protection of the curtains. When he next dared to peer out they had turned their backs to him and were looking across the far length of the piazza. And then they had gone, absorbed back into the murky depths that had spat them out just moments before.

One could have power with no friends and no supporters. Or friends but no power and no supporters. Or supporters but no friends and no power. But with power, you are an island, and it is only a matter of time before your friends and supporters merge into one beast whose sole purpose is to wrestle your power from you. And then new power will be dispensed, and the person with the most power will quickly find himself alone too. The job of the leader is perhaps the loneliest job in the world. Better to be an influencer than a leader. An influencer can achieve so much of the role of the leader without setting himself up to fail through the futile acquisition of power. A powerless influencer is more potent than a leader without influence. As such the influencer has power, but only as long as the influence is never promoted as power. Then his influence can thrive

and take on many of the properties of true power
without the inevitable downfall.

Sergio chewed the end of the pencil. His writing was becoming more and more illegible as his ideas tumbled ahead of him, his pen furiously chasing across the page in a desperate bid to capture his last thoughts as president.

As his working day drew to a close, the periods of time during which he felt able to concentrate were diminishing. After just a few minutes back at his desk he rose for another break, this time taking to the well-trodden paths around his chambers. At the first circuit of the room he caught sight of himself in the mirror. His face was haggard, drawn and grey. His hair was pasted to his scalp with sweat, making him appear much older than his years. His clothes were creased and tired-looking too.

He pulled himself up straight in front of his reflection. His image sneered back at him. Ringing in his ears he could hear the mocking derision of his father.

'So, my son, this is what you have amounted to, is it? A snivelling wreck of a man, not fit to wear the shoes I left for you to fill.'

Sergio looked at himself in the mirror, his own face merging with his father's. 'Father, I have tried my best, but I can no longer tell my friends from my enemies. I am alone now, alone to make the decisions that will settle my fate.'

His father glared back at him, contempt written in his small, dark pupils.

Sergio strained to listen, using his powers of concentration to separate the cacophony of crackles and hisses from actual thought, until, like tuning a radio set, he was able, out of the confused noise of his inner turmoil, to decipher the clearly enunciated words of his father speaking to him. 'A great leader has neither friends nor enemies! I bequeathed you a small country, son, not a vast empire, just a nugatory scrap of land that should have presented no challenge even to a man with so few obvious qualities. Is it to fail now? In your custody? You should be ashamed of yourself. You dishonour my memory and the memory of your forebears. Look at you! You are no longer worthy of your title and you are unworthy to be called my son.'

Sergio examined himself slowly from head to toe. His father was right: he was a pitiful excuse for a man. And yet, and yet, his mother had found in him so much to be proud of even when he was a child. He pulled himself up a little taller and looked deeply into his reflection until he could see the light of his own eyes begin to replace the dark, contemptuous glare of his father's. Within the lightness, he saw a glimmer of something familiar, a suggestion of the man he had once known and liked, a man with more integrity, more love, more friends than his father before him.

It took only a few moments to find the clarity he sought. He nodded, determined once more. 'If I am going to be destroyed, then let me face that moment with dignity and a clean shirt.'

He headed to his bathroom to busy himself with pampering. Beginning with the feet that were not fit to wear his father's shoes, he filed away at the cracked skin of his heels, shedding the sordid version of himself that clung to him parasitically. After oiling his newborn skin, he turned his attention to his toenails: snipping, filing, buffing to remove all traces of the tired yellowing toes that had begun to sicken him. From his feet, he moved upwards, carefully examining the nooks and crannies of his neglected self. He washed, scrubbed and preened while conjuring up long-forgotten memories of maternally applied ablutions. He shaved carefully and thoroughly, then plucked stray nose and ear hairs with a deft and determined hand. He applied moisturizer until his face shone. He doused his clean neck in cologne until it stung with the sting of a reawakening. At last, resurrected, he dressed in his finest suit and shirt, picking out his best cufflinks and strongest, most self-assured tie.

When, a couple of hours later, he presented himself to his mirror for inspection he liked what he saw. 'Now I'm ready,' he said to the mirror, and as he straightened the knot on his tie, there was a soft knock on the door.

Sergio's stomach lurched. He opened the door, the condemned man facing his executioner for the first time.

'Angelo, it's you, just as I thought.' Sergio greeted his oldest friend sadly.

'Well, of course it's me – who else might you expect at this time?'

But time had long been unharnessed, as far as Sergio was concerned. A few weeks of increasingly troubled sleep had allowed all measures to slip and he was no longer able to distinguish the routine from the outlandish.

Angelo spoke to him softly, kindly, and placed a protective arm around Sergio's shoulders, holding him as a priest might comfort a dying man. 'There is something you and I must do in preparation for tomorrow's big day. I would like you to come with me. No questions asked. Would you do that for me?'

Sergio squeezed his eyes tightly shut, removing any trace of sadness. When he reopened them he was able to look Angelo in the eye with calm resolve. 'I understand. I am ready.' He spoke with barely a tremor in his voice.

Angelo propped up Sergio's elbow, then guided him out of the room and along the dark corridor, taking the unofficial exit down the stairs, through the private door and gate into the piazza. Just before they stepped out from the cool of the palace interior, hovering on the threshold of the past and an uncertain future, Angelo moved in front of Sergio and turned to face him. Calmly, kindly he put both hands on Sergio's shoulders and looked deeply into his friend's eyes. Behind him it was dusk. The light was fading but the sky above remained the bright dark blue of midsummer. Sergio looked back at his friend and his heart ached for the pathos of the moment. All of their summers, their winters, their shared losses and loves were caught in those few seconds of eyes locked together.

'Now, Sergio, I am going to ask you to trust me completely. Can you do that?'

'I am beyond fighting, Angelo. I am in your hands now.'

'Good. Please, to make this easier for us both, may I put this blindfold on you?'

Sergio nodded his acquiescence. 'Here, let me do it,' he mumbled. A resigned submission had overcome him and, with shaking hands, he prised the black cloth from

Angelo's hands and secured it firmly across his eyes, adjusting it back and forth until he was sure that all light had been extinguished.

'Let us go, Sergio.' Again Angelo steered his leader with a light touch to his elbow, manoeuvring him through the gate and onto the rough cobblestones.

They walked across the piazza, and Sergio quickly became aware, from the acoustics of his own footsteps, that he was being led into the centre. All was quiet. He was sure he could feel the presence of other men and women around him, but there was no noise to suggest this was anything other than a sensation. As they walked he began to falter, his feet occasionally catching on the cobbles. His instinct was to turn and run or to rip the blindfold off, but he took strength from Angelo's quiet leadership and allowed himself to be led forward. After what seemed like an interminable time Angelo steadied him to suggest they had reached their destination. A firm hand on his shoulder pushed him downwards, not, as he anticipated, into a kneeling position but instead onto a chair. He recognized, from the soft give of canvas, the chairs they usually set out for parades and other formal occasions.

That he was seated gave Sergio a whole host of other supposed outcomes to imagine. But, straining his ears, he could hear whispering: there were other men around him and they were awaiting a specific moment. He swallowed noisily, reminding himself that he would face his fate with dignity. Now the thing he feared most was that his terror would betray him in the presence of witnesses. These moments would be recorded in the annals of time so he must give a good account of himself. He had to acknowledge, though, that if he had been asked to walk any further his legs would not have carried him. The seconds ticked by. Occasionally Angelo gave his shoulder an encouraging squeeze but otherwise his hand remained firmly in place. It might have resembled friendship but there was something commanding about that hand: its presence was a comfort but there was no doubt that its true purpose lay in keeping the president from bolting.

The atmosphere around him changed. Something clanged to the ground, perhaps from a great height – it sounded as if it bounced a couple of times. Angelo tightened his grip. Sergio flinched. Someone swore quietly. Someone else stifled a laugh. The president's heart was thumping, threatening to explode at any moment. He wanted to appeal to Angelo to put him out of his misery quickly, but the seconds passed slowly, each one seeming to stretch ahead of him indefinitely.

Suddenly out of the darkness a voice barked, 'Now!'

Sergio stiffened and leaned forward, an instinctive shrinking away from a blow. Angelo pulled off the blindfold with one hand while using the other to tilt Sergio back to an upright position, then tip him further back to face upwards. Sergio let out a gasp. In the semi-darkness he was struggling to interpret the scene ahead of him. Footlights on either side of the piazza shone upwards, momentarily blinding him and masking the structure lurking in the shadows – scaffolding ... perhaps gallows? At that moment a tremendous noise started and further lights were thrown on, picking out the clock face on the tower. A bell was clanging defiantly, loud and true, ringing with a purity of tone that had not been heard for a quarter of a century. As it tolled its ninth clear stroke, the ancient doors to either side of the clock face sprang open and from each a pair of painted wooden figures leaped forward.

From the left, Humility and Altruism emerged and shyly made their smooth journey towards the front of the clock where they met their fellow travellers, Fertility and Liberty, at the centre. Here, they performed a perfunctory greeting, Humility saluting Liberty and Altruism acknowledging Fertility with a stiff bow that tilted her from the ankle. Creakily, Humility raised her right arm, leaning forward to tip the teapot she held to touch the cup in Liberty's now outstretched hand. After a few moments, in which Liberty lifted the cup to her lips, they bade each other farewell and, with a mechanical jolt that Pavel very much hoped to coach out of them in time, they continued their onward journey, disappearing into the darkness of the tower's recesses. As they dissolved from view, the doors closed upon them, leaving them to the privacy of their own quarters. There they could continue to converse at leisure while they readied themselves to re-emerge exactly an hour later to remind the citizens of Vallerosa of the virtues to which they should all aspire.

Sergio's jaw dropped. It was all too surreal. He was alive, he was sure, but was that possible? Was this Hell or Heaven or both? That the clock was working surely meant he was no longer in Vallerosa as he knew it. But at the same time, there was cheering and laughing, and Angelo was pulling him to his feet and shaking him and hugging him, and there were men all around him clamouring and laughing and one word, again and again, was being shouted in his ear. 'Surprise, surprise!' they roared, and Sergio burst into tears.

Later they celebrated in Il Gallo Giallo. Sergio hadn't drunk with his men since his father was alive, but now he pushed through the crowded bar, his arms linked with Alix's and Angelo's. There, the rest of his men gathered with bottles of wine, decanting them generously into beer and wine glasses and toasting the success of their grand unveiling. They were pouring and drinking fast, refilling in time to file out to check the quarter-hour strike. Sergio still had tears rolling down his face but he had given up wiping them away. His friends were equally moved to hear the bells ring out in the square after such a long absence so they were not taken aback to see their president overflowing with emotion. The backslapping and laughter hadn't stopped and Dario had to shout across three rows of customers to take orders from newcomers as they arrived.

'There is somebody you must meet,' Angelo shouted into Sergio's ear. 'Come quickly. He is in the next bar.' Sergio was dragged through the crowd and across the alley into Il Toro Rosso. Pavel stood quickly to attention but Angelo put a friendly arm around his shoulders.

'This is the man you really have to thank. He is the one who fixed your clock.'

Pavel shook hands with the president and quickly introduced Elio. 'This is Elio, the potter. He worked on the figurines and did a remarkable job on their features. You will see when you look more closely that he has already made some improvements. Humility has had that smug smile wiped from her face while Fertility is looking a little less licentious. Altruism's basket is full again, but we need to do a little more work on Liberty – the way she wields that key makes her look like she's ready to incarcerate Humility, rather than liberate her. We didn't have as much time as we'd have liked and Signor Bianconi was determined that this should be a surprise for you, which meant working under the cover of darkness for much of the restoration process – not easy when we knew your quarters have a direct view of the clock tower!'

Sergio laughed at the clockmaker's joyful enthusiasm and shook his head at the audacity of the plan. Once again he used his handkerchief to wipe the perspiration from his head and the tears from his eyes. 'I can't thank you enough, or express how glad I am to have the clock restored. To me, this symbolizes the rebirth of our country, demonstrating that we can move ahead in step with time once again. I am for ever in your debt. You are a remarkable man to achieve this when so many of my own men have failed. Thank you.'

Pavel shrugged. 'The mending of the clock was not difficult. The true skill, perhaps, was not the horological demands but getting to grips with the mechanisms of the government and for that you must thank our British visitor.'

Sergio had not noticed Lizzie sitting quietly to one side. Now she looked up with bright, anxious eyes, biting her lip and hoping she had not overstepped the mark.

Sergio stepped towards her and took both of her hands in his. She drew herself up to her full height so that he had to look up to meet her eyes.

'I really hope you don't mind me interfering, but it seemed that everyone wanted to fix the clock but nobody seemed to be actually doing it. I took it upon myself to help sort it as it was just about the only thing in the whole country that wasn't functioning well. I hope you're not angry?'

Sergio smiled. 'Absolutely not, Miss Holmesworth. One day you must tell me the full story of how you unlocked the secret of time, but now I believe the half-hour is approaching. Shall we all go and observe?'

They left the bar together. Sergio, Lizzie, Angelo, Pavel and Elio joined an expectant crowd gathered at the foot of the tower, craning their necks to look at the spectacle above them. As the hour hand clicked into place, a single strike sounded and a spontaneous cheer rose from the crowd. Pavel checked his wristwatch and his face broke into a broad smile. Good. He nodded.

As they began to drift back to Piper's bar, Lizzie fell into step with Sergio and allowed them to drop back a little from the others.

'Pavel is the son of your father's clockmaker, who had the contract to run the clock until it was withdrawn and reissued to the palace workmen twenty-five years ago. I think it might be diplomatic, if you don't mind me suggesting it, to engage Pavel to look after this clock and any others you might have. Then you can ensure your country always runs on time. He is a good man. I don't think you could find a better one.'

She had barely finished her appeal before Sergio broke away from her and hurried after Pavel. 'Pavel, this weekend is a time of celebration but you and I have some business to discuss on Monday. Be sure to make an appointment to see me at my offices with Giuseppe Scota. Let's make sure that this country runs smoothly from now on, shall we?'

Pavel nodded gravely and shook his president's hand.

Sergio linked arms with Angelo and they headed back to the palace. 'Was it a surprise, or did you get a hint that something was afoot, Sergio?' asked Angelo, teasingly.

'Well, it is hard to keep anything a complete secret, but I can honestly tell you that was the very last thing I expected to happen this evening.'

'And you're happy? The surprise was worth the secrecy?'

'I'm very happy. I can't remember ever feeling so glad to be alive. But next time, Angelo, I would be even happier if you could let me know when you're planning to surprise me.'

'I'll do my best.' The men hugged and went their separate ways, each carrying equal doses of relief and joy in their step.

CHAPTER 43

In Which Lizzie Explains the Birds and the Bees

LIZZIE HAD ONLY A FEW HOURS at her disposal, and she knew better now than to lose them to a complex maze of protocol.

She leaped out of bed as soon as she heard the clock strike six and headed directly for Angelo's house, where she rapped impatiently on the door. Nonna Ada had already left the house for the day but a bewildered Angelo greeted her, rubbing his eyes sleepily.

'You do know it's Saturday, don't you?'

'Yes, of course. That's all the more reason for starting promptly – we have so much to do before tonight. Do you know where Giuseppe Scota's house is? And Civicchioni's?'

'Of course.'

'Come on. Let's go and get them.' Lizzie grabbed Angelo's arm impatiently and attempted to haul him into the cobbled alley.

He motioned to the lower half of his body. 'I suppose I may get dressed first?'

Lizzie paused long enough to process the striped pyjama bottoms, then the white T-shirt he had obviously slept in. 'Ah, yes, I suppose you must.' As the door slammed in her face she shouted, 'No longer than five minutes, though!' And laughed at her own daring. She waited in the alley, tapping her foot and looking at her recently returned watch, calculating all the time the enormous amount they had to achieve before that evening.

Angelo emerged, and they immediately hurried off, stopping briefly at Dario's bar to allow Lizzie to arrange for breakfast to be delivered. 'A good selection, if you don't mind, and a pot of honey on the side – I know him, he'll never serve it if I don't ask. Delivered to Sergio's in twenty minutes, OK?'

Angelo looked around him at the bar, taking in the tablecloths, the fresh flowers, the selection of tantalizing breads and pastries laid out under glass domes on the counter. Dario, sporting a pristine white apron and a colourful tie, was whistling as he swept the bar. Angelo shook his head. 'I sometimes wonder if your arrival coincided with the general madness that seems to have gripped this town ...' He wondered alone: Lizzie had already skipped out of the bar, leaving Angelo to chase after her.

Fortunately, breakfast with Lizzie was already on Sergio's agenda – she had suggested as much the night before – so he was not surprised, as he stood on his balcony, to see her marching across the piazza in his direction, with Angelo and Giuseppe Scota in tow. Every few steps the two men had to break into a little trot, just to keep pace with her determined strides. Sergio smiled to see his ministers so completely emasculated by their British visitor.

Before long, they were in his quarters, assembled around Sergio's desk. Sergio was dressed for business. In front of him a blank sheet of paper and a full ink pen betrayed their purpose. He had enjoyed a restful sleep, and the steady chiming of the clock throughout the night, rather than interrupting his slumber, had helped to keep the demons at bay.

Now Lizzie paced up and down. Angelo and Giuseppe Scota took their seats opposite Sergio, who sat patiently awaiting instruction.

'You know there are jobs, don't you?' said Lizzie, eventually, having mulled it over for a while.

'Jobs? What jobs? Where?' said Sergio.

'Everywhere. But you're going to have to let some students graduate to fill them. It's a chicken-and-egg thing.'

'There is nothing keeping our students at their studies. They are free to enter the job market as soon as they graduate. They just haven't quite fulfilled their full academic potential as yet.'

'Well, Woolf wants to be a writer.'

Sergio scowled. 'What do you know of Woolf? He is a low-life reactionary, not a writer. Has he been putting far-fetched ideas into your head?'

Giuseppe Scota's ears had pricked up at the mention of one of his favourite students. 'Woolf wants to be a writer? Why didn't I know this?'

Lizzie shrugged. 'Yes, he wants to be a writer. But his full-time studies prevent him giving it the time it needs. And apparently you're lining him up for a post-post-graduate degree.'

'Well, he's a good student with much he can offer to academia, but he cannot fulfil his true potential without having completed his studies.'

'But he wants to be a writer and he's got things he should be sharing with the world now, while he's a driven young man with the promise of life ahead of him – not when he's a cynical old professor.'

Scota winced at the reference, but Lizzie continued unabashed.

'And imagine what happens when Woolf is a writer. He finishes a book and he'll need it published, won't he?'

Sergio's imagination immediately leaped to the baskets of loose-leaf manuscript he himself was storing for some such event.

'It will need printing and then selling, won't it? And a bookshop would be a huge boost to the – to the buckets and rope you've got on sale currently.'

Scota and Sergio each frowned for separate reasons. Sergio was imagining the many steps he'd have to take before he could be signing freshly printed copies of his own memoir, on sale in a bookshop visible from this very balcony. Scota was imagining the steps he would have to take to release a tranche of students to start fulfilling these new roles.

'You're going to need a printing press, some editorial staff and designers anyway. For the newspaper.'

'The newspaper?'

'Of course. There's a great guy at the university who's practically running a newspaper already. Edo is his name. He's full of ideas and passion. He just needs encouragement, and perhaps a little investment. And Maria wants to be a florist.'

'A what?'

'A florist. She'd like to sell flowers from a shop here – and maybe make arrangements for special occasions. She's already making the floral arrangements for Dario's bar, and Piper's been enquiring for some bigger and better ones for his place too.'

'Flowers.'

'Yes, but, of course, that's a little way off.'

Sergio thought for a moment. 'There used to be a florist … What was her name? Angelina? Yes, Angelina used to run a florist's shop, didn't she, Angelo?' Sergio suddenly recalled his mother walking into a room, her nose buried in an armful of blooms.

'Yes, but Angelina died and nobody took over. The shop has been empty ever since. I think the women here have been a little, er, preoccupied, for a while now. Certainly too busy to think about such trivia as floral arrangements.'

This comment drew Lizzie up short. She addressed the men with fire in her eyes. 'Flowers aren't trivial. They're fundamental. When you make space for flowers in your life, it means you're on top of all the other aspects. Well, that's what my mother always says.' She paused, searching for the link that had so neatly presented itself. 'And they're fundamental in other ways too. They help the other stuff happen.'

There was a knock on the door.

'Right on cue!' announced Lizzie, and ran to welcome in Civicchioni, without even checking with Sergio that this was acceptable.

'Enzo's here,' she called, over her shoulder, as she hugged him. 'Leave the door open, Enzo. Breakfast should be right behind you.'

'Good. Excellent,' said Civicchioni, his delight at Lizzie's warm greeting evaporating at the sight of his president, slack-mouthed, shaking his head.

Lizzie skipped back to the desk, gaiety in her step and voice. 'We were just talking about flowers,' she explained, leaning heavily on the last word as if that would make everything clear to the newest arrival.

'Flowers,' he confirmed, an edge of uncertainty creeping in.

'Yes, flowers. And I was just getting to the bit about how fundamental flowers are to, you know—' She was interrupted by a polite cough from the open door.

'Ah, breakfast. Perfect.' The clock chimed half past six and Sergio, Angelo, Scota and Civicchioni exchanged baffled looks behind Lizzie's back. Sergio raised his eyes to the heavens, but he was smiling broadly.

Lizzie moved an occasional table out from against a wall and began to unload the trolley, setting out plates, knives, a butter dish and a mountain of pastries and breads. 'Tuck in, everyone. I'll be mother.' She poured a cup of tea for each of the assembled men, making much of the filtering process as she sloshed it from cup to cup, straining it as she went. She took a cup to each man perched around Sergio's desk and then, as she was about to sit down, pulled herself back up to her full height, sighing loudly. 'Silly me. Honey.'

She went back to the trolley, came back with the pot and allowed the men to follow her movements. She stirred in a full spoonful of honey slowly and deliberately.

'If you stay here long enough, young lady, you'll learn to drink our tea as Nature intended,' muttered Sergio, taking a full sip of the scorching, bitter liquid and sucking it through his teeth noisily.

'No chance. I don't actually take sugar in my tea at home – but here? Sorry, I really do find it too bitter.'

'But tea is our symbol, and to dilute it is to dilute its message, its symbolism.'

'There's a point to be made here,' argued Civicchioni. The extraordinary, awakening property of his first sip had immediately set his brain in motion and he sprang into action, taking his lead from Lizzie's strangely exaggerated movements. 'Honey is nearly as important to our nation as tea. It could easily justify its place as a national symbol too,' he pronounced, reaching over to help himself to a generous spoonful.

'Honey? Since when?' Sergio looked suspiciously from the minister to Lizzie and back again.

'Well, without bees, we probably wouldn't have any tea,' answered Civicchioni, now deliberately stirring the honey into his own cup.

Sergio looked sharply up at this new development. 'We wouldn't?'

'The tea plant, in its own right, is actually sterile. It relies entirely on the bee for its fertilization,' he explained, slurping from his cup happily.

'Yes, of course. Simple science,' agreed Sergio, cautiously, uncertain of the direction in which this might go.

'And if we were to do anything to deny the bees a good habitat in which to thrive, they might suffer. Perhaps that is what Lizzie referred to as the fundamental task of the flower.'

'But we wouldn't allow such a thing, would we?' Sergio glanced nervously around the table, but the men seemed focused on their breakfast, examining the pastries with great care.

'Well, I suppose there would be a risk posed if we were to over-cultivate the tea plantations – we might quickly find that a monoculture might be self-destructive quite quickly. If the bees didn't thrive …'

Sergio, anxious now that another unforeseen disaster was about to befall him after the rigours of the last few days, felt desperate. 'But isn't that what we're about to do? Have already done? Aren't we in danger of planting the bees out of existence if we follow the American's demands? Perhaps we've passed the point of no return already …' He scanned the room wildly for hope. He found it in Angelo's eyes, which met his.

'Well, I think you'll find that your minister has anticipated this type of threat and is already putting in place some contingency plans to mitigate any risk.'

'Contingency plans?'

'Well, it's important to ensure we don't do any lasting damage to the eco-structure, you know. I'm just talking about a bit of set-aside to keep the insect world happy.'

'Well, thank goodness for that. Good work, Enzo. Good work. How much should we set aside?' Sergio relaxed and brightened, feeling in control once more.

'Enough. Plenty. Enough to ensure the continued safety of the tea crop. Our American consultant has his agenda, obviously, but it is up to us to ensure the ongoing security of our country's natural resource. I'm not sure these delicate matters, the intricate balance between flora and fauna, fall within his remit. And our own experts feel that perhaps we ought to protect our national interest from unforeseen forces. Complex issues. The maths alone ...' Civicchioni reached for the right words and appeared to find the answer, after a few moments of silent contemplation, in the depths of his teacup.

'Sometimes, Sergio, it is the job of government to protect the people from the acts of government,' he said conclusively, satisfied that nothing more needed to be explained.

Sergio followed the logic of the argument and readily concurred. 'Yes, yes. So we set aside some land to allow the insect world to flourish. Excellent. I'm very happy to hear it.'

'Which is why you have bees, and why I can add honey to my tea. It's all part of the same cycle, really,' offered Lizzie, encouragement in her voice.

'Yes, yes, I'm following the argument, Miss Holmesworth, but my men have yet to furnish me with some detail. You'll have to be patient with me. I expect you're used to legislation passing at speed but here we have a process that is accompanied by a lot of debate and a quorum. My immediate problem is that I'm not absolutely following the government procedure. My government's procedure, that is. Where would we set aside the land, Signor Civicchioni?'

'Oh, we haven't consulted extensively but possibly the upper north-west, sir,' he answered, perhaps a little too quickly.

Sergio thought of the area and recalled the beauty of the land. 'Haven't needed to go up there myself for a while. Bit busy, you know how it's been. But hasn't that recently been cultivated with more intensive planting? I seem to recall that was where we were achieving the maximum number of plants per hectare.'

'Yes, but the tea there hasn't always been first class. We're getting a better quality from the upper south side now.'

Sergio took an appreciative sip. Yes, it had certainly never been finer. 'So you are masterminding this initiative, are you, Signor Civicchioni?'

Once again, the minister couldn't quite meet his eye. And Sergio understood he was getting close to the crux.

'And supposing we do set aside some land for some more diverse planting, how long will this take? Have you a plan?'

'Well, not exactly. But I consider myself to be very fortunate to be surrounded by people who are instinctively very good at this sort of thing.'

'Such as?'

'My wife, Augusta? Angelo's mother, Ada, a few others.'

'Let me get this clear. Your wife and Angelo's mother are helping you to anticipate our government's potential short-sightedness and guarantee the safety of our entire country's tea crop by singlehandedly planting some flowers?'

'Well, yes, I suppose that's the short version.'

Sergio allowed this information to sink in again, and tried a couple of times to voice some sort of intelligible response. But his mouth just gaped and nothing at all came out.

'The important thing, sir, at this precise juncture, is to use this information to our advantage, politically speaking,' chipped in Angelo.

'Quite,' agreed Civicchioni. 'I mean, we're fine, aren't we? We didn't risk the crop, we've done no long-term damage and perhaps if we could find a way politically, publicly, to recognize the people who masterminded the operation, we could turn this very much to our favour.'

'You mean tonight, in my speech.'

Lizzie chewed her lip, barely able to contain her excitement as realization spread across Sergio's face.

'I publicly acknowledge their part in this and by doing so I publicly acknowledge our collusion.'

'I think,' said Angelo, 'if I might be so bold, it may be politically useful to go one step further.'

'By doing what?'

'By making a gift of the set-aside land back to the people. Allowing them to take ownership of the land for themselves. It might help them feel compensated for the land that they have lost over the years to the great tea experiment.'

'And a scrap of land would serve as compensation, would it?'

'Well, to be fair, I haven't measured the exact curtilage. It may be a bit more than a scrap. It may even, by chance, somewhat match exactly the area of land lost to the tea plantations on the north side.'

Sergio nodded, wondering if perhaps, like his men, the less he knew about it the better.

'And I think we may want to go one step further in your speech, sir, if we can. I'm wondering if perhaps you might want to backdate the gift of the land.'

'Backdate it? To the start of this fiscal period? I can't see that being a problem.' Sergio, animated now, was scribbling notes as he spoke.

'I was rather thinking by about a decade.' Angelo kept his eyebrows raised high as he looked squarely into the face of his president. Now was not the time for a weakening of resolve.

'Backdate a gift by ten years? Are you serious?'

'I think it would make people feel very comfortable with the decisions that have had to be taken. If you backdate the gift, it will allow them to make more long-lasting plans, the better to protect our tea crops. Without actually breaking any laws along the way.' Angelo spoke with confidence; Civicchioni backed him with enthusiastic nodding. Lizzie fiddled with her ponytail, barely able to contain the grin that was trying to spread across her face.

'Is there anything else you want me to do, other than give away what sounds like a substantial area of land to the people of this country and to backdate that gift by two presidential terms, even though I knew nothing about the need to protect this land for all these years?'

'Well, we may want to allocate a few resources to that area, sir. The land is valuable. It really is the land that keeps our tea, and therefore the whole country, safe. Not to mention the fact that most of the country's foodstuffs could – hypothetically – come from that area.'

'Of course, if it's to play such a vital role in our future prosperity I agree entirely. We can protect it immediately, build some walls, station some men, now that we're investing such a huge amount of money in the area, let alone attaching so much importance to it. This is surely a job for Alix. We must consult him.'

'I wasn't really thinking along the lines of security. We may just want to employ a few of the women who are already working very hard voluntarily. I think if we were to allocate a few resources to it, perhaps a bit of irrigation too, then we may get some of our women back. We're rather missing them, sir.'

'So you're suggesting we've lost more than just Augusta and Ada to the project.'

'I think you'll find that's where all the women spend most of their time. And when they do get home, they're exhausted. If we can find a way to help them out a bit, perhaps they'll have a bit more time for – for dancing.'

Sergio smiled to himself and began at once to craft his speech.

CHAPTER 44

In Which the Bell Tolls

IN THE FINAL HOURS before the celebrations were due to commence, a stillness hung in the air, punctuated every fifteen minutes by the proud toll of the bell. Each clang reminded the citizens of their appointment that evening, stirring up the thrill of anticipation and sending it rippling through a city gripped in the final throes of personal preparation – the dresses and suits, the shining of boots, the braiding of hair.

And, to Sergio's watchful eye, it seemed that the city was indeed ready. It glistened and gleamed as if, with the reparation of the clock, the fabric itself had begun to heal. The paint was a little less flaked, the stonework shone with a new lustre, the windows gleamed and bounced the early-evening sunlight around the piazza, adding to the overall sparkle. The stage was laid out beneath the clock tower. Red and black bunting framed the set and the proud flags of Vallerosa swayed gently in the cooling evening breeze. The band had already been out to practise, to the satisfaction of all concerned, and had now left the sheet music pinned to their stands, ready for the opening ceremony. Chairs were neatly set out, those flanking the stage for dignitaries and special guests, while row upon row of chairs facing it were for the city folk, those who had braved the queue at Remi the postman's horribly disrupted post office to buy tickets for a comfortable seat. Other onlookers would simply crowd into the piazza and fill the space around. Loudspeakers had been rigged to allow the voices of the orators to ring out around the town.

On previous occasions, Sergio – as his father before him – had addressed the crowd from his balcony, keeping himself a little aloft and aloof. Tonight, however, he had arranged to speak from the stage on the piazza and had arranged for three chairs to remain on it throughout the proceedings.

As he watched the minutes click satisfactorily by on the clock opposite him, he read and reread his speech. Angelo had helped him to prepare it and he was satisfied with its intent and purpose, though something niggled as he tried to perfect its delivery in his mind. Occasionally he scribbled a question mark in the margin or underlined a word for stress, but he knew in his heart he was merely scratching at the surface: he had an underlying doubt that needed to be addressed before he could comfortably take to the stage. He paced backwards and forwards and continued to do so as the people of Vallerosa began to appear from each alley and file into the piazza beneath him. A noisy murmur grew in volume until the excited hum of conversation filled the air and he was unable to contain himself any longer. Checking his reflection once more as he hurried to the door, he left his chambers and descended the stairs, exiting Parliament Hall through his private gate while Angelo, the guards and the rest of his men awaited him at the main entrance. It was only when the men heard the cheers of recognition from the crowd that they realized their leader was making his way unchaperoned through the throng, shaking hands, patting backs and pinching the rosy cheeks of small children as he snaked towards the clock tower.

Pushing through the horde, Angelo hurried to catch him up, anxious that he was alone and almost invisible in the masses that crowded around him. Once he caught sight of Sergio's beaming smile and shining eyes, though, he relaxed and held himself back. The president, confident and rested, looked both distinguished and accessible, and the people of Vallerosa were thrilled to be in such close and unguarded proximity to their leader.

Lizzie made her way to the stage at just before seven o'clock, as instructed. She, too, had made an effort with her attire, wearing the smartest outfit she had travelled with, an ankle-length skirt, short-waisted jacket and sparkling sandals on her feet. She hovered nervously by the stage, unsure of where to sit or stand to draw minimal attention to herself – but she needn't have worried. Sergio spied her and made a beeline for her, the crowd parting to either side deferentially as they realized he had switched his attention from them to the tall blonde visitor. As he reached her, he hugged her warmly.

The noise around them made it almost impossible to have a quiet exchange, so she bent down and he spoke directly into her ear, his hands cupped around his mouth so that she could hear clearly. 'My dear, I shall ask nothing of you that makes you uncomfortable. You have already done enough and you may consider your official duties discharged.'

Lizzie squeezed his arm gratefully, and pushed back, ready to take her place in the wings to observe the great spectacle.

'But,' he said quickly, grabbing her hand, 'you would do me a great honour to sit on the stage, as my friend and most special of special guests.' At that moment, Lizzie would have liked nothing more than to disappear quietly into the background but she looked at the appeal in his eyes and was unable to refuse him this most simple request. With a resigned smile, she took to the stage and sat on one of the three chairs facing the swelling crowd. She fidgeted with her skirt, tugging it down towards her ankles, then immediately fiddled with her blouse, deciding to do up one extra button. Once she was sure she was dressed with as much decency as she could muster, she raised her face to study the crowd in detail.

CHUCK WHYLIE and his colleague Paul had been unsure whether to join in with the evening's celebrations and had shared several beers at Whylie's apartment while debating the issue. Paul felt strongly that since he had only recently established the broadest outline of a consultancy agreement with the government, his purpose would be better served by retaining a healthy distance and maintaining an arm's-length relationship until the agreement was cemented with the time-honoured tradition of a financial commitment. Whylie, on the other hand, felt he'd pushed the president quite aggressively in recent times and would need to work on his softer skills to encourage a further extension of the contract he had enjoyed for so many years. Besides, he argued, he was a valued member of the wider team and his absence would almost certainly be noted. These Vallerosans were sensitive to protocol and he certainly didn't want to snub Sergio at this delicate point in their negotiations. In the end the two men agreed that their different stages each required a slightly different approach and Paul went to the university to check his email while Whylie grabbed a couple of beers from the fridge to ensure he didn't have to risk the local brew.

When he had arrived in the piazza he had been surprised to discover that no formal seating had been arranged for him at the ceremony. He had gone back to his apartment to reflect upon the meaning of this affront. No answer sprang to mind, so he drank a couple more beers for clarity. By the time he wandered back outside to join the throng, his surprise had morphed into outrage. Now, as he mingled with the crowd, pressing a cold beer bottle to his forehead to fend off a headache that was tiptoeing quietly behind his right eye, he caught sight of the blonde on stage, in a chair that, by right – when you took into consideration everything he had already achieved for the country – should have been his.

Their eyes met. She looked embarrassed. He rustled up a disarming smirk.

AS THE AMERICAN CONSULTANT took a long swig of his beer, his eyes never once left hers. She detected a challenge. She half smiled back, in the hope it would deflect some of the unpleasantness aimed at her, then allowed her eyes to sweep across the crowd where she soon met the smiling face of Pavel. He waved and signalled his delight with a thumbs-up. Lizzie breathed a sigh of relief. As she did so, Angelo bounced onto the stage and took the seat next to her, then reached out and squeezed her hand. Her heart swelled with joy. She was surrounded by many more friends than enemies, and the American's power, if he had any, seemed to evaporate into thin air, subsumed by the goodwill that emanated from everyone around him.

The band played the National Anthem, and the crowd stood to attention, singing the chorus loudly:

Vallerosa, Vallerosa,
Red valleys, green hills,
My cup overflows
With sweet, sweet tea.
Vallerosa, Vallerosa,
You mean the world to me ...

As the final notes died away, a hush fell and Sergio took to the stage. He adjusted the microphone, tapping it with his finger. Once he had commanded complete silence, he turned his back to the crowd and looked up at the clock, raising his arms as if to conduct an orchestra. After only a few seconds the minute hand clicked up to the vertical. Sergio allowed both arms to drop dramatically and the seven chimes rang out across the piazza. The hush remained until the seventh stroke, at which point the entire audience erupted into applause, shouting, whistling and throwing caps into the air. The jubilation continued while Liberty, Altruism, Fertility and Humility performed their merry dance, and Sergio's clapping thundered out, magnified by the microphone and exciting the crowd even further. Eventually, the noise petered out and Sergio cleared his throat.

'Ladies and gentlemen, honoured guests, people of Vallerosa, I welcome you here tonight to this most auspicious of occasions.' He looked down at the swimming text in front of him and faltered. The crowd sensed that this was more than a dramatic pause and held its breath. Angelo readied himself to help, and stared intently at his leader, searching for the reason behind the cavernous silence. The hush held as Sergio folded up his speech and placed it carefully in his pocket.

'Ladies and gentlemen, friends. I can't do this. I can't stand before you and read a prepared speech, when I have so much in my heart that I want to share with you today. My speech, had I delivered it, was designed to make you feel confident in me. Designed to make you vote for me. Designed to make me your president again for the next five years. But I don't want to make that happen. I want *you* to make that happen. I don't want to use words and promises to trick you into believing in me. I want you to believe in me anyway. Without the words and without the promises. Is that too much to ask? I suspect it is, because I have not always been honest with you. I have not always kept my promises.'

Sergio let this thought hang in the air, but the crowd were not yet shuffling nervously: they seemed intent on allowing the speech to deliver itself and were willing to let the president confess in this public space.

Angelo had begun to tense, but something in the air was shifting and suddenly he felt that the outcome of this election was not perhaps as important as the health and happiness of his dear friend. If Sergio's moment of lucidity failed to convince the crowd, would he suffer any more than he was already prepared to suffer for his country? While he pondered this, with hope in his heart, a curious sense of calm descended on him.

Sergio continued: 'I made a promise to you recently that I would throw a party and invite our royal visitor to address you. But that is not a promise I am prepared to keep.' Here, he turned to Lizzie and smiled. 'This woman has already made great changes to our city and I am not prepared to ask anything more of her. I have, just this evening, allowed her to relinquish any further official responsibilities.'

The groan was collective and audible, the disappointment almost palpable: the highlight of the evening had been revoked and the crowd had sensed the loss of something rare and irreplaceable. They turned their expectant faces towards Lizzie, who shifted uncomfortably in her seat.

The disconcerting moment was broken by the sound of glass shattering. And again. And again. Chuck Whylie had been drinking Budweiser continuously from the bottle and now he was deliberately dropping the empties on the ground, drawing concentrated attention to himself.

'Imposter!' he shouted, his fist raised in Lizzie's direction. 'Imposter!' he yelled again, his voice slurring as he flipped the cap of another bottle of beer. The guards from beside the stage became alert and started to move towards him. But they were frozen in their tracks by Sergio's roar, a shout of disgust that reverberated around the piazza with enough power to send pigeons scattering and force Commandant Alixandria Heliopolis Visparelli, lurking in the shadows of the clock tower, to reach for his handgun.

'Imposter!' Whylie yelled again, but this time his outburst was cut short by a scuffle. Pavel had fought his way through the crowd to the American and now held him in an arm lock. In the meantime the guards had quietly edged their way forward and were waiting for permission from a senior figure to deal with him.

'Imposter?' Sergio bellowed. 'Imposter, he says!' Sergio threw his head back to laugh at the absurdity of the claim and pointed a stern finger at the drunken American. He was aware that his words would reach the far corners of the piazza and perhaps down through the labyrinthine alleys to the river below, and even up to the sun-baked tips of the tea plants in the north. Nonetheless he addressed his words to Whylie alone, jabbing a finger in his direction as if he were the only man in the crowd. 'You insult my men. You insult my people,' Sergio hissed, gesturing wildly at the gathered crowds. 'He insults me,' he said, with equal passion, thumping his right hand on his chest. 'And, most traitorously, he insults our precious visitor.' The crowd hummed in approval. 'And who is the greater imposter?' He searched the crowd for an answer. 'This woman who arrived here in the middle of the night, who appeared like magic to remind our women to dance, and our men to sing, and our clocks to chime?' Here, the clock tolled the quarter-hour, and the audience's voice of approval stepped up a notch in volume.

'Or this man, who comes here from across the sea to tell us how to run our country!' Once more Sergio jabbed a finger towards Whylie. 'You dare to come and tell us what to do with our tea? You are the imposter. You don't even like tea!' Sergio bellowed this final insult, inciting a similar reaction from the crowd, who spat their disgust to match that of their leader.

As quiet fell again, Sergio appealed directly to the guards: 'Take that imposter to his rooms, oversee him as he packs and escort him to the railway station. Commandant? Ah, there you are, good man, ensure that we remain on Code Red until the American has left our land. Vinsent Gabboni! Where is Vinsent Gabboni?' Sergio scanned the crowd until the stationmaster raised his arm and stepped forward. 'See that both of our American visitors board tomorrow's train and ensure that neither of them is ever again issued with a visa. From now on, the imposter and his dangerous friend are banned from our country.'

Gabboni hurried forward, bristling with pride at being tasked with such a momentous responsibility. Confident that many drinks would be bought for him at the bar as he recounted each detail of the American visitors' exodus, he bustled away in the company of the two guards and their prize.

Remi the postman was torn by his sense of duty to his president and to his country but intuited that more drama might yet unfold as the unwanted visitors were ejected from Vallerosa. After a moment's hesitation, in which he hopped from foot to foot, feeling the equal weight of both responsibilities coursing through his body, he decided he, too, could risk missing the end of the speeches in favour of bearing witness to this event, perhaps even with the eventual release of a further commemorative stamp. It seemed appropriate, after all, that having played such a crucial part in recent Vallerosan history, he should continue to influence the proletariat from his unique perspective. He hurried after Vinsent Gabboni in order to ensure the smallest details of the eviction were accurately recorded and meticulously related in the bar later that night.

As Remi scurried away, silence had once again fallen upon the crowd and they waited expectantly to hear the rest of their president's address.

'Yes, my people, I owe you an apology. It's true. I have not always seen clearly and on this occasion I have been blinded by an unhealthy ambition. Greed is a dangerous breakfast and I have allowed myself to taste its promise too often.

'But I have learned some valuable lessons, taught mainly to me, at the expense of my pride, by the women of Vallerosa. But in order for my wounds to heal, I must deepen them a little further. I must expunge all trace of the rot I have harboured within me by reassuring you, in public, just moments before a crucial election, that I'm prepared to admit I was wrong.' He drew a deep breath and allowed, for the briefest of moments, his eyes to travel to those of Angelo, who was now sitting forward in his seat, nodding and silently urging his president to continue along this path. Sergio read Angelo's face and took courage from what he found there.

'Tea, you see, is a unique crop. I listened to the American consultant because I wanted to believe that his great tea experiment might be a panacea. What did I want to achieve? I wanted so much to provide greater opportunities for you and I suppose, yes, I wanted to put us on the world map. Who knows what I was trying to prove and to whom? But I expect that my own ego played a starring role in that process and, if that is the case, I apologize wholeheartedly. The American consultant urged us to follow his long-term strategy and we did – or, at least, we nearly did. But what he failed to understand is that in the life of the tea plant, long term extends well beyond the life of a contract, or a presidential term. Those plants we put in will last for over a hundred years, so when we commit to a planting strategy we are locking ourselves into a plan that must outlast us all. Ultimately it is our grandchildren who will be the judges of our success, not this year's election results.

'But, just as a president is nothing without his people, a tea plant is nothing without its vital partners: the bees that pollinate it and allow us to harvest our beautiful crop for many decades to come. The relationship between the worker bees and their queen is complex, and they live in a society that can be brutal and hierarchical but, without external influences getting in their way, they flourish both magnificently and enviably.

'The country from which our special guest hails,' here he gestured to Lizzie, whose eyes, like Angelo's, were trained determinedly upon Sergio, 'once at the helm of a great empire that controlled much of the world's wealth, is allowing its own bee society to die. Not just figuratively, but in reality. Whole communities of bees are being wiped out because those good people of the United Kingdom of Great Britain have interfered with nature to the point that essential layers of the food chain are being eliminated.

'It is what happens when we get greedy. We try to make nature work for us in a way that does not suit it. Once crops are farmed too intensively, the natural eco-structure begins to collapse. My minister of agriculture, Enzo Civicchioni, is an expert on this subject, and very recently he and I have had many interesting conversations about this very point. Signor Civicchioni, I must tell you, is an excellent minister who shares my ambition for our country's export potential.

'But we must be honest and admit that political gain blinded me and my expert advisers. However, unlike my government, the women of this nation had the wisdom and foresight to allow a safety net to be cast to catch us should we fall.

'It is the women, Nonna Ada, and, may she rest in peace, Evelina Civicchioni, with countless others under their expert guidance, who have shown us the way. Not through talk but through action, action undertaken not for personal glory or for the amassing of power but out of an instinct to do the right thing for the good of us all. They knew, as perhaps we failed to see, that not only do the bees require pollinators and a diverse landscape in which to survive, but they also require diversity within their gene pool if they are to be successful. Similarly, we must take our ideas from a wide source and not just rely on the thinking and actions of a few men in power. Rather, we must draw upon the wisdom of the many to inform ourselves and strengthen our thinking. And I'm not too proud, I hope, to recognize that help can come in many forms and in most unexpected guises. Lack of diversity in bees, indeed in any species, can lead to reduced levels of fitness in future generations, and just as within the bee population there can be tens of thousands of drones awaiting the accidental flight of one virgin queen, so we, a proud small nation, must take advantage of the accidental arrival of …'

Lizzie was blushing furiously at the allegorical reference to both her implied virginal status and to her pseudo-royal one, but the intensity of her embarrassment surged as Sergio stumbled over the reference. Realizing he was himself flying into very dangerous territory, he simply threw his hands into the air and altered his course.

'That is why my minister of agriculture, under the guidance of some of Vallerosa's finest minds but taking his own counsel too, has been persuaded to allow large swathes of land to be set aside for you to preserve the varied crops that give your country its colours, its flavours and its smells. So the bees are happy and they'll continue to pollinate your tea. So the bees make honey and the visiting foreigners, with less refined palates than our own, may add some to their tea.' Here, he turned to smile with warmth at Lizzie, now visibly at ease, relieved by his change in direction.

'If I had continued to trust our American consultant, before long we would have destroyed not only our tea crop but everything else that is associated with it. Fortunately, however, the women of this country are far too intelligent to allow that to happen. They ensured that the right steps were taken to keep the balance of nature in harmony.

'Speaking of balance, I think the men are finding the number of hours the women spend tending the farmland just a bit too taxing and are hoping they'll come down from the hills to dance a little more often. It's not all about tea and honey, is it?'

As a ripple of laughter spread through the audience, Angelo whispered to Lizzie, 'I think the people need to hear from you.'

'You want me to speak?'

'It feels right.'

Lizzie swallowed, licked her lips and stood up a little unsteadily. Sergio frowned for a second, wondering if she might be leaving the stage, but when he saw she was moving towards him, he smiled broadly and took her hand, drawing her to his side and making room for her at the podium.

Lizzie wrestled with the microphone, raising it several inches until she could speak comfortably into it. 'Ladies and gentlemen, your president did indeed let me off the hook, because he knew I was dreading standing up on stage and talking to such a big crowd. But I don't intend to let anyone down, not after you have shown me such warmth and kindness.

'And I'm not sure your American consultant was right about many things. But he was right about something,' she said. 'I am an imposter.' Sergio slumped a little, accentuating their difference in height even further. 'I am here under completely false pretences.' She allowed this to sink in, then continued bravely, 'Your president wanted me to address you because he thought that a visitor from the United Kingdom might have something to offer you that he couldn't offer you himself. He thought that my addressing you might deliver something above and beyond his reach. But he's wrong. There is nothing, nothing at all, I can teach you or your country. I arrived here with no knowledge at all of Vallerosa and will leave with my heart full of it. But I am simply not who you think I am. I am not qualified to lecture you, to teach you, to influence you, because everything you do here, you do so well. Here, I have learned about community – something I think my

417

own country has long forgotten. Here I have learned about taking responsibility for your own life, rather than relying upon and then blaming the state. Here, I have learned valuable lessons about life that will help me as I decide what I want to do with the rest of mine. Here I have met real warmth and real love and I feel very honoured to have been part of it.

'While here I have learned some incredibly important things ...' She paused to gather her thoughts and to ensure her next words would not be swallowed by the emotion that was close to the surface. 'Leading a country with honesty and integrity is harder and harder the bigger your country becomes, the more successful it becomes, so I would urge you now to follow your hearts. Don't try to introduce hordes of visitors with marketing gimmicks and bargain flights. They'll come, of course they will, but they'll come for the cheap beer and the wrong reasons. Let them discover Vallerosa the hard way, like I did. Let them find it for themselves and, like me, I'm sure they'll leave a bit of themselves here when they go.

'I stand before you, your humble servant. Nothing more, nothing less. And I am proud to be at your service. I think, I hope, I have met people here who will be my friends for life. And I hope I will meet even more people who will be my friends for life before my stay is finished.

'So I thank you from the bottom of my heart, for your warmth and generosity. And long may you live peacefully.'

She would have liked to say more but tears were forming in her eyes and a lump in her throat was threatening to stop her speaking. She hugged her arms tightly around her and looked at Sergio, who had resumed his position in front of the microphone. Sergio put his arm tightly around her, squeezing her, then releasing her. She returned to her seat, her colour rising.

Sergio looked out at the sea of faces in front of him and found nothing but warmth in the eyes shining back. Unburdened now, and feeling stronger than he had for years, he continued swiftly, 'Ladies and gentlemen, my business tonight is not yet concluded. I have some important announcements to make.

'I was saved, on this occasion, by the women of this country who ensured the safety of our tea crop. And I've been saved too, by my young friend here.

'Miss Holmesworth does herself a great injustice by referring to herself as an imposter. Never a wiser woman have I encountered, or a more honest one. It gives me great satisfaction to award her the freedom of the city and to bestow upon her the title of "Grand Duchess of Vallerosa", a new title specially coined to recognize the contribution that visitors can make to our country, providing their motive is to further our country's standing rather than to erode it. She uniquely fits the bill, and I would ask that you continue to respect her as a most venerable visitor.'

The crowd cheered, Pavel beamed and Lizzie blushed as she accepted the medal that Sergio was now draping around her neck.

'Ladies and gentlemen, in my pursuit for honest leadership I seek much counsel, and I look for it in the most unlikely places – some places that I know I should leave well alone. Particularly as the counsel I have at my side is of the very highest order. Signor Angelo Bianconi is my most special adviser, and is loyal to the nation and loyal to me. If you should decide to replace me at the next election, then you could do no better than to seek the highest office for Angelo, but in the meantime I shall be asking the Presidium, when it next convenes, to promote Angelo to deputy president, a position he holds in everything but name. In this new post he will be even better positioned to act as my moral and political guide.'

As Sergio spoke, Signor Mosconi, who had been growing increasingly anxious, politely pushed his way from the edge of the stage into the midst of the crowd, excusing himself as he passed, apologizing for his intrusion and making himself as small as he could. He ducked between the members of the enraptured throng and on one occasion crouched low beneath the held hands of a couple who seemed unaware of the minister for tourism's urgent need to pass. He had a clear idea of the direction in which he needed to travel and, after a few nervous moments, by peering low and looking for the glint of light on glass, he spied his prize, swallowing his mounting excitement. As he reached down to grasp the empty Budweiser bottle, so recently abandoned by the American consultant, he recoiled in shock, his hand meeting another's. From his stooped position he raised his head angrily, defiance in his eyes, ready to defend his trophy with force if necessary.

Nose to nose with his adversary who appeared equally determined to hang on to the empty bottle, he found himself staring into the eyes of the curator of the Museum of Things Left Behind. 'Mine, I think,' the curator said, extracting the bottle from Signor Mosconi's hand. They unfurled themselves to a standing position and the minister kissed the curator loudly on the cheek.

'But of course it's yours!' he cried, to the irritation of the crowd around him, who were straining to hear every word spoken by their president. 'I knew this would be an extremely important exhibit – I didn't want to risk such a treasure being broken underfoot. But you were vigilant as always. Excellent work.'

The minister and the curator were loudly shushed by their neighbours and, satisfied with their work, they turned their attention back to the president, as the curator slipped the bottle into the safe haven of an inside pocket.

Even though he was drawing his speech to its conclusion, the president showed no sign of slowing down. 'So, you are spared my prepared speech tonight, but I would like to mark this historic day by adding it permanently to our calendar of holidays so that we can celebrate it for ever, and so that our children and our children's children can, too.'

The bell chimed the half-hour, drowning the sound of Sergio's voice and ending his speech just as he had gained enough confidence perhaps to deliver a further twenty minutes or so of rhetoric. There was so much he wanted to share – his thoughts on leadership, on education, on reform – but it could wait until the next occasion, because now the band was striking up, chairs were being cast aside and the dancing was already beginning.

Acknowledgements

My love and thanks go to my very earliest readers, Eoin and Poppy, whose unenviable job it was to let me down gently if they thought this book should go no further. Thank you to you both – not just for this but for everything else, too.

My love and eternal indebtedness also go to Jon Stefani who not only read the book but has taken charge of it (and me) ever since.

Thank you to my Great Aunt CC Rendel whose name I borrowed when I sent the manuscript out. I think she would have liked to know that all those hours I spent at her beautiful little typewriter using up her carbon paper were not entirely wasted. While thanking the deceased, I must also acknowledge the many names I've appropriated from the notices that appear around villages in Italy to announce a death and to celebrate a life. I was at pains to mix and match the first and second names to ensure I didn't reference any real people but by interlinking their names in this way I hope I haven't invoked any old wounds or caused any offence in perpetuity.

Thank you, Doctor Hogg, for the Latin. Not just for the Latin within this book but for bringing alive a couple of dead languages that I suspect will stand my daughters in very good stead.

My thanks to Clare Reihill and to the formidable team at Fourth Estate who combine all the right elements of fierceness, kindness, gentleness and prowess. They really are fabulous and I feel very fortunate to be in such safe hands. They're an elegant bunch, too.

Thank you Faye Brewster and thank you Becky Hardie for your unbridled enthusiasm which, if nothing else, gave me the impetus to take the next step. And thank you, too, to the very inspirational Gail Rebuck, not just for the breakfast, but for making the world a much better place, both behind the scenes and on centre stage.

And finally, to Millicent Divine and Sonny Solomon. I know you're busy scanning the dedication and these acknowledgements to see if you get a mention. You are thanked here not just because I am a fair and just parent, but because you have improved my life immeasurably. Thank you.